The Potency!

by
Ben Garrido

First American edition published in 2017 by Lucky Bat Books

Cover design by Nuno Moreira

Manufactured in the United States on acid-free paper

FIRST AMERICAN EDITION

Garrido, Ben
The Potency!

1 2 3 4 5 6 7 8 9 10

ALSO BY BEN GARRIDO

The Blackguard
Critical Thinking for Leaders
Anglo-American Culture

Chapter One

From my office overlooking the choirs of heaven, I checked my omniscient calendar and took note of a certain master of unintentional comedy nearing his final hour. I would not normally concern myself with human death—it does happen all the time—but I made an exception for this particular gentleman. I did so because my previous diversion in Enclave had come to a conclusion, because this man's long and eccentric career had provided me with a great many chuckles, because I can only tolerate so many divine ambrosia requisitions a day and, most importantly, the great man's passing will serve as the instigating incident for a heroic venture I arranged.

Allow me to digress for a moment and pull on a thread I've noticed running through the history of your species. You see, I am very interested in greatness and it seems that for every great man and worthy woman you'll find some coincidence, some tiny little accident or distant catastrophe, to set them on the path of immortality. There's no Dante without Beatrice, no Stalin without seminary school, no Buddha without beggars and so forth. Greatness tends to require an initial coincidence, some fortuitous accident. This day's death, conveniently, will provide a great plenty of happy incitements.

I leaned back in my throne of glory, set aside the property insurance policies of infinite wisdom and opened the heavenly gates. I stepped over a sloppily drunk Dionysis, threw a bone for Cerberus' amusement and castigated Saint Peter for neglecting shuffleboard the day before.

I descended into the new capital city, Chongjin. I came to palace number 16 and drifted through the heavy, reinforced walls. I floated over a grey jumpsuit so hideous one has to wonder if the man's tailor took secret revenge during its design. I crossed in front of a nude companion girl covering her fear with a veneer of lust, over a bounty of expensive liquors and under a chandelier made from Italian crystal. My fingers ran lightly through the man's fabulous bouffant. My spirit penetrated his skull and passed harmlessly through his occipital lobe to the juncture where the tiny old drug abuser's cerebellar artery branched off from his ascending carotid.

From this vantage point I watched an event of inestimable beauty. The man's blood and matrix, plasma and hemoglobin pressed upon his vessel with just one dyne too much force. The cerebellar artery opened like a zip lock freezer bag and spilled forth a scarlet flower adorned with tiny yellow cholesterol plaques.

The man's face froze in a posture of strained astonishment. The companion girl dropped her spoon and spilled cognac as she fled into the great hall. Doctors rushed into the gilded bedroom and attempted to rescue the man. Their efforts, I'm happy to report, came to naught.

Later that evening I passed unto the fourth floor of the People's Nuclear Armory of Glorious Liberation. I tolerated the crumbling concrete and brutal, hideous architecture of the type which only communists seem capable of constructing—a sort of pseudo-efficient dreariness so thick it poisons the air. I did so because I wanted to watch as the man's son and chosen successor negotiated his ascension to the heights of leadership. A square jawed, glowering army general spoke first.

"Should we tell the people that our beloved leader has passed?"

A thin, severe marine general answered.

"We should not. If it remains a secret then nothing has to change and we can rule without any concerns over legitimacy."

An air force general, whose gravity exceeded even that of poor Persephone, answered his companions.

"While the great leader of yore is both dead and the official head of our country, it is most unusual for a nation to maintain as its *acting* head of state a man deceased. This does not preclude the possibility of our doing just so, but some may accuse us of absurdity should the matter come to light later."

The son's many ample chins jiggled with the force of his high ideals, his jelled hair jounced sympathetically with each earnest gesture as the young man's strong, slightly congested voice shook the air.

"Of course we should announce my father's death!" the son said. "The sooner we tell the people the faster I can consolidate my own power. But I do not say this for my own sake. You must know that when I rule I will modernize our nation and help us to join the ranks of respectable countries."

The silence fell like a wet blanket over the heaving busom of the goddess Ishtar caught, as she often is, in a moment of extraordinarily passionate lip synching.

The marine general scratched his chin as the air force general and army general executed a subtle encircling maneuver.

"He speaks the truth."

The air force general's head bobbed slowly in agreement.

"Doubtless he is right."

"Would you, my esteemed colleagues, be so kind as to lend me your assistance?" the army general asked while clubbing the new leader over the head with a lead-lined rice bowl.

"Certainly," they said.

"One, two, three," the army general said.

The military heads of North Korea defenestrated the great man's son. His plump, young body sailed through the high window and took on the globular elasticity of a falling loogey as he fell. He bounced once, twice on the concrete below.

"We can arrange a body double with no great difficulty," the marine general said. "Let us move on to matters of greater importance, such as tonight's excellent broadcast of exceptional forthrightness."

The air force general agreed.

"A newscast regarding our leader, in excellent health, mourning his son's horrible, disfiguring skiing injuries should serve our truth nicely. Or, failing that, we can always make up something else."

As the generals deliberated, physicians rolled the man's body away to a secret morgue. Morticians cremated the son's remains and flushed the ashes down their finest, Soviet-made toilette.

I could have observed the generals further but, growing bored, flew back unto the heavenly host. The instigating events had finished. The generals' plan would unravel not even two weeks later and, following on their failures, would bring the idiocy of men to such heights as to necessitate my direct intervention.

Heroes

I must make a fresh start in life. I must hide the truth deep in my wounded heart and advance silently, taking oblivion and falsehood as my guide.

-Lu Xun

Chapter Two

The Dear Leader's death remained unknown in South Korea and, unsurprisingly, the rest of the world as well. And since we are traveling to South Korea anyway, we may as well visit the greater of our two heroes in his 14th story apartment. And since we are visiting him, we might as well take advantage of my omniscience to peer inside this intense little man's head, poke at his thoughts with a divine stick and plaster the passions of his heart to the insides of the unnecessarily weighty book you even now hold in your hands.

Choi Chul began that day as he normally did, throwing away the previous night's beer bottles, boiling water and turning on the TV. He left his wife in bed without a second thought. Mrs. Choi required an act of divinity before she'd wake up and, I'm afraid, moonlighting as an alarm clock is well beneath my dignity.

I could fill our washing machine with screaming pigs and she'd sleep through it, our hero thought. He thus stomped this way and that without the least concern for waking his beloved. Chul had fallen asleep more easily than usual the night before and so only had three empty bottles of Stout brand beer to trash.

Our hero set a fire under the family's mold green kettle and pulled down the individually packaged cylinders of dehydrated instant mix——the Korean approximation of coffee you might say. He decided on Folgers with lots of sugar and cream, tore open the packaging and then set the empty plastic tubes beside the stove. For a moment he had nothing to do. A feeling he refused to call loneliness rose and fell in his breast as he searched for a distraction.

Chul struggled to find his remote control. Someone had put it on the bookshelves in the front room for reasons unknown. The nearly empty shelves reminded him of his son, recently taken from college into the army for two years of mandatory service. Not long ago Choi Min-sung's pocket-junk covered these shelves every day—MP3 player, loose change, electronic dictionary, bus and subway tokens, wallet. Now only Chul's favorite light reading, a weighty hardback called *Fuck Japan, An Objective History of the Imperialist Shitheads* remained.

Chul turned to his modestly sized but brand new Samsung flat screen and flipped it to CNTV's endless parade of medieval soap operas. The kettle shrieked like an elderly banshee and he poured the hot water into a coffee cup with "Dokdo is Our Land!" written in multi-colored Korean script. He finished one cup, then a second while the heated floor chased the night chill from his bare toes.

On CNTV an ancient prince sporting a fake beard wooed the cleanest possible peasant girl with sweet nothings so contrived they could hardly please anyone except the infinitely vulgar Mrs. Choi. Chul switched the thermostat from floor-heating mode to shower mode and went back to the TV while he waited. A short blast of the remote control banished CNTV's chin-wigs and brought him into a limbo of "advertising broadcasts." Our hero finally settled on KBS News.

He was about to get a third cup of coffee when the anchor broke through the normally sacred life insurance commercials to display images from the lush forests and rusty minefields separating North and South Korea.

"North Korean garrisons facing the DMZ are in chaos this morning. Witnesses say it looks like some of the North Korean units have turned their weapons on their comrades, while a large percentage of the guards appear to have vanished completely. Chinese sources indicate similar unrest along the northern border. We go now to Lim Ho-joon for the latest on these shocking developments."

"Hello, as you can see over these flower pots, anti-tank munitions and Hyundai advertisements, the North Korean 42nd division is firing to its rear against the 81st cavalry division. Oh no, it now looks as if the cavalry has pushed the infantrymen into the Demilitarized Zone. Wildlife is fleeing everywhere! The animals are setting off land mines left and right! This is really terrible, viewers, really disgusting. It appears we are being showered with deer viscera."

Chul ran into his wife's floral-themed room and laid hands on her. He shook the woman like an electronic pet that just won't shut up as her head bounced back and forth against her shoulder.

"Wake up! We are reunifying!"

Mrs. Choi rolled onto her face and gurgled. He punched her softly on the arm and tickled her ribs. Her head sunk ever deeper into the powder blue comforter.

"Uh-ouch," she said.

"They are falling, *yuhbo*," Chul said. "The rift in our nation will not last much longer. Look, get up and look."

Silence.

He left her to rise or remain. He could celebrate by himself anyway. Our hero rushed back into the kitchen where he, remembering the army did not allow phones, sent a message to his son. The boy's messenger service defaulted to some sort of music concerning "chocolate love." *Why can't my boy listen to better music, like trot?* The young man was not available to chat so Chul had to content himself with sending this message instead.

!!!!!! ☺ !!!!!!!OUR NATION WILL BE ONE AGAIN!!!!!!! ☺ !!!!!!

Mrs. Choi had retreated into her preferred comatose state and her husband attempted no further intrusions on her sleep. Instead he jumped on the heated floors and slid in his socks——an overgrown and unshaven kinder-gartener somebody left alone with the espresso. *Work,* he thought. *I must shower and go to work.* Chul nearly tore his pajamas with violent undressing and ran into the bathroom where he slipped on the polished tile. His happiness was so great he took mind of neither the rising welt on his buttock nor the sudden itching between his toes.

(For the sin of using emoticons, I sent a plague of ath-lete's foot down on the Choi family's bathroom floor.)

Chapter Three

Let us now leave Mr. Choi aside and move to an entirely different part of the world. On the tenth day of September the lesser of our two heroes, a short, thin 48 year-old named Carver Jefferson Smith, came to the front counter of a New York City McDonald's.

"I will take my usual seat," he said to the manager. "Please don't let anyone disturb me."

"No problem, we're not busy anyway."

He ordered, as he had in each of the previous six annual visits, an Egg McMuffin and hash browns. He took the previous drafts of his letter from a small computer bag and set about reviewing them for grammatical errors or less than elegant sections of prose. He would not settle for any failure, any outcome short of perfection.

The McMuffin and hash browns were ready. CJ folded the old manuscripts under the tray and went to the deepest, farthest reaches of the restaurant. His hands, hard and gnarled as rod iron, pushed aside the food and left oily prints on the pile of napkins. He removed sheets of thick, high quality writing paper and an ivory engraved Waterman pen. CJ took a deep breath and set to work.

He looked first at the front page of the *New York Times*. He saw only a small item addressing the coming 9/11 anniversary and a much larger story about some triviality in Korea, wherever that was. He had not needed extra motivation, but this slight to the victims of 9/11 renewed his resolve and strengthened his will. CJ took up his pen with great fury and awesome vengeance. The seventh in his series of annual letters to the *New York Times* read thus.

Dear So-Called Editor,

I realize you probably won't print this letter, as you've similarly refused to print the six preceding messages I've written you. It would take courage to publish what I submit and your organization has precious little in the way of valor. Still, I continue on because there will never be a time that is right to forget the outrages Osama bin Laden perpetrated against this city. I write because you and your readers are not truly remembering the horrible events of 2001.

The nonsense with ground zero and annual 9/11 remembrances infuriates me endlessly. More than a decade has passed and there's still nothing here beyond a waterworks. 2,605 civilians lost their lives on this very ground, in the most terrifying act of terrorism my country has ever witnessed, and we memorialize their deaths with a leaking garden hose. Unbelievable.

In case you've forgotten exactly what happened, or if you think it's time I moved on, I want you to remember those people who, trailing broken glass and smoke so hot it boiled blood, jumped from the highest towers ever constructed by man because they couldn't stand to burn. The ones near the top spent seven seconds falling, seven seconds to feel the pulverized concrete dust and smoking death before they splattered onto the concrete below. Jane Alice Smith was one of those who couldn't bear to die by fire. She was 35 years old and had dimples when she smiled and when she jumped it probably never occurred to her that she'd break a police officer's neck on the way down. Nine years, two hundred four days and six hours of marriage when her falling body killed a twenty seven year-old hero as he guided survivors out of WTC 1.

My wife, reduced to not only suicide but manslaughter. That sweet woman with a wonderful daughter and a budding career in business appraisal left this world with blood-smeared hands because those turban wearing fucks had some point to prove with Muhammad or Allah or whoever it is their Abrahamic death cult tells them to believe in.

Now it appears we're done fighting the camel jockeys who caused this suffering to begin with. And no, I do not feel even the slightest need to adopt less offensive names for the people living in various failed states stretching from Morocco east to Pakistan and from the Sudan north to Serbia. They are all murderers as far as I'm concerned. There was a distinct shortage of black Africans flying hijacked airplanes into the Twin Towers, nary one Indian or Irish Republican, not a single Mexican or Enclavian had even a hand in those attacks. Arabs did it and until they give up their terror-loving, dictator-heavy corrupt theocracies I will have exceptional difficultly remembering to respect cultural differences with the Middle East.

So, did we catch or kill all those responsible before we stopped blasting the towel heads? Of course we didn't. We are far too busy building madrassas and fighter jets half way around the world, for the benefit of people who hate us, to find those upstanding fellows.

So drop the self-congratulatory memorial services and stupid floral arrangements and convince your liberal elite buddies to do the two things that will truly honor the first casualties in our War on Terror. Rebuild the World Trade Center and drop bombs on Whateverthefuckitisastan until every last man and woman involved in 9/11 is dead and in the ground. That is if you and the rest really do care about the victims of 9/11.

Righteously yours,
C.J. Smith

CJ folded the note into an envelope, swallowed his Mc-Muffin in two largely unchewed bites and went out to the sidewalk. He hand delivered the letter to *New York Times* headquarters. The envelope whooshed into the drop box's darkness and made a clunking noise against some unseen metal liner. CJ then climbed the heights of his one ton dually truck and set off into the Manhattan rush hour.

Chapter Four

L et us exclude both Mr. Smith and the Choi family from our attentions for a short while. I have not yet introduced myself and our conversation has progressed to the point where only one of shocking crudity would continue withholding his name. You may call me the God of Potency.

The day 400 days from now will come to be known as P-day. They will thus memorialize my arrival because in a little less than 14 months I plan to spritz my dominance on the world entire. Think of me as a water-retaining greyhound and the people of earth as unspoiled fire hydrants.

They will know I've come when my sparkling cloud descends over a colony of hypochondriacs in New York City. They'll panic, they'll rejoice, they'll make a great deal of noise.

I forsee pointless questions, digitized and translated by orbiting satellites, dominating all the varieties electromagnetism mankind uses to communicate. Methodists from Texas will claim that Jesus, the incurable slacker, is coming back to take the righteous away to heaven. Quat chewers with dental hygiene like antique sewer pipes will wade through their chronic intoxication and determine that I've come as part of Allah's plan to strike against the infidels. A phalanx of apocalypse fantasies will penetrate the Vatican's ruddy halls. Self-proclaimed white witches in Scotland will turn up the volume on their reruns—"Mother Earth is sending her essence to protect the sacred feminine"—bullshit of that sort. At least one of the Mafiosos moonlighting as an Italian parliamentarian will try to claim me as a 3300-year-old bear-man hybrid. I'll enjoy these diversions for a while, but I do get bored.

Lest I forget, there is one more item we must discuss. I've picked two gentlemen for a heroic mission to free the world from my tyranny. One's a South Korean with an unresponsive wife and the other an upstate New Yorker with extremely impractical personal transport. You've already met them. They will whisper their plans, pilot a boat and travel the globe attempting to kill/smite/punch/inconvenience me. The whole affair has the potential to entertain for years.

Chapter Five

Since the 9/11 attacks CJ Smith had made his home in the small town of Selfsevere, New York. Dust covered laborers coming home from the porcelain factory and farmhands smelling gently of desiccated cow dung always left CJ feeling real, grounded, human. Where cities like Chicago ran on electrons, binary code and invisible currents of money, this place actually made things people could touch and see. It also helped that the residents of Selfsevere drove liberals crazy with their bountiful old time charms and patriotically themed wind chimes. It was thus natural that when the rituals of the 9/11 remembrance deepened his wrinkles and caused his eyelids to droop, CJ sought refuge in Selfsevere's homiest diner.

The Eagle's Pride Grill served fresh coffee, thick t-bone steaks and enough transfats to clog every artery within 30 kilometers. CJ took a seat near the unstained wooden door, opened a slightly rusty iron framed window and waited quietly for the staff to notice him. *No hurry,* he thought. *I just want to sit.* The waitress saw CJ after perhaps three minutes and approached to take his order.

"What'll it be, hon?"

"Gimme a chili burger with seasoned fries," CJ said. "And coffee. I need coffee."

"Arabica okay?"

He grimaced and rubbed the grime from his eyelashes. Sweat mixed with tears and stung CJ's eyes.

"You got Folgers?" he asked.

"It'll be right out," the waitress said.

CJ had neither companionship nor reading material and so, both tired and bored, he tore open a sugar packet and crushed the tiny crystals between his fingernails. The resulting sludge soon forced him to find another tick lest the sticky mess subsume his entire place setting like mold on old bread.

The proprietress, who also served as head cook, came out from her den and walked straight to CJ's booth. He briefly panicked when he could not remember the woman's name. *Might be spending too much time locked in my own head.*

"CJ, sweetie, you don't look good," she said. "You wrote another letter to the New York Times, didn't you?"

"I did."

She sighed and patted the heavily restrained bangs covering her forehead. They bounced back to their original position in mere microseconds——oh the joys of Aquanet.

"Mind if I sit down?"

He did not mind. On the contrary, CJ welcomed the chance to talk, to listen, to vent——mostly vent.

"They're never going to print your letters," the proprietress said. "You'll have more luck beating your head against these walls."

CJ answered in a low voice that split the difference between anger and resignation.

"Ain't not give a fuck."

"Language!" she said.

"I'm sorry."

"You're far too intelligent to speak that way. Truly CJ, in addition to the vulgarity you know full well 'ain't" is not a proper word."

"You forgot the double negative."

"I did," she said. Her voice picked up and gained power, like a long jumper easing out of the gates. "And you know what? That is beneath you, too. Far beneath you. Sweetheart, what's wrong?"

The waitress interrupted their conversation with one perfect chili burger and a small mountain of garlicky french-fries. The proprietress quickly dispatched the help with instructions to fetch more coffee. CJ ate a french-fry, wiped the salt and oil from his mouth and spoke.

"I'm not going to let those bastards beat me."

The proprietress pursed her lips and shook her head side to side.

"Listen to me. You know I'm the last person on earth to defend liberals, but you've got to realize there's nothing you can do to make the New York Times care about your wife. They aren't going to pay you one bit of attention now and they never will."

"So I should just let those pin-heads ignore 9/11 until everyone forgets? Hell, even the good people around here are letting it go. How long has it been since we had a memorial parade?"

The proprietress did not answer her guest directly, instead opting for metaphysical ruminations.

"In the whole world, I only see two kinds of things. The ones you can control and the ones you can't. Newspapers and parades, liberals and posterity; you're better off letting them go."

CJ bit into the burger and spilled a drop of chili on his cuff. The proprietress produced a handkerchief and passed it to him.

"Thanks."

It was not clear for which gift he gave thanks, the napkin or advice.

"I don't just hang onto stuff for fun," CJ said. "I'd have let this go a long time ago. But I can't because every time I try to close the wound some politician talks about how it doesn't matter if we catch the terrorist leaders or one of our military kids gets blown up while building some goddamn orphanage for the towelheads. It brings me right back to that day. It shows me that no matter how much we pretend to honor the victims, we don't and never did give a goddamn."

"Language!"

"Fuck!"

"Language!"

CJ's rage burned like a spicy fart, held in overlong and released to the world from between sweaty buttocks.

"Niceties! This is about justice, not manners."

"Justice is the Lord's responsibility," she said. "Your job is to live a good life and take care of that wonderful daughter Jane gave you."

Dear reader, pardon my intrusion at this point. As a god, though admittedly not the Lord this woman spoke of, I would like to make clear that those of us in the pantheon of deities, we who are the very forces of nature, laugh at remarks such as the one above. Justice is something your species conjured from the ether and it would be a lie to say we understand this human fixation or pay it any attention except as the butt of divine jokes. Enough digression, back to CJ's conversation.

"God helps those who help themselves," CJ said.

"Yes he does."

The powerful cliché left the woman silent. CJ saw this and smiled the bitter smile of a triumphant nihilist. She finally replied.

"It's killing you."

"Justice delayed is justice denied," he said.

CJ hoped this well-worn truism, this good old-fashioned bit of common sense, could shut her up again. Better yet, perhaps it would convince the owner to join him in a wholesome condemnation of Osama bin Laden, liberals or Arab culture. He was instead disappointed.

"Nobody cares. Someday you'll learn that. But until that day you will be a very miserable man."

(For the sin of using two clichés in one conversation, I rained down an affliction of acne upon CJ Smith's scalp.)

Chapter Six

Choi Chul's Saturday began at work where he arranged a driver's license for his boss' secretary and ordered new business cards to commemorate his recent promotion—"Choi Chul, Assistant Manager, Three Castle Finance." He tended to several loan applications and looked over a proposed marketing scheme targeting middle aged women interested in gardening. He began at 9am, worked through lunch and finished before 7pm. With the last memo done, he rubbed his head and loosed his tie and left for the Daegu Foreign Language Café.

Long ago he'd scored 4th out of 2,109 students in his middle school's English speech contest. Our hero had always been proud of his language competence. He took a certain flippant joy in flaunting said competence before the jealous Korean students and those bug-eyed Westerners whose cluelessness did nothing to curb their invincible confidence.

To get there Choi Chul had to climb to the sixth floor of Gwang-woo Byeong University's tallest structure. Students called it the Nude Building because any passersby could see through its expansive glass facades and observe those inside. He pushed the buttons to all four elevators and waited no more than 10 seconds before the first door opened. Choi Chul joined a young woman in the elevator and heard a chorus of bells, like slightly peeved Buddhist monks chanting slightly out of tune.

"I am going to the English Café to speak with the *wey-gooks*," our hero said. "Where are you going?"

The woman said nothing.

Chul grew angry from being so rudely ignored and turned to chastise the disrespectful cur. He only quieted himself when he saw the young woman's earphones and MP3 player. Chul sighed, muttered "moron" in English and disembarked on the 6th floor.

His favorite *weygook* sat alone in the corner drinking from an espresso. Nelson had a fear of heights and therefore preferred to take a table far from the windows. Our hero joined him.

"You are sad?" he asked.

"No, only tired," Nelson said. "I took my girlfriend to a baseball game, she drank too much and I had to spend all night holding her hair back while she vomited."

Chul nodded his head knowingly and elected to show-case his vocabulary.

"Ah yes, emesis can endanger the severely inebriated's respiratory integrity. It is good you ensured the security of her person. How is she appreciating her sojourn in Korea?"

Nelson stifled a laugh and Chul decided to dial back on the vocabulary.

"She's had fun here but she wants to go home," the Australian said. "She misses her parents and her dogs."

"You should comfort her."

Nelson interpreted that remark as sex advice of the sort middle aged Korean men are very prone to giving, smiled, took a dainty sip from his espresso and changed the subject.

"I can't remember. Is today English day or Korean day?"

"Korean day."

"I was afraid you'd say that," Nelson said. "I forgot my homework."

Our hero grinned with the full knowledge of his superior organizational skills, studiousness and preparations. *The best parts of our Korean national character,* he thought.

"Then today we will study English. I have prepared enough for us both."

The pair proceeded to discuss the use of archaic 2nd person familiar pronouns such as thee, thou and thy as they appeared in our hero's King James Version Bible. Next they moved onto the economic problems caused by Japan's heavily subsidized farmers and the importance of water policy in Nelson's native Australia. Together they nodded and grimaced in the manner customary for all great practitioners of intellectual masturbation.

After twenty minutes the spent foreigner announced his need to piss and left for the restroom. Choi Chul took this opportunity to pick up *The Economist* magazine and hold it in such a way all the others could admire his worldliness.

A different *weygook* sitting one table away from our hero closed her cell phone and laughed. The Korean college student sitting opposite her asked what was so funny.

"I swear," the foreigner said. "Three quarters of the people I know from back home couldn't find Korea on a map!"

The two laughed together and did not notice when Choi Chul grew angry. *The ignorant, disrespectful foreign bitch glorying in the ignorance of her fat, hideous kin. And her friend, may the traitorous whore choke on her own filth, rushing to throw dirt on the face of our nation!* He wanted to vent this outrage, he wanted to slap those two, to lead a mob that would point and shame those fools. He looked right and left and despaired. In this, too, he was alone.

While it would be tempting to follow our gallant hero as he fought through traffic, my dignity prohibits mentioning the many vile references to interspecies concupiscence, eternal damnation and anatomically unlikely orifice insertions Choi Chul shared with his fellow motorists. Furthermore, an occurrence of even greater interest was unfolding at the very same time, some 700 kilometers north, in the middle of a communist controlled rice field.

Colonel Moon Doong-lee's rebel forces ran low on fuel, ammunition and bodies. The imperial puppets, capitalist pigs and traitors from South Korea blocked his every escape, threatened him from every side. This left him with only one option—a phone call to Liu Hwang of the People's Liberation Army. If the Chinese could be persuaded to intercede, the traitors would have no choice but to retreat. The satellite phone rang three times as mortars exploded and jet planes flew low overhead.

"Captain Liu, my army is on the verge of destruction. Send your jet planes at once and we shall survive."

"You are besieged by the South Koreans and not the Americans," Liu said.

Moon mistook the captain's statement for a question.

"I can see only traitors. The imperialists are too cowardly to fight against our people's army."

"Then I suggest you surrender. We will send you no aid so long as the Americans remain south of the DMZ."

"What noise is this? You know the traitors fight only because the imperialists command it."

"We have made a deal with the Americans. They have yet to renege and therefore I cannot help you. For the sake of your brave men, surrender now."

"It is thus?"

"It is thus."

The phone fell silent but the colonel held onto his mouthpiece for several seconds longer, hoping for some further instruction. Moon finally set the receiver on the arm rest as one would lay a beloved mother to rest. He turned to look out of his command car's window. A shell exploded in the distance and laid waste one of his last heavy guns. The colonel imagined the men operating the artillery. The soldiers nearest by torn to small pieces, those a little farther away gashed by shrapnel and the survivors staggering about, dazed by both the shock wave and their broken eardrums. Moon wished to share their fate as he sent out the order to throw down arms.

It occurs to me that Captain Liu's agreement came about largely due to the politics inherent between proxy states and their masters. Perhaps because modern world powers do not consider themselves complete without a puppet regime, the proxy has proliferated of late and made the comparative study of said marionettes more practical.

The United States has Israel, Hitler's Germany had Franco's Spain, China had North Korea, Iran has Hezbollah.

The proxy serves to rankle its parent's enemies, represent the parent's preferred ideology—whether democracy, jihad, fascism, capitalism or communism—and to generally do as it is told. Most vitally though, the proxy state must furnish its own land as the battlefield for whichever conflagration the parent deems most pressing. Suicide bombers in Israel, republican rebels in Spain, encirclement in North Korea.

In return the proxy can expect immunity from the UN Security Council, cubic dollars in military aid and the freedom to crush minorities and dissidents like the mint in a tourist's mojito, perhaps even as mojito-drinking tourists look on. In some cases the proxy can use its status as a symbol of the parent's national power to extract even greater benefits like subsidized economies.

The danger to proxy states emerges when they forget their real purpose and begin to believe in things like national friendships and so-called special relationships. When their behavior begins to resemble that of a needy ex-girlfriend—when the late night, wheepy phone calls grow too numerous and the emergencies too frequent— puppet regimes have a way of finding themselves alone and on sale to the sorts of folks who butcher nations, take the choice cuts and leave the rest to rot.

Just such a fate befell the military leaders, fighters and rebels in North Korea. The chaos created by their power struggles left China holding back a tide of more than 10 million refugees, afraid of American or Japanese designs on the entire Korean Peninsula and facing a wave of criticism for the human rights crisis—pardon me as I chuckle at the mention of "human rights"—that grew worse every day. It was thus with a sense of relief that the Chinese gave up their North Korean proxy and delivered that massive headache to South Korea.

News of Colonel Moon's surrender spread quickly. The American president, predictably, called it "a great day for freedom." The Japanese set about finding the children Kim Jeong-il had kidnapped during the 90s and the South Koreans got drunk. Choi Chul heard the wonderful news when he clicked on his office radio.

"… the reclusive communist regime may have finally completed its long collapse," the newswoman said. "I'm Yoo Mi-gyeong, reporting live from an embedded position within the 14th army division near Kuumni. Stay with me as I further explain North Korea's turmoil."

At this point in the announcement Choi Chul leapt from his desk and toppled a cup of Happy Digestion brand barley tea. Joyous faces turned to our hero and the office workers rose as one. The radio announcement concluded as Yoo Mi-gyeong described the last of the North Korean rebels laying face down in the dirt with wrists tied behind their backs.

"There is only one proper course of action," the office supervisor said. "Let us go to the *noraebang*, sing patriotic songs and drink *soju* until everyone has fallen over!"

All those present rushed downstairs to the nearest singing room. They threw open heavy white doors and descended upon the bar. The supervisor bubbling with excitement like a heady beer, reserved the largest room— enough space to hold off other revelers soon to flood Daegu's streets. Choi Chul watched this and grew reflective. He stretched out on the *noraebang*'s vinyl-clad, red sofa and took a drink from his *soju*. His coworkers blasted off-key destructions of Korea's most famous songs and he joined them without shame. More than three hours passed before any thought to rest.

Our hero let the sound and intoxication wash over him. It was finished. He was together with his people, all his people. The ugly gash running from Incheon to the East Sea had closed. Roads, trains and electrical cables would soon bind together the two halves of a nation so brutally divided decades before. Rod iron tendrils, concrete scars and fresh new copper nerves would sprout from every town and join every road. A knot in Chul's chest released and our hero felt as though some ingenious surgeon had reunited him with a long severed hand or a hastily amputated foot.

It was then after he stumbled home and kissed his unresponsive wife that Choi Chul remembered an end to war also meant the safe return of his son. United nation, united family, the future seemed limitless.

(For the sin of referencing freedom in a speech yet again, I afflicted the American President with a mild form of rabies. For the sin of calling North Korea "reclusive" in a broadcast yet again, I afflicted radio announcer Yoo Mi-gyeong with acute agoraphobia so that she might meditate on the true meaning of reclusive.)

Chapter Seven

P-Minus 300 Days

I passed the next several months in quiet solitude, tending bonsai, collecting stamps, rearranging the matches in my divine humidor. It would have been longer had CJ's semi-estranged daughter not invited him to her marriage. When CJ received the invitation he did not recognize the groom's name and became anxious. *What if Patty married a loser?* he wondered. *After all, she's been locked down in that embassy for years, surrounded by hippies.*

He reached for his cellular phone and called his supervisors at the Solid Lead Plumbing Company to ensure the availability of sufficient vacation time. They could see no problems with his request and thus granted CJ six working-day's leave. He'd not had much work in recent years anyway.

Smith set about gathering the proper garments for a wedding. He had nothing beyond blue jeans, tank tops and polo shirts with farming logos in his closet but was pleased to find a forgotten bundle of dry cleaned dress shirts and pants hanging in his wife's old dresser. A phone call to his travel agent likewise produced a reasonably priced round-trip ticket to and from San Francisco International Airport. He even remembered his free parking vouchers.

Scarcely an hour had passed before CJ completed his arrangements. This left him in the unfamiliar situation of having nothing to do except think about those in his family who had not died in terrorist attacks.

CJ was a man unable to sleep while sitting. I mention this not out of some perverse love for intimate artistic portraiture but to hint at the misery he felt while flying six hours from New York to San Francisco, riding a Greyhound bus for another five and then meeting his daughter Patty for the final 180 minutes of driving through the redwood forests in northeast California. Combine these burdens with his newly erupted scalp pimples and CJ was in an altogether sorry condition as Patty filled the trip with small talk and nothingness. Dim sunlight filtered through the forest canopy as the young woman finally made clear her real concerns.

"Dad, please behave yourself."

CJ sat straight and glared at his daughter. *Who the hell does she think I am?* Patty grimaced and muttered under her breath.

"Guess not."

"What do you think I'm going to do?" CJ asked. "Huh? Shoot somebody? Smear blood on my face and ululate in front of the in-laws?"

"I was worried more about you being a dick," Patty said. "Sort of like you're being right now."

"How am I a dick?"

Patty looked like she might bite her tongue and accept the berating her father was building up to. The young woman gripped the steering wheel and locked her eyes onto the road. CJ pressed his point.

"How am I a dick? How is your father a dick?"

CJ's daughter shook her left hand and struck down the psychic levies holding back years of accumulated wrath, stifled frustration and festering resentment.

"Well let's see, you start fights with everybody you disagree with on anything, you have this stupid god-damn vendetta about Mom, you physically intimidate my friends and you think it's really funny to make racist comments in public. Other than that, you're a swell guy. I can totally see why Mom was so happy those last couple years."

CJ could not have anticipated his daughter's disrespect. The shock at her temerity rendered him silent for several seconds. When he'd collected himself, he decided that since haranguing Patty into submission had not worked he would try guilt.

"I'm sorry to hear you feel that way about me. I wish I knew what I'd done to give you such a low opinion of your father."

Patty took a sharp breath and rolled her eyes.

"Whatever. If you want to help you should just pose for pictures and talk about the weather."

She turned into her fiancé's driveway, switched off the car and walked into the house without waiting for CJ to follow. He let himself out and heard his daughter talking to somebody inside the home.

"Inviting him was a mistake," she said. "I'm sorry."

CJ felt a pang of sympathy and decided to take a short walk around the neighborhood before introducing himself to the people inside.

(For the virtue of successfully using the verb "to ululate" in a sentence, I blessed CJ Smith with an entire day of pleasant, honey scented flatulence.)

The next 36 hours passed quietly enough in Patty's company. CJ had mercifully followed her advice about the weather and, as a consequence, had yet to challenge anyone to a fist fight, pistol duel or jousting contest. She had even begun to relax in his presence.

The marital tent went up in a confusing bundle of rope, aluminum and torn sod. Patty walked between two of those supports and thought less and less of the man who'd begotten her. She turned her thoughts instead to the man with whom she hoped to beget her own children. *Was John really comfortable in the tuxedo I picked? Will the reception music be to his taste? Was it his grandmother or great aunt who couldn't eat fish?*

These thoughts occupied her young mind to such an extent she found herself at the crowded dinner table—father tucked in a far corner, John nearby and grandmothers scattered randomly—without exactly remembering how she'd arrived. A second cousin or nephew's girlfriend—Patty couldn't remember—nudged the bride.

"I'm so curious about your work," the distant relation said. "John tried to explain it but he just made me more confused."

"I work in an embassy," Patty said. "I moved back to San Francisco from Pakistan in January."

She saw her father's increasingly furrowed brow and tried to end the conversation before CJ could say anything stupid.

"I just do paperwork. Do you like the pasta? We made it with abalone and goat cheese, believe it or not."

This strategem failed and her father began discourse on a subject only tangentially related to the weather.

"I don't understand why we need an embassy in Pakistan, or Iraq, or any of those camel humping countries. If we were smart we'd just nuke that place until it was one giant glass parking lot and be done with them all."

The guests fell silent and Patty could not decide who she more wanted to strangle, her father or the cousin/niece/whoever-the-fuck-she-was. But her anger did not last and she quickly set about salvaging the dinner.

"Ha-ha, you're such a joker Dad."

The others forced awkward smiles and twittered their humorless, brittle laughter. Patty could feel the guests hoping, praying, that CJ would accept the conversational life line. No such luck.

"I'm dead serious. Those bastards were harboring Osama bin Laden. The Pakistanis were aiding and abetting a mass murderer, and that makes them accessories to murder."

Patty clapped her hands together loudly and spoke directly to her father.

"Fascinating. Let's talk about this later when there aren't dozens of guests to humiliate me in front of."

CJ answered loudly enough so that all the squirming dinner guests could hear.

"Why are you embarrassed? You embassy people must talk about this stuff all the time."

Patty had a progression under duress. First she attempted to retreat. If she found her escape blocked, Patty naturally tended toward a caustic, brutal sarcasm. If that didn't work, her impulses turned to direct confrontation of the sort involving bulging veins and off duty police officers. In her professional capacity as a diplomat, Patty worked to avoid steps two and three but in CJ's case, she no longer saw the point in civility.

"Yeah, Dad. We spend all day pulling the wings off flies and feeding mice into wood chippers. And then, when we run out of animals to torture, we drink blood and fantasize about how fun it would be to fry the skin off 170 million people."

He missed the point and, evidently eager to impress everyone with the power of his conviction, raised the volume of his reply.

"170 million accessories to murder! Murder! Those sons of bitches are buddies with the men who killed your mother, and you don't even care. Do you know what that's called? That's called treason!"

She grabbed her father's sleeve and yanked him from the table with sufficient force to send a broken cuff link flying into one of the grandmothers' wine glasses. She opened the nearest door and jerked CJ's arm in the hopes of bashing him against the door jam. He connected and thunked a little bit but suffered no major injuries. Patty had to content herself with walking too quickly for CJ's arthritic knees. Only when she had finished dragging her father to the driveway did she speak.

"Get out! Get out of this house and don't come back. And I am not going to let you crap on my wedding either. If I see you I swear to God I'll call the police."

Chapter Eight

In the greater part of a year, patriotic euphoria had still not yet deserted the former South Korea. Both the first week and first month reunification anniversaries attracted nationwide attention. News outlets retained their nearly exclusive focus on Korea's newfound unity and citizens persisted in decorating their public parks with thousands of flowery wreaths. Decorative cabbages arranged in the shape of "통일"—unity—sprang from every highway onramp. National pride had constructed a mighty dyke against dissention, bedazzeled it in a shrubbery of elation and encased it in the concrete of loyal citizenry. But already cracks were beginning to show.

Rescuing the northerners from starvation drained the southern treasury like a monstrous babe tearing the flesh of his mother's breast. Much of the aid never reached those in need and corruption sucked at the channels of distribution like aphids clustered round a strawberry stem. Rail shipments ran very slowly along lines built by the imperial Japanese seventy, eighty, ninety years before. Pyongyang, jewel of the North, had scarcely fifty kilometers of paved roads and, compared with the neighboring cities, it was Silicon Valley.

Even those northerners with decent education found themselves out of work or reduced to the most menial labor. Years spent languishing in the communist regime, working with outdated equipment and under the supervision of managers who usually didn't pay salaries, had lowered their productivity to sub-Zimbabwean levels.

And so they moved south en masse. Whether in Seoul, Daegu or Busan, the northerners found themselves on welfare, in crap jobs or homeless in a culture they did not understand, speaking southern dialects so different as to be unintelligible and under the care of people who increasingly considered them burdens.

Dealing with the rebellious remnants of Kim Jeong-whatshisface's army also cost both blood and treasure. Although the number of outright gunfights fell to near naught, Seoul could only look on as the North Korean military leaders reinvented themselves as Pan-Korean crime bosses. For the first time since the 1960s, young women found it unwise to venture out alone at night. Middle and high schools, for the first time ever, had to deal with *mayakjaengy* students, their used needles poking through plastic garbage bags and pot clouds billowing from bathroom stalls.

Foreign investors fled for fear of the economic carnage 20 million peasants and 2 million potential insurgents would surely inflict on the world's 11th largest economy. With them went billions of dollars and the solvency of millions of pension funds. President Yeo Ju-han announced that, while certainly worth the price, unification had undone Korea's hard won balanced budget and necessitated higher taxes. Now was the time to sacrifice for the Korean race's sake, he said.

Choi Chul knew this but would not normally allow such trivialities to disturb his routine. Beggars could be ignored, taxes paid and criminals imprisoned. None of these wise and good expedients, however, stopped his friends and coworkers from endlessly bitching about each little thing. Even Nelson, his favorite *weygook*, groused.

"How ugly is that river project construction?" Nelson had asked. "Because of the damned commies, it will probably never get finished. What a blight. And all of this crime, my family wants me to come back home."

"Because of those lazy stone heads my grandmother's retirement benefits have fallen by half," Choi's secretary had said. "Who do you think must pay to erase this difference?"

"It was foolish to take the Northerners in," our hero's supervisor had said. "Their uselessness has reached such heights that the government can no longer afford to maintain our busses and subways. We will all have to buy cars…from where will that money come?"

"I do not know for how much longer I can afford to maintain this office," Chul's employer had said. "The foreigners have pulled out all of their money and it is only with great difficulty we convince our customers to buy."

Our hero's tolerance for such treasonous talk extended only so far. It was a Tuesday when he finally castigated the secretaries, supervisors and managers during lunch.

"How dare you speak of our nation's triumph so disparagingly," he said. "Did you think the restoration of our people would come without cost?"

"Spoken like a man who has not yet paid," the secretary said. "Your parents are dead, your wife rich. Not all of us are so lucky."

Our hero fashioned a dagger of contempt and poisoned its edges with loathing.

"Who could ask for more than dead parents? Why not cut your mother's throat if doing so would bring such blessings?"

The secretary cried and Choi Chul basked in the glow of righteous vengeance. He continued.

"We are one people," he said. "If you cannot abide the loss of pensions for the sake of your race, then you are truly beneath contempt."

The office supervisor suggested our hero still himself.

"Ya! Son of a fuck, shut your flapping pig mouth!"

Chul did not accept this advice and instead went on for several minutes more. As a result, he found himself on three month's involuntary unpaid leave. This left our hero free to fully experience the sacrifices necessary to restore the Korean race.

I do not like having you at the house all day," Mrs. Choi said. "Why do you not take up a hobby?"

"I need no hobby," he said. "I need rest."

"You should rest elsewhere. It makes me nervous when you lurk in the home."

"I do not lurk."

"You always lurk."

Our hero could see no further point in arguing and thus did as his wife requested. Chul's new Ssangyong Chairman W waited glistening in the car park and its loveliness lifted his spirits. He spent more time touching this lovely car than perhaps anything—certainly *anyone*—else. Chul ran his fingers over the mirror smooth paint and felt the solid, heavy key fob in his pocket. He remotely unlocked the doors and slid behind the steering wheel with great care. *It would be a shame to scuff the leather.*

The navigation screen offered such a glut of possible destinations as to overwhelm him. Our hero responded by turning the GPS system off. He drove at random through the streets of Daegu and paid more than the normal amount of attention to pleasing reflections, cleverly executed advertisements and carefully designed public parks. Choi Chul, as if by magic, found a mildly upscale bar with plentiful parking and elegant shrubs in plaster pots. The lure of neon mood lighting and velour seats proved too strong to resist. He parted the cushioned, vinyl-clad doors and sat at the bar. A bartender in her mid thirties with small eyes, porcelain skin and full lips came to his stool.

"What will you take?"

"Give me a Hite," he said. "Your bar is not busy this night."

"It is thus because tonight is a Wednesday."

He bowed his head and grimaced.

"I had forgotten."

"How can a man with a car such as yours forget which day it is?" the bartender asked. "Certainly the North Korean problem has made every day precious to businessmen and officials."

Chul became annoyed and thus delivered his reply with less than customary deference.

"There is no North Korean problem and I forget in exactly the same way any other man forgets."

The waitress forced a grin and turned quickly to walk away.

"Your Hite will be ready after a short time."

Our hero looked at the liquor shelves made of backlit Plexiglas and noticed a 300-dollar bottle of sake. *Damn the Japanese and damn their pride. If it wasn't for the island bastards with their infernal occupation, their cruel destruction of Korean society, this reunification would never have been necessary. And even in modern times, those dirty children of dogs had the nerve to claim Dokdo as their own!*

He called to the waitress once more.

"Here."

She responded promptly but with the absolute minimum of courtesy.

"Yes, customer."

"I want to buy that bottle of Japanese piss water."

Our hero could see the confusion in her eyes but did not mind. The annoying woman deserved, indeed had earned the foggy, perplexed cluelessness now enveloping her.

"Uh, yes customer. Did you notice the price?"

"Of course I did. Men who drive cars such as mine can hardly be expected to forget pricing. Bring me that garbage."

The bartender bowed and returned with both the sake and Hite. It was with a great deal of befuddlement that she uttered the customary "take the deliciousness."

Choi Chul cradled the unopened sake bottle for several hours as he drank a dozen cold rimmed Hites. He tasted the aluminum and felt the alcohol in his mouth. He swayed to and fro under the weight of his mighty drunkenness and spoke with a tongue dry as cotton balls.

The bartender took note of his obvious intoxication and would normally have stopped a customer in such a state from driving. However, she was a vengeful woman and 'forgot' to call the *daeri-oonjun* men that deliver drunken customers and their cars safely home.

"I'm leaving!" our hero said. "And I'm taking this bottle of Japanese shit with me!"

"Yes customer," the bartender said. "Go well and be safe."

"Where is the *daeri-oonjun*?" Chul asked.

"I am sorry," she lied. "I did not understand you."

"Fuck it, I need no help."

"Sleep well, customer."

Our hero stumbled into the night, threw his bottle of sake at a Honda dealership's glass pane window, took to his car and failed a field sobriety test.

(For the sin of wasting liquor, I afflicted Choi Chul with both a screaming hangover and a sudden craving for sake.)

Chapter Nine

I was so horrified by Mr. Choi's wanton mistreatment of spirits that I fled to the other side of the earth, into the head of a man who would never dream of throwing sake at Hondas. I seated myself safely upon his optic nerve that I might observe a wilderness of cheap tile and exposed ventilation ducts, plumber's crack and tragic perms.

CJ Smith was at that moment browsing the magazine shelves at the Selfsevere Wal-Mart. He picked up the new edition of *Guns and Ammo* in order to admire Glock's recently released, .84 caliber, 25 round, semi automatic hand cannon. The civilian model gun, according to the article, could fell 7 home intruders with one bullet so long as the criminals formed a single file line. It could pierce body armor, penetrate bullet-proof glass and stop small but vicious whales in a single hit. The author then speculated at length on its anti-zombie efficacy and what would have happened in Enclave if the natives had been properly armed. CJ finished reading the specs on the enormous firearm and re-shelved the magazine.

As he did so he knocked several copies of *Foreign Policy* magazine onto the tile floor. Normally he would not concern himself with worthless, liberal-propaganda garbage like *Foreign Policy*, but his respect for order and cleanliness compelled him to rectify the mess. The magazine cover depicted a giant grey mushroom cloud spreading out over an otherwise plain black landscape. The feature story's title read "India and Pakistan, the Future?" *Who gives a damn?* CJ put the magazines back.

It was not until the cashier scanned CJ's beef hamburger patties that he remembered his other Patty and her connection to Pakistan. *I should call her,* he thought. He pulled the cell from his Wrangler jeans as he walked away from checkout. Perhaps 10 yards and four rings passed before his daughter answered.

"What do you want?"

"Are you somewhere we can talk?" CJ asked. "I really think we need to discuss your safety."

"I'm at the airport."

His soft concern juxtaposed amusingly against his daughter's impatience like waves of goose down against a razor wire coastline. It had taken a mere three sentences of discussion to firmly establish the rhythms of awkward conversation.

"I want to make sure you're safe. I worry about you."

Patty said nothing.

"No, really, I'd like to talk about your safety. No ulterior motive, I swear."

"I'm headed to Islamabad right now," Patty said. "I don't have much time to talk."

CJ stifled his irritation. *Why does she namedrop these backwaters halfway around the world, like everybody should know Islamisbad off the top of their head?*

He continued.

"That place is in the Middle East?"

"More or less, it's the capital of Pakistan."

CJ could barely stand the thought of his daughter living among all those blood-thirsty terrorists. *They must drool and swipe the ground with their claws when they think of a nice white girl. They could cut off her head like that liberal bastard. They could rape her. They could kidnap her and put her in front of one of those terrorist flags and make her denounce America!*

Why Patty's time in the Middle East had not bothered him before, he couldn't tell, but this did not stop him from continuing.

"Why are you going?" Smith asked. "It's dangerous."

"How touching. I'm going because it's my job. It's not like I haven't been to Pakistan before."

CJ persisted with the goose down approach.

"I saw a magazine and it scared me. I think the terrorists will probably start something with India. Nobody can reason with those terrorists. How could you possibly help?"

Patty's short little laugh came through the phone and CJ could feel her taking on the role of a 3rd grade social studies teacher.

"We're trying to talk the Pakistanis out of building up troops in Kashmir. That's not unusual, the Pakistanis and Indians threaten to nuke each other about once every other week. My job is to make sure they don't."

CJ could not contain his joy.

"But imagine how many terrorists that would kill!"

"You are really missing the point."

It was CJ's turn to try his hand at social studies pedagogy. His voice deepened and his words slowed. It was like the Goddess of Wisdom had descended from heaven for the sole purpose of lifting his weighty maxims in divinely cupped hands. Athena, actual Goddess of Wisdom, was then eating cheesy poofs from her divinely cupped hands, but close enough.

"They aren't like us. They will stop at nothing to kill or convert every last person on earth to Islam."

"You do know I lived in Pakistan for three years?"

"You lived in an embassy, that's different."

"Dad, I lived in an apartment and worked in an embassy. I talk to dozens of Pakistanis every day."

"All the same, it's different out in the real world."

"Right," she said. "I have to get on the plane now so I'm going to hang up."

CJ's concern took the form of a seldom used expression in the Smith family.

"I love you."

Patty blew him off.

"Yeah, I'll talk to you later."

(For the sin of reading gun magazines, I afflicted CJ Smith with a priapism. For the virtue of comparing one's daughter with ground beef, I reduced his scalp acne to dandruff. For the sin of using zombies in a narrative, I cursed the *Guns and Ammo* writer with torrential diarrhea, sudden male pattern baldness, a broad assortment of skin rashes, fungal toenails, loud and unending next door neighbor sex, a demonically possessed shower nozzle, kidney stones the size of ping pong balls and a year in which, for entertainment, he can access naught but Stephanie Meyer novels and the most recent films by M. Night Shyamalan. At the conclusion of that year, I further curse him with being thrown into an active volcano by a tribe of cosplaying teenagers.)

CJ's perturbation, aching groin and itching head made stillness impossible. He dropped his groceries off at home and drove aimlessly through the Selfsevere hill country.

He mulled over the many outrages towel-head camel-fuckers had committed against his loved ones. They murdered his wife, endangered his daughter, humiliated his country and harbored terrorists! His blood pressure rose and his indignation grew so full it made breathing difficult. His rage finally spilled out in a flood of incoherent obscenities and flying spittle.

"Fucking cunts fuck with my fucking family!"

CJ became aware of his outburst's silliness and grew even more morose. *I can't even cuss correctly.*

He turned on the radio but could not stand the thought of music. CJ changed to his favorite talk radio station and listened as the *Michael Barbarian Show* ramped up a new hour of programming.

"You know what?" Barbarian asked. "The Muslims are always calling our brave young men and women in uniform crusaders. They say that like the crusades were somehow worse than the savage outrages Muslims commit every single day.

"Did the crusaders strap bombs onto themselves and then explode on city busses? No! Did the crusaders randomly murder Jews as they went about their daily lives? No! Did the crusaders kill thousands of their own people to make a political point? No! Did the crusaders stone women for violating medieval modesty codes? No! Maybe the real reason they call us crusaders is jealousy. Maybe they wish they were half as civilized as the crusaders were. Let's take a caller. Preston from New Jersey, you're on the air."

"Hi Michael, long time listener first time caller here. I just wanted to say first of all that I love your show. You're the only one out there in the media with the stones to say what we're all thinking."

"Thank you Preston," Barbarian said. "So what do you think about the Muslims trying to slander our brave troops?"

"I think it's disgusting for a bunch of cowardly suicide bombers to make any attack on our troops," Preston said. "If they had one tenth the integrity our troops did their 'civilization'—if they even deserve to call themselves a real civilization—wouldn't be so backwards."

Smith pounded his fist against the plastic dashboard of his Chevy truck. The impact felt righteous, glorious.

"You speak the truth," Barbarian said. "But let's talk about the crusaders, since the Muslims brought it up."

"I agree 100% with you. The crusaders may have been nasty dudes, but they were nothing compared to the terrorist scum running around the Middle East. And if you study history you will see that they are the only thing that saved Western civilization from the Jihadists. If it hadn't been for the crusaders buying time against the Muslims, Europe would not have survived long enough for the Renaissance. We should thank the crusaders for saving us, and so should the Muslims, because if it wasn't for Western Civilization, the whole world would suck just as much as Iran. Even though the crusaders didn't win, they saved us. We just need a similar total war to finish the Muslims off for good now."

Hell yeah, CJ thought. *Finish those sons of bitches off.* Maybe India was on to something. Maybe it would only take one spark before the forces of righteous vengeance swept aside the terrorists!

(For the sin of saying "long time listener, first time caller" on a radio program, I caused Preston from New Jersey to suffer from three years of intensely homoerotic dreams.)

That edition of *Foreign Policy* magazine, the cover art of which had so upset CJ, led that month with a story concerning new tensions between the long time enemies, Pakistan and India.

In it, Indian sources accused the ISI, Pakistan's not always obedient intelligence agency, of coordinating a series of assassinations against India's civilian leadership. First they sent a sniper to kill the undersecretary to the director of demography and caste research's liaison to the oversecretary of regional electoral sales and management, Sikh Khan. Next, Rajesh Sing, India's greatest racing cow breeder, fell to a mysterious poisoning, laid waste by a toxin the ISI was known to use. Finally, India blamed the evil doers at ISI for the asphyxiation death of Sunil Patel. Patel had gained notoriety as a Bollywood star after singing—through the use of a poorly understood technique called circular breathing—a perfect, continuous b flat for more than an hour straight. It is a truly monstrous enemy that would strike down such a man, the Indian authorities said.

The Pakistanis, under new President Generalissimo Mohsin Bahawalanzai, fired back by accusing India of once more scheming to flatten Pakistan like they had in the humiliatingly brief 1971 war. "There will be no walkover this time," the Pakistanis warned. "We have more determination, more will and nuclear weapons just as potent." President Generalissimo Bahawalanzai clarified the ISI's role in the undersecretary slayings, racing cow breeder assassinations and circular breather strangulations.

"I'm not entirely sure what the ISI is doing," the President Generalissimo said. "But I'm positive that whatever it is, it's for the best."

Within a week of publishing *Foreign Policy* magazine's prophetic article, India massed more than 100,000 troops, 400 tanks and 200 mobile missile batteries at the border near Lahore. Outside analysts estimated that such a force could sweep through all of Pakistan's rich southeastern provinces within a week. Imagine the Soviet Union conducting full fleet attack sub exercises along the United States' eastern seaboard and you come close to realizing the gravity of India's military maneuvers.

Pakistan responded by performing seven nuclear tests in short succession and by moving their long range missiles to the border region where they could strike any part of India. Imagine al Qaeda opening a dirty bomb facility in Paris and you still greatly underestimate the gravity of Pakistan's nuclear experimentation.

Firebrands whipped their followers into mouth-foaming frenzies. Calls for pre-emptive bloodletting rose like melanomas from Central Asia's mountainous skin. Disaster seemed but one idiot soldier away.

Chapter Ten

P-Minus 16 Days

Our hero looked forward to seeing his triumphantly returning son this day. Choi Chul had planned a
night of heavy drinking and dancing girls, going so far as
to personally select the entertainers beforehand. Therefore, when his son did not arrive that evening, our hero
grew angry and spoke thus under his breath.

"The little bitch makes me a fool."

Still, any reasonable man would shudder at the thought
of putting dancing girls and alcohol to waste. Several
phone calls resulted in our hero's office supervisor meeting with Choi at the bar. The man walked through the
vinyl padded doors and loosened the black tie hanging
from his hard starched collar.

"You have chosen our meeting place wisely," the supervisor said. "The velour curtains are most tasteful and I
cannot help but chuckle when I see these miniature umbrellas in lieu of drinking straws."

Our hero smiled and thanked the supervisor. *Now
would not be a bad time to build upon* wanjangnim's *favorable impression,* Choi thought.

"I arranged this in your honor to illustrate how dearly I wish to reenter your favor."

These words hurt the sensitive supervisor and he spoke as one wounded in the pursuit of love.

"You never departed from my favor, but your evil words and insubordination made me to punish you. I know your mind is good."

Our hero expressed his thanks, nodded and called out for sake—he meant to say soju—and dancers. The girls, probably 30 years old but looking much younger, appeared wearing nothing save their bikini bottoms and serving trays.

"Consider these my formal apology," Chul said.

"And what an excellent means of expressing your remorse."

The supervisor partook in Choi Chul's hospitality for many hours. The dancers gyrated, the spirits spilled forth and time seemed to evaporate from the hot surface of our hero's happiness. The celebration did not conclude until well after 4 AM. When Chul laid down his weary body, he did so hoping that the supervisor would restore his post very soon.

It is best if we now change venues and turn our attentions to the salty waters separating the cold, rocky beaches of Yamaguchi Prefecture and the great Korean steel mills in Pohang. There we will find a tiny Japanese vessel and a naval captain of great interest.

Suzuki Tojo's patrol boat had but three crewmen and a hull so thin it echoed with every wave. The iron had not been treated and thus, even in spite of the maintenance crew's continual efforts, the sailors were forever finding new pockets of rust.

Even the feeblest enemies could scarcely help but sink it. Rocket propelled grenades would surely destroy it, not to mention any of the commonly available surface skimming missiles. Even small arms fire posed a credible threat to the *Gymkhana*. To command such a vessel did nothing to bring Suzuki honor and in fact caused him to blush when in the company of his fellow officers. *It is inexcusable how impotent the* Gymkhana *renders my men*, he thought. *We are well trained, sturdy fighters with large caliber firearms. We should be feared and yet this boat makes us pitiful.* He scraped a rust bubble from behind the boat's rev counter and felt the horrid, wet grinding under his fingernail. He thought of his young twin daughters and gritted his teeth. How frustrating to be here.

He would have continued scratching rust bubbles from behind the instrument displays and hating life if not for the clumsiness of Neptune. Just hours after our hero left the dancing girls behind, the Japanese boat captain found himself battered by great foam-tipped waves and wind seemingly driven by the very hand of Satan!

(The Prince of Darkness was actually, at that moment, washing the planting soil from his Crocks. He's growing rhubarb, chard and kale this year. The conflagration, as I mentioned previously, actually arose from Neptune slipping in the bathtub.)

The tempest passed quickly enough, but floating debris and high waves battered the little vessel. A log perhaps, something blunt and heavy and vaguely soft, crashed into the starboard flank and opened a hole of about five centimeter's diameter. Suzuki summoned his gunner and threw open the thin bulkhead separating the engine room from the wheelhouse. He flicked on the bilge pumps and went to war against the in-rushing water. The water was cold and salty and itching against his skin. Suzuki attempted to stop the leak with a large bottle of emergency expandable foam, though largely in vain. He cursed and returned to the wheelhouse. Anything potentially compromising—navigation logs, orders from on high, briefings on Korean, Chinese and maritime traffic—he put into the safe box along with a lit flare.

The *Gymkhana's* damaged electrical systems, communications capabilities and weakened hull integrity precluded limping home and the remote location made rescue unlikely. The *Gymkhana* sank into the water like a fat man settling into an over soft bed. With no means of navigation and the sun rapidly setting, the captain ordered his men into to the emergency raft. As they set off in the direction of two small islands just visible over the horizon, our captain looked back at his sinking boat and muttered "good riddance."

I fear I must put Captain Suzuki's miserable, wet and wind-blown raft ride to the side. Completely unbeknownst to our brave captain, he was stumbling into a territorial dispute of infinitesimal practical significance but enormous symbolic weight.

He, like most Japanese, was only vaguely aware that Korea and Japan had vied for control of those two islands, collectively known as Dokdo, since the end of World War II. He, unlike the Korean citizens who take this sort of thing very seriously, had not familiarized himself with the tortured history of those two rocks. Suzuki, like most Japanese, knew little about the debate that had devolved into the Koreans' ever more bizarre protestations and the Japanese governments' obfuscating stupidity. He knew even less of the maddeningly vague ancient documents thrust this way and that as "proof."

South Korea bases its fiery, passionate claims—about which Suzuki neither knew nor cared—on territorial records from the 6th century, during the Shilla Dynasty. These are the first historical mention of Dokdo and they clearly show Korean, or rather a kingdom in what would several centuries later become Korean, ownership. The Koreans further bolster their case by referencing the An Yong-bok incident of 1693 wherein a small contingent of *Joseon* fishermen drove their Japanese counterparts from Dokdo through a combination of intimidation and abduction. The Edo government in Japan publically concluded the An Yong-bok matter by banning its fishermen from Dokdo and recognizing Korean sovereignty. Lastly, that Japan saw fit to annex the island in 1904, the Koreans argue, means that even they recognized Korea's historical ownership. After all, what sort of country annexes land that is already its own?

The Japanese, favoring a more "we don't really care about Dokdo but will still put up a fight because we're in denial and also, fuck you" rhetorical style, doubted the veracity of Korea's documents, insisting that they instead refer to rocky outcroppings near Ulueng Island. That rocky outcroppings could be confused for Dokdo will give you some idea of how small the territory in dispute really is. The Japanese also point to a 1677 report in which the Tokugawa Shogunate gave dominion over Dokdo's seas to a handful of privileged Japanese fishermen. Further, maps dating from 1785 denote Dokdo as the territorial boundary of Japan. Finally, Japan most certainly took control of Dokdo in 1904 and, with their 41 years of administration, felt it was entitled to what the

Korean monarchs ceded, even if the ceding took place at almost literal gunpoint.

In the course of the dispute, a few southern Japanese counties declared poorly understood and sparsely attended "holidays" to celebrate their ownership. Korean protesters, invoking a symbolism they only vaguely understood, decapitated live birds in front of the Japanese embassy. The spat continued to hamper trade, mobilize militaries, complicate diplomacy and generally get in the way of a great many things that actually do matter.

Lost in the hubbub is the small matter of Dokdo's crushing insignificance. Both islands combine for a little over 40 acres. The soil is poor, the total permanent population consists entirely of one octopus fisherman and his wife, the terrain is rugged and the surrounding reefs hazardous. And while the waters have plentiful fish and the seabed natural gas, those valuable commodities take a distant backseat to the more dramatic elements discussed above.

This all leads the thoughtful but only quasi-benevolent trickster god of impossible grooviness to wonder, is the Dokdo controversy more than the physical manifestation of a patriotic pissing match? Is it more than a case of dueling inferiority complexes bred from the fertile humiliation of Asia's most brutal empire and the resurgent jingoism of its former colony? Our brave captain Suzuki Tojo would soon find out.

The emergency raft crashed into one of Dokdo's eastern reefs. It settled unsteadily on its Kevlar coated flanks, ripping a little against the limestone with each wave. The storm surge threatened to turn the boat, and Captain Suzuki therefore decided to take his men quickly ashore before the raft capsized. The captain removed his shirt, pants and shoes and threw them into the water. He felt the tiniest bit of regret as he watched his gilded, white captain's hat sink. The others likewise cast off their heavy, water-logged uniforms and leapt into Dokdo's angry tidal pools. They held their weapons high overhead while wading through knife-edged reefs and stinging jellyfish, one of which lit Suzuki's foot on fire. A concrete dock jutted through the brine into the bay. The Japanese took advantage of it to avoid the sharp rocks and came ashore. Once securely on the "beach," Suzuki's men took stock of their surroundings. The captain noted a signaling tower higher up on the island, just visible over the cliffs. He pointed, shouted orders and sent his crew toward the light source. They had not climbed more than three minutes when something disturbed the party.

"I hear something," one sailor said.

"It's just the waves," Suzuki said. "Let's continue on."

The sailors came round a ferocious, jagged boulder and faced at least a dozen armed men. *Maybe paramilitary, maybe police, maybe smugglers or Chinese.* The enemy nearest the sailors shook his M16 rifle and, yelling so loudly his voice cracked, called out the following.

"손들어!"

"I don't understand you," Suzuki said. "Put down your weapons."

"야 씨발, 지금 당장 손들어!"

The enemies attempted an encircling maneuver and a Japanese sailor to Suzuki's left opened fire. He felt something burn through his cheek and when he bit down, pulverized bits of tooth cut his gums. Suzuki hunched down in blinding white pain and used his left hand to cradle the broken remnants of his face. He raised his other hand to signal that his men should surrender but had no time as another bullet destroyed the metacarpals and phalanges of his palm. Suzuki fell silent as blood moistened the earth and his strong, military legs crumpled under the weight of hemorrhagic shock.

Chul's son Min-sung wished to spend his day at Kyobo bookstore so that he could pretend to read and inconspicuously spy on the checkout counter. He liked one of the cashiers—perhaps 22, tall, cute glasses, perky butt, no breasts—and was working up the courage to ask for her phone number. He flattened the tiny wrinkles on the bottom hem of his button-down shirt, checked his face for pimples and cursed the military for mandating such an unfashionable buzz cut hairstyle.

After more than an hour, the young lady had still not stepped out from behind her post. Min-sung grew impatient and thus did not hesitate to answer the phone when his friend Jo Dong-hyeok called.

"Min-sungah, we float in a sea of shit."

"What noise is this?"

"The stone-head junior police shot four Japanese navy men," Dong-hyeok said.

"Have the commanders ordered us to come?" Min-sung asked.

"It is only a matter of time."

Min-sung slapped his open hand on the wall. The resulting sound startled the nearest customer. He apologized and spoke once more into his phone.

"What should we do?"

"I do not know," Dong-hyeok said. He paused and added the following with a most uplifting tone of hopefulness. "Maybe we should stretch our muscles to prevent injury?"

"You are a moron," Min-sung said.

"Why does your anger go to me?"

"Because you are a moron. Let us meet in two hours under the Samsung Tower. In this way we can talk more clearly."

Jo Dong-hyeok agreed and Min-sung's phone went dead. He felt the urgent need for action, an anxious desire to fight or flee, but could make no judgments as to which he should choose. Min-sung saw the young woman at the bookstore checkout counter and remembered his purpose. He wrote his phone number—forgetting to include his name—on a scrap of paper and went to her. His hands shook and his jaw flexed as he stepped into her checkout line. When the customer in front finished, Min-sung thrust the paper at the cashier, said, "this is my number," walking briskly away with no further explanation.

Chapter Eleven

R-Minus 15 Days

CJ Smith normally got his current events from Fox News Channel. Everyone knew Fox was most free from the pervasive bias, sensationalism and shoddy reporting that pervades the mainstream media. However, Patty's departure had the unexpected side effect of rendering Fox News insufficient. While they made valiant efforts to cover the crisis in Pakistan, their previous brave stands against the corrupt faith of Islam had left Fox noticeably thin on local correspondents. CJ decided to try CNN International for the first time.

Settling down with a beer and notepad, CJ went about making his observations. Socialists had clearly taken control of this channel and they had very little information on important matters like gun rights or global warming hoaxes. Further, the on-air personalities were obviously affirmative action hires and CJ could not stand all the so-called "football" coverage. *Fucking European lawn fairies.* Still, Smith wanted very badly to make sure his daughter remained safe, and CNN International had much better penetration into Islam's blackened heart than did Fox. Not the best, but CJ could persevere.

His first day post-Fox contained a great deal of coverage about tensions and Kashmir and the massing troops. The second day brought more of the same, the third a seeming thaw. But the fourth day...

(For the virtue of taking notes on newscasts, I bless CJ Smith with absolute immunity from carpel tunnel syndrome.)

Patty woke to the sounds of many people running quickly in the small, enclosed area outside her first floor Islamabad apartment. She threw off a white, 500-thread Egyptian comforter her fiance John had given her and pulled on a huge T-shirt emblazoned with "Columbia." Pajama bottoms and tennis shoes without socks followed in short order. She thought first of a building fire and second of a car bombing, maybe another coup. Part of her knew fear, sensed the danger and urged panic. Patty felt it, owned it, took a breath and shoved all that down somewhere it couldn't get in her way.

So many Pakistanis had filled the narrow hallways that Patty had to strain when she opened the door. She knocked an old man onto his ass while he passed by and made her way into the hall. Quick efficient thoughts helped Patty keep that fear buried, keep hold of that self-possessed pragmatism that prevents smart people getting trampled in hallways.

Stick to the walls. There's less of a chance to get trampled next to the walls. Keep your knees bent. Push out with your elbows and hands, give yourself space. Don't stop, don't stop for anything.

Patty looked back at the stairwell from whence so many had come. Seventeen stories worth of residents packed into the first floor walkway. Cracks on the old ceilings looked bigger than they had just a day before and Patty wondered if the mass of humanity was literally spreading the walls apart. An exit came into view. Patty's elbows went back to work and it was not long before she'd gotten outside, grabbed hold of a decorative streetlight and pulled herself clear of the throng.

Her building emptied ever more and the flow of people on the streets showed no signs of slackening. Patty spotted an older woman with apparent difficulty breathing.

"What's happening?" she asked in precise if accented Urdu. "Why's it that the people flee?"

"The Indian army attacks!" the woman said. "They took Lahore and now it's for us that they're coming! We must go to the shelters!"

Patty stuck a hand in her pajama pockets and searched for the cell phone she'd left inside her apartment. "God-damn it," she said in English. She soon reached the corner convenience store. A tiny bathroom window served as her hand hold, the top of a fence a place to wedge her foot. Patty used her free hand to break one of the store's large second story windows and pulled herself inside.

Her hands shook and she shivered twice—not so much from fear, which had passed, but a glorious sensation of life. Some strange confidence sated her, made her laugh at her mastery of danger. Patty dialed the embassy and smiled as the cuts on her hands turned the phone red.

M y awesome powers and sublime intellect enable me to explain this incident far better than Patty's embassy co-workers ever could. I had watched as Sheik Yar-haz, unofficial head of the ISI and the man India believed responsible for killing innocent undersecretaries, circular breathers and racing cow breeders, secretly visited Lahore the day before. The Indian military leaders, whose coffee I lightly sprinkled with horse laxatives, had long been eager to strike against Yar-haz. When they learned from their spies exactly when and where he would appear, it presented an opportunity too good for their rumbling bowels to ignore. Lahore's very close proximity to the Indian border caused these Indian officials to imagine that a small team of hyper-trained super ninjas could descend from an ultra high-tech helicopter, fire their top-secret weapons into the murderer's low-tech nasal cavity and make a glorious escape while trailing clouds of pure awesomeness. I would never miss anything involving Indian super ninjas and thus immediately decamped to the secret super ninja's headquarters. That which follows is a nearly objective, 80 percent accurate account of their activities.

Pilot Singh Kareshi loved his new, American-built Mohawk helicopter. Its interfaces were perhaps too numerous, its controls were a monument to confusion and its occasional reliability problems aroused suspicion amongst the Luddites, but Kareshi gladly suffered these shortcomings in exchange for the craft's immense capability and leading-edge technology.

Enjoying the sunset from beneath his Mohawk, Kareshi greeted the team of super ninjas with a friendly smile and cordial invitation to "rip that goat fucker Yar-haz's head off."

The first roguishly handsome, two-meter tall and heavily muscled super ninja chortled before answering.

"Yes, of course we will rip the goat fucker's head off. This night we will use his blood to practice calligraphy while trailing clouds of pure awesomeness."

Kareshi laughed and motioned to his Mohawk.

"Indeed, let us set off."

The prototype engines spun each million-dollar rotor blade through the air like a sword through adipose and lifted the Mohawk lightly from the earth's scalp. The supremely high-tech machine slipped through the air without making anything as low-tech as noise. Bleeding-edge processors and the latest sensors fed Kareshi's 563 instruments and displays at more than seven terabytes per second. Active camouflage, carefully calibrated for the night sky, duplicated Home Depot brand black spray paint so convincingly you could hardly tell the difference.

However, all was not well. The Possible-Insurgents-With-High-Blood-Pressure-Who-Have-Suspicious-Chemicals-On-Their-Hands (PIWHBPWHSCOTH for short) scanning radar system suddenly sprung a leak. Even if he had noticed it, this cooling system's failure would not have alarmed Kareshi. After all, Sheik Yar-haz didn't have high blood pressure and was known to prefer Dove hand soap, the one soap in all the world capable of masking all suspicious chemicals from PIWHBPWHS-COTH. But with the amazing helicopter's 99.2 kilometers of wiring and 6,214 sensors, some systems were bound to operate nearby others. The PIWHBPWHSCOTH cooling circuit happened to mount less than three millimeters above the helicopter's cutting edge carbon fiber and titanium winch. A shower of coolant fell into the top-secret relay switch that operated the winch's controls and shorted it out. The significance of this tragedy will soon become clear, but let us now return to the super ninjas.

Lahore's nightly rolling blackouts provided the perfect cover for Kareshi to slide his craft over Yar-haz's compound. The super ninjas patted each other on the backs, adjusted their platinum-plated-carbon-fiber-diamond-lenses night vision goggles and began roping to the safe house roof.

"Away!" the first ninja said.

"Avast!" said the second.

"Ahoy!" said the third.

But they weren't moving. Due to the previously mentioned problems with PIWHBPWHSCOTH, the supremely crafted winch would not respond to Kareshi's high-tech commands. The pilot did not worry, though. He could simply engage the autopilot's hover capability and release the winch manually. With the press of a button, the Mohawk's 877 hydraulic circuits activated in a perfectly perfect ballet of impeccably impeccable balance and precisely precise precision. Kareshi grabbed ahold of the forged and shot peened titanium override lever (machined to within .00003 millimeter tolerances and treated to resist ocean depths of up to 50,000 meters) and slid the super ninjas to their insertion point.

At this exact time, or more specifically, eight minutes before this exact time, the sun emitted a slightly above-average burst of neutrinos. In a process far too scientific to explain, these neutrinos interfered with the magnetic fields generated by the craft's 109 gyroscopes. This magnetic interference then altered the mean rate of electrical resistance in one circuit of one of the 72 processors devoted to autopilot, causing the Mohawk to veer left by 16 meters.

A combination of Kareshi's surprise and the autopilot's sudden exercise in free will deposited all three super ninjas noisily into Yar-haz's swimming pool. As they splashed about, the terrorist leader's bodyguards rushed out of the building and opened fire. Our brave pilot had to retreat and the super ninjas were left with no choice but to fight. The first super ninja called out to the others.

"We must find cover. According to my nearly instant and completely excellent battlefield calculations, fighting from within this swimming pool puts us at a disadvantage tactically, mathematically and, I dare say, grammatically as well."

Another super ninja almost hit eight different body guards with a single burst of high-tech nano-tube coated bullets from his experimental ultra lightweight GPS and microwave equipped machine gun. As spent shells poured from the rifle, he answered his fellows.

"He's speaking truth. We should retreat to that concrete abutment filled with inflatable pool toys."

The third ninja leapt from the pool in a single bound. Before his feet even touched the concrete, a stream of nano-tube encrusted lead issued forth from his gun. The suppressive fire was, if not entirely accurate, at least highly intimidating. Terrorist bodyguards rushed to hide behind corners and low stone walls and the remaining ninjas likewise bounded to the abutment. The first super ninja brutally cast aside a pink, plastic giraffe and called out to his companions.

"Remember your training. We've got to hold off these terrorist goat fuckers until reinforcements can arrive."

A sudden grenade landed inside the concrete abutment. The impeccably prepared and ultra athletic power warriors did not panic. Instead they leapt out in a burst of rock-hard quadriceps, twitching pectorals and slightly mussed hair. They narrowly avoided both the explosion and dozens of shredded water wing fragments. Using the latest tactics and stealth so stealthy you could hardly believe it, all three ninjas quickly escaped the terrorist goat fuckers. Diving dramatically from the terrorist compound's roof onto the street below, the first super ninja round house kicked a young woman off her motorcycle. The second super ninja jumped on the seat behind the first and the third super ninja sat on the handlebars. They rode until nightfall when they found hiding spots in the basement of a Victoria's Secret for Pious Muslim Wives. They would wait, crouching beneath lace prayer brassieres and astride skin tight hijabs until the rest of the super ninja forces could come and rescue them.

(For the virtue of successfully employing modest lingerie in a battlefield situation, the dread god Hades blesses each super ninja with ten straight years' smooth, supple bikini areas. For the sin of using grenades against pool toys, I rain down a plague of perpetually foul smelling tap water on the Pakistani bodyguards.)

Back in America, the lesser of our two heroes sat unbelieving before his television. He watched as an affirmative action news anchor rambled on about India's humiliated, enraged leaders. He listened to talk of India's plans to occupy Lahore until both Sheik Yar-haz and the super ninjas were given over.

CJ wished desperately that CNN International had simply made a mistake, perhaps a very late April Fools' Day joke. *How could the Indians take such horrible risks to rescue three goddamn soldiers? Would they really chance an all-out war with Pakistan? Would the Indians really put good people like Patty in danger for something so insignificant as their third world hellhole's national pride?*

CJ could stand no more and walked away from his TV. His kitchen window, overlooking grazing land and the gardening hut, offered a temporary reprieve. *Relax, relax,* CJ thought. *It'll be okay. Patty's probably right about this being just another bluff, another dick waving contest.*

Cows chewed their cud, licked their nostrils and crapped delicately in the distance. Mightily stupid creatures for sure, yet CJ could not help thinking that if the kingdoms of earth fell to bovine rulers there would be no chance at all of India killing Patty. Smith spoke aloud.

"They can't be this dumb."

Chapter Twelve

P-Minus 2 Days

In a way, Choi Chul welcomed the Dokdo conflict. Certainly only a monster could take pleasure when the evil island monkeys sank Korean fishing vessels. The Japanese cruise-goers imprisoned by Korea's mighty navy elicited some compassion. Anyone with the least amount of humanity would extend their sympathy to the sailors drowned defending Korea's territorial waters—the Japanese soldiers who died leading their hateful incursion could of course go straight to hell. So while our hero was not blind to the sufferings caused by the Dokdo conflict, he could not help but feel these evils well worth the glorious—if tenuous—sense of solidarity the invaders had given his countrymen.

If only the skirmishing escalated into war, the traitors bemoaning unification's economic cost would fall silent, the boorish parents' groups and trembling women, the cowards fearful of northern gangs would silence their whining. Even the damned, weepy secretary might shut up about her mother's pension. If only the heat and smoke of war could burn away all those decadent luxuries, it would forge the North and South into the cohesive whole they were so clearly destined to become. *If things go just a little bit farther, the Korean people will come together like a quarrelsome family united by villainous neighbors. No more standing alone, no more alone at all.*

Shik In-jong, advisor to Korean President Yeo Ju-han and director of the Department for Patriotic Feeling, needed to make a plan for rescuing his political party. The economic repercussions of unity had savaged President Yeo's approval rating and, sadly, none of the advisors could conjure any strategy except waiting. If they didn't do something soon, public discontent would surely destroy all the many glories the Large Nationalist Party had worked so hard to achieve. Another day's meetings loomed and Patriotism Minister Shik In-jong had not yet conceived any ideas worth a damn. The president addressed him as soon as the director entered the party's great velvet-lined Hall of Wisdom.

"We cannot continue along our current path of steady patience," President Yeo said. "To do so will surely deliver Korea into the hands of the Populist Party."

Minister of Domestic Affairs Lee Soon-bin answered President Yeo.

"We have no choice. It is obvious that no matter what course of action we take, the North will remain a millstone about our necks for years to come."

"Then shall we cede our power to the unspeakable curs in the opposition?" President Yeo asked.

The meeting was turning into the sort of damned-if-we-do, doomed-if-we-don't quagmire the previous seven meetings had. Patriotism Minister Shik In-jong came to the edge of despair before an idea of infinite brilliance lifted his spirits.

"Can we not use Japanese aggression to turn the people's eyes away from their economic plight and onto the lively, brave course of national resistance?"

"Surely it is not your suggestion that we should escalate our conflict with Japan?" Domestic Minister Lee Soon-bin asked.

"It is my suggestion," Minister for Patriotic Feeling Shik said.

All present fell silent to consider these words. After a small delay, President Yeo spoke.

"This path is indeed our best chance to retain leadership."

Minister of Domestic Affairs Lee looked like a man who, after consuming far too much water in a single gulp, chokes and spits in equal measure.

"You cannot be serious!"

"To strike against the Japanese is not even indefensible on its face," Minister of Patriotic Feeling Shik said. "Invading Dokdo and driving the monkeys back to their islands will do much to advance our nation's self respect."

"You know as well as I that Dokdo has very little practical significance," Domestic Minister Lee Soon-bin said.

Patriotism Minister Shik sensed his opening and gathered breath with the ferocity of a honey badger in musk. His fists crashed onto the table and his lips quivered with passion.

"That is beside the point! Now is the time to move beyond practical significance. If we do not use this opportunity, then surely the Populists will soon. Now is the time for bold action! Now is the time we must put to work the fine pride of our countrymen to both heal over our divisions and take back Dokdo once and for all!"

Now they will applaud me for these fine words, Patriotism Minister Shik thought. Alas, the infernal Domestic Minister Lee Soon-bin persisted in his protestations and delayed Shik's richly deserved praise.

"Move beyond practical significance?" Domestic Minister Lee asked, then, turning away, continued. "Mr. President, you cannot take these rantings seriously."

The president did take those rantings seriously.

"Mr. Lee, it is not to your credit that you continually underestimate the value of symbolism. If there are no further objections, I wish to put into action the plan of Shik In-jong."

Only Domestic Minister Lee Soon-bin spoke further.

"Long experience has shown me no surer way to bring about the ruin of a republic than to suggest a bold, patriotic course for the people. The people will always find appealing any notion that presumes their own greatness. Look how the Americans, after more than a decade, are still unable to extricate themselves from their wars of patriotic revenge. Look also to Sri Lanka, consider also the Basque. It is the duty of men such as ourselves to limit patriotic suggestions, not to inflame them. Dokdo is of small importance, that we can coexist with Japan is of large importance and…"

Patriotism Minister Shik cut him off.

"It will be a simple matter to limit the scope of our war with Japan."

Domestic Minister Lee picked up his papers and threw them on the desk.

"Your idiocy knows no bounds!"

Minister for Patriotic Feeling Shik leapt to his feet and fired back.

"If it is idiocy to love your country, then you are indeed many times the greater intellect than I," he said, then waited half a beat. "Traitor!"

Patriotism Minister Shik threw a plastic cup at Domestic Minister Lee. He stood ram-rod straight and glared at the spineless Domestic Minister. After a short pause he threw his pencil, then a notepad, then an entire paper file. The Minister of Domestic Affairs was ready to strike back but by this time a chorus of advisors had joined Shik in pelting him with office supplies. Domestic Minister Lee stood strong against the assault and opened his mouth to speak. Only when the blunt base of a flying lamp struck his nose and broke his glasses did the valorous Domestic Minister retreat. Lee's assistants grabbed hold of a large drapery and, holding it over the Minister of Domestic Affairs' bleeding nose and watery eyes, shuttled him away. On this note, the debate came to a close. Patriotism Minister Shik In-jong breathed out more noisily than decorum would demand and addressed President Yeo.

"I do believe we have brought this matter to a satisfactory conclusion. Now we have only to decide which sort of dramatic gesture will best arouse the patriotic feeling of our country."

(For the sin of retreating in the face of office supplies, I cause Minister of Domestic Affairs Lee to arouse violent and generalized hatred in small dogs for the duration of his life.)

Chapter Thirteen

P-Day—The Morning Of

On this day the idiocy of men reached such heights as to require my direct intervention. The great intellects of the East and West, North and South, failed to prevent folly on so great a scale that the entire world might perish for the sake of two tiny islands and a mildly pretty stretch of Himalayan watershed.

As the sun rose over the Eastern Sea, Korean President Yeo summoned an air of importance, gravity even, as he stood behind the great, gold-trimmed lectern and addressed the press. He told the world that Japan would never see her soldiers, her tourists or her captured vessels until Dokdo lay unchallenged in the possession of Korea. The president pounded his podium with such force it jiggled his jowls, and he spoke with such authority the very air appeared to tremble.

"We, the strong, unified people of Korea will never allow Japan to enslave her neighbors again. We will never again permit those who raped Asia to steal our land. We will not waiver, we will not fail, we will not cease confiscating Japanese maritime assets and we will not return that which we have taken from Japan until Japan returns that which it has taken from us!"

Around the same time, in a secret ISI missile installation buried within the hill country of eastern Pakistan, Sheik Yar-haz delivered a speech of his own.

"Those anus-sucking Indians think they can reach down and touch whomever they want. Attack my home? Shoot at my bodyguards? Brutalize my daughter's pool toys? I want you to blow every undersecretary they've got into a thousand pieces!"

Just as the security men readied 23 medium range, high explosive missiles, Japanese President Ichiro Nomo received word of Korean President Yeo's defiant proclamation. He summoned the highest commander of the Japanese Self Defense Force and issued an order.

"We will see if the Korean remains so bold a kidnapper when our defensive forces crush Busan. Put emergency plan 'Take Back the Colony' into action immediately."

At 2:00 pm, the eight million people of Busan fled as Japanese battle ships fired their heavy guns into the harbor. By 2:30, the first of Sheik Yar-haz's missiles left the Pakistani hills and rose into the heavens, trailing a column of fire and smoke. Butterflies took wing en masse, jays and crows and bees all bracing for the fiery retaliation soon to blacken their homes. Yar-haz took this moment to smell the burning phosphorous and smiled.

"To hell with your ninjas," he said.

Back in India, helicopter pilot Kareshi received an urgent order to get his Mohawk up immediately. The commanding officer spoke thusly.

"The goat fuckers hunger for war? They'll be very happy then because we're going to give them a mushroom cloud curry!"

At 2:33, the first Pakistani missiles killed 144 people in Bengal. At 2:37, Korean President Yeo ordered a massive rocket strike on Kyoto. At 2:38, Korean Minister of Domestic Affairs Lee Soon-bin overcame a vicious poodle attack and beat Minister of Patriotic Feeling Shik In-jong to death with a stapler. 3:03 saw the first Indian nuke rise from its silo. Just 4 minutes later Pakistan launched its own atomic weapons. At 3:16 pm on P-Day, the Pakistani and Indian missiles passed by each other in midflight, Japan's twelve inch guns bore down on Korean skyscrapers and Korean rockets drew near the ancient Japanese capital. At 3:17, I intervened.

Chapter Fourteen

P-Day—The Afternoon Of

It came to pass that George Tenetive, director of the CIA, was watching CBS in his office when a reporter broke through the sportscast with footage of Indian missiles launching from secret silos. The director immediately rang the satellite department over his communications link and demanded all available intel on the Indian missiles, their likely targets and whatever American assets remained in the area.

"What attacks?" the satellite tech asked.

"Check CBS."

The satellite tech swiveled in his chair, turned on his TV and demanded the underlings rotate all available space cameras to central Asia. The underlings set to furiously tapping keyboards and clicking mouse buttons in the dim, blue light of their top secret bunker.

"But we're surveilling a terrorist cell in Germany," an underling said. "They are plotting to buy fertilizer."

"This is higher priority," the tech said.

The underling rose up in his righteousness and fury to strike back at the satellite tech.

"Nothing is higher priority than terror!"

The satellite tech responded with what I consider the utmost in gentle courtesy and well bred sophistication.

"Turn the satellite before I skull fuck you to death."

Soon the flotilla of billion-dollar machines rotated their lenses and sensors away from nefarious fertilizer purchases and onto to the air over Kashmir. The tech located seventeen of the weapons and beamed live footage to Tenetive's office. Large missiles of a type and design Tenetive did not quite recognize—were they furry?—flew through the heavens. The director spoke under his breath.

"Those look big enough for nukes."

He reached for the secure phone line to the Joint Chiefs of Staff and was about to dial when something amazing happened on screen. The Indian missiles seemed to disappear. In their place were thousands of flying pieces; pink and soft, seemingly organic. At first Tenetive thought them some sort of new multi-target nuclear warhead—but no. The director barked into his communications link.

"Zoom in on those fragments."

An underling rushed to adjust the satellite image. The picture expanded, went out of focus and then became clear enough for Tenetive's straining eyes.

"Those aren't missiles," he said. "I think they're…pigs?"

Tenetive acted decisively and showed many of the fine qualities that had made him a leader of men. I came near to blessing him as he spoke.

"If the Indians want to shoot pigs into space that's the least of our goddamn problems. Show me the Pakistani response right now."

The techs and underlings set themselves into a flurry of keyboard tapping, cursing and phone calls. The spy satellites rotated yet again while the hyper-advanced targeting systems went to work. Tenetive was getting the earliest images when CBS once more caught his eye.

"This is Lewis Lavaliere in New Delhi. As you can see behind me, the heavens have opened and the city is being bombarded by thousands of what appear to be cows. I have no explanation. I cannot begin to imagine the source of this tragedy. Ladies and gentlemen, the situation might seem merely gruesome, but I shudder to think what would happen if one of these cows were to land on a person. And with this many cows falling, there almost have to be deaths."

An underling called to Tenetive.

"We can't get a visual lock on any of their missiles."

"Check CBS," Tenetive said.

"Ah, okay. I see it now."

Tenetive rubbed his bald head and put a hand up inside his shirt and over his heart. *What the hell is going on?* He pinched a nipple just to make sure it wasn't all a dream. *Nope.* The tech called over the communications link.

"NBC is reporting some very strange happenings in East Asia."

Tenetive—letting his focus slip and causing me to retract that blessing I had all warmed up—went off on a seafood themed cliche.

"We've got bigger fish to fry, don't you think?"

"NBC's reporting dozens of warships down. Japanese fighter jets are falling out of the sky...I just received word they launched an invasion of Korea."

While Tenetive couldn't afford any appearance of weakness in the face of adversity, he also couldn't understand one damned thing going on. As such, he uttered the most authoritative bit of nothing he could.

"Get our best men on it right now."

Chapter Fifteen

P-Day The Night Of

When our hero arrived at Gwang-woo Byeong University's Nude Building he found a scene of turmoil. Professors rushed from office to office, students huddled in corners and staff members whispered with such urgency that Chul initially feared a cicada infestation. He turned to an elderly sweater-vest enthusiast as he passed along the hallway.

"Please explain this."

"The Big Nationalist Party finally got the war it desires with Japan," the sweater-vest enthusiast said. "And the world has become insane as well!"

"By the world you of course mean the damnable Japanese island thieves?"

"No, I mean the people who believe in magical goo storms. I mean people who say that an army of sea creatures have destroyed the Japanese navy."

Choi Chul scratched his head. He decided to take on an attitude much more mirthful than that of the others milling about. Our hero asked the man from where the confusion originated.

"I think it is from the Internet. Follow me and we can solve the mysteries of this day."

"Interesting," Chul said. "Worthy sir, which subject do you teach?"

"I am a professor of emotion-based psychology."

Our hero could not stop himself.

"And how does that make you feel?"

The educator missed the joke and instead, with strong hands and sudden violence, snatched a student from the passing throng.

"What is your major?"

The student stuttered before answering.

"I s-study art history."

The professor said "useless garbage" and released the art historian. He did not wait long to grab a young woman from the crowd.

"What is your major?"

"Computer science. Professor, please let go of my collar."

The professor ignored the student's request and pulled the youngster into an office. When the party arrived, the bold educator compelled the computer scientist to sit by pushing down upon her shoulders with furious anger.

"We need very much to know from where this madness emerged," the professor said. "Do that computer stuff I always see in the movies."

The young woman held her hands palm up and looked to our hero for guidance. *OMFG, WTF?* she seemed to ask. Choi Chul bit his lip to keep from laughing and then clarified the professor's request.

"We wish to know where reports of goo storms, tuna attacks and whales sinking the Japanese fleet are coming from. Perhaps you can show us from which fraudulent corner of the Internet these rumors emerged?"

"I do not need a computer," the student said. "It is on KBS, CNN, MBC, everywhere."

"But that has to be fake," the professor said. "Find the backdoor virus or Trojan worm that is controlling KBS's computers and doctoring the footage."

The student stared uncomprehending at her attacker.

"Do it now!" the professor said.

"I am sorry professor, if it is even possible to take over this many broadcasters simultaneously, the person responsible will have abilities far surpassing my own. And further, I usually write the programming for word processors and spread sheets."

The professor called the student useless and made off towards the door.

"I will get to the bottom of this mystery. I do not care if it disrupts my emotional equilibrium for a week!"

When both had gone, our hero finally felt safe enough to laugh out loud. He sat down at the computer and opened Internet Explorer. Choi Chul could hardly wait to see all the hubbub.

(For the virtue of assaulting art historians, I bless the professor of emotion-based therapy with rock solid equilibrium for an entire week.)

When the Korean people wish to search online content, they most commonly go to naver.com. Less commonly, they visit daum.co.kr or nate.com. They very occassionally use Google. I mention this so that you may appreciate just how archaic and unusual a man our hero was being when he surfed to the even less popular aol.

com and clicked on MBC's streaming account of the East Sea incidents.

Video shot from the deck of the Korean fishing boat "Ddong-jeep" showed a sea boiling. Japanese destroyers and frigates, submarine hunters and battleships rocked in the water. Spray like that which trails behind a jet ski splashed from the sides of Japan's greatest warships. Some unseen force wrenched them side to side through the waters with sufficient violence to make the creaking of metal audible even to the crew of the Ddong-jeep.

Chul looked to the surface of the sea and beheld hundreds of enormous creatures pressing their fleshy noses into an invading aircraft carrier. Minke whales, reef sharks and blue fin tuna coordinated their attacks to maximize the ship's side to side momentum and soon achieved a powerful, resonant frequency.

Helicopters and fighter jets spilled off the lone aircraft carrier's flight deck and into the water below. Invaders fell from their observation posts and splatted upon the flight deck, bodies followed the aircraft into the sea and the bridge collapsed onto dozens of remaining Japanese below. Our hero cheered aloud as the Yushin Maru capsized.

"Even nature revolts against you!"

An "urgent news" button flashed in the corner of Choi Chul's browser window. Still exalting, he clicked the link without thinking.

A different video, taken from the heights of a Busan air traffic control tower, showed a sky filled with clouds of white, quivering goo. A news crawler at the bottom of the screen read "Mysterious storms down at least 17 Korean fighter jets. All commercial flights canceled." Choi Chul stopped smiling as the footage cut to a reporter huddling under an umbrellain the middle of a different goo storm.

"I'm Song Sung-jung reporting for MBC News. As you can see, the mysterious substance is coming down here at the rate of several centimeters per hour. Commuters are reporting it is impossible to drive in this downpour and the government has already advised the elderly and infirm it is not safe to walk in these slippery conditions. If you must…"

A small jet plane entered the frame from the right corner, nosed up momentarily and then smashed into the goop covered ground at what must have been 200 km/hour. The forward compartment bounced up once and Chul thought that the flight crew might survive. However, the jet's huge intakes caught on the wet earth below and wrenched the plane's cockpit back to the ground like a snapping mousetrap. The fuselage broke behind the bubble top and rolled over the severed front half. A fire followed and enveloped the wreckage. Kerosene fuel blossomed into red and black wisps of fire and smoke and spread over the ground. Soon the goop and plane, pilot and navigator crackled and caramelized like the world's least appetizing stir fry.

The reporter and his cameraman ran to the scene and attempted a rescue. They were rebuffed, however, by the intensity of the heat and the scalding heaps of what looked like fried tofu. The reporter said "I'm sorry, I'm sorry, I'm sorry" and our hero shut off the computer.

Patty didn't like the way her office air-conditioning filled the air with dust and the smell of mold. She called the building maintenance man's extension but could not reach him, getting this charming message instead:

"This is Badir. I'm out of the office. Leave a message for me and I'll pretend to care about your problems at whichever time I return."

Unable to stand the air any longer, she stepped out of her office and into the hall. Patty stretched her arms, breathed in and was going to visit the water cooler when she heard the scream of an enraged hog. The embassy roof failed and crashed down over the bathrooms. She took three running steps, prepared to open the stairway doors and heard another boom. A wave of plaster and wood, blood and viscera came through the ceiling like a shotgun blast and rendered her instantly parallel to the floor. Patty hit the ground so hard she could feel the concrete bend beneath her elbow. She coughed once, felt immense pain of shocking clarity and fell unconscious.

In the face of my "strangeness," the citizens of Japan and Korea, Pakistan and India could conceive of no course of action but to set aside conflicts and get to the business of repairing their nations. Japanese leader Ichiro Nomo sent a message to Korean President Yeo Ju-han suggesting the two most prosperous of Asia's nations put Dokdo under joint administration and focus instead on preparing the Pacific for future attacks from whatever evil (me!) had caused the wildlife insurrection and tofu precipitation. Yeo had little choice but to accept.

In central Asia the Pakistani president, Generalissimo Mohsin Bahawalanzai went on television to address both his own people and the citizens of India.

"As you know, on this day a tragedy most bizarre has stricken our people and the people of India. This mysterious force has smitten our land with the blood of a thousand unclean pigs and covered India with the remains of countless holy cows. We may have had our differences in the past, we may have launched missiles at each other, we may have invaded each other's territory and we may have massacred each other's citizens but we are not so insensitive as to defile religion. I say now to the people of Pakistan, it is certain that India did not pollute our country with pig blood. I say now to the Hindus of India, it was not us who slaughtered those magnificent beasts above New Delhi or Bali. Please do not take offense, know that instead of your sacred cows we intended to send cleansing fire."

The Indian president responded in kind and offered a hand of friendship towards the Pakistanis that they might unite and prevent such a horrible violation of religious taboo from ever occurring again.

It seemed certain an era of peace and stability would soon visit Earth. Some short span of solidarity and pragmatism to soothe man's fevered passions before the people could conjure new outrages, new and ingenious methods for destroying themselves in the next clusterfuck of self-righteous myth building. I would not allow such a boring outcome.

And so I called into existence a sticky red cloud, took up residence in its center and prepared to descend into New York City. Angels appeared on either side and blew their magnificent trumpets. Hades called forth the spirits of the valiant dead and let loose Cerberus to chew through untold thousands of reclining sofas. Quetzaquatle spread his mighty wings and blocked out the sun as I prepared to come down. My divine arms thrown high, my legs straight and powerful—heavenly light shone from my every orifice.

Chapter Sixteen

The Day After, Morning

The cellular phone played two verses from The Who's "American Woman" before CJ could mute the television, find a suitable place for his coffee and fish the buzzing, singing box of plastic from his pocket. *International call,* he thought. *I can hardly wait to pay the bill this month.*

"Mr. Smith? Is this Carver Smith?"

"That's me."

"Mr. Smith, I am Dr. Muhammad bin Feisal at the Islamabad Surgery Center. I regret to inform you that your daughter, Mrs. Patty, has been gravely injured."

CJ could not speak.

"Mr. Smith, are you there?"

"Yes, I'm here. I'm sorry—please go on."

"Mrs. Patty has sustained severe blunt force trauma to her legs and pelvis," Dr. bin Feisal said. "She has numerous fractures and your daughter's internal organs have not escaped injury either."

"Is she going to live?"

"I would be very surprised if she does not. But I expect her recovery will be both long and difficult. She will certainly never again have the mobility and flexibility to which she has grown accustomed. If at all possible, we would advise you to fly here to Islamabad. She will need all the support you and your family can give her until such time she is strong enough to return to the United States."

CJ's heart sank in his chest. *Drop everything and go to Pakistan,* he thought. *Oh joy.* He disguised all hints of self-pity before answering the doctor.

"Yes, of course. Thank you and please take care of my daughter."

"Certainly, Mr. Smith. In the course of my business dealings I have worked with Mrs. Patty on several occasions. I flatter myself to think I am her friend. The world needs more people like your daughter, not fewer."

It does not take as much effort as you would think to prepare a levitating, sticky red cloud. I fashioned mine from several tons of finely spun cotton candy and 17 kilograms of iron dust. With these two ingredients properly mixed, all you need to maintain whichever shape you desire is the proper means for magnetic bottling. If you have ever spent time contemplating how Zeus called down lighting, Jesus walked on water or Buddha Boy caused light to shoot from his forehead, know that we of the divinity are very adept with this technology.

I chose the design for this cloud based on two desires. Firstly, I enjoy the company of flying insects in the same way you might enjoy a case of dysentery. That my sweet, sticky cloud will murder houseflies by the millions causes me little sorrow. That any uninvited guests will find it necessary to push through these layers of rotting insect remains likewise brightens my mood.

Beyond that, there is no better way to establish my brand, so to speak. I could make my designs clear and spread out, buffet style, a list of reasons for my actions. I could stage debates with the brightest, most famous and loudest among your species. I could even hire a press secretary but to do so would make the whole process inestimably boring.

Instead I intend to shroud my visit in enigma and menace and the music of Tiny Tim. I want people to look upon my cloud and ask themselves questions such as these:

Will the God of Potency help me in my time of need or will he worsen the situation in order to improve the irony of my suffering? Is he saving the world from Pakistan and India, Korea and Japan, or does he merely intend to prolong our death throes? What will he do next, lead an uprising of pretzels and bratwurst? If he is here to save us? Do I even want salvation?

And so a ball of candy, covered in the carcasses of household pests, forced the people of New York to flee as it encompassed all of Manhattan. None could penetrate its mysteries or divine its purpose. Why, if it were my desire, I could conduct a massive construction project inside this cloud without a single soul noticing.

CJ drove his dually pickup truck to Albany, New York. While not as large as JFK International Airport, Albany Airport had considerably less congestion and CJ thought himself less likely to get stuck in traffic. He was refueling just outside the city limits when he received another distressing phone call. The proprietress at the Eagle's Pride Bar and Grill—Shirley, that's her name—spoke loud and fast.

"I don't even know if I should tell you this, you aren't very reasonable about this stuff at all and I don't want to make things worse but on the other hand, I guess you're going to find out anyway and I think there are going to be a lot of people who need help."

"What happened?"

Shirley suddenly clammed up.

"Come on," he said. "I'm going to find out anyway."

"Are you sure?"

"Yes, tell me."

"I'm gonna regret this," she said. "They think some-body—something rather—is attacking New York City. They think that whatever it was dropping cows from the sky in India and making the whales go crazy in Japan is in the city now. I guess it's a poison cloud and for some damn reason 'Tiptoe Through the Tulips' is playing real-ly loudly inside it."

"Is everybody okay?"

"I don't know. There's this red goop floating over downtown and I don't know if it's hurting the people in-side."

"Damnit, I was hoping it wouldn't happen to us. What are you going to do, Shirley?"

She paused for a beat. CJ read the subtext as something along the lines of "I don't exactly know the protocol for this situation, hon." Her actual words were as follows.

"My husband has two big trailers and we're filling them up right now with water and food. We've only got one truck, though. If you come by we could hitch the other one to your Chevy and take two loads in at once."

"God damn it. I'm in Albany right now."

"What for?"

"I'm flying out to see Patty," he said. "She thought she could help the goddamn terrorists and got herself hurt. To be young…"

He had intended that as a "kids these days" type incursion into the land of delusional nostalgia but ended up cringing instead. *Wow, I sound like a retard.*

"Can't you get another flight?" Shirley asked.

CJ had to stop and think. *Any real patriot knows times like these demand sacrifice—action on behalf of the nation—even if the victims were mostly liberals. And anyway, Patty is probably sedated and won't know if I stay here a day or two longer.* CJ was about to answer when the proprietress broke in.

"Sweetheart, I just had a thought, my friend Jeff is still in Albany and he's trying to get to the city. He's just got a little car, but if you meet him at the airport and give him your truck, the problem's solved."

Smith grit his teeth and silently cursed this Jeff character for stealing his chance at heroism.

"Ah, alright. Tell him to meet me."

Not an hour had passed before CJ had surrendered his truck, checked his luggage and discretely kicked a water fountain several times before boarding his plane. Much later that day he landed in Islamabad and set about giving Patty his tender if not entirely focused attentions.

Chapter Seventeen

The Day After, Evening

In the détente following my initial interventions, Choi Min-sung's commanders felt secure enough to send some of their charges on leave. Like most of his companions, Min-sung took this opportunity to visit home. Our hero met with his son at East Daegu Train Station and drove him to a Homeplus department store for lunch. They pulled into the parking garage just as night fell upon the people of Korea.

When Min-sung opened the car door, a gust blew across the lot and sent biting cold air into his fashionably unbuttoned shirt. The young man pulled his jacket closed, fumbled with his gloves and rushed to the automatic doors before his father had finished locking the car. *Why could my family not move to Hawaii?*

At the food court, Chul ordered a vinegar, rice and raw fish meal with a side of fried pork cutlets. Min-sung opted for beef, soy and thick noodles. The smells of industrial cooking wafted gently as Chul began their conversation.

"I assume you are ashamed on this day, as am I."

"What noise is this?" Min-sung asked.

"The chance to restore our nation's territory has passed and now Dokdo lies even further from our grasp."

"It is very nice to see you as well, father."

Koreans don't really do sarcasm and thus the joke completely escaped our hero's notice. Chul's face scarcely moved as he continued on.

"Because of our failure, the world once more sees our weakness in the face of Japan. Surely it will not be long before the monkeys again denude Korea of all her land."

Min-sung said nothing.

"You must be ashamed as am I."

Min-sung pushed the beef and noodles across the table and threw up his hands.

"Do you know the things I want?"

"Now is not the time to discuss selfish desires," our hero said.

Min-sung bit down so hard his teeth hurt. The young man struggled to keep his voice at a reasonably low volume.

"I want a girlfriend with dimples and to finish my schooling. I want real Nike shoes and a scooter with chrome plating and I want to grow my goddamn hair out. I want to eat duck for dinner and drink 100 dollar vodka with Red Bull mixed in. And do you know what has nothing to do with any of those things? Shit-eating Dokdo."

Choi Chul nodded his head and took a bite from the crispy, lightly oiled pork cutlet. He set the chop sticks carefully to one side and put his hand over Min-sung's clenched fist.

"You have no plans for tomorrow?"

Min-sung felt his knuckles popping. His voice barely rose above the fryers and dishwashers working behind them.

"I have no plan."

"I want to show you some things. Now enjoy your food, relax and prepare to sleep. Tomorrow we go south together."

(For the virtue of horrifying vodka enthusiasts, I bless Min-sung with chill-resistant nipples. For the virtue of staging a reunion at a supermarket food court, I bless Chul with the ability to telepathically communicate with starfish.)

At the southernmost tip of the Korean peninsula lies a village known as Ddang-Ggeut, or Land's End for monolinguals and their hilariously incompetent online translation programs. A lighthouse marks the southern extremity of the township, and it was to this tower our hero brought his son.

A vicious winter wind tore through the village and moaned against the lighthouse's sheet metal and aluminum exterior facades. Chul and his son walked quickly from the car and ducked inside the lighthouse. They ignored the elevators and, wishing to demonstrate manly fortitude, took the stairs to the eighth story. When they arrived at the observation platform, they first looked toward the unspoilt islets and ocean to the southwest.

"What do you think of this place?" Choi Chul asked.

"I think it is savage."

"We agree perfectly. Look out at these war-like clouds as they turn the ocean black. Not more than 500 meters long and yet so dark that when they pass before it, the sun is blotted completely from the sky. Do they not resemble jellyfish dragging poison tentacles through the air?"

"You could say such a thing," Min-sung said.

"And what of these rocks and small islands sprouting from the ocean? Each one sharp like scissors, merciless as the cold. Have you ever wondered what the first people to cast eyes on this place must have thought?"

"I have not."

Our hero cupped his chin with his left hand and gestured broadly with his right. Min-sung's eyes followed the arc he traced through the scenery.

"They must have asked to themselves, 'How am I to survive in this land?'"

"It is clear they found some method," Min-sung said.

"It is thus," Chul said. "Let us now look to the north. Do you see those roads built into the coastline, the cellular phone towers straddling mountains and the fish nets drifting in the bay?"

"Of course."

"And when you see these things do you think of savagery?"

"I do not."

"That is because we, the people of Korea, have tamed this land of sharp stones and stinging skies. First those men long ago who built dirt mounds and hid in the earth. Then their descendents who saw fit to erect stone bridges and wooden buildings and now we who have made fishing fleets and tour busses. This land is not like Madagascar, where nature provides all you require. It is not like Singapore, where the traders of many nations every day bring more civilization for the people. We took this peninsula through the exertions of three hundred generations; working together that the Korean race might bend this harsh place to its will. Think of this and ask yourself again why I cannot abide even a single piece of our land falling into Japanese hands."

Min-sung, at a loss for words, nodded and looked away—struck silent by the mighty traditions of which he was heir. Chul saw this, put an arm around his son's shoulders and smiled.

Chapter Eighteen

14 Days After

The United Nations Building in New York City shone blue in the sun. While the unenlightened may bemoan the kilowatts of energy wasted on heating and cooling such an inefficient glass building, the luminous minds contained therein surely require bounteous light that they may convert sugars and O_2 into pure genius, geopolitics and trade into treasure and arugula salads into pungent gas. It would be a shame if I changed the essential character of this magnificent edifice.

With this in mind, my spirit ventured out from the cotton candy ball and over the elegant, flag lined boulevard serving the UN Building's main doors. Ahead the day shimmered cold and bright. Behind me a stream of blue and green and red glass, liquefied and silent, descended from the sky like hot caramel dripping from the clouds onto the parking lots and flag poles. I paused to concentrate the flow over the structure itself and smiled as the gelatinous blobs of molten glass engulfed the UN Building. My glass hardened and rendered the world leaders inside an instantly captive audience. Those wandering the inner sanctums suddenly found themselves bathed in twisting sunbeams, as if the bastard children of two thousand stained glass windows and a kaleidoscope had suddenly replaced all their windows.

At this time I took on a human form in order to lessen the necessary shock to my prisoners. I thought my normal appearance too outrageous. My small horns might invite comparisons to Satan, my powerful right leg and withered left leg might confuse and my extensive tattoing might lead you mere humans to assume I feel sympathy for pirates, punk rockers or, even worse, the arch villain Miley Cyrus.

I decided on the face of Jean Claude Van Damme, the hair of Bruce Lee, the torso of Saddam Hussein and the legs of Cameron Diaz for the organic portion of my appearance. A red polyester business suit, closely tailored with a white necktie and matching plastic belt would serve as my costume. I materialized on the marble floored halls of the UN Building, looked upon the glorious light-show created by my molten glass and listened to the soft creaking of my shiny red shoes.

I laid my hands upon the great wooden doors that separate plebian from patrician and came into the main assembly hall. Above me the domed ceiling and exposed metal supports housed dozens of recessed lights. The effect was very much celestial and I could not help but make a warm space in my immortal heart for the architect of such a place. A golden mantle towered above the podium and divided two enormous video screens designed to ensure all those in attendance could see the presenters. All of the decor more than 3 meters above the floor delighted my eyes.

However, I can hardly describe that which stretched out below as anything other than hideous. Extremely hard sea foam carpet stretched wall to wall. Someone had seemingly built the doors from the crushed dreams of small children. Another had clearly chosen the wallpaper based on a deep and abiding love for chicken bones. Only particle board desks and chairs taken from the nose bleed section of the old Yankee Stadium broke the vast plains of polyethylene fiber.

The honorable representative from Ghana turned to look upon me. Her white eyes contrasted beautifully with jet black skin and I blessed her with 14 days free from email spam. I continued down the central aisle. The Mongolian representative turned to look, then the Uzbekistani and Australian. The German health minister, upon seeing my godly visage, fainted and, in doing so, brought the blessing of new, much more amusing names to all Germans with below average marijuana consumption. Those assembled were reluctant to speak and so I reached the podium without further incident of any sort. Upon arrival I asked the Czech Environmental Secretary, so recently presenting on the state of Canadian forests, to step aside before commencing my first earthly speech.

"Ladies and gentlemen, I am so very happy to come here before you. As worldly and sophisticated people such as you surely know, it was not long ago that bizarre events befell the warring nations of Pakistan and India, Japan and Korea. I beg you allow me to explain the source of these anomalies. It was I who covered India in steak tartar and led a sashimi revolution in Japan. It was I who fried the tofu skies of Korea and sent a million porks falling from the clouds of Pakistan. It is from me that your united and confused leaders wish to defend themselves, though I hope before long you will not consider me your enemy."

The representative from India stood up and pointed her finger at me.

"Listen, whatever your name is, you cannot crap on a people's heritage and expect them to treat you like a friend. You need to leave right now."

I smiled at the representative, caused her to smell strongly of cheesy snacks and continued on as if I had not heard.

"I come here today because my work is not yet done and the completion thereof concerns you all. Please direct your attentions to the area above me. Your video screens are certainly of high quality and so please do not think me presumptuous for replacing your human televisions with a device of my own invention. I shall of course make further modifications to your world and I think it better if you experience these alterations with the maximum clarity of my 7 dimensional, wide screen, scratch and sniff optimized holographic projector.

"Some of your nations will change a great deal; some will feel only the indirect effects of my will. I have unilaterally decided on the changes for some of your nations, while others will choose the nature of these little tweaks. Whether, when I allow you to leave, you take advantage of my changes or hurl yourselves into cesspools of victimhood shall of course depend entirely on you."

Directly over my head and in front of the human-built displays I called into existence a divinely powered sound, smell and light-shaping device the effect of which is to render extremely realistic copies of whatever scene I command to appear. My prisoners gasped and murmured in their alarm. I called out to them once more.

"Let us now consider England."

Sir Ethelred Leofric Westminsteringham III Esq. PhD held his breath as the divine projector rumbled into life. The domed assembly hall burst into a flash of light and sent the smells of Mexico's mesquite brush, agave cactus and open sewers flooding through the assembly. The mayor of Chiapas City came into view first, then a very poshly dressed man carrying a woman's hat, next a group of Mexican well wishers. Finally the Queen herself materialized. In her hands Westminsteringham III could see an uncommonly clean shovel holding perhaps 300 grams of soil. She turned the shovel over and thus "planted" a pine tree that would forever more symbolize the friendship between Great Britain and this south Mexican state.

The Mexicans clapped and waved their hands and the queen waved back in that strange royal fashion that, for some reason, prohibits bending one's wrist. The mayor brought forth a stately leather bound book inscribed with the following:

"I have seen the living history of this place on a fine spring day. May our nations forever more unite in mutual disapproval for Spaniards in sailboats."

The queen signed this paper, received another round of applause and readied herself to depart. Royal skirt servants rushed to remove sub-visible wrinkles from the matriarch's pastel pink dress. A regal man took the shovel from Her Highness' precious hands and inspected her fingernails for any sign of damage. Westminsteringham III's chest swelled with pride and he, like a charismatic pastor reducing his audience to tears, combined the acts of head-nodding and smiling. His pleasure did not last long, for when the royal shoe attendants had wiped the dust from her majesty's pumps, a stream of flame shot out of the imperial soles.

The queen's body straightened, rigid as a ruler edge and twice as androgynous. She rocked gently back and forth as the servants and Mexicans—yes, my friends, there is at least sometimes a distinction—screamed and flailed about. The thrust grew strong enough to launch her skywards. Glamorous purple flames came down and scorched the tree of friendship. Ornate hats and lace gloves swirled in her wake and soon those below lost sight of Her Excellency.

Westminsteringham III stood and pushed aside his chair with violence so great it bounced three times before settling in the aisle. His voice trembled and he addressed me with such vehemence that even the other dignitaries shrank from his wrath.

"What is the meaning of this? How dare you molest Her Majesty the Queen? What have you done with her?"

I answered with the gentlest of manners and the softest courtesy.

"The meaning, sir? It would spoil the fun if I were to share the meaning so soon. As for how I dare to interfere with her majesty—I dare because, while the queen may enjoy the great power of a figurehead, I enjoy the power of a deity. Just as an owl does what it pleases with the sparrow, I toy with human beings. Now, what have I done with her? I have frozen her for safe storage. Your beloved regent is now whistling about the earth at more than 1,000 kilometers per hour, in geosynchronous orbit, mere centimeters behind the Hubble Space Telescope. She will, naturally, bump it from time to time so that NASA has greater opportunity to release photos in its "comedy of astrophysics" series. I thought it fitting that one of the most modern human inventions should be so near one of its greatest anachronisms."

The Englishman covered his eyes and wept on the floor of the assembly hall.

"What has the Queen ever done to deserve this? What have we ever done to deserve this humiliation?"

A fat man representing Iceland came to Westminster-ingham III's side and comforted him with these gentle words.

"At least she won't age any further."

The British representative cast piteous eyes about the room and glared at me with such hatred as to leave little mystery about his desire for revenge. This was turning out to be even more entertaining that I'd hoped.

To my right the delegate from France attempted to suppress her laughter. Genevieve de Sade whispered to her secretary and did not think I could hear.

"It serves those sanctimonious bastards right. Always lecturing the world on what is proper and what is fair, so eager to lift themselves above Europe. If anyone deserves to lift themselves above Europe it is we, the French!"

I considered this and caused the divine television to change channels. It flickered for 3 seconds before resolving into an aerial image of Paris. Cool, fresh air wafted from the display and covered all those present in the pleasant odors of baking bread, wine and the ever so slight whiff of unwashed armpit. The image then descended past the Arc de Triomphe and through the open windows of Professor Michel Marceau's university office. In the right hand corner stood a sign reading "burqas forbidden" and to the left another member of the French academic elite settled into Marceau's overstuffed cheval-skin sofa. In poetic and linguistically pure *francais* the men discussed which foreign words they should exclude from their language.

"It is a travesty so many words from English and Spanish, German and Arabic should sully our speech," Marceau said. "Have you prepared a list of these pollutions I might present to the Loi Toubon Commission, Professor DeTamble?"

"I have indeed found several…ordswey and phrases… even…olewhey entencesey that omecey omfrey glisheney."

At this point Professor DeTamble's eyes opened wide and he covered his mouth with both hands. Professor Marceau saw fit to scold him and spoke.

"Atwhey si-ey ongwrey ithwey ouyey?"

Marceau likewise covered his mouth and at this time I caused the divine image shaping device to shut down with a deep, electronic thunk. In the far reaches of the UN assembly hall a brave Australian commerce secretary raised her hand. I smiled, pointed at her and asked her to please say whatever she wished.

"Sir, did you do that? I mean, did you make them speak that way?"

"Of course."

The Aussie shook her head before continuing, disbelief and befuddlement twisting her face in equal measure.

"I really wish there was a better way to say this, but, did you change the French language into Pig Latin?"

Before I could answer Genevieve de Sade, French representative to the UN, rose from her chair and yelled out to me.

"Ogey otey ellhey!"

Those assembled tried to combine quiet, private laughter with soft concern for a people so tragically afflicted. I moved to comfort the Gauls.

"Fear not, your precious and ancient tongue will continue on in the protective embrace of those French speakers living in Haiti, northern Africa and the Caribbean. Now, let us move onto the next stage of my Godly presentation."

Is there here a representative from Israel?" I asked. "Yes? Excellent. Is there here a representative of the Palestinian Authority? Oh, there are six of you. Wonderful. I mentioned before that I will offer some representatives the chance to choose the nature of your nations' alteration. You both will enjoy this privilege, but, well, you will see exactly how this works soon enough."

I paused long enough to survey the audience. Every set of eyes pointed my way, little white globes with tiny black spots tracking my every movement. I smiled and continued.

"I have decided to squeeze dry your festering, gangrenous pustule of a conflict. I shall, with thunderous finality, end your ridiculous wars and your colorful ambitions. The Islamic Caliphate and ersatz Israel, those great stupidities of your ancient heritages, are very, very unlikely to survive my judgment."

Shimon Netanyahu, Israeli minister of agriculture, curled his toes inside his shining, $300 shoes. The Hebrew's lips turned white and his hand rose with great timidity.

"You think I am qualified to decide the fate of Israel?" he asked. "It is true I have risen to the heights of bureaucracy but that is mostly due to my overbearing, traditionalist father and highly questionable conduct in wars past. This hardly marks me as a fitting representative for the will of my people."

"I'm afraid that doesn't matter," I said. "The will of your people had near as makes no difference seven decades in which to conclude this matter and everyone has grown impatient. I therefore present you with two choices.

"In the first scenario, I will grant the Jewish people the ethnically cleansed homeland they have so long craved. I will guarantee the safety of your ancestors for centuries on end and ensure that you retain racially pure control over your governance. I will also more than double the size of your territorial holdings."

Netanyahu could not help but smile. I noted his mirth and continued.

"However, you shall quit the Holy Land and establish Krakow as your capital. Your eastern boundary, should you accept my terms, will extend from Auschwitz-Birkenau in the south to Vilna in the north. I grant you the land surrounding Lodz and Buchenwald, Dachau and Nuremburg. You will dwell in these lands so long as your nation is to last."

Netanyahu recoiled in horror, clutching at his collar and curling his ample lips.

"You mean to establish as our homeland the very concentration camps we, my father, fled during the Second World War? You cannot expect me to accept this!"

I nodded with great solemnity and extended a sympathetic hand to the Jewish bureaucrat.

"You certainly need not accept this option. You may defer to your counterparts in the Palestinian Authority but I warn you, they also have a choice to make."

Abu Yassin, foremost among Palestine Liberation Organization's olive lobby, stood up from his bleacher seat and addressed me.

"I can see that you are intent on humiliating us as you have humiliated the others. What torture have you devised for my people?"

"An excellent question! I offer you a trade. I will give you Palestine and complete power therein. You may do with the Jews as you wish. You may do with Hamas as you wish. You may do with Hezbollah as you wish. Further, I will confer enough military jets and tanks, missiles and what may or may not be nuclear weapons to ensure your territorial integrity far into the future. The settlements will evaporate before your eyes, the checkpoints will check no more and you may trade with Egypt to your heart's content."

"The horrible price you demand?" the Palestinian asked.

"Your people must abandon the faith of Mohammed and convert to Orthodox Judaism."

I paused for dramatic effect. The dignitaries and lobbyists looked to the seafoam floors and spoke no more. I saw their trembling lips and downcast eyes and smiled. The energy commissioner from Norway saw this and spoke.

"You're enjoying this, aren't you? You are a sadist, aren't you?"

I smiled again before continuing.

"If only you could see the silliness of your priorities, my dear friends, then you might understand why I grin at you. But let us finish the business with Israel and Palestine. If you ladies and gentlemen of the Palestinian Authority agree to my terms before the Israeli makes his decision, your deal will take force, the terms I offered to Israel will become moot and the fate of the Hebrew nation will fall entirely into your hands. Likewise, should the Israeli bureaucrat accept my terms first, you of the

Palestinian territories will revert to your former state as Syrian peons, free to behold the glory of New Israel from beneath the oppression of yet another occupier. Should you both defer, I will of course resurrect the spirit of Nero Caesar and reinstate his famous rule over your lands."

I had no sooner finished than Shimon Netanyahu, Israeli bureaucrat, thrust his hand into the air, called out and accepted my terms. No one else had the courage to speak.

"Please take this time as a recess," I said. "Stretch your legs, enjoy the egg salad on offer in the cafeteria and help yourselves to the cots stowed along the walls of Auditorium E. Take care to ensure a comfortable night's sleep. We will resume these proceedings tomorrow morning at 8 AM."

Chapter Nineteen

Fifteen Days After

CJ held his daughter's left hand. He felt the rough, calloused skin of Patty's palm and wondered if she would ever again have the ability to ride a bicycle, climb a fence or move her kitchen table. He looked at the ragged, scabby canyon running down her forearm and shuddered. The sutures snaked left and right and puckered the inflamed skin over her wrist. Rusty bandages covered the black and blue wasteland of Patty's abdomen. His index finger brushed one of the stainless steel pins holding her femur in place.

Patty took a sudden rushed breath and her eyes bulged wide. Mouth open, vessels straining against the skin over her neck, the young woman spoke a single word before lapsing back into the fog of sedation.

"Dad!"

CJ stood up from his chair and placed one careful hand on Patty's forehead and the other on her good arm. He did not want her to pull at tubes or injure herself further.

"Shh. Shh."

Patty fell still and CJ did not have to wait long before a nurse opened the door to their hospital room. She stood no higher than CJ's shoulders, had a round face and a pleasant if slightly bulbous body. Smith saw her hair net and wondered if a medical requirement for hygiene or Islam's hatred for women motivated her choice in wardrobe.

"My daughter is having panics. Could you please increase her pain killer dosage?"

"Yes sir, it will take me just a moment."

The nurse turned to a facility phone mounted on the wall and spoke quickly in some language CJ had never even heard of. *Why can't these people just speak English,* Smith wondered. Then he remembered where he was and stopped. Still his indignity would not go quietly. The nurse turned back to CJ.

"An orderly will stop by shortly to provide Ms. Patty's valium."

"How do you know I couldn't understand you just then?" CJ asked.

The nurse looked to the ground and shuffled her feet.

"It is my experience, sir, that the people of your nation cannot be bothered to learn our customs or languages, regardless of how long you remain in Pakistan."

Night fell and CJ faced the choice of finding a hotel by himself, seeking help from the embassy or simply melting into the Little America surrounding Camp Justice and Freedom. He sought to solve this problem by walking in the general direction of the embassy. If he were lucky this would afford an opportunity for creative distraction—a circus, heathen funeral rites, McDonald's—at worst it would still give him a chance to observe the terrorists in their natural environment.

CJ turned into the Saidpur Model Village and came to Café 199. The "roofs" made from silk and hanging partitions combined with neon lighting and a group of white men smoking near the door to make him think "bar." Smith reached for the door and took care to avoid the greasy spots and suspicious smears when he entered. To his right, three men, only two of them Westerners, sat smoking a large, brass bong with braided hoses and plastic tips that belched quietly whenever the men exhaled. To his left another six Westerners alternately poured tea, smoked cigarettes and pinched the Pakistani waitress's buttocks. CJ nearly felt sorry for the woman before remembering her national allegiance to suicide bombing and depraved autocracy. *I'd feel so much safer with a Glock in my pocket,* he thought. Smith was about to leave when one of the men at the bong called out to him.

"Hey gringo, where you headed?"

CJ turned and saw a muscular man, perhaps 35 years-old, with a flattop haircut and a small goatee. The man motioned for CJ to join him, another possible steroid abuser with graying hair and the only towelhead customer in the 199.

"Would I be wrong in supposing you're not from around here?" the first meathead said.

"Just got in from New York," CJ said.

The grey haired Westerner answered.

"Business or pleasure?"

"I wish it was business or pleasure. My daughter is in the hospital—pins poking out everywhere—she looks like something out of a fucking horror flick. And they pumped her so full of drugs she can't remember her own name."

The goateed man rubbed his whiskers and shook his head.

"I'm sorry to hear that. We've both lost friends in Waziristan, so I'm sure I know how you feel. How did it happen?"

"One of the flying pigs."

"That's awful," he said then, smiling. "But you have to admit that would have been funny a week ago."

"Pardon me if I don't see the humor."

The older of the two men spoke.

"Why don't you stay awhile and we'll get you some tea and hookah?"

CJ looked at the one terrorist seated with the Westerners and frowned. He saw the younger Westerner pick up the bong nozzle and quickly thought up an excuse.

"I don't smoke marijuana."

The younger Westerner followed CJ's gaze onto the native and laughed.

"Hey Ahmed, why don't you get lost?"

The Muslim cultist finally spoke. Ahmed had a very thick accent the type of which CJ often encountered in American convenience stores.

"But I am comfortable."

The older Westerner pushed him gently on the arm and continued explaining why it would be best if Ahmed found a new diversion immediately.

"It's American time, buddy, and you don't belong. Get some food or pray or something. We'll call you when we need an interpreter again."

CJ watched happily as Ahmed groaned, stood up and muttered what was probably some sort of voodoo curse. When the intruding native had left, CJ sat down in Ahmed's seat.

"Well, stranger," the grey man said. "I'm Leon and this ugly fucker next to me is Cody. What's your name?"

"I'm CJ. Hey, thanks for getting rid of the Taliban, but I wasn't lying when I said I don't smoke marijuana."

Hideous Cody laughed and held the bong tip up for the others to see.

"This, sir, is hookah. Think of the big tub here as the world's fanciest cigar. Tobacco, honey, spices and who knows what else they put in it. Tasty stuff."

CJ smiled. While he would not want others to see him smoking a cigarette, brass bound, honey flavored cigars would have a certain panache. CJ took hold of a nozzle and held the fumes inside his mouth. Cody continued.

"Good, isn't it? Almost good enough to make you forget what a shithole this place is."

"Nothing is that good," CJ said. "You know, if it wasn't for the fact my daughter lives here, I would have been happy about the pig stuff. These sons of bitches deserve worse in my opinion."

"Can't say I disagree," Leon said. "What do you think is happening with all this weird shit going on recently?"

CJ felt the hookah going to his head. He got the distinct impression that someone had inflated his brain with helium and released it to bounce lightly against the roof of his skull. Still, this did not prevent him answering.

"I think somebody has one hell of a sense of humor. Anything that pisses off the Muslims makes me happy and I couldn't believe how stupid the Indians were. Same thing with the Japanese and Koreans. Two tiny islands that nobody gives a shit about? I mean goddamn, how much are these people really willing to sacrifice over their stupid historical shit?"

Ugly Cody agreed and told CJ about the recent happenings in France, England, Palestine and Israel. CJ laughed out loud.

"Poetic justice right there!"

"I agree with you," Cody said. "I'm just worried the US might be next."

Leon took a giant drag off the hookah and sent spiced smoke pouring from his nostrils. He leaned back against the soft couch and spoke.

"We're the good guys in this. I don't think there's anything to worry about."

Cody and CJ likewise took up the smoking nozzles and soon the tobacco fog grew so thick the Americans could barely see each other. CJ finally spoke.

"And what can they do to us anyway?"

I again took my place at the pedestal and looked down on the haggard representatives. Very few had slept.

"Ladies and gentlemen. Thank you again for attending our little meeting. For today's agenda we shall concern ourselves with Korea and Japan, the United States and China's countless disputed territories.

"Let us begin with Japan. Please direct your attention to the screen above me once more. As many of you know, the Japanese have, unlike the Germans or Italians, persisted in honoring their WWII barbarians."

Fukashima Tsuchiya, Japanese secretary of historical preservation, objected to my characterization.

"Those men fought and died just as bravely as any others! Not even their enemies denied their courage. Is it really barbarism to fight for the glory of your homeland?"

"Of course it is," I said.

I turned to the rest of my hostages and continued.

"This image materializing on the divine screen is the Yasukuni Shrine. Contained inside are memorials honoring luminaries such as former president Hideki Tojo, venerable minister Sadao Araki, famous Manchurian adventurer Kenji Doihara, marketing genius Kingoro Hashimoto, noted ladies' man Seishiro Itagaki, development guru Iwane Matsui, Akiro Muto—known the world over for his great exploration of Sumatra, Shumei Okawa, that most generous organizer of the festivities in Mukden and of course Ishii Shiro, who advanced the cause of science so greatly. If you do not know them, ask one of the representatives from China, Singapore, the Philippines, Korea or the War Crimes Court in The Hague to help you. Or, failing that, make like a freshman and hit Wikipedia.

"Now, please turn your noses to my projector. As you can no doubt smell, I have caused a massive bloom of carrion flowers on the surrounding hills. My horticulture will soon cause the tourists to flee and then we can move on to the most important of our business here in Japan."

Fukashima's face grew cold and his lips tightened into a thin line. The historian folded his hands across his lap and spoke no more. The English delegate, Westminsteringham III, moved from his seat and hunched near the Japanese representative. Genevieve de Sade, Shimon Netanyahu and Abu Yassin took up their chairs and moved them to Fukashima's side. Those who believed themselves victimized held hands and looked into my eyes. "Our solidarity and humanity unite us against you," they seemed to say.

At that moment I elected to detonate a small thermonuclear device inside the Shinto monument. The pressure wave sent the Yasukuni's glistening black wood, golden calligraphy and finely etched stones flying through the atmosphere like a sea anemone throwing out its luminescent tentacles.

The Chinese delegation would have laughed or cheered at this display had they not seen my judgment against the French. Instead they huddled together and sent fearful text messages to their families. In my wisdom, I chose to direct their attentions onto that hated enemy to all patriotic Chinese, that most evil of Tibetan monks.

"Friends, since there are so many disputed territories ringing your nation and we have but limited time, I have decided to appoint His Holiness the Dalai Lama representative for all the separatist movements. Yes, you are quite right in pointing out that he is not present at our meeting. Pardon me as I digress slightly.

"There are living in your swamps and jungles a few dozen species of plant that supplement their phosphorous intake by killing and consuming animals. The venus flytrap is of course most famous, but I am more interested in the organisms of the genus *Drosera*. These amazing vegetables slay their victims through the use of sticky tentacles, digestive juices and a primitive nervous system. What would happen, I wondered, if you were to increase the *Drosera*'s mental capabilities and cause it to grow several thousand kilometers in length?"

At this moment hundreds of delicate, waving stalks crowned with sugary purple tips grabbed hold of the UN Building's roof, delicately cut away a portion of my glass entombment and opened wide the sky lights. A longer, fleshier stalk, reminiscent of the aloe vera plant's arms, then came through the skylights and uncoiled. When the *Drosera* released its grip and withdrew completely, all those present cast their eyes upon the only slightly digested and very much alive leader of the Tibetan Buddhists.

"You of the Chinese delegation no doubt remember the rules under which I cured the Israeli-Palestinian cancer. Your Holiness, I trust that *Drosera* has availed you of all the necessary details regarding your duties?"

"That incredible thing has indeed told me of your ways."

I nodded with marvelous magnanimity and bountiful benevolence.

"Since my carnivorous plant has already briefed His Holiness, I shall move directly to the Chinese delegation. I have grown weary with your insecure nationalism and territorial squabbles and thus propose to forever solve the issues of Taiwan, Tibet, the Uyghur territories and the hundreds of maritime dots and niches you claim from the likes of Vietnam, Japan, Myanmar, India, Russia, Korea, Laos and Cambodia. Truly, could you have picked more fights if you tried?

"In the first scenario, I offer you that which you claim to desire. All those territories, filled to bursting with subversives and undesirables and rebels, shall fall silent and submit to your rule. I will even solve your smog problem. In exchange, you will sacrifice all future territorial claims and, during the next 50 years, appoint for your Chinese Communist Party leaders only those currently or previously imprisoned for sedition. And when I say sacrifice all future territorial claims, I mean I will convert your entire military into an army of Chia Pets should you disobey.

"Choose quickly, for His Holiness has only to accept the farcical Chinese Dalai Lama as his successor. Should he agree, I will grant overwhelming power to the Tibetans, Uyghurs, and Vietnamese. Should you both refuse, I will of course turn all your territories into Mongolian vassal states filled with third rate barbeque restaurants and a new species of fish that lives in water pipes and severs the nipples of all who come near."

The Dalai Lama rose and addressed the delegates.

"I accept your proposal. In doing so I have partaken in the vilest of lies, for that boy you Chinese appoint is no more the reincarnation of our beloved Lama than I am the reincarnation of Mao. However, I will never sacrifice the happiness of my people, nor will I ever allow China to massacre Tibetans again, for the pure continuation of my religion. I pray that when it is we who control the levers of power we use these for the causes of justice. I pray we can restore that which I have on this day destroyed. It is my greatest hope…"

I interrupted the Dalai Lama.

"Yes, yes, of course, but now on to more important matters. You see I have two remaining countries to judge, and I must do so in such a manner as to make possible this heroic quest I've arranged."

I turned my gaze onto Alcohol, Tobacco and Firearms agent Mac Kaczynski and smiled.

"What the hell do you want?" he asked.

"I am willing to wager that two days ago, when you prepared your PowerPoint, created your audio files and searched the databases on the weapons trade, you did not envision yourself representing the entire United States."

Mr. Kaczynski seemed surprisingly unfazed.

"I can kill a man with my toes. I have eaten live rattlesnake and own one of the three diesel-powered Gatling guns in the world. If anyone is ready, I am."

I sighed and pursed Jean Claude Van Damme's lips.

"Then I am sorry to say that I will give you absolutely no choice as to the manner of judgment befalling the United States. But first, is there a representative from Korea in attendance?"

Expert on authoritarian princesses Baek Geun-hye raised her hand and said nothing. Her grim, grey face registered little and her unmoving gaze remained on my godly countenance. I directed her attention to the heavenly screen as it flickered into life again. On it Japanese President Ichiro Nomo stepped behind a podium and addressed the world.

"Ladies and gentlemen of the press, citizens of the world, my countrymen, I would very much like to speak to you about the tragic explosion today at the Yasukuni Shrine but find myself curiously unable. Instead, I will talk about the completely unrelated issue of Dokdo Island. I have drafted and signed an executive order ceding this territory to Korea. You might think there is some malicious spirit controlling me, but I assure you this decision is 100%, completely and thoroughly, purely and truly my free will. Once again, absolutely no power, divine or worldly, has interfered with me in any way whatsoever. Thank you and that is all I will say today."

The Korean representative's mouth opened and she said, "*hul.*" A flicker of hope restored the color to her cheeks and the glimmer to her eyes. I addressed her thusly.

"I am very glad this news makes you happy. Please do enjoy it while I am otherwise engaged. I will return to the judgment of your nation in precisely 1,945 seconds. In the mean time, we shall concern ourselves with the United States."

I turned back to the ATF representative.

"Mr. Kaczynski, please remind me exactly how your nation's war on melancholy, or indigestion—or was it frumpiness?—began."

"Al-Qaeda terrorists flew airplanes into the World Trade Center and Pentagon. That started the War on Terror."

"And pray tell what happened in this War on Terror?"

"You know what happened."

"Please humor me lest I am forced to convert your undergarments into gelatinous blobs of habanera pepper sauce."

Kaczynski's anger softened and he covertly scratched at his gentleman's sausage before answering.

"We fought wars in both Afghanistan and Iraq."

With that I whirled my hands and willed a baton to materialize. I pointed the baton skyward and spoke with the great gusto of a circus master.

"Ladies and gentlemen, I would ask you to once more direct your attention to the screen above."

The gently decaying insect carcasses completely encrusting my cotton-candy cloud flickered into view as the spray of brackish water crashing onto concrete embankments and soggy piers moistened my captives' cheeks. A mighty wind blew in from the east and tiny chunks of red spun sugar spiraled off my earthly home and into the petrochemical refineries of New Jersey. Flies and mosquitoes, gnats and spiders drifted from my candy cloud like ash from the wreckage of a house fire and fell into the Hudson River where the currents and eddies subsumed them forever more. The wind intensified and soon only a sticky residue remained from my cloud. The ATF agent gasped when he laid eyes on my newest construction.

"You rebuilt it?"

"Yes I have indeed re-erected your beloved World Trade Center. That singular outrage, that most traumatic of all traumas, most horrible of all horrors—eclipsing the Stalinist Purges and Armenian Massacres, overshadowing the Cambodian killing fields and making the Rape of Nanking the mere play of children by comparison—I have set right. I have even seen fit to improve the exterior walls of your great landmark."

Our hero and Mrs. Choi sat in front of their TV and watched in astonishment as the resurrected World Trade Center emerged from a cloud of mysterious candy goo. Those strakes and concrete ribs shined and the blue glass windows once more glinted in their tall slats. Choi Chul sat in wonderment, unable to understand what America had done to deserve reward while the rest of the world received punishment.

The TV cameraman zoomed in on the slick, black strips running down each of the new Trade Center's ribs.

Millions of tiny electric diodes flashed into life and bathed the building in light for a second before resolving into a clearer set of images. Happy digitized people tumbled down the diode strips from the greatest heights of the New World Trade Center down to the sidewalk like babies frolicking in a ball pit. Other cartoon people swung from the wings of animated airplanes in the manner of idyllic rural children clinging to rope swings.

Our hero could not help but laugh at the Americans' symbolic misfortune. That the great arrogant power whose people obsessed over 2,600 dead and whose tantrums shook the earth would every day relive its greatest humiliation tickled Chul's sense of irony. He turned to his wife and spoke.

"It is fitting punishment for people who did so much evil, only to avenge stupid historical shit that is best forgotten. How much of their own blood have they sacrificed, how much blood of others have they sacrificed over but one small misfortune? May it be covered in urine and garbage every day anew."

The TV cameraman turned his attentions to a plump middle-aged woman and her balding husband. The couple strode past a "vandalism will be prosecuted to the full extent of divine law" sign and grabbed hold of the LED strips. The woman's permed hair bounced with exertion and reminded our hero of mattress springs. Her husband sweated and grunted through his business shirt and khaki and exhorted others to help.

"Bring this down! Tear it down! Tear it down!"

It was not until lightning shot from the LED screens and rendered the vandals a mosaic of seizing, tongue biting and, finally, comatose slobbering that Choi Chul ceased to find it funny.

I turned my attentions once more to Baek Geun-hye and addressed her.

"Please share your thoughts regarding my actions in New York."

"I fear you."

"You are wise to do so, for it has now been 1,908 seconds since I returned Dokdo to Korean control and you have less than 1 minute before I complete the judgment of your nation. What is the greatest humiliation your people have ever suffered?"

The representative went quickly to her answer.

"The rape of our nation by the Japanese. 1910 to 1945."

"I thought as much. What, pray tell, would you think if their presence— oh, I am sorry to say it is one thousand nine hundred and forty three seconds, one thousand nine hundred and forty four—my dear friends, look now as ground about Seoul quivers. Watch as the earth turns crimson in this place and bleaches white in another. Cast your eyes on the burning red circle rising but a few centimeters in Suwon and the alternate spokes of scarlet and alabaster racing through Itaewon and Incheon, Gimpo and Namdaemoon."

My divine display vibrated with the heaving earth and the scent of topsoil came to dominate the UN Building. When all had fallen still, I caused the display to zoom out and reveal the brilliant modifications I had made to the Korean capital. The Burmese secretary for the ethical management of precious stones said "it's worse than I could have imagined!" and spoke no more.

The Distance

Seosi

Until the day of my death I will

look to the sky without shame.

As the leaf blowing in the wind I too suffer.

As clearly as the singing stars I know

I must love all things wandering toward death.

And I too must walk the road I've been given.

For tonight as well the stars brush past the breeze.

-Yoon Dong-joo

Chapter Twenty

Thirty Nine Days After

I saw fit to leave the United Nations Building behind and return to the heavenly ether. However, before departing in a cloud of glory, I deigned to once more address the diplomats and support staff and thus more thoroughly elucidate upon their situation.

"Dear Ladies and Gentlemen,

"I have grown weary with the stereotypical hostage crisis. You know what I mean—gaunt cheeks and disheveled hair and unresolved traumas leaking out all over the place. I want to put your minds at ease, for you will suffer no such fate. Look to the rear of the great hall and you will find a bounteous plenty of Mountain Dew, pork rinds, and Big Macs. I have taken the liberty of removing the lettuce, specifying bacon, ordering extra sauce, even going so far as to compel the McDonald's staff to withhold the onions and pickles on said hamburgers. In addition, I leave you in the presence of this glowing, throbbing Twinkie, floating through the air and casting its benevolent light down upon you at night. You may wonder about the Twinkie's significance but I assure you, all will become clear.

"I have modified your dietary intake thus because you will remain enclosed here until each and every honorable representative becomes obese enough to make me laugh. Please do eat up."

The hostages shook their heads and headed to the buffet line. Many a whisper of "asshole" drifted across the forum and I was well pleased. And so I went away that those vital to my heroic quest might resolve their personal difficulties.

Patty Smith needed time to recover sufficiently and reunite with her husband in Northern California. CJ also required a period of quiet that he might visit the new World Trade Center. Likewise,Choi Chul wanted rest and a period for stewing in anger within which to plot his revenge against me.

You would of course be correct in noticing these things do not preclude my staying in New York unnoticed. However, in addition to intervening in the idiocy of men, it is also my duty to manage the other deities' real estate claims. This is not normally difficult work. We gods are, by human standards at least, practically immortal and therefore less prone to speculation than your average human. That we can call lands, palaces and gaggles of Ishtar's sacred whores into existence at any time does much to grease the rails of serenity. But immortality, a wonderful hedge against death, is not nearly so effective a barrier against senility.

This brings us to Hades. Shortly after my judgment against Korea, the Greek master of the former underworld called to me in a voice that shook the ground and set the ice-capped mountains trembling.

"Damn usurper," he said. "Shiva knows full well I command all the spirits of the dead. Chiron answers to me alone! You need to fix this, Quezalcoatl."

I pressed my divine palm into my heavenly forehead. I answered with the sort of teeth-gritting strain typically only found in those attempting to navigate automated phone answering systems.

"I'm not Quetzalcoatl. I'm the God of Potency."

This aroused Hades' mighty anger and he chastised me grievously. He'd somehow gotten ahold of Poseidon's trident and, holding it backwards, shook the terrible weapon while he spoke.

"Don't question me, pup. All you feathered bastards look the same anyway."

I was about to argue with the master of all lands beyond the Styx. I was near to pointing out my complete lack of plumage but relented that he might move more quickly to the source of his complaint.

"I want my souls back, especially Tupac. Persephone's bingo night hasn't been the same since. Too quiet, no hippity hop, no…"

Hades burst into song.

"No fucks given,
no choice, I'm stacking bills
fuzz on my tail, I bail til I lose em
Done busted my black ass,
brag about the nigga they got to blast…"

The great master of the underworld paused to gather in his breath, and I interrupted that he might not continue the funky beat. Hades, no longer rapping but hardly contented, moved on to a new subject, or rather, subjects.

"Too many light bulbs! Stupid clappers—and where are my damned pants?"

"Perhaps you should ask the nymphs about your pants. St. John is really not my department. What do you wish me to do regarding Shiva?"

"Not your department? Boy, you will make it your department! I am the earth shaker! I am the master of thunder and the scourge of man! I am the giver of wisdom and light and swords and grain and wine and party favors and modest lingerie and—"

I interrupted Hades, who was not the earth shaker (that would be his brother Poseidon), not the master of thunder (Zeus), not the giver of wisdom (his niece Athena) nor the scourge of man (his nephew Ares). However, as evidenced by the fate of our previously mentioned super ninjas, Hades had indeed taken on the proud office of modest lingerie godhood..

"Let's focus on Shiva and Tupac. What would you like me to do?"

"Get my damned pants before I kick your backside into the cycle of reincarnation!"

And in such a manner those two long weeks passed by.

Our hero did not wish to leave Daegu. He could not stand the thought of seeing Seoul desecrated and would not dream of carrying on while the stinking pro-Japanese pollution lay covering his nation's capital.

Choi Chul's powerlessness ground against the bone and sinew of his neck, frustration festered beneath his fingernails and he could think of no salves more soothing than sake (he meant to say soju), solitude and *samgyupsal* at his uncle's traditional restaurant.

Our hero parked his car on the sidewalk and took a plastic seat under the "SAMGYUP-LOVE" banner. A part-time waitress took the cover from the table's BBQ pit and lowered a crucible of glowing coals into the hole like a blacksmith setting fire to her forge. Chul waited for the grill to bend the light with its heat before laying down slabs of thick pork belly and setting raw garlic to boil in the fatty runoff. He looked to the waitress and spoke.

"Bring to me a bottle of sake—soju. Bring my uncle as well. Go quickly and do not waste time fucking around."

The waitress, taken more than a little aback, returned with the liquor. Our hero poured it viciously so that the spillage sizzled in the pit and the shot glass slipped slick between his white fingers. He drank with equal malice and slammed the glass's rim against his teeth. The table shook with the violence of Chul's refilling. The uncle came soon after.

"You are not well?"

"I am fucking unwell. I wish to drink much and hope to suffer from vomiting in the morning. Join me as is your duty or leave me alone."

"What noise is this? When if not in times of trouble should men make themselves hard like iron, ready for action?"

The uncle gestured to his employees for more side dishes, pulled another plastic chair from a neighboring table and sat with our hero. He struck the table with his knee and all of Chul's remaining soju spilled out onto the ground.

"*Hul*," our hero said.

"It is better this way. Fewer passersby will know your weakness."

Our hero was unimpressed with this line of reasoning and rolled the empty soju bottle toward his uncle.

"Bring me another. I will not pay for this one."

Chul's uncle muttered "little bitch" and summoned the part-time waitress once more. She returned shortly and poured two shots. Chul lifted his glass for a toast and spoke.

"Take the deliciousness."

"You are a little bitch."

The samgyupsal began to burn and our hero quickly set about cutting the pork and moving it to cooler sections of the grill. The garlic had blackened beyond the point of rescue. They ate and said little until the coals died and the mosquitoes emerged from the creeping dusk.

"What are men of action to do in times like these, uncle?"

"You are a business man well accustomed to discord and strife. Think of something."

Chul held up his arms with disbelief.

"Why scold me if you can see no other road?"

"You are supposed to be smarter than I. It is right that the mind of a businessman surpasses the mind of a restaurateur."

"My mind, so great as to surpass even Uncle's, can imagine no cure for this calamity. I cannot even know the source from which this evil emerges."

"It is the Chinese and the Jews, making conspiracy."

Our hero feigned outrage.

"May their sordid conspiracy-rubbing result in ugly children!"

"Aye, little bitch, you know my meaning."

Chul rolled his eyes.

"Yes uncle, the Chinese, having nothing better to do with their time, made a pact with the Jews to humiliate our nation. In this plan they must be so brilliant as to create high technology of unfathomable expense and great ability. They must be so competent as to assemble hundreds of scientists and manufacturers, security professionals and spies and do so with perfect secrecy. Then they must also be so stupid to do this that the Jews may gain nothing and the Chinese might honor their greatest enemies."

"Nephew, it is only my opinion."

"Your opinion is a waste of air. The Chinese and the Jews have not laid the Japanese pollution across Seoul."

"How do you know?"

"Give credit to a mind greater than your own. Conspiracy theories are for idiots who dream of grandeur and have no recourse less desperate."

The uncle pushed the table perhaps 15 centimeters and stood before Choi Chul.

"You will drink for free and suffer no more of my criticism if only you promise me action. When we know this evil, when a target for our revenge reveals itself, swear to me you will act."

Our hero did not require any further negotiation.

(For the virtue of spreading conspiracy theories, I bless Chul's uncle with a lifetime's supply of tin foil. For the virtue of drinking violently, I bless Chul with exactly the raging hangover he wanted.)

Chapter Twenty One

Forty Three Days After

The plane circled in preparation to set down at JFK International Airport. CJ could see the runway extending into the horizon and heard the landing gear drop. The pilots worked to scrub speed and altitude, pointing the nose skyward. The flexible wings shuddered and woke Patty from her thin, medicated sleep. 386 tons of aluminum and composite, people and luggage, dishware and hot towels compressed the balloon tires onto rough concrete at just under 200 miles per hour. He thought of heavy titanium springs compressing and huge carbon-ceramic brakes glowing red beneath the plane. *Do Patty's own surgical titanium and ceramic meshes shudder, compress and rattle in the same way?* This made CJ imagine surgical screw heads rubbing against the cartilage in his elbows and he quickly searched for a distraction, a way to change the subject in his own internal dialogue.

"Patty, we landed in New York," he said. "The weather is really nice."

Patty's eyes looked like marbles covered in motor oil. The tacky residue from dried tears formed crystals on her eyelashes and when she spoke, CJ could not help noticing how her tongue tripped over her teeth.

"Is John here? I need to see John. I need to see John."

"He said he would wait at the customs checkpoint."

"That's good. I need to see John."

She receded into the haze of vicodin and sat unconsciously staring at the air-mall catalogue. CJ retrieved both his and Patty's carry-on luggage, slung the straps and handles over his body and waited for the other passengers to leave. He didn't want anyone to bump Patty's wheelchair or tweak her spiky osteo-corrective apparatus. He breathed a huge sigh of relief when they finally cleared the final seats and entered the connecting walkway.

Patty woke again just as they arrived at customs. She looked scared and set her good hand searching around her lap. CJ correctly guessed what was perturbing her and dropped a passport onto her leg. She pulled her lips back and sucked the air. Her one good hand tucked the passport into her pocket, out of CJ's reach.

Patty asked for her husband once more as they cleared customs but nodded off before CJ could answer. John came to meet them in security. CJ saw the fashionable, square frame glasses hanging from an overlong nose and laid eyes on the green wool jacket draped over sloping shoulders. He hated this yuppie, this "son-in-law ." John was about to say something to Patty but stilled himself when he saw she could not answer. He instead addressed himself to CJ.

"Thanks for bringing her back. You have no idea how much this means to me, and her too."

CJ wanted to be rid of John more than he wanted to breathe and thus went straight to the day's itinerary.

"I understand. I need to take care of something this evening. Please take Patty to Selfsevere yourself. I'll meet you there tonight."

John did that infuriatingly sincere *I feel your pain* nod and grimace like he was a goddamned daytime talk show host comforting an orphan. CJ wanted to hurt his son in law.

"Not a problem," John said. "Thanks for letting us stay at your house. We can be out as soon as she feels better."

CJ was about to lie and say he didn't mind and that it would be a good opportunity for him and John to get to know each other and that he was sure they'd both like spending time out in a genuine small American town. He said this instead:

"I will make sure you're both taken care of. I'll see you later."

John's soft, dainty little faggot hands brushed against CJ's fingers as CJ turned Patty's wheelchair over to his son-in-law. CJ shuddered, turned and left before the temptation to speak frankly overcame him.

It's like a sewage pipe ruptured, CJ thought. The pedestrians turned right or left and detoured at least a block away. Cabbies and motorists too. Old people, bums and Goths walking aimlessly with their depressed girlfriends, alone among all New Yorkers, saw fit to pass near the new World Trade Center.

Smith parked his truck in the empty underground lot and took an unadorned industrial elevator to the first floor lobby. There white marble floors reflected the sunlight up and into the rows of potted trees. The vegetation erupted from what looked like enormous, decapitated beer cans. He ran his fingers over the marble and concrete, aluminum and leather. It smelled like cleaning solution and dust.

CJ looked toward the rotating glass doors and thought it was perhaps time to go and face the outrage I'd left on the building exterior. Indeed, a part of him wished for yet another fresh wound, another confirmation that he would not forget the death of his wife, but it didn't feel right. *Now is not the time,* he thought. Instead he turned to the elevators and chose floor 109, the offices of Underwood and Sampson. The elevator accelerated up the shaft and delivered CJ to his goal.

The carpeted halls and cherry wood doors spoke of affluence and sophistication—triumphant Americanism of a shiny, globalized sort that CJ did not quite approve of. The black marble Underwood and Sampson sign's spelling began with a V, like Smith had seen with BVLGARI. The lesser of our heroes pressed a button and listened as the automatic glass doors wafted along their well-greased runners. CJ breathed deeply and stepped inside what, at this time, felt very much like a holy sanctum.

Air conditioning blew icy little darts across the lobby. The ubiquitous water cooler bubbled twice near a brass-trimmed reception desk. He couldn't see a single stray paper or discarded staple. *If anybody has been in here since the towers went back up,* CJ thought, *they did a very good job cleaning up after themselves.*

He turned to the right down the hall and read the name plates next to each office. Cecil Roads, Foreign Acquisitions Chief; Ellen Greenbridge, Economic Forecasting; Barry Stearns, Office of Accounting; Bertrand Mancoff, Oversight; Don Ggaseu, Human Resources; Jane Smith, Valuation. The exquisite handle clicked once when CJ pressed down and the door opened silently on its expensive hinges.

He smiled for a second. Her desk was a tangle of chipped aluminum trays, beaver board, scattered cell phones, USB ports and family pictures. CJ thought it likely Jane was the only Sampson and Underwood employee who had made a habit out of shopping at Costco. He picked up one of Jane's Nokia brick-phones and tried to call his wife's voicemail.

"I'm sorry; service is no longer available for this model."

CJ put the phone back and walked to the conference room. He wanted to see the spot she'd jumped from—to understand what she felt and imagine what she thought.

They must have used a whole tree to make the conference table. Beautiful, burled mahogany so smooth and shiny that CJ could imagine women checking their makeup in its reflection. With the brushed titanium protecting the wood on each side, the solid, stainless steel-framed chairs and retracting flat screen displays, CJ thought they had easily a million dollars in furnishings alone.

It had been the second window to the left. There was a small lip perhaps one meter high and 30 centimeters deep separating the glass pane from the interior façade. Smith tapped the window with his knuckles. He felt no bend, no vibration, not even the slightest hint of fragility. They must have really gone at it, perhaps a strong man swinging one of those steel-framed chairs.

CJ stepped back and let his mind fall silent. One step, two steps, Smith put his boot on the window lip and braced himself against the frame. *She must have seen blue sky and New York's countless towers, felt the smoke rising and heard the wind rushing.* CJ looked down at the bums and Goths and old people below and saw them reduced to the size of wood lice or krill. *She must have closed her eyes and counted to three. She must have felt a sense of freedom as she broke through the heat and poisonous gas. She must have looked down.*

Patty's new husband, John of the soft little hands and hipster glasses, opened the front door with a finger to his lips.

"Shh," he said. "Patty's asleep."

CJ grimaced and led John to the kitchen. Cows crapped delicately in the distance, birds sang of love and the last of the day's sunlight shone through the windows as he spoke.

"How are you?" John asked. "After the visit, I mean?"

"I went into the WTC through the basement. Never even saw the light strips, or at least, not up close."

John puckered a little.

"Really?"

"Yeah, you seem surprised."

John puckered a lot. CJ took pity on him.

"What did Patty tell you?"

"She said you don't pass up many opportunities for outrage, especially about stuff like that. I don't know. Maybe she's wrong."

CJ felt the exact outrage Patty foretold rising in his chest. It pressed against his sternum and tightened the muscles of this throat. Then, for the first time in years, it relented. CJ metered out slow, careful words.

"That stuff on the outside is a cartoon. It doesn't matter. I went to where Alice jumped and it was something else—sacred."

"I see," John said, clearly not seeing.

"Profound. I touched the things she touched and saw the sidewalk below the same way she must have and I got to thinking. In that last minute before she died, my wife went from poison filth to perfect cleanliness and back to the dirt."

John, looked even more confused and so CJ explained.

"That office must have been disgusting. Ash everywhere, bits of paper flying around, burning plastic. She must have felt positively infested. So she went to the window—maybe somebody else broke it, maybe she did—and put one foot on the window sill. She told herself she would not die by fire and leapt out.

"Imagine that for a second. More than three hundred meters up and you just jump. She must have felt so clean in that ocean of fresh air. It must have blown her hair back and pulled tears to the corners of her eyes."

CJ paused and looked at John. His son-in-law replied.

"I'd never thought of it like that before."

"Neither had I, not until I visited. But we're not finished with the story. Jane ends up back in the dirt."

John said nothing.

"It's probably true she didn't know what would happen. But that doesn't change how things ended. The last thing my wife did in her own life was deprive that boy she landed on of his. So I think about that and I realize something new. They didn't just kill her. They didn't just take my wife and Patty's mother away. They made her into a murderer as well...."

John bit his tongue and said nothing. CJ spoke after what felt like minutes.

"I'm not going to let some cartoon overshadow the profundity of the death she chose."

Chapter Twenty Two

58 Days After

Patty hated pain medication. Vicodin, percocet, morphine—it didn't matter what the doctors prescribed. The pills always left her stupid but not so stupid she couldn't recognize her idiocy. This fog, this state as a self-aware simpleton, frustrated Patty and so she preferred to trade pills for pain much sooner than most.

This was day two without the vikes. The day before, she'd contented herself with daytime TV and teasing CJ's cat. She would have done the same this day had she not noticed a pile of legal pads stacked beside the armchair.

Patty picked up the first and flipped it open. The first page was nothing more exciting than a shopping list. The second page had sketches for an irrigation system and some other mechanical device she could not identify. She was about to put the pad down when she noticed a scribble on the bottom that said "CNN stuff: AA Bob said the Tibetans are on the rise. Tibet!?!?!"

Who the hell is AA Bob? Alcoholic's Anonymous maybe? Patty dismissed that after a few seconds. *Dad drinks less than anyone else I know.* She flipped the page and saw the following:

"AA Bob says that Tibet wants control of Afghanistan. I say let 'em have the towelheads. But what if they also want our bases? What if they want new-Israel? We've got to show these fuckers who's boss sooner or later."

"AA Bob quoted the Dalai Lama today. DL said something about peace growing from the barrel of a gun. Don't think that's original. Find out who said it first. Use Wikipedia."

AA, AA. Patty grabbed her Internet phone and did a search for "Bob CNN International Dalai Lama Tibet Afghanistan Barrel of Gun." All it turned up was Robert Umbaku, an anchor on the network. Patty gave up trying to figure it out alone and sent a text message to her father asking for some explanation.

She set her phone aside and went back to the notepads. The next page had information concerning her own hospital address, how to clear Pakistani customs, phone numbers and contacts. She caught herself smiling at this point. Patty put the notepad aside and resisted the urge to trust, to feel anything beyond suspicion, in her father's presence. The cat jumped on her lap and asked to be petted. Patty dumped him on the floor.

Page four had CJ's notes on new-Israel, France and the Queen of England. Patty considered turning the TV on and ignoring her father's weird, handmade news chronicles but could not stand the thought of yet another romantic comedy. She settled her legs more comfortably on the foot stool, scratched her armpit and resumed reading.

Shame what happened to Israel, but the forests around Birkenau do look nice. I think I like this Netanyahu guy... said they might not have gotten this homeland without killing so many Palestinian leaders"

Heard about the French language. Gonna order some freedom fries tonight.

Queen of England still in orbit. Supposedly you can see her with a home telescope. Next fly-by is Tuesday at 3 a.m. Stay up and watch?

Patty let her head fall back against the pillows and cast her eyes upon the ceiling. Her phone buzzed and she checked her inbox.

"AA Bob = Affirmative Action Robert -Dad"

Patty's thoughts coalesced around one unendingly odd question. *How the hell did I come from him?*

(For the virtue of paraphrasing Mao Zedong, I bless the Dalai Lama with 20% thicker armpit hair.)

Chapter Twenty Three

59 Days After

I had been six days removed from Hades' hellish senility when it struck my fancy to take over the organs of human mass communication. I began with a few small incursions, such as divinely mandating absolute honesty during this sports talk interview of Miami sports star Tiger W. Roethlisberger.

"Mr. Roethlisberger," James Roman said. "It's a pleasure to have you on *The Manly Show*."

Tiger rubbed the whiskers of his tightly cropped goatee and answered.

"I would normally say that it's my pleasure, but you know as well as I do that anything's better than a televised sausage fest aimed at entertaining an audience made entirely from fat dudes who couldn't do a hundred-yard sprint if there were pussy-shaped beer kegs at the finish line."

Roman frowned and moved on to the first question.

"A lot of people say the Alligators are in a great position for championship run this year but only if you play like you did with the Industrialists last year. How are you dealing with that kind of pressure?"

"Call girls."

"Excuse me?"

"The occasional porn star, coeds, those drunk chicks who do the butt jiggle dance at night clubs. What do you call that, twinking or something? Anyway, they really help me relax…what?"

Roman extended an accusing finger out to Roethlisberger and worked himself into a lather of righteous fury. He would likely have said something terrifically boring.

To prevent this I caused a flood of My Little Pony dolls to engulf James Roman and sweep him away to the set of *The View* where blood-thirsty producers forced him to opine endlessly on, and I quote, "the new(ish) theory by well renowned Marxist feminist historian Sherry Sherrill concerning the ethics of unnaturally curvy and idealized Barbie Dolls and how those unjustly sexy children's toys might affect the endlessly delicate and vitally important psyches of the very same young girls who would, should they survive mentally intact the many depredations and social manifestations of the perfidious patriarchy, one day lead a world more free and verdant than that which they inherited under the discriminatory and unhealthy domination of old white men not only unconcerned with the fate of femdom but actively seeking to undermine the very female fruit of their own loins in a suicidal quest to retain the tyrannical hierarchical domination of their unworthy, sexually, physically and spiritually—you might even say metaphysically—abusive sons and sons-in-law who, like their fathers before them, sought not to achieve the just and verdant world we all strive for but to institutionalize the late-capitalist system of systemic oppression and worker exploitation that was even then dooming their nations to squalor and disarray of the type unseen since the fall of the Roman slave oppression system of oppression—surely a fate worse than death and desirable only to those depraved men, yes, the appropriately named and infinitely despicable monsters of the One Percent recently exposed with great eloquence and through the glorious and growing sense of proletariat class consciousness inevitably preceding the fall of the entire oppressive capitalist system of bourgeoisie oppression." James Roman wept and I was well pleased.

I naturally followed this salvo with an army of sapient intra-uterine devices that, latching onto his head, caused Tiger W. Roethlisberger to immediately crash his motorcycle into his wife's Cadillac while perjuring himself in front of the American Congress, failing a drug test, getting an awful tattoo and attacking his fans with a cricket bat.

Well pleased once more, I followed this first dalliance with the mass media by lighting Celine Dion's hair on fire during a Diane Sawyer interview and re-animating the corpse of Michael Jackson on TRL. For a final touch I caused Bill O'Reilly to adopt the new moniker "Steve the Midget Fucker." With these practice runs complete, I elected to make my first public appearance on earth.

Wolf Blitzer walked that day into the *Situation Room* and scanned the magnificent set. He looked upon the towers and skyscrapers sparkling in the darkened Washington skyline. The large flat screen TVs flashed one by one into life and cast a subtle blue glow on his central news desk. Blitzer picked up his notes and spread them carefully near his chair but below the cameras' line of sight. Not too many that day. He was well pleased and went to the dressing room where a team of Georgetown

University interns set about perfectly coiffing his hair. He spoke as the first brush touched his wizened head.

"My how the Dalai Lama has changed."

The interns were afraid and said nothing because they suspected Blitzer of covert Buddhism. The newsman smiled and drank his coffee. He would have interrogated the fact checkers one last time and reminded the producers to run though the all the feeds had I not caused *Drosera* to once more open the way for my divine will.

The glass windows burst open in a frenzy of sugar-tipped, fleshy stems. The mighty plant pressed gently on the *Situation Room* screens until they had slid from the cameras' view. A talking head walked in and I commanded *Drosera* to grab hold. The commentator shrieked when my elegant vegetable caught him round the waist and called out once more when *Drosera* sent him flying towards the Potomac River, trailing a stream of stage makeup, digestive juices and talking points. An intern spoke upon seeing this.

"I didn't know you guys were doing special effects. Awesome!"

I heard this and blessed the intern with four years immunity to mosquito bites. The talking head made a faint splashing sound in the distance. I materialized on the slick, marble floor in a cloud of fuschia mist. I commanded the heavenly choir to descend into the set, ablaze in divine glory, and play a short rendition of "La Cucaracha" that all might know of my arrival. The staff stood amazed and I let loose my mighty voice.

"You, cameraman, turn on your camera. Sound-guy, ready your microphones. Mr. Blitzer and I have business of an incredibly weighty nature to discuss."

The Wolf emerged from his lair and, in a manner most manly, screamed upon seeing my godly personage. He laid eyes on the glowing choir behind me and called out once more.

"Ah! Are you going to kill me?"

"Certainly not yet. I've not even introduced myself."

I removed a chair from behind the news desk and settled in while Blitzer spoke.

"Who are you and what do you want?"

"I am the God of Potency and, Wolf, I would like to congratulate you because I have just caused every television in the world, every Internet video and navigation device to display your program. You are starring in the highest-rated show in all history.

"Before you ask, yes, I am the one responsible for the irregularities in Korea, Japan, China, New York, India, Pakistan, Israel, France and the Mexican desert."

Blitzer covered his mouth and leaned away from me. However, it did not take the intrepid newsman long to recover his courage.

"I suppose you will wait until after the production to murder us?"

I approved of the way he used this moment to create tension with the audience but, sadly, could allow no further indulgences. I became so serious, in fact, that I motioned for the heavenly host to retreat quietly to the cafeteria.

"No, my dear man. I have not ended a single human life since my interventions began. The more interesting question is why, bearing my benevolence in mind, do you fear me yet? Why only last week you, with no obvious signs of discomfort, braved the roads surrounding Kandahar that you might interview General Bob O. Gateun, a man responsible for thousands of deaths."

Blitzer rocked back in his own chair and harrumphed as the last angel made his way into the snack room.

"It's because you've wreaked havoc."

"What wonderfully dramatic phrasing! Truly Wolf, you missed your calling. Surely you would do better in poetry, literary criticism or soap operas. But fantastic wit aside, I must ask in what sense have I caused havoc?"

Blitzer frowned and summoned an air of gravity at least as deep in profundity as his "wreaked havoc" comment had been in ominous drama.

"I really think you know, Mr. God of Potency."

While his showmanship would have cowed any human, and indeed 47.3% of all divinities, I felt nothing beyond the natural and good urge to, as the great poets of your time are wont to say, "bitch slap" this "fuckin' ho" back into his proper place. I moderated this impulse somewhat before continuing.

"And I really think you're dodging my question, Mr. Blitzer."

Blitzer smelled blood and prepared to crush me under the weight of his righteousness.

"You denuded China, turned the Dalai Lama into a militarist, launched the poor Queen of England into orbit, caused the Israelites to suffer humiliation and shame every day of their lives, deepened the sufferings of the Palestinians, mocked the victims of 9/11, destroyed an ancient Japanese shrine in the least sensitive manner possible, embarrassed the Koreans and offended both the Muslim and Hindu religions, and that's just off the top of my head!"

I ran fingers over my jacket sleeve before reaching up to flick a single strand of Jacky Chan hair from my Jean Claude Van Damme forehead.

"Use your journalistic training, Wolf, specifics. What did I actually do whilst committing those outrages? How exactly did I wreak havoc in all these places, against all these people?"

"Do you mean instance by instance?"

"Of course not."

Blitzer leaned towards me and crinkled his brow in the puckered grimace of a power-lifter.

"Are you asking me for something more metaphysical?"

"You could say so."

He breathed deeply and paused.

"Everything you've done was designed to humiliate large numbers of people."

I began to grow frustrated with Mr. Blitzer. I considered setting *Drosera* to the business of digesting him, but, from the depths of my near infinite mercy, decided to give the Wolf one last hint before I handed him over to the metabolic harshness of plant intestines.

"This is technically true but hardly illuminating. Under what theme have I united these many outrages and humiliations?"

Wolf said nothing.

"Take your time, Mr. Blitzer. Do not worry, my plant is friendlier than it looks."

He paused a good 15 seconds.

"Well, I would say, maybe—you seem to have searched for the rawest national nerves and then used those weak spots to torture people."

I clapped Saddam Hussein's hands and smiled like the Old Testament God at a smiting.

"Yes, Mr. Blitzer, yes! These nerves, they are all symbols and traditions, are they not?"

Blitzer drew his reply out over several seconds.

"Yes ..."

The smile vanished from my divine mouth and I spoke with the intensity of a man navigating a magma field.

"So you fear me because I am a slayer of the symbolic but have no particular problem with General Gateun, who controls nuclear weapons?"

Blitzer pounded his perfectly manicured fist into the desk.

"It's a matter of intent! You've been nothing but malicious. In comparison, Bob O. Gateun does not seem to be a sociopath."

My mirthful expression returned, my martial artist's eyes softened and I crossed Cameron Diaz's shapely legs before me.

"I would be interested to hear if the Pashtun tribesmen he bombed this morning share your opinion regarding intent."

The breeze of certainty fell, like a frozen turd, from the sails of Blitzer's arguments.

"Perhaps I should rephrase."

"Perhaps you should."

Blitzer grimaced and held his outstretched hands open, palm down, in the manner of a frazzled mother attempting to debate a toddler.

"We humans are used to war. We are not used to giant, predatory plants. We don't know how to deal with tofu rain. We don't have any traditions for dealing with a man/god/thing that launches our royalty into space. We understand General Gateun, but we can't make heads or tails of you."

"So it is a matter of social customs, completely divorced from the actual, physical survival of your species, or indeed, divorced even from your prosperity and comfort, that causes you to fear me while holding General Gateun in high regard?"

"I never said that."

"Are you going to disagree?"

"No, but—"

"Then it doesn't matter what you were going to say."

I pushed aside Saddam's ample forearm hair and looked at my tasteful gold/silver/diamond/dollar-sign themed Rolex.

"I'm afraid we must move on." I said. "While I confess I could continue philosophizing with you in this manner for hours, my larger purpose demands we shift our attentions to the delicious pastry I am now causing to materialize."

A creamy, spongy brick of disastrously unhealthy desert flickered into existence in the air above Blitzer's desk. Hovering there, it caught the light and cast a heavenly aura across CNN's drab studio audience.

"Is that a Twinkie?" Blitzer asked.

"Yes, but no ordinary Twinkie. This is the great, exalted Twinkie of Destiny."

"I'm afraid I don't follow."

I caused Jean Claude Van Damme's eyes to glow red and sent lightning shooting from the tips of my fingers. Thunder sounded in the distance as I spoke.

"All will be made clear in a moment, Mr. Blitzer. This pastry will soon hold the key to earthly omnipotence, power exceeding even my own. Whosoever consumes this Twinkie shall enjoy dominion over the land and seas, men and beasts, god and mortal, if for only 15 minutes. It will not allow resurrection, immortality or time travel, but these are the only limits I will impose. The delicatessen who engorges this might make himself unendingly wealthy, stunningly beautiful or powerful like none before. Why, should they wish, they might even undo all that I have done."

None could speak in the face of such awesome oration and so I stuffed the special effects and continued in a normal voice.

"However, I must warn you that I will do nothing to lower the cholesterol content or saturated fat levels, nor shall I moderate the radioactivity resulting from the operation I am about to perform."

Blitzer rose up against his terror and awe to speak.

"Who will you give it too?"

"I'm afraid it's not going to be so easy."

With that I caused the Twinkie to shake violently in its levitation. Interns screamed and *Drosera* wilted in fear. A mighty wind blew in the open windows and set Blitzer's tie fluttering. Lightning came down from the ceiling and a polar bear roared in the sound-mixing room. A great flood swept across the studio audience. Wind and water and beast and predatory plant met in an almighty collision. Spray and fur, lightning bolts and windblown debris swirled around the quivering Twinkie and obscured it from view. Those present heard a mighty booming and saw a brilliant flash of light. The Twinkie of Destiny had vanished.

I turned once more to the cameras and gave my final address of the evening.

"The Twinkie of Destiny, the Pastry of Power, the Junk Food of Everlasting Glory, it awaits you. Go forth and make yourselves legendary!"

Chapter Twenty Four

60 Days After

Our hero reclined on his sofa. He bunched together lumpy cushions and set them under the back of his head. The TV glowed unnoticed in the distance. Empty bottles of Stout formed an aluminum cityscape in miniature atop the table. Choi Chul felt only a pleasant swimming intoxication and an encroaching, fuzzy sleep descending upon his leaden eyelids. He would see, hear… feel …! BRRRRRING! He yawned and took up the phone.

"This is Choi Chul."

His uncle's voice came triumphantly through the speaker phone.

"Yah! Little bitch, the time has come to earn your soju. We know who laid the Japanese pollution across our greatest city and it is time to take action!"

The uncle proceeded to describe my appearance on *The Situation Room*. He referred to me as a "large bitch" several times and for this sin I sent a plague of unusually loud mosquitoes to buzz around his ears and suck the blood of his knuckles every night so long as he should live. The sinner continued on.

"The part-time waitress at my restaurant has a rich father. You must know of Hwang Nara, the reclusive cell phone charm baron. In any case he has prepared a boat to pursue the Twinkie of Destiny and seeks a man skilled in foreign language."

"The what of what?" Chul asked.

"The details are not important now, but this Twinkie is the key to the God of Potency's destruction! You must find it before some Chinese Jew uses it to further insult our nation."

"The what god? You are making dog's noise, uncle. No one of sound mind would believe this fantasy."

The uncle sighed before speaking.

"Turn on the television." His voice picked up considerably. "An unemployed man such as yourself will have much time in which to follow current events."

"I am not unemployed, uncle, merely on suspension until the economy improves."

"The details are unimportant. Turn your television to the news and let me know your decision in the morning. I must arrange your place on Hwang Nara's vessel."

Our hero pressed the red key on his cellular phone and laid his head back. *What foolishness.* The chin wigs babbled uselessly on the TV in the distance. Chul flipped the channel to CNN International. *May as well discover the root of uncle's ranting.*

Chul saw heavenly hosts, sapient plants, the torso of Saddam Hussein and a rampaging polar bear. His mouth fell agape. He first asked himself what Korea had done to offend heaven. Then, consumed with even greater horror, our hero moved on to the most terrifying question possible.

What sort of disaster awaits a world in which Uncle makes sense?

Patty Smith sat up on the couch, used the remote control to turn off the radio and called to her father in the kitchen.

"You going to be busy?"

"Not really. What do you need?"

She gathered her strength and uttered words she thought very likely to haunt her later.

"I'm feeling good enough that John and I were thinking about flying back to San Francisco this weekend. Could you give us a ride to the airport? If you have to get back to work or something, I completely understand."

Her father seemed, rather than annoyed, excited by this news. Patty grew fearful as her father spoke.

"How are you going to get your stuff back? The embassy has flown most of your Pakistan stuff here—that's a lot of stuff."

Patty grimaced. *How awesome is it going to be paying to ship a queen-sized bed, a safe and a quarter ton of books across the country?* She turned to her father.

"Could you keep it here for a while? I should be walking in a couple months and I'll come back for all my crap then."

CJ shook his head.

"Listen, there's not a whole lot of work for me right now and it doesn't make sense for you and John to run back and forth while you're still recovering. Let me load all your stuff up in the truck and I'll deliver it for you."

Patty's bullshit sensor went off. *What is he up to?* She answered her father with the calm propriety of a society lady, newly acquainted with a business partner of uncertain character.

"Oh, I wouldn't want to make problems for you. You don't have to trouble yourself for my sake."

"I insist. Let me help you out."

Patty shuddered. *What if Dad is trying to use my house to look for work in California? What if he stays?*

"If you come, I'm afraid we can't give you much of a welcome. There's only one bedroom and we're both going to be really busy."

"I'll be out of your hair the same day I arrive. Don't worry—honest."

This sounds almost benign, she thought. *It must be a trap.*

"Won't you need something in return?" Patty asked.

CJ smiled and answered.

"Pay for my gas and we'll call it even."

Chapter Twenty Five

62 Days After

As CJ revised the latest in his series of annual letters to the New York Times, Choi Chul stepped out of his glistening luxury sedan and looked over the sand beaches of Pohang. The cold ocean waves pounded in the night, red and green under the fireworks displays. To his left the coastline turned rocky and harsh, curling around the horizon in a jumble of fishing boats and tidal pools. To his right the mighty POSCO steel plant poured steam up into the night sky, like milk tumbling through a glass of hot, black coffee.

The Marado Raw Fish Restaurant nestled into foothills behind Choi Chul and soon the smells of *dwinjang jiggay, bulgogi* and *hwey* tempted him inside. Hwang Nara, the boat-wielding avenger of Seoul and captain of phone-charm industry, would not arrive for ten minutes longer. Chul saw no harm in going ahead that he might survey the menu and ensure sufficient seating.

Our hero stepped over the threshold and saw tables of knurled wood, covered in varnish and gleaming beneath low, glass table tops. Partitions wrought from rice paper seeped gentle, yellow light onto the rough, shale floors.

The faint sound of sloshing seawater issued forth from some unseen holding tanks and offered welcome competition for an irritating American pop song about calling me maybe.

… I grew some fish that do smell; don't ask, I'm in a well, I cooked your dentist now you know feng-shui …

Chul was about to sit down when the sight of a tall man with hard cheeks and a tailored grey suit, cut with a severe taper from over-wide shoulders to an impossibly slender waist, stopped him. *Could that be the great cell-phone-charm-industrialist Hwang Nara?*

Another man, this one with dark glasses, long hair and a stringy black mustache came to the suit's side. A woman with a shaved head and prayer beads followed close behind, her padded gray jacket wrapped over the orange vestments of a Buddhist nun. The three turned in unison to look upon our hero. The mustache spoke first, stones seemingly grinding together in his throat.

"This must be our linguist," he said to the others. "He looks pathetic to me."

Chul pretended not to hear and stood to shake the suit's hand. Instead of a friendly greeting though, he received this harsh rebuke.

"Do not go near our leader," the mustachioed man said. "Even now conspirators seek to end his life."

… and this is greasy, but here's my member …

Our hero wished to express his disbelief but the nun broke in and spoke.

"Sit, my son. We will ensure the benevolence of your mind but you must be still while we perform the arcane rituals."

This all transpired faster than our hero could think. *What the hell did Uncle get me into? Arcane rituals? Conspirators?* The nun spoke once more.

"You must not move. The rituals do not take a great length in time. However, we require all of your cooperation. Do not resist unless you wish for this situation to get *chemical*."

Chul, for reasons unknown even to himself, assented and sat cross-legged upon the floor. His eyes glazed over with the profound film of confusion. The suit and mustache looked down upon him with curled lips and furrowed brows. The nun produced a suitcase full of red, white and yellow powders, strange herbs shaped like warts and a blow torch. She mixed the powders in a marble bowl and set them ablaze with her torch. The cauldron rattled against the table as it belched noxious smoke. *Plastic, eggs and laundry detergent? … and all the other toys, try to please me, and this is greasy, but here's my member, slap me crazy …*

The woman drew herself up and, eyes wild with religious passion, began a sacred incantation.

"A-woogie woogie woogie," she said. "Woo woo woo."

At this moment, a different woman, perhaps 50 years old, came into the restaurant and, laying eyes upon this scene, turned to flee. The mustache saw this and produced a blow gun from his long coat. She yelled but could not reach the door before he shot her in the back. The woman plunked down onto her face and said "ugh." This caused no disruption whatsoever for either the nun or the suit.

.. baked beans, belly bubblin, big bite, gas is flowing, what you think I'm showing baby?

The nun threw down yet another powder into the crucible. The mixture exploded in a flash of blinding light and purple smoke. Our hero, for a moment only, could not see and so groped along the ground. His eyes adjusted. He beheld the nun once more, flapping her arms like a fearsome ostrich in the heat of a territorial battle. The reflections of a hundred burning powders smoldered in her eyes and she looked ready to pounce when, all of a sudden, she stood up and addressed the others in a voice casual and strong, quiet and serene.

"No demon of potency has polluted his mind. Now, Sahal, let us see if he allies himself with the global conspiracy."

The suit nodded and motioned that the mustache should do further violence to Chul's dignity. The man bounced with each step, bending at the waist to leer at our hero. He circled behind and spoke aloud.

"How did they recruit you, assassin?"

"I am—"

The mustache slapped Chul's face. This shocked our hero to near the point of paralysis. The mustache grabbed ahold his chin and held his head straight.

"Did I tell you to speak? I care little for your lies. Know this, assassin, I have learned all your vile society's ways, including where you hide your suicide capsules!"

"Suicide? Why would I—"

The suit pounced on Chul's back and pinned his arms. The nun followed closely behind and twisted his leg painfully. Chul cried out for help.

"Help! Help! I need help—rape!"

A waitress ran from the kitchen and Chul, for a moment, held out hope of rescue. However, the mustache once more struck with swift precision. Whoosh. A dart protruded from the woman's stomach and she fell groaning to the floor.

"My ovary," she said, losing consciousness.

The blowgun enthusiast continued into the kitchen and the sounds of two more people falling to the floor thudded like nauseous burps through the restaurant.

Choi's eyes opened wide in terror. Each of the 656 sphincters in his body clenched with crushing force. *Do not let me die this way. Please God, do not let it end at the hands of these lunatics!*

The mustache returned and squatted in front of our hero. Chul could smell the kimchi and cigarettes on his breath, see the sweat beading between his eyes.

"Now, assassin," the mustache said. "I am going to break your suicide capsules. Any final lies before I take your filthy life?"

Chul breathed so fast, so shallow, that he could barely form words.

"Please, I am no…I do not…"

… before you came into my life I missed you so bad, I missed you so bad… I missed you so, so bad …

The mustache leapt forward and, with vicious force, twisted both our hero's nipples.

(For the virtue of ovarian husbandry, I bless the waitress with reproductive potency unprecedented in all vertebrate history.)

Patty's furniture and books bounced slightly in the truck's bed as the Great Plains stretched out before CJ like an enormous, grass-carpeted stadium floor. Dark green and yellow, the fertility of Middle America seemed infinite—infinite in grain, infinite in scope, infinite in sameness.

The hulking, 8.1 liter engine devoured the laser-straight miles 300 at a time. Only the need to fill the truck's 40 gallon fuel tank and the corresponding need to empty CJ's much smaller organic tanks broke the monotony.

The old, deep-fried burritos and Coke in plastic bottles waged war on his stomach and caused his belly to bulge painfully against his ribs. Greasy residue spread to the overused tuning buttons on his radio. A radio news station, spreading some nonsense about hundreds of pregnant men in South Korea, was the only thing playing. *Why can't the good stations ever broadcast outside of main cities?*

A deep discontent settled over CJ. A vague yearning for life beyond double yellow lines and sixth gear, a hope that somewhere out in the expanse a grand adventure awaited him yet. *Something sexy, something dangerous, something to make the grandchildren of my grandchildren remember my miserable, insignificant life.*

As the sunburnt eastern flanks of the Rocky Mountains emerged into view, I smiled down from heaven and blessed CJ with a surfeit of entirely digestible roadside food. It would not be long before I answered his prayers.

Chapter Twenty Six

64 Days After

CJ passed through the austere suburbs and harsh sterility of Salt Lake City and came unto Nevada's Great Basin. The mountains and valleys stretched before him like an enormous, wrinkly rug. A highway, never bending so much as one degree to the right or left, rose and fell as far as he could see.

Hours passed and CJ often went 20 minutes or more without seeing another living thing. He thus pressed a little harder on the accelerator pedal. 75, 80, 85 mph.

The truck's massive tires hummed faintly in the background. The engine and wind noise settled into a soothing drone and CJ smiled as the miles melted away into the rear view mirror.

A sign reading "Dayton, 32 miles" came into view in the last, orange-red vestiges of daylight. This sent a wave of nostalgia washing over his dandruffed head. His body pulsed with righteous triumphalism and he pressed down the gas pedal in celebration.

Out here are some good, honest people, he thought. *These folks don't need handouts from the goddamn federal government like the liberal brainwashed ghetto bunnies back east. If these men and women get hungry, they can jump in their trucks, load their rifles and shoot dinner. I'd like to see some liberal vegan in his fair trade Prius try that!*

Blue and red flashing lights interrupted CJ's glory. He looked down and saw 87 mph on his speedometer. "Shit," he said aloud.

He let off the gas and felt the warning strips rumble through the Chevy's hulking chassis. He had scarcely come to a stop when the cop behind aimed a spotlight at CJ's mirrors. It must have been in order to limit his vision. *Do cops really get shot at that often?*

Smith put his hands on top of the steering wheel, safely and in plain sight so that the nice officer would understand just how considerate he was being. Soon, the familiar tap of a Maglight on window glass set CJ in motion.

"Good evening officer," he said. "How can I help you?"

The cop, a 40-something fat man with a bushy mustache, severe buzz cut and some mirrored sunglasses straight out of 1973 responded by hitting the button on his Maglight and setting CJ's retinas ablaze.

"License and registration," the cop said.

CJ complied as quickly as he could, smiling and handing over his neatly arranged paperwork.

"Here you are, officer."

The cop turned the flashlight down onto the papers and chortled.

"New York, eh?"

CJ was about to answer when the lawman again shined the Maglight directly into his eyes. Smith heard a dull click and immediately imagined the 9mm, a gun he'd always thought of as slightly effete, sitting on the cop's hip.

"Are you carrying any drugs or weapons?" the cop asked.

That sudden left hook of evil insinuation and unprovoked hostility clipped CJ's psychic jaw and left him stumbling, dazed against his seatbelt.

"No, not at all," he said. "I'm just going to deliver this stuff to my daughter in—"

"Sir, I need you to step out of the vehicle."

CJ's mind went blank. *What the fuck?* The seatbelt latch felt like a jailer's lock, the door handle like rolled steel, the air a stinging nettle.

"Put your hands behind your head."

The handcuffs made a solid, hard clinking as the cop tightened them down.

"You have the right to remain silent—"

CJ ignored the policeman's stupid sermon and broke in.

"Officer, I don't understand what's going on. I'm a God-fearing patriot and I want to know right now what this is all about!"

The cop's expression remained utterly unchanged, a sort of mid-point between angry and stoned. The fuzz continued his lecture.

"Anything you say can and will be used against you in a court of law. "

CJ could stand no more.

"My daughter needs her things and she needs them soon. I'll be damned if I let some cop who has got no idea what he's talking about stop me!"

(For the sin of prefacing an empty threat with "I'll be damned if," I caused Satan himself to prank call CJ Smith at least once a week for the duration of the year.)

The female police officer responsible for processing inmates at the Dayton Prison, one Michelle Dosen according to her name tag, practiced uncommon methodologies. I could, in my godly wisdom, enumerate the many ways she manifested these singularities but I judge it better if we leave CJ Smith to illustrate.

CJ leaned against the loose chain-link fencing that separated him from the fingerprint machine, the short, black-haired female officer and the jail proper. The chain restraint around his waist linked to his handcuffs and forced him to adopt the pose of a particularly modest beggar. *So stupid.* He looked down with loathing at his prison pajamas and wanted to tear those idiotic, no-suicide plastic flip flops into foam confetti.

"I don't even know why I'm here," CJ said. "You guys don't have a bench warrant for me. I couldn't have failed to appear for a speeding ticket because I couldn't have sped in Nevada. I couldn't have sped in Nevada because this is the first time I've ever set foot in your state."

"I've heard it all," the officer said. "And I don't care about your slick, big city tricks. We've got a warrant for a CJ Smith and that's you. You're going to the slammer and it don't matter how big an east coast elite you think you are."

Smith tried to throw his hands up, but the restraints stopped him. He had no choice but to give up and sit down.

"Do you even care if I committed a crime?"

She responded to this poignant, morally and philosophically brilliant question by ignoring it completely.

"Now," she said. "I'm gonna take you out of that cell and process you right here. But listen, I don't want any funny business. I don't wanna hafta hurt you, understand?"

CJ thought this might be an attempt at humor——she could not have weighed more than 100 pounds—but her angry face and threatening demeanor indicated not. He stifled the urge to laugh.

"I'm gonna open this door," she said. "I want you in the opposite corner, facing away from me. If you move, I'll taser your ass."

CJ rolled his eyes. *I'm here on a fucking traffic citation, what does she think I'm going to do?* He obeyed and, answering, tried to hold the sarcasm to a minimum.

"Whatever you want."

He heard heavy chains clink against the galvanized steel posts of his all-expenses-spared holding cell. Finally, a hulking dead bolt somewhere inside the mechanism retreated from the door frame into the battered, square lock.

"Turn around and face me," she said. "Come slowly towards me."

When CJ had crossed over the threshold the officer commanded that he once more go stick his nose in a corner while she dealt with the door.

"Remember, I'll tase you" she said.

Finally the matter of the door came to a conclusion and the matter of fingerprinting began. The woman grabbed CJ's pajama sleeve and led him to the machine. A clear glass plane in front, an ancient computer screen above and hideous orange painted metal to each side.

"I gotta take off your handcuffs," she said. "Be nice."

She stood close behind and pressed her hips against his backside. He felt the hard, plastic shock gun poking at him like some creepy, gender confused version of dry humping—the sort of moves convicted rapists use to woo leotard-wearing meth addicts. He looked down and saw the woman jamming the tazer prongs into his butt cheek.

"Like I said, be nice."

CJ once more repressed the urge to laugh, or cry, or perhaps both. He offered up his bound hands and prayed it might all end. The infernal woman unlocked his right hand and motioned to the glass. CJ complied and watched on the computer screen as his vital, identifying marks leaked out onto the police network. *Wonderful, sure am glad Uncle Sam has another way to track me now.* He would have groused more if not for the sudden pulling he felt on his waist chains.

The officer had unlocked the right-hand manacle and now struggled to feed it through CJ's waist loop. She bent low in order to more perfectly see the mechanism but still could not solve intricacies of that steel semi-circle. As she crouched below, CJ reflected on her many braggadocio threats and briefly, in a flight of whimsy, considered beating her to death. *No, no, that would be rash.*

"Would you like me to help you?" he asked.

"Go to hell!"

The clicking sound continued on for perhaps 15 seconds and still the handcuff would not go through that perplexing loop.

"Are you sure you don't need my help?"

"Shut up!"

Another minute passed while CJ's smug condescension blossomed. Finally the woman stood up and looked at him with great vengeance and furious anger.

"Fine, fix it."

The lesser of our two heroes squeezed the ratcheting mechanism until the prongs collapsed and slid the cuff, with very little effort, silently and cleanly through the loop. He handed these restraints to the officer and smirked. Oh how delicious is conceit!

The cell was a rough pentagon, squished on one side with the public shitter placed in the back so that passersby could watch the prisoners defecate. Two iron bunks bolted to each of the four other walls for a total of eight beds. CJ's was the top bunk on the back right, beside and above the toilet. He sat cross-legged on his thin, meager mattress and looked his cellmates over.

A blond kid, maybe 22 or 23, reclined on the lower bunk opposite CJ. His thin but doughy-soft body, the lazy muscle tone around his slow eyes and moist lips couldn't have said "pothead" more clearly if Bob Marley tattooed a dooby on his cheek. CJ tried briefly to make eye contact but gave up.

Above him, an older man with a handlebar mustache, beer belly and hairy arms sat on the bunk reading a Tom Clancy thriller—"Team Rainbow, Assault on the Closeted Precinct" or something to that effect. This one occasionally paused to chitchat with the final prisoner, a well groomed little man in his 60s.

The stoner surprised CJ by snapping out of his trance and speaking first.

"Hey dude, what they got you for?"

CJ grit his teeth. *I am NOT one of you!* He soothed his badly strained sanity before answering.

"They said I had a bench warrant," he said. "They're wrong."

All CJ's ill will passed unnoticed over the young stoner's head.

"Yeah, they got me for possession."

CJ's rage overflowed the banks of decorum and swept towards the stinking human detritus like a tsunami.

"No shit? Possession of, let me guess, marijuana. Anybody else would think securities fraud by the look of you."

The old man and the guy with the beer belly smiled uncomprehendingly. Fatso decided to chip in with his oral autobiography.

"Chris there can't turn down no roach," he said. "I can't turn down no Bud Light. You know if you get enough, them DUIs can be a felony? Done blowed my mind. Well, live and learn. What kind of bench warrant you have?"

CJ's appetite for conversation had hardly improved but he answered nonetheless.

"They say I have an unpaid speeding ticket from the 80s."

An intelligent person would surely answer this revelation with disbelief. They would sympathize and laugh bitterly at the absurdity of incarceration following so minor an infraction. The older man spoke.

"I pled down to solicitation," he said. "My wife still supports me."

Great, a pederast, death on wheels and an "herbalist," CJ thought. *The sooner I can get away from these inbred hillbillies, these insults to the very idea of human decency, the better.* He sought to end all further attempts at socializing.

"I just want to think now. Be quiet and leave me alone, please."

The sex criminal and drunkard looked at each other and shrugged. The stoner set about examining the hairs sprouting from his toes and CJ returned to his thoughts.

I want my fucking phone call, he thought. *Yes, my rights! These assholes will never take my constitutional rights from me. I'll hit these assholes with the fucking CONSTI-*

TUTION!…Who am I going to call? Not Patty. No, I can't make her come all the way out here. Bail bondsman? That's someone shitheads like Mr. Solicitation use. Maybe a lawyer, though I don't want to. I don't want to pay some ambulance chaser but, I do want—I'll make these fuckers wish they never crossed me if I have a lawyer!

The stoner and old man started a new discourse and led CJ away from his musings and onto a topic at once more metaphysical and, shall we say, earthy.

"Dude," the stoner said. "I just thought of something man, about like, about God."

The old pederast perked up and nodded, like an over-earnest teacher encouraging a gifted but hitherto unmotivated student at the first sign of effort.

"Really? I'm fascinated to hear your thoughts. I used to study theology at the Dayton Community College."

The stoner cocked his head to the side and warmed up for the big finale.

"So like when you go for a long time without jacking off, you know how it comes out all, like, tapioca? Why is that? Like, I can't think of any reason 'cept for like, you know, God."

CJ turned and buried his head in the pillow. Morning and the lawyer couldn't come fast enough.

Chapter Twenty Seven

67 Days After

Our hero woke from a mucosal, anesthetized sleep. A sort of vague, humming sensation, halfway between sound and feeling, ran through the bed's metal frame. Choi put his hand against a hard wall, covered in paint and much colder than the surrounding air. He tapped it and heard, in place of the expected metallic echo, a ceramic ticking sound. *Where am I? Is this a prison? A basement? A ship?*

Somebody turned on a light bulb in the hall outside Choi's room and he saw the glow escaping under a previously unseen door. He swung two unsteady feet onto the grated floor. As soon as he stood up he had to reach out and brace himself against the opposite wall. He noticed an IV drip attached to his right arm and pulled it out. His head swum and he nearly fell over. However, no amount of drowsiness could make him surrender. He slid along the wall until he reached the door. He pounded and pounded and felt the harsh, slapping impacts bruise his palms.

"Hey, you, let me go!"

Someone in the hall ran away and left our hero in silence. *Do I really want out?* He ran his hands over the door and found no handle, no means of escape. *I suppose it does not matter what I want.* Despair, like a blast of furnace air, washed over Choi's face. Sadness and fear, drugs and darkness gathered together and surged through his groggy skull. Our hero could stand no more and thus fell in a clump on his backside, starring into the darkness and breathing heavily.

Two people returned to the hall outside Choi's room. He reached for the door and pounded his fist against it. Finally, our hero heard the familiar clacking of a brass key against steel tumblers. With a poorly lubricated growl and sudden clunk, the door popped open and let loose blinding, artificial light. A man, perhaps the mustache or maybe the suit, reached down and took Chul by the arms.

"Let us take our interpreter above deck and get him some ginseng. He will need the endurance. Go quickly and send Sahal to secure the armory."

Choi could not recognize the voice. Before his eyes adjusted, the narcotics and exertion once more conspired to rob him of consciousness.

W arm sunlight appeared yellow and red through our hero's still closed eyelids. Cold spray washed over his skin time and time again, leaving behind salty little crusts where the water had evaporated away.

"Welcome to the *Gunham*," a man said. "May your strength return quickly and fully. We have much to discuss and many great things to do."

Choi felt the thin layer of moisture between his eyelids—ever so slightly viscous, ever so minisculy adhesive—part as those heavy curtains pulled asunder. The sun once more shone through steel grey winter skies, illuminating the stinging tentacles of precipitation streaming down beneath each angry storm cloud.

He turned left and looked upon the *Gunham's* deck. He sat upon an upper deck in a plastic reclining chair, the sort tourists find beside luxurious hotel swimming pools. Beneath him a sleek, wooden floor richly varnished and stained dark red extended perhaps 3 meters in each direction. An elegant railing made from shining black carbon fiber rose wherever the wood stopped. Behind him glass doors shut firm against the wind and protected a minimalist cabin trimmed in metal and furniture covered with suede leather. *This is a boat most exceptional,* our hero thought.

He turned the other way and beheld the severe, high cheeks and jarring, triangle cut business suit of that first man. Chul squinted and took a long look. It had to be cell phone-accessory-baron Hwang Nara. Chul's heart rate climbed and he reached down to rub his brutally twisted nipples.

"Mr. Gun-sauce," the Mustachioed man said to Hwang Nara. "Should I stay to protect you?"

"No, Sahal, you may go."

Two questions immediately appeared in our hero's mind and, addled as he was, he expressed them in a rush almost at the same time.

"What have you done with me? Why the shit did he call you Mr. Gun-sauce?"

Dangly-phone-doohickey-magnate Hwang Nara frowned and looked beyond the guard railing into the gray expanse of ocean.

"I shall answer your questions in many ways, Choi Chul. In the physical sense, you now recline upon the highest deck of my boat, about 2100 kilometers east of the Japanese mainland. I must apologize for that. We overestimated the dosage for your anesthesia and you have, indeed, slept for nearly a week. In order to prevent your death by dehydration, we provided you with a drip of ritually blessed saltwater and the sedative so loved by Michael Jackson. However, let us move on. If I answer in terms of your own history, you now stand at the precipice of the greatest doings in your life. Should I answer from the wider perspective of world history, I can answer only that you now might strike back against the vile conspirators and evil demons who have shamed our nation."

Our hero considered these words and, moved by their splendor, answered in the only logical manner.

"But I did not accept a position on your vessel," he said. "You have kidnapped me. Also, Mr. Gun-sauce?"

"We have protected you," master-of-molded-plastic Hwang Nara said. "Those very same men who shamed our nation laid their evil eyes upon you. They learned of our great purpose and, knowing we required your language skills, sought to snuff out your life. We only narrowly escaped those assassins."

Chul closed his eyes and shook his head. *Uncle, damn you and damn your conspiracies.* Hello-Kitty-on-a-small-smart-phone-compatible-rope-maker Hwang Nara continued.

"We had need to spirit you away. It is only thanks to our bravery and mercy you live yet."

Chul answered with furious eyes and raging lips. His feet sounded hard against the deck as he rose and issued forth his reply.

"I am a serious man! I work in a large office (if even on temporary suspension) and I conduct important business for a real company. I have no time for your Gun-sauce idiocy. I will not waste my time pursuing the agents of some imaginary alliance between the Chinese and Jews!"

It only then occurred to our hero that, should the conspiracy theorists come to despise him, he was far more likely to return to the mainland in the belly of a fish than a cloud of triumph. *Perhaps it is best not to irritate them.* His fear, though, proved unfounded as be-winged-spongy-phone-case-creator Hwang Nara laughed and pounded his hand onto his perfectly creased slacks.

"Ha! Chinese Jews!" he paused to gather his breath. "Only a fool could believe such ridiculousness. No, no my friend." He grew suddenly serious. "We saved you from no Chinese Jew. We plucked you from the grasp of the *Mongolian Illuminati.*"

Chapter Twenty Eight

A different guard with a silver mustache and fluffy hair came to CJ's cell and spoke quietly so as to let the nearby pederast continue sleeping.

"Smith," the guard said. "We're gonna get you out of here. Your attorney just arrived to pick you up."

CJ was so full of random hatred by that point he nearly spat at the guard. He managed to keep this urge locked away, but not by much. The cell door swung open. He stepped into the powder blue hallway and wished death upon all those he saw. Finally CJ came to the processing room and met the same woman, *that whore,* who'd shown him into this jail.

"So I see they're turning you loose," she said.

Her smirking, twinkling little rat's eyes bore into what little grace remained in CJ. He glared at her and bit down hard. He could feel the veins in his neck bulging and taste the metallic tingle of his tongue pressed against teeth.

She approached and unlocked the handcuffs. The cold steel bonds dropped into her hands and CJ spoke.

"I see you figured out how to use a key," CJ said and gave her a short round of applause. "Well done."

This shut her up and CJ smiled for the first time in three days. She went to a closet in the wall and took out the green polo shirt, two lace-up leather boots and a pair of straight-cut Levi's jeans he'd been wearing before.

CJ pulled off his shameful, striped jail shirt and threw it against the chain-link fence. The black and white pants, burning at his skin with their fetid otherness, their humiliating marks of the untouchable underclass, followed soon after. He stood there, on the concrete floor under the cameras.

Wearing nothing but his white elastic underwear, CJ should have felt vulnerable but that could not have been farther from the truth. No, he looked at that awful woman and held his shoulders high, his head back. *I do not fear you. You have not broken me!* She must have seen his resolve and, frightened, turned her head away.

His polo shirt felt like heaven, his jeans and boots like a refreshing breeze across fevered skin. The woman spoke once more.

"Pick up the prison uniform and put it in the laundry basket."

CJ looked at his tormentor, kicked the hateful garments under a mop bucket and answered.

"No."

CJ's lawyer was a white-haired, square- jawed man of perhaps 50. He drove a new Mercedes SUV and invited CJ into his car.

"You made a good decision, calling me."

CJ winced a little bit. *Innocent people aren't supposed to need lawyers.*

"Did I?"

The lawyer took a moment to check traffic and pulled out onto the street, interrupting their conversation. CJ took advantage of this lull to check his phone and noticed a text message from an unknown number, area code 666. "Soap on a rope, sugar-ass!" it said. CJ rolled his eyes and closed the phone. The lawyer grunted a little and resumed his speech.

"Absolutely. They would have gotten you for a whole bunch of money if you had just paid up. They'd make you pay for that original speeding ticket, the recent speeding ticket, there'd be the fine for failure to appear, jail costs—if I had to guess I'd say you'd be down around 1,500 bucks. And they would have suspended your driver's license for six months. By the way, it's not common knowledge but, being that this is Nevada, your license is almost certainly suspended right now."

"But I didn't do anything wrong, that ticket from the 80s cannot belong to me."

The lawyer laughed and didn't answer. He had a difficult left hand turn to make and fell silent. A few minutes passed before the lawyer pulled into a crowded strip mall and parked. At last they got out of the Mercedes and he said "let's get you some breakfast" to CJ.

They walked to a little restaurant called The Litigious Legume. On the patio CJ saw metal tables with large, collapsible umbrellas. People with dogs lounged and talked quietly lest they frighten the swallows and pigeons. Eggs Benedict, judging by the other customers, seemed like a big hit. *They sure smell better than anything those damned cops gave us.*

The lawyer held the door open and invited CJ in. Here were sun drenched tile countertops and chairs made from thatched reed. They sat next to the window and ordered two cups of coffee before the lawyer decided to pick up the nearly abandoned threads of his legal lecture.

"So CJ," he said. "You're thinking about this all the wrong way. Innocence and guilt don't really matter when it comes to your situation."

He raised his hands in a defensive posture, surely in response to CJ's exasperation.

"Let me explain, Dayton has no economy to speak of. It's just a bedroom community with a few small farms and gas stations. Anything that makes real money is off in the big cities. So how do you think the township of Dayton survives?"

"I would have assumed hard work and a lack of welfare bums," CJ said. "You know, salt of the earth small town goodness."

The lawyer laughed. He took a sip from his coffee, added creamer and sipped again before answering.

"You have a very high opinion of small towns, but no. We need money for our roads and schools so we squeeze travelers. People from the big Nevada cities, the rich states—anybody we can find, especially if those people can't vote for a new sheriff. You, my friend, are a revenue stream in the eyes of our fair town, nothing more."

This explanation clashed with CJ's notions of rural goodness and so he ignored it. Instead he frowned and twirled the stirring straw in his drink. The lawyer continued.

"You are actually an ideal target. Because you are from out of state, you're less likely to fight your charges. That means more guilty pleas. More guilty pleas mean more revenue with less expenditure. It's also probable that you don't have any friends or family in the area, so they can stick your truck in the impound for a week before you can get it out. That can mean hundreds or even thousands of dollars in impound charges."

CJ threw up his hands. *What the hell is wrong with these people?*

"I'm innocent! I didn't speed in the 80s because I was never in Nevada before this week."

"They don't care." The lawyer stopped to dab his tie with a napkin. "Listen, I can get your charges dismissed, but it's not because you're innocent. It's simply no longer profitable to go after someone once they've lawyered up. Like I said, you made a very good decision calling me."

The waitress came and asked "can I take your orders?" The lawyer wanted blueberry waffles and country potatoes. CJ preferred something a little gamier.

"Steak and eggs," he said. "Make it bleed."

(For the virtue of violating health codes, I bless the Litigious Legume with a vast, nesting colony of swallows.)

Choi Chul came down to his cabin and could hardly believe the luxury. Leather like butter covered the swiveling chair. Brushed aluminum veins curved and twisted one against the other in the shapes of a tree over a background of rich dark cherry-wood ceiling. The king-size bed had a matching wood frame and stood beneath panoramic glass windows ever so often splashed with sea water. The shale-stone flooring gripped pleasantly at Chul's feet. His L-shaped desk, hewn of billet aluminum and granite, stretched three meters long and a meter deep. A plasma television larger than any he'd seen rose up beside the door and connected with 15 discretely hidden surround-sound speakers. *At least my kidnappers have good taste,* he thought.

He considered turning on the TV and seeing if his abduction had made the news but decided to do so could provoke the conspiracy theorists. Instead he changed out of the wrinkled and smelly blue business attire he'd worn to the restaurant a week ago and into the all-white jumpsuit the conspirators had left on his bed.

"It symbolizes the purity and virtue of our purpose," happy-dancing-angel-tied-to-your-antennae-progenitor Hwang Nara had said. *It symbolizes the emptiness of your head,* Chul had thought. Regardless, our hero would wear a tutu and leotard if only he could banish the smell of month-old yogurt.

Balsa wood doors swung out on electric hinges and let the air rush out into the Gunham's tan and black hallways. He walked slowly, running his hands over the metals, stone, wood and expensive ceramics that seemed to cover every inch of the boat. Our hero saw sunlight down the long hall and went to it, near the nose of the boat. Inside, the mustache hunched over a dozen navigation screens.

"Ah, you are awake again," the mustache said. "I am very glad we did not have to end your life. It is because of the Mongolian Illuminati's devious machinations that we require such drastic countermeasures. But I have not introduced myself. Call me Sahal. I know your name perfectly well, indeed I have pried loose all the private informations in your life while you were drugged and semi-conscious—incidentally I had never thought of using jumper cables in the shower—so there is no need to reciprocate with an introduction of your own."

This caught Choi by surprise and he let the silence stretch uncomfortably. He finally brought up a new topic very much of interest to all kidnapping victims in transit.

"Where are we going?"

Sahal wasted no time in answering.

"I am uninterested in that question so, instead, I shall tell you what I know of the Mongolian Illuminati and the beneficent leader of our expedition. I will start by explaining my own involvement with the conspirators."

Chul responded by blinking three or four times more frequently than is strictly necessary.

"I come from the far north of Inner Mongolia," Sahal said. "My father herded yak and gave tender care to each of his thirteen wives. My mother kept the third tent with two other wives and fed the horses. My 19 brothers and 22 sisters played soccer upon the idyllic steppes and sought knowledge from all the wandering scholars who came to seek my parents' endless expertise. We enjoyed perfect happiness in all matters until the night of my 8th birthday.

"I sat in front of the charming campfire beneath a rock ledge and looked upon my amazingly attractive and supernaturally intelligent siblings. My 12th brother, only seven years old, was working on differential equations near the pot of boiled sweet potatoes. My 11th and 20th sisters likewise huddled under their yak skins and theorized on the behavior of the Higgs Boson within a gravitational event horizon. This struck me as a singular way to pass the afternoon and so I put down my copy of *On the Origin of Species*—written in Latin, naturally—to address my inestimably wise and good father.

"I asked how our family came to know so much, how so many so young had mastered the greatest scientific, artistic and spiritual endeavors of man. My father, I will never forget the benevolent twinkling in his eyes, said but one thing—'we seek illumination!'

Chul was having difficulty maintaining his arsenal of credulous facial expressions.

"At this moment I heard a great boom and the rumbling of stones," Sahal said. "The same ledge we had used to shelter against the wind gave way and fell upon my father, my mother, the co-wives and all 41 of my siblings. You must understand that it was only through the most fortunate coincidences of micro-geology that I survived. The stone beside me supported the stone above, the stone at my feet protected my legs from the bolder crashing down to cripple me.

"It was then I looked up and saw a man upon the ridge, pointing at the scene of devastation and sending out his evil cackle. I can remember how the lightning flashed as he said—"

Sahal paused to gather his breath. His voiced dropped two octaves as he came near to shouting.

"'None are illuminated like the Illuminati!'" Sahal's catharsis spilled on the floor and caused a mess. "It was then I began this sacred journey of vengeance."

Our hero hardly knew what to say. While he took Sahal's amazing story about as seriously as a Murdoch family tabloid, he also did not wish to aggravate the blowgun enthusiast. *Be conciliatory.*

"It is most regrettable you suffered in that way."

Sahal had little use for sympathy and instead moved onto the sufferings of his mentor.

"The Mongolian Illuminati injured Mr. Gun-sauce as well," he said. "When Hwang Nara launched his Foundation for the Illumination of Celestial Morality, the conspirators began a campaign of torture against him."

He wants me to ask how, he thought. *Right?* The words burst from Chul with rather more force than he'd intended.

"You must tell me!"

Sahal furrowed his brow and nodded with all possible solemnity.

"The conspirators torment Mr. Gun-sauce's dreams even to this day with psychic energy. They cause him to suffer horrible nightmares. Each night he wakes, chilled in his sweat, sure that a dog has urinated on the bed, sure that lobsters have removed his testicles. This is why we travel with the nun."

Chul nodded once more and searched for escape routes. *Perhaps we are near an island?* He again asked Sahal where they sailed.

"We go to strike at their headquarters, the source of the Mongolian Illuminati's power," Sahal said. The blow gun enthusiast paused to both increase the dramatic tension and to puff up his chest. "Northern Chile."

Our hero made for the door but stopped when he heard Sahal's words. The man had turned to his computers and spoke over his shoulder.

"I apologize for brutalizing your chest in the restaurant. Rest assured it was I who lovingly rubbed balm, for an hour each day, into your nipples while you slept."

(For the virtue of lovingly rubbing balm into the nipples of a stranger, I bless Sahal with cake. Lots of cake.)

The Great State of Nevada saw fit to immediately suspend the driving licenses belonging to those accused of a huge number of perfidies. As such, CJ had little choice but to follow his attorney's advice and bed down in the Dayton Motel 6 for one or two days until the DMV problems could be ironed out.

CJ thought on the time in jail, thought of the oozing globules of power those fucks had dangled over him. He remembered clinging to the dignity those cops had tried to pry from his hands and grasping so hard he could feel the very center of himself bleeding. All in a second, those feelings evaporated. He slid the electronic safety key into the appropriate slot. He felt the brutally air-conditioned breeze slide out like frozen yogurt through an auger. The chill knocked him back a step and caused him to wait a moment before going in.

The unnatural alliance of purple squares and red squiggles on his comforter did not create the relaxed atmosphere he desired but CJ paid them little heed as he flopped down. The spackled ceiling above looked like a cave roof covered in tiny stalactites and he imagined each one falling and skewering him onto the purple squares and red squiggles, a suitably absurd and grotesque ending to his time in an absurd and grotesque town.

He felt around and soon laid fingers on the cold, low-quality plastic remote some rapacious, job-stealing Chinese peasant had made, probably with total indifference, months before. The TV clicked into life and CJ flipped to a sports channel. Kazakhstan vs. Lichtenstein in the first round of the world pairs ping-pong championships, evidently. A suspiciously hairy and overly-muscled Liechtensteinian woman smashed home the volley before CJ's attention again wandered off. *What an exercise in triviality.*

He considered checking CNN International again but decided against it. With his personal world gone so inescapably wrong, he could not bear to think about my next potential alteration. Would I cause Sri Lanka to explode? Would I turn Alaska into strawberry jam? CJ didn't want to know.

Kazakhstan victorious. *Who gives a fuck?*

The air in Dayton smelled bad, like that idiot prison guard's perfume. Over sweet, a hint of decay and utterly lacking in sophistication. Everything in that town sprawled out in big block letters, formed into small words and grammatically simple sentences so that the cloudy-eyed shit-farmers with fleshy noses and patchy stubble could sound out where to buy their rot-gut domestic macrobrews. CJ pulled off his shirt and unbuttoned his pants. He could feel himself building up to a big condemnation and wanted to pass the righteous denunciations in comfort. The feeling got so strong he decided to speak aloud.

"Are these people even capable of perceiving the profound?"

That didn't come out as amazingly as he'd hoped, but no matter. CJ grabbed the comforter and balled it up in his fist and continued on.

"When they look at the clouds of ionized gas 11 light years out from the huge, hot center of the Crab Nebula, can these idiots appreciate their own smallness? Can they ponder the immensity of a light year? Can they sense the glory of creation? Can they look to the heavens and feel the power of the universe swirling above their heads?"

CJ liked the way his rant was building and sat up straight for the grand finale.

"I'll bet when these dumbshits hear of the Crab Nebula the tiny thoughts in their shrunken, malformed little heads run straight to the fucking seafood buffet."

He almost wished he'd had an audience. Even without a cheering section, though, CJ felt better. He laid back against the headboard and returned to the TV. The next game would feature a "grudge match" between Slovakia and Laos. CJ turned the damned TV off. He would leave this shithole and head west on I-80 as soon as that license came through. *I'll go to Reno, Sacramento, San Francisco—places with things. Places with serious people.* Then something hit him that made him stop. *Places that are nothing like Selfsevere.*

CJ felt an unpleasant, unfamiliar void from where he normally drew certainty and conviction.

It would be better if these people didn't fly the flags of rugged independence, small government and traditional values. Would it? It would. Embarrassing. Yeah, too embarrassing. These small town folk let us down, they let me down, let down the ideals they were supposed to stand for.

Uncertainty, dark and immense, came over CJ. A belief, strongly held and rightly professed, crashed against hard experience. He wanted to deny, to avoid. Anything to escape the conflict. Sleep did not come easily to him that night.

Chapter Twenty Nine

70 Days After

It was that night I first revealed myself to the greater of our heroes. He had gone from the kitchen, past the well-stocked armory and to the top deck in order that he might speak with the nun. The stars shone down on the carbon fiber hull and twinkled against the aluminum trim. The nun was lecturing Sahal on the significance of her shapeless, traditional overcoat when I materialized above their heads. My red leather shoes glimmered in the reflected light of my glowing skin and my red suit pulsed with the divine glitter of immortality. The nun's mouth fell agape and she spoke no more. Chul too gazed up at my personage in dumbstruck silence. I decided to capitalize on their awe and, having always suffered from a weakness for the epic and indeed sesquipedalian loquaciousness of all sorts, emphasized the ancient terror of my being.

"And lo," I said. "Thou shalt not travel unto the lower continent of the Americas, going neither to Peru nor Chile, Patagonia nor Panama. Thou shalt sail instead unto the golden land of California! Thus spake the God of Potency."

The nun reached into her vestments and produced a cup, which she shook at me.

"You have no place on this holy vessel, Potency Demon! I will send you back into the darkness from where you came. I have cut the sacred chicken's throat. I have squeezed the blessed bile from the holy bear's intestine. I have gathered my holy estrus in this goddess cup, which I raise before your evil person. I now banish you with this incantation—"

For the sin of being that damned nasty, I cursed the nun with sudden, uncontrollable hiccupping. Punishment complete, I spoke thus.

"Go not unto the land of Chile. Obey my words lest I strike down furiously upon thee."

The nun, popping with each step, gasping with every gesture and grunting beneath the weight each exertion, continued her assault.

"Demon, gulp, you cannot stop us, gulp, going to Chile. The Mongolian, gulp, Illuminati will not go un—gulp— punished for conspiring with you and the, gulp, forces, gulp, of, gulp, evil."

"Woman, thou art a moron," I said. "Whosoever, what sort of crackhead, would conjure such shit from the arse of a bull?"

She was about to speak further but I caused an army of sea cucumbers to fly from the deep and carry her overboard. A trail of noxious bubbles rose from the ocean and we heard her idiocy no more. Chul had still not spoken, preferring instead to stare with his mouth open, breathing slightly less than needed to continue normal brain function. In order to engage our hero in conversation, and because I was running out of imagination with regard to the

Old Testament talk, I came down to the Gunham's deck and spoke more normally.

"Listen, my friend," I said. "You are not going to Chile. You will not be battling the Mongolian Illuminati, which, as I'm sure you suspected already, does not exist."

Chul coughed, speech still eluding his overworked credulity.

"Look," I said. "I'm sending you to California. Don't worry about the conspiracy theorists. If they interfere, I'll send them to the Antarctic Peninsula with that nun. Forgive me, I should be honest. I'll probably send them to Antarctica regardless of what they do."

He finally mustered the sense to respond.

"Why have you shamed my nation?"

"You have such strange priorities," I said. "But it doesn't matter. Concern yourself with important things like— well, you'll see. Suffice it to say, we have more important matters than the honor of your nation, far more important matters. Go to the port of San Francisco and I will arrange a more suitable companion for your journey. The Twinkie of Destiny is not beyond your grasp."

Chul's ample and ever-present pride emerged from behind this unaccustomed sense of flabbergasted submission.

"How could you cover my nation's capital with such a shameful and pro-Japanese disgrace? I will not leave this crime unpunished. I will strike against you!"

My immortal heart leapt with joy. How exciting, how gloriously dramatic—how wonderfully was our hero embracing his role? Granted, he seemed to have ignored my admonition about more important matters but I do not expect perfection from human beings and, as far as drama went, Chul could hardly exceed his current performance.

"I will give you the opportunity to punish whomever you please," I said. "Should you find the Twinkie, you may restore all I have set askew, you may right all I have changed and you may, if only for 15 minutes, have rule even over myself. I'm *here* for *you*."

Chul compared me unfavorably with dog excrement and was coming near to striking my godly countenance when Sahal emerged from below. The mustachioed blowgun enthusiast drew back his lips and snarled.

"Demon! Damnable dastardly dirty deranged despicable destructive diabolical devilish demonic demon!"

I used my immense intellect to deduce that these words would not likely preface an interesting conversation and thus brought about swift action. Enormous waves sprang from the sea and a huge wooden boat came into view. Our hero and Sahal fell to the ground as the Gunham shot up the face of a 15 meter, white tipped roller. The boat's prow crashed down upon the valley of sea with the percussive bounce of a clumsy pedestrian falling on the ice. Wind driven water, hard as concrete, sprayed over the Gunham.

The wooden boat came near and an epic-looking, generously-bearded gentleman with many creatures in his company leaned over the railing of his much larger craft and called out thus.

"Head north! Head north or the deluge will wipe away your sins, and everything else!"

Sahal turned to Chul and grabbed his arm that the two would not fall over the Gunham's slick, shimmering decks.

"We must not let the Demon of Potency stop us!" Sahal said. "We must continue west and strike down the Mongolian Illuminati."

At this moment I caused a mighty wind to sweep a mating pair of giant New Zealand moa birds off the epic-looking, generously-bearded gentleman's wooden boat and into the air where they swirled high among the clouds.

"Damn," the epic-looking, generously-bearded gentleman said. "Another extinction."

Sahal set off with determination toward the Gunham's pilothouse. He was near to opening the door when I caused the first giant moa bird to plummet posterior first into the mustachioed conspiracy theorist. He said "oomph" and dropped over the starboard rails, into the raging froth below. I descended once more and spoke to our hero so that he would not thrash ignorant against the immovable will of divinity.

"You will have your chance, Choi Chul. You will have your chance."

With that I caused the other giant moa bird to whip quickly through the breeze, falling in just such a manner as to strike our hero's head with its own amusingly tiny, avian skull. Chul registered the concussive crack of bone hitting bone, saw the world drain away to blinding whiteness and fell onto the deck. Wind more powerful than any he'd ever heard, gusts unparalleled—a feeling of flight.

(For the sin of employing a spiritual advisor that damned nasty, I caused flippy-floppy-pot-metal-phone-dealy-whopper-entrepreneur Hwang Nara to develop every psychological ailment listed between pages 126 and 194 in the Diagnostic and Statistical Manual of Mental Disorders. For the virtue of glorious whiskers, I blessed the epic-looking, generously-bearded gentleman with enough surplus chest hair to lavishly carpet his wooden boat's living quarters. For the virtue of extensive alliteration, I bless Sahal with sudden, massive weight gain so that he might better pass the winter in Antarctica.)

CJ came onto the Bay Bridge and briefly worried. He had no idea where Patty lived and had not arranged any precise location to meet. The bridge offered him rescue as, halfway along the span it set down on a tiny spec of earth called Treasure Island. CJ pulled the giant Chevy down from speed and nearly crashed against the unconscionably sharp and poorly sighted exit ramp. He drove slowly from the off ramp to the retired naval station below. He parked on a pier where rust bubbled from every fastener and blue paint clung like fungus to salt-ruined wood pilings. Wind and storm surge pounded the piers.

CJ unlocked his smart phone and dismissed an alert regarding some unprecedented tempest sweeping north from the seas off Central America. His driver's license even then sat upon the truck's dashboard, still awaiting its rightful reunion with CJ's wallet. Fishermen threw dainty hooks into the ominous breakers and seagulls battled the wind as CJ dialed his daughter.

"Hey Patty," he said. "I'm parked on Treasure Island. Is there any place in particular you'd like to meet?"

Patty's voice rose like an oceanic wave gathering up in the shallows.

"I thought you'd flaked."

"No, I didn't flake. I just got stuck for a couple days. There was nothing you could have done so I just fixed it by myself."

CJ very much wished to avoid talking about his adventures in Dayton. The burnt odor of shame trailed behind that topic like particulate smoke after an old bus.

"Oh, okay," she said. "I can just meet you at the deli on Treasure Island. It's next to the old barracks if you want some lunch."

"Sounds good. I'm awfully tired of sitting down, so take your time getting here and I'll walk around."

"John has to come get me so we'll need about an hour," Patty said. Then she paused for a moment before changing the subject. "How much do I owe you for gas?"

Let's see, CJ thought. *10 miles per gallon, roughly 6,000 miles round trip makes 600 gallons of fuel. Four bucks a gallon…shit, that's too much.*

"Gimme $500 and we'll call it even," he said.

"Sounds good. I'll be down in about two hours."

CJ thought of his 401K and immediately regretted that show of generous, if impulsive, score settling.

Patty felt the car rock back ever so gently as John engaged park and let off the brake. The clear, defined pain of a hundred surgical incisions—incompletely healed and chafing against dissolvable sutures not yet dissolved—ran through her knee and hip, her belly and neck. She reached to John and folded down his unruly collar.

"You ready?" he asked.

Patty gathered her breath and looked at the ocean below, the barracks beside and the forested hills above. John was reaching back to get the wheelchair, a device Patty had already come to hate.

"Yeah, I'm ready."

She slid from the bolstered leather car seat to the springy canvas bottom of the wheelchair. The drop sent a small shock up her back and forced from her lungs a small puff. It did not hurt and for that Patty felt strong. *No way I'm gonna be an invalid forever,* she thought.

John pushed her across the concrete towards the small, tourist-trap deli where they'd be meeting CJ. She braced for the smell of old grease but, door opened and warm air rushing out, instead smelled fresh bread and meat well preserved with vinegar, salt and smoke. *I'm pleasantly surprised.* She looked around and didn't see her father. *Another pleasant surprise.* That last thought seemed a little cold and she smiled. John saw this and spoke.

"You ready?"

"Yeah, I'll be fine. He's been surprisingly nice recently, anyway."

"So how do you want me to be around your dad?" John asked. "Anything special or do you just want me to make small talk?"

Patty looked out from under the electric sign reading "Heineken" and onto the parking lot. Her father was even then rounding a row of tan Quonset huts.

"Just be friendly and vague," she said. "Here he comes."

He looked tired, a condition Patty associated with a slightly a less venomous sort of rage than her father normally brought to social engagements. She reached for John's hand and squeezed. *I don't want to owe him anything.*

Small bells hanging from the glass door jingled as CJ came into the restaurant. Patty braced and extruded conversation like lard through a pasta strainer.

"Hey Dad, thanks for making that trip for me," she said. "I know you said $500, but I really want to make you whole. The State Department is taking good care of me—I can handle it."

CJ answered immediately.

"I think it's probably going to be around $2,500. No, more like $3,500."

Patty involuntarily jerked her head back a little. She could pay, that was not the issue, but three and a half large? *What happened?*

"Oh, that's a lot," she said. "I mean, no problem, I'll write you a check."

"If that's too much money," he said. "You can pay me back later."

Patty paused to consider a little interpersonal calculus. *Dad might blow up if I take this conversation beyond small-talk, but I am curious, and he does owe me an explanation if he wants three grand out of us.* She looked around the restaurant and saw only one cook, a waiter and John—not much collateral damage if the big guns came out. *Fuck it.*

"Not at all, I'm just curious what happened. Did everything go to plan?"

She watched her father's face pucker into that eternal, familiar canker of vitriol. CJ looked to John, as if he didn't want the younger man to hear. John noticed and, quickly glancing to Patty, excused himself to use the restroom. Patty watched him disappear out the door and spoke.

"Now you have to tell me."

"Most of it's gasoline. You know, it takes a big truck and all."

Patty tilted her head and pressed her father just that little bit more.

"Most of it, huh?"

How honest should I be? CJ wondered. He could feel that eternal familiar cornucopia of acid building pressure in his core, steaming out through a tight throat and clenched jaw. He could feel the fury bidding him to partake, offering him safety and righteousness. He had only to fume at the crippled young woman sitting to his side and the entire humiliating episode in Dayton would remain locked harmlessly away. There seemed little to recommend against such a course of action. Why, if not for the wreck of a relationship that anger had left in place of normal father-daughter love he would have, but he could no longer, indeed he had to...

"I had to hire a lawyer," CJ said. "I got arrested."

He cringed in preparation for the smirk and ironic laugh Patty would surely unleash. Like an honorable, brave hero assaulted on all sides but unwilling to surrender, CJ prepared for a painful martyrdom at his daughter's hands. Her lips, seemingly dripping with poison, opened and let loose.

"That's awful, Dad. If you're in trouble, John and I would really like to help."

What had that been? Had she really seen his fetid weakness and disgusting shame and passed over the chance to mock? The cringe would not entirely release. He could not speak, could not overcome her unexpected kindness.

"Patty, I don't know what to say. I can't believe you're being so nice—I mean no, not that you're not usually nice—it's just that I thought you'd be..."

CJ paused to consider his next words. *Embarrassed to be my daughter? Vindicated in your hatred? Eager to exploit my vulnerabilities?*

"…ashamed of me."

It was like somebody covered his eyes with gauze and stuffed cotton in his ears. Feelings so strange they almost tickled coursed through him as the conversation ran cool and strong along paths he'd forgotten long ago. Hours passed while they spoke of workplace frustration and smallness and the tiny, twinkling spots of hope that kept old plumbers and crippled women afloat. They and ate brisket and drank imported beer. As dusk fell, they left CJ with this offer.

"We have a guest room," John said and paused, waiting for Patty to finish his thought. "You can use it as long as you like."

Chapter Thirty

76 Days After

The greater of our heroes had woken three days earlier in his bed. Legendary tinkly-trinket-tycoon Hwang Nara, huddled in the corner, had been unwilling to speak or indeed do anything other than glance furtively right and left, nibble piteously on a blanket and weep from time to time. With the sole remaining conspiracy theorist so thoroughly incapacitated, Chul had had little choice but to ignore his bulging, bruised cheek and evaluate the situation alone.

With the cranes and tanker ships of the San Francisco harbor bobbing in and out of view with each wave, finding safety demanded little of our hero. He had tied the Gunham to moorings near the city zoo, searched in vain for edible kimchi and called his wife and son back home. It would be a matter of a few days, they assured him, before Korean government agents arrived to both incarcerate floppy-phone-flappies-founder Hwang Nara and return our hero to Daegu.

On this, the third morning since regaining consciousness, Chul heard the crying of his charge and went to the traumatized man. The conspiracist clung to the sink in his fashionable, marble and granite bathroom and pulled at the titanium spigot with knuckle whitening force.

"Do not let the demon take me! You must protect me, you must save us from the, whoever they are!"

Chul felt some pity for the wretch, indeed it pained him to see one so proud as the phone-wiggly-biggly-builder Hwang Nara reduced to a second infancy, but our hero's pride could not look upon one so badly beaten without a natural, inevitable contempt. *He wears his weakness like a woman's jewel-studded necklace, flashing and shining for everyone to see. It is worse that he does so knowingly, unforgivable that he does so in the spirit of cowardice.*

He went to the fantastic—no, this was no captain of the phone dingleberry industry, this was a creature beneath contempt—Hwang Nara and grabbed the conspiracy monger under the armpits. Someone had to put the man to bed, if only to quiet the ranting. Hwang Nara resisted, screeched like a badger cornered and dug his fingers into the slick metal with such force that Chul imagined the fixtures crumpling under crazy Hwang Nara's death grip. Our hero bent his knees, not his back, and pulled with all the power he could muster. He could feel as the conspiracy theorist's individual fingers popped free from the bathroom fixtures.

He finally prised uninspiring Hwang Nara free. The conspiracy theorist fell backwards onto Chul's ribs and forced the breath from his overfilled lungs. Our hero's torso compressed like a spring and launched broken Hwang Nara back into the air. The frightened conspiracy monger landed on his feet and, with surprising athleticism and impressive speed, reattached to the sink.

"Do not let them take me! Do not go over to the Mongolian Illuminati when we are so close to victory."

Chul stood and cursed. He saw that unexceptional Hwang Nara's clutching had broken something inside the sink. What at first appeared to be urine spilling from the conspiracy theorists' trousers was in fact grey, contaminated water. Our hero said, "you are a little bitch" and walked from the room.

He wished to go far from below average Hwang Nara's madness and so emerged onto the top deck, stepped to the wharf and set off in search of lunch.

CJ, in a way that didn't make 100 percent sense even to himself, felt naked walking the streets of San Francisco. He suspected that the feeling all came down to his daughter. Not that it was entirely bad, indeed the mini-renaissance with Patty had several perks. He hadn't felt so light in years and the air had somehow become thinner to inhale and more nourishing to breathe. That moment of vulnerability with his daughter had done his body incalculable good. Like a knight removing his fetid armor and slipping into a hot springs, CJ felt cleansed, free from the accumulated years of sweat and blood and pus but also distinctly at risk for stab wounds.

And Patty had the knives. She could turn on him and use those nights of incarceration to undermine his dignity. She could, the next time he took a valiant stand against lenient judges, quickly and efficiently poke at his "hypocrisy," as if there were no difference between those in jail over real crimes and his own perfect innocence. More frightening, she might use this weapon to pick at his assumptions, to perforate the fabric of his belief. How Patty could attack his notions of rural goodness, how she could pry open his mouth and force moral ambiguity down his throat—he shuddered to think how she might apply the injustice of his own imprisonment to the so called "regular people" she lived with in Pakistan. He might as well have painted himself orange and walked onto a live shooting range.

These direct threats Patty presented to CJ were not the worst. She could die or disappear or get sick and fall into coma and rob him of a real person, a real relationship and not just some comfortably abstract notion of distant but sacred family. If this détente continued, she could, without malice or forethought or anything more than the force of chance, do to him exactly what Jane had back on September 11, 2001.

He craved anonymity and solitude if for no other reason than to hide away from anyone with the slightest hint how to injure him. He looked right and then left and then behind. *That Asian place on the corner, nobody will know me there.*

Choi Chul came to a Korean restaurant unimaginatively called "Han" and sat upon a cheap metal chair behind a small aluminum table with a charcoal pit in the center. It was not an impressive place and Chul worried about the way Americans, *migukindeul,* would look down upon this poor representative of his nation. The short and chubby waiter, probably a Korean as he was neither slightly hairy in the Japanese mold nor flat faced like a Chinese, appeared after an unconscionable delay and, in English, asked what the customer would like.

"양념 오리 구이 일 인분요," Chul said.

The waiter's eyes opened a little wider and he called out to the kitchen in English.

"Mom! Come talk to this guy. I can't understand him."

Chul blushed and grabbed the waiter's sleeve. *Did the imbecile see no value in his Korean heritage? Is he so lazy he cannot even learn the tongue of his fatherland? Does he think so little about causing a scene?* He pulled the waiter down a little bit and switched to English.

"Aygo, do not bother your mother. I want seasoned duck, one order."

"Oh," the waiter said. "I totally thought you didn't speak English. My Mom speaks Korean but I only know how to ask for the bathroom."

Chul did not wish to continue the conversation any longer.

"It is thus. Bring me sake, I mean soju, as well."

The waiter disappeared into the kitchen and our hero leaned back in his chair. He almost preferred Hwang Nara's company to this. Then he thought of the leaking sink fixtures aboard the Gunham and decided to persevere through lunch. *I will exchange madness for ignorance,* he thought. *The variety will at least rest my spirit.*

Our hero looked around the restaurant and saw only two other tables occupied. In the corner a morose black couple argued about child support and ignored the *bulgogi* steaming off to the side. Nearer to the front door a white man who, had his skin been hairless, his hair black and his face higher-cheeked, could almost have passed for a Korean born in the 1960s. He had the familiar bony, harsh hands and flat body that grew slightly thicker at the hips and ever so minisculy thinner at the shoulders. This one struggled with a bowl of *sullungtang,* a bland soup with boiled beef and flavorless noodles. He attempted to take this soup with none of the kimchi, salt, and black pepper that makes such a meal delicious. *Why has the useless waiter not instructed this* Migookin *on how to eat that which he has paid for?*

Our hero's disquiet increased and his stomach rumbled. *Where is my damned duck?* The staff seemed to have vanished and the man with the *sullungtang* still hadn't figured out how to eat properly. Ten minutes, fifteen, Chul stood and thought *I will not have the foreigners thinking less of our national food on account of these horrible restaurateurs.* He went to the white man and spoke thus.

"I see that the waiter has abandoned you as well. Let me help you with this dish so that you may enjoy Korean food."

(For the virtue of learning naught but "bathroom" in a foreign language, I bless the waiter with a 12% less demanding mother.)

CJ startled when the stranger addressed him. *Who is this man and what the hell is that accent?* However, the stranger was right about poor service and not particularly enjoyable food. CJ welcomed the chance to indulge in some manly anger after so much time caught in Patty's unsteady sphere of emasculating calm.

"The waiter is busy texting somebody," CJ said. "Why should he interrupt gossip with something trivial like his, you know, job?"

"He should do his duty," the stranger said. "But because he is worthless, I will do his duty and mine as well."

CJ got the very strong sense that the stranger had missed his joke but, tired as he was of the flavorless soup and happy as he was to embrace a passing bit of hostility, decided to continue on.

"This soup is very bland," the stranger said. "You must add these side dishes until the flavor satisfies you. Do you eat spicy foods well or can you not take peppers?"

CJ smiled. The stranger's mush-mouthed accent, partially mangled liquid consonants and strange phraseology emerged amusingly from a face both stone hard and continually scowling. It reminded him of the 90's when Mike Tyson threatened to eat Lennox Lewis' children in that squeaky little girl's voice of his. CJ bottled the good cheer up lest it offend this gentleman before answering.

"I can handle spicy food," CJ said.

"It is thus."

Odd phrase. The stranger picked up the scissors—CJ had initially thought their inclusion in his place setting an accident—and cut the strong-smelling, sour cabbage. The scissor blades scraped against the stone bowl and soon no cabbage leaf longer than four centimeters remained.

"Put these in your soup," the stranger said. "You may put in a little now. It is a simple matter to add more if the flavor pleases you."

CJ complied and emptied two spoonfuls into the soup bowl.

"You should add black pepper and salt," the stranger said. "Stir them and take the delicious soup. It will taste much better."

Black pepper spread out over the surface of the milky white broth and salt disappeared into the red cabbage poking above the surface. CJ stirred and what resulted looked like a pink version of the cabbage soup like his mother used to make. What had before tasted like a little bit of boiled beef in a lot of water now filled his mouth with savory, subtle heat, a gentle crunch or two and a little bit of sour.

"Holy crap, that's good!"

"It is as *sullungtang* should be served," he said. "That the waiter did not teach you is insulting to our nation."

CJ thought this comment disconcertingly jingoistic but decided to let it slide. *I guess it's okay for foreigners to love their countries, even if America is better.*

"So you're from the former South Korea?" CJ asked.

"I am."

"What brings you to San Francisco?"

Choi Chul considered the ways he might answer such a question. The truth was obviously unsuitable. Should he say "I was kidnapped by conspiracy theorists and blown into your port by the God of Potency" it would cause the white man to both doubt his sanity and cast dispersions on Korea. Any mention of the Mongolian Illuminati would be even worse. An impenetrable vagueness seemed the best course of action.

"I am waiting to meet with government officials," he said. "There is a legal matter to which I must attend."

The white man slapped his thighs and laughed. Chul thought this a mildly crude way to express humorous irony but still did not refuse when the stranger offered him a seat. *Why not? In any case I must find some way to pass the great spans of time these fools require to prepare my meal.*

"I'm here, or at least I'm here at this time rather than three days ago, because of a legal matter of my own," the white man said. "My name's CJ. What's yours?"

"Choi Chul. My family name means greatest and my given name means iron. My family wished for strength in their sons."

"That's interesting. In my name the C stands for Carver and the J stands for Jefferson. I'm named after George

Washington Carver who used hard work to lift himself from poverty and low origins to become a great inventor. The Jefferson part comes from Thomas Jefferson, who knew how dangerous the state could be and designed protections so that the central government couldn't take away our god-given freedoms. So I'm named after hard work and a small minimal federal government."

Chul thought this a ridiculous thing to name a child after, but crazed people must name their children something and, in any case, it did no good to pass judgment. He considered his childhood and the state-run industrialization programs of President Park Jung-hee. *Had these not lifted Korea from the shameful poverty of the 1960s? Why would the people of a democracy fear their government? Can they not replace it whenever they wish?* He did not understand and thus changed the topic.

"Fascinating. However, I must ask you for help in a different matter. There is a sick man on my boat and he has broken the pipes. Do you know anyone I might speak with regarding repairs?"

Chul liked the way that "my boat" part sounded. It would certainly not hurt anything if others believed him the owner of such a fine machine.

"I'm a plumber by trade," CJ said. "Would you like me to look at it?"

"We should meet later and I will show you *my* boat," he said. "The Gunham may interest a man like you."

The two exchanged phone numbers and promised to rendezvous the next evening.

(For the sin of naming her son after a limited federal government, I cause CJ's mother's Social Security checks to bounce for three consecutive months.)

Chapter Thirty One

While it is true my wisdom stretches to near infinite lengths, my intelligence dwarfs that of your greatest scientists, philosophers and taxidermists, and that my foresight forms the actual basis of the myths surrounding the Oracle of Delphi, even my own frankly awesome brilliance from time to time fails to predict the totality of consequences following on miracles. Such a case arose this day regarding the matter of *Drosera*'s suddenly enhanced size and cognition.

Looking back, I should have foreseen the problem of its appetite. Not only should I have know that the increasing proportion of volume relative to surface area on *Drosera*'s grasping tentacles—indeed its entire being—would reduce its feeding efficiency, but I had access to Rick Moranis' excellent documentary "*Little Shop of Horrors.*" The inescapable conclusion, confirmed with the Dalai Lama's partial digestion at the "hands" of my sentient plant, is that *Drosera* would not long subsist on its diet of insects, slugs and my spare Twinkies of Destiny. Considering that the two most successful animals on earth, by bio-mass, are overwhelmingly humans and ants, and that ants require a great deal more effort in harvesting, well—I think it becomes increasingly obvious what will happen if I do not intercede.

Less apparent but no less inevitable is the matter of my *Drosera*'s erratic psychology. While humans have profited from nearly a billion years of evolutionary progress with regards to neural networks, ganglion and multi-cellular sensory apparatus, the predatory plants must rely on what amounts to a network of electrically linked pumps and tubes. After all, more than one and a half billion years separate your lineage from that of plants and the last protist-flagellate from which you both descend. I had elected to preserve these pumps and tubes as the basis for the super *Drosera*'s new sentience in a fit of nostalgia, which might have been a mistake in hindsight.

The effect is not unlike the hydraulic computers first developed in the late 1940s—only a bit more wieldy than the early sewing-loom based computers first built in the 18th century. A consequence of this poor space efficiency and the inherent limitations of analogue computation—whether artificial or organic—meant that my helper plant's intelligence required a "brain" so large as to account for almost 40% of its body mass. The necessarily diffuse nature of this "brain" further resulted in direct and near passionate stimulation of the central "nervous" system whenever *Drosera* touched anything. This physical sensitivity manifested in a linked emotional sensibility far more profound, far more…passionate.

Alas, my glorious *Drosera*, using a language wherein vowels come from the rapid inhalation of carbon dioxide and consonants are expressed through the sudden expulsion of phosphate-rich mucosal streams, came to my heavenly office. With the most heartfelt feeling and the heaviest vibe imaginable, *Drosera* poured out the contents of its delicate and artistic soul.

"My despair is as deep as the ocean, as wide as the cosmos," *Drosera* said. "My loneliness inescapable, my desires unsated—how am I to go on?"

I should, at this point, explain that in addition to intervening in the idiocy of men and managing divine real estate, I am also the god of plant psychology. Thus, while it was largely my own lack of planning that caused *Drosera's* suffering, I was at least the one best able to alleviate its pain.

"Where are these feelings coming from, *Drosera*?"

The plant blew out its mucous in a touching display of vowel-free vulnerability. I reached out and touched one of its trembling branches and patted. *Drosera* seemed to gain both emotional strength from my simple act of empathy and physical strength from the spare Twinkie of Destiny I pressed into its sticky tentacles. The plant continued.

"When I was digesting the Dalai Lama I felt so—so intimately connected. It was like all my acidic excretions were made specifically for his multi-chain epidermal proteins. It was like my sticky tentacles could see into the very depths of his soul. I have never wanted to dissolve and absorb something—I mean someone—so badly. Not in the violent sense—oh how I abhor violence. If anything it was love. I wanted him to be part of me forever."

I held a tissue to *Drosera's* weepy light sensing spots. It continued.

"Even when I threw the talking head into the Potomac River, even for our brief time together, I felt such a spiritual bond with that commentator. You obviously had no use for him, why not let me absorb his fantastic nutrients and beautiful soul into my protoplasm of love?"

I considered *Drosera*'s words with care. No doubt the plant proposed a difficult ethical problem. Who was I, his creator, to deprive *Drosera* of that which it naturally required? On the other hand, human beings, even talking heads, deserve something more than the flies and gnats *Drosera* normally consumes. They deserve the opportunity to amuse me, for starters. The question of human rights arose as well, but I didn't have time for make-believe in the midst of so profound a vegetable's crisis. No, I would need to probe much deeper into the matter.

"My dear friend, I appreciate your needs and sympathize," I said. "Believe me when I say that I regret preventing your consumption of the talking head but, I must emphasize, we are working here together for a larger purpose."

Drosera's weeping increased and my immortal heart nearly burst with pity.

"You don't understand the depths of love I feel for each creature I digest," it said. "Imagine holding your own child as the babe breathes gently against your chest. Imagine that child ripped away forever while you stand powerlessly by. That's what I feel like!"

This metaphor, beautiful though it was, required me to break briefly from my pattern of unalloyed empathy.

"I understand your feelings, *Drosera,* but parents do not usually consume their children."

Drosera responded with more insight than I could have possibly predicted.

"Their affections are so limited?" *Drosera* asked. "It is then obvious my love exceeds that of a mother for her child a hundred fold. You must appreciate the depths of my suffering now?"

I answered with the most tender caution and sincere empathy.

"Perhaps I could offer you Hwang Nara? He looks delicious and I have no further use for him."

"You would do that for me?"

Drosera threw up its magnificent tentacles and sprayed phosphate rich mucous over the shimmering gates of heaven. I reached out and touched one of its glorious stamens. To extend such mercy, though boring in and of itself, did lend the exciting matter of my adventure an exciting new solution to the ancient problem of conspiracy theorist disposal.

CJ gasped when he first laid eyes on the Gunham. It looked like something out of a Bond film, like Platinus von Sliverass should pop out and assassinate somebody with a space laser. Almost 100 feet long, the boat nonetheless left CJ with an overwhelming impression of sleekness. A carbon fiber shark, a glistening black gadget-dick. He suddenly doubted his qualifications in the face of a machine so magnificent.

"Shouldn't you get an expert from the factory?" CJ asked. "I've never worked on anything like this before."

The Korean grimaced for a second before restoring his customary stoic quasi-frown. CJ saw this and smiled. Perhaps Mr. Eat-That-Weird-Soup-The-Right-Way wasn't all he made himself out to be.

"I am sure your skills will suffice," Chul said. "In any case, it hurts nothing to check. Please wait here and I will prepare the room."

At this point Chul went ahead of CJ and into one of the exquisite titanium and stained wood passengers' quarters. CJ heard a tussling and then an inexplicable, panicky pleading in one of those Asian languages nobody can understand. Dread and curiosity in equal measure collided on the surface of his consciousness and boiled against the fierce heat of his heroic aspirations. *Times like these demand action!*

CJ burst into the room and saw Chul grabbing at the waist of another Asian man. They spoke quickly in their unintelligible gibberish—Chul seemingly annoyed and the other man the very picture of horror. CJ had initial problems deciding who required his heroic bravery but, without really knowing why, picked the frightened man.

"Let him go!"

Chul looked up and noticed, for the first time, CJ standing nearby. CJ could see the Korean's surprise and—what? Embarrassment maybe? CJ crouched and made as if to tackle Chul. He would have commenced an attack had the mighty bonds of caution not caught him. Chul saw this, let go of the victim and started to speak. *Damnit!* CJ thought. *I almost rescued somebody.*

"Please," Chul said. "He is sick and he will not let go of the pipes. I have to return him to my country so that—"

A great rumbling emerged from beneath the boat. Tasteful paintings with velvet backgrounds and poignantly exposed breasts rocked on the walls. Commemorative plates smashed against the sandstone floors and tinkled expensively with each gyration. CJ grabbed hold of the aluminum bedpost and bent his knees so as to maintain balance. The Gunham crashed down suddenly and the impact forced CJ's head toward the floor. When he looked up he could scarcely believe his eyes.

At this point in the narrative, I have elected to give *Drosera* direct access to you, my cherished and impossibly groovy audience. Please, listen in hushed reverence as the mightiest plant the world has ever known grants you an unfiltered look into its deepest secrets.

Hello? My name is Drosera and I love you. I want to bond with you and everyone you know. It's more than that, I yearn for you like a badger yearns for honey, like a virtuous lawman yearns for justice, like a pop starlet yearns for cutting edge analysis of post-modern memetic evolution. I tremble imagining your strength. My tentacles tingle with anticipation every time I think of your beautiful spirits. If I could, I would breast feed you all until your stomachs burst in joy and you fell to the ground in the exhaustion of extreme contentment. I love you. I love you. I love you.

My first true experience of this love—and I do love you—came on the night when CJ Smith, whom I love, first went aboard the Gunham with Choi Chul, whom I also love. The God of Potency, whom I love, sent me up from the oceanic depths to greet them and clear the way for their glorious and uplifting journey. I love inspirational things. And when I say clear the way, I mean come together with Hwang Nara in the most spiritual, intimate way possible.

My tentacles burst free from the salty sea water and into the wondrous, radiant sun. My chloroplasts—I love my chloroplasts—nearly jumped free of their cell walls. They set about absorbing the glorious solar radiation, which I love, in a refreshing and beautiful burst of photosynthesis. I could not help but bask in the gentle light and carbon dioxide gas, to respire as all plants seek to do.

But I could not relax long without seeing to my work. I took hold of the Gunham. I do not love that awful boat because it is inorganic and cold and ghastly and horrible and I weep every time I think of wonderful, lovely people locked away inside its lifeless hull. But I am one who will endure any torment if only I can fulfill my duty, so I held the nasty boat and shook it back and forth.

Chul, who I love, fell down and rolled around inside the largest of the bedrooms. I saw him bounce from divan to ottoman and finally come to a stop, wedged beneath the bed. I know he used the vilest language during this time but, I must assure you, I could feel the affection and love behind each word. How else could I be a "son of a fuck" unless I was the product of physical love? How else could I be "a massive bitch" unless I had the potential to fill the world with wondrous, glorious offspring of my own? I wept again when I fully realized the beauty of Chul's comments—he thought of me not only as the product of love, but a fountain of life!

CJ, whom I love, kept his balance longer but he eventually fell down as well. I gave the boat one last jolt and CJ bounced into the bathroom. This left Hwang Nara alone to my attentions. A deep, fizzing sensation emerged near the base of my two longest branches. Anticipation ran up and down my tentacles in a spasm of unbearable ecstasy. To touch—to consummate that ultimate expression of love! I placed a single sticky pad on Nara's trembling shoulder and drew back. Surely he would not love me as I loved him, surely he would reject me and, truly, am I worthy of such love? I would have retreated, spurned and alone had Hwang Nara not looked up into my light sensing spots at that moment. Such beautifully formed epidermal protrusions, such fragrant lipid excretions and what delightful traces of urea!

I sent out my tentacle again, this time without a hint of hesitation and held him, held him like he yearned to be held. Warmth spread from my slender protrusion into the very womb of my stamens. I squeezed tighter and felt the delicate, rippling contractions of Hwang's musculature driving my sensory glands to the edge of erotic combustion. Oh to be in love as I was ...

I nudged the spiteful boat and its two lovely passengers out into the Pacific and focused my entire soul, my entire body and spirit onto Hwang Nara. Our love lasted hours— the sun rose and fell and rose again whilst we were yet comingling in the dance of love. To be fulfilled, to feel our bonding complete! I can still feel him swimming through my vasculature. I still taste his leather shoes on my chemical receptors. I still feel his polyester slacks tumbling through my excretory ...

W hat the fuck just happened?" CJ asked.

This question, more even than *Drosera's* rendition of conceptually entangled love and digestion, troubled Chul. How could he answer without losing face? Any lie would insult the *Migookin's* intelligence. Any truth would make him seem ridiculous or weak. And this did not even begin to address the problems of his increasing desire for vengeance, the way he could feel himself sliding ever so slowly into the heroic role his uncle had envisioned at the Samgyeop Love restaurant those months before. Chul decided on truth but only because nothing else had the slightest chance of success. *If the* Migookin *will ever see fit to believe the fantastic, it is now.*

"The God of Potency sent his attack plant to retrieve the last of my conspiracy theorist kidnappers," he said. "He did this, I assume, because he wants you to act as my companion while I search for the Twinkie of Destiny."

CJ stared at Chul and blinked as one would expect from a brain trauma victim. Chul could not think quickly enough to devise any cunning strategy and thus piled on the already overwhelming weirdness.

"I have good chance to find it," he said. "The God of Potency said as much before he plucked an extinct flightless bird from the deck of a passing ark and struck my head. He promised to arrange a more suitable companion in San Francisco. Though I did not expect you to fill this role, I would prefer traveling with you to hunting the 'Mongolian Illuminati' as those idiot conspiracy theorists wished. You will, I expect, leave my nipples in peace?"

CJ's expression remained fixed in equal parts astonishment and horror, like a beautiful woman desperately trying to escape the amorous attentions of her 14 year-old second cousin. He finally responded with the greatest of alacrity and most awesome of fluency.

"Yeah, I mean—what?"

"These things overwhelm you," Chul said. "We should go to the kitchen and I will explain."

(For making context-free demands regarding the treatment of his nipples, I bless Choi Chul with massively improved skill at Dance-Dance Revolution.)

CJ's desires bifurcated at this point. The rational side of his nature, the side so carefully nurtured by inspirational daytime talk shows and advice columnists who preface their stories with "Dear [Vaguely Old Fashioned Woman's Name]," wanted to escape the boat, swim to the coast and drive slowly to the marginal employment and security of Selfsevere. This part of CJ thought of warm couches and darkened bedrooms awash with gentle candle light. It tightened his stomach with nostalgia.

The glory-seeking, villain-slaying, damsel-rescuing destroyer-of-all-worlds part of CJ felt differently. Phrases like "fuck yeah!" and "bring on the pain, motherfucker!" issued from this corner of his mind. A natural but dialectically confused desire to avenge his wife or, at least, avenge the way I "cheapened" her death, reemerged from days of hibernation. A great swelling of righteousness bore him away from Patty's humiliating détente and raised him far above the pathetic vulnerability of emotional ickiness. This side of CJ imagined consuming the Twinkie of Destiny in a single jaw-clenching bite. It fantasized of calling up the oceans and sweeping aside all my vile pollutions, striking down my "villainy" in some—as of yet unexplained—way that would both destroy me utterly and leave me the object of mockery and derision for all eternity.

The bifurcation produced no dominant branch and the lesser of our two heroes had little recourse but to seek clarification from Chul. CJ opened the door to the kitchen, sat on an aluminum mesh seat of exquisite craftsmanship and spoke thus.

"I need to know what I'm getting into."

"Surely you have seen the television. The God of Potency has—"

"I know about the deal, but how did you get involved?"

Chul seemed to retreat from this question, as if CJ had asked him something unseemly and private. This reaction did little to quiet his rational side's many objections. *Not much reason to trust this guy so far.* At this point CJ's cell phone let out the beginning of "Hell's Bells," a ringtone he had not actually purchased.

"I'm sorry, just a second."

He pushed his phone's green button and said, "CJ speaking, who is this?" A decidedly male voice answered thus.

"Your mother!"

"What?"

"Your mother," the caller said. "I'm pulling a cock out of my ass! Thought I'd say hello before I put it back in."

A string of laughter followed and CJ hung up. He rolled his eyes and tossed the phone onto the table next to Chul. The area code read 666, though neither man took notice.

"Prank call," CJ said. "But please, tell me how you got involved."

"My uncle is a very silly man," Chul said. "He believes in these stupid conspiracies. However, he loves our nation as do I and we agreed that, should the opportunity present itself, I would pursue whatever agent laid the Japanese pollution over our capital."

Why would he care? CJ wondered. *Those Asian countries are all so similar.* He kept this thought to himself and gestured that Chul should continue.

"One of my uncle's friends—the plant attack victim that I did not suspect of conspiracy theorism at the time— owned the boat you are riding now. When I met this man he kidnapped me and committed outrages on my nipples with his followers. It is only due to previous attacks from the God of Potency that I have gained my freedom."

CJ disregarded Chul's penultimate comment, deciding it best to leave some mysteries unsolved. However, a different and much more important matter needed discussing.

"So you want me to avenge Korea?"

"I would wish you to do so, given the opportunity. You may find this Twinkie before I. It is possible neither of us finds it, but why should we not try? For if I find the Twinkie I will, as soon as I repair my nation and strike back against this Potency God, act as your agent. I only ask you do the same for me."

CJ could almost feel the brutally air-conditioned offices, empty and mocking, from whence Jane had leapt. He imagined the dripping disrespect with which I'd fashioned those cartoon strips running down each strake. He imagined throttling the life from my immortal throat and bit so hard he could taste blood. Chul continued.

"This Potency God spits upon my ancestors and mocks the greatest of our sufferings. He makes a joke from untold misery. He steals away our land. All that my race has achieved he mocks. My culture he treats like a dog's plaything. I have a boat, I have my resolve and I have a goal. I see no reason I should not strike against this villain."

While the specific causes for Chul's outrage struck CJ as being very abstract and not a little silly, he could certainly sympathize with the desire for vengeance. Rational side be damned, CJ Smith would leave behind his distinctly and disturbingly disarming daughter, take up the spiritual armor of wrath and strike out against me.

Bume's Dilemma

Burying You Next to the Corn Field

While Gyeon-woo and Jiknyeo meet on Chilseoknal*

I return only to bury you in the ground.

I return to bury so many baby's breath flowers.

During your life I never bought you a dress and yet

Upon your death I clothe you in funeral robes.

How many funeral clothes do I weave upon the loom

When I return to bury you next to the corn field?

Crossing the galaxy, crossing the clouds for one night a year,

The galaxy's expanse stretches east and west so far that

I can know the distance between heaven and earth.

You soon become dirt and later I become wind

So that when we meet again I may know the distance.

My remaining field I sow with seeds

And while I sweat I must live another year

So that when I meet you again I may know the distance.

-Do Jong Hwan

*This poem makes reference to the myth of Gyeon-woo and Jiknyeo. In the legend Gyeon-woo, the herdsman of heaven, falls in love with Jiknyeo, the garment maker of the gods. Those gods, in their wrath, separate the lovers and banish them to different stars. Their lamentations are so great the gods eventually relent and allow them to meet one day a year, Chilseoknal, or July 7th.

Chapter Thirty Two

78 Days After

Choi Chul awoke the next morning and called home. His wife answered after the fourth ring and spoke thus.

"This is whom?"

"It is Chul," he said. "I have called so that your worrying may extend no further regarding my disappearance."

Very little pause followed after Chul's explanation. The lady, it seemed, had spent precious little time worrying about Chul's disappearance.

"You had not taken up a hobby?"

Chul's voice took on the operatic quality typical of Koreans grievously injured or unjustly accused.

"Ya! What noise is this? I disappear for 16 days and you think I have merely taken up a hobby? Conspiracy theorists shot me with poison darts, assaulted my nipples and took me near to Chile. An extinct bird crashed into my head and rendered me unconscious. An enormous plant ate the head kidnapper and stranded me in San Francisco. I have *not* taken up a hobby!"

She paused at this juncture. Chul's heavy breathing looped through the airwaves and echoed in his ears.

"You must have learned many things about biology," she said. "Perhaps that can be your hobby." A pause followed on this before she continued. "Do you wish to speak with Min-sung? He made mention that he wants to talk with you."

Chul said nothing.

Our hero heard the receiver click as Mrs. Choi set it down on either a table or counter, something hard. Footsteps, a vague banging noise, the sound of a younger person catching his breath.

"Father, where are you?"

"I am on a boat, near to San Francisco."

A recap of Chul's adventures followed and left Min-sung speechless. Chul broke the silence with a question.

"What has transpired during my absence?"

"The God of Potency, or whatever they call him, has sent his plant out to cause many strange happenings all over the world," Min-sung said. "It kidnapped a French yodeling instructor and placed him in a train. His situation resembles to your own. This Frenchman now scours Europe in search of the Twinkie. I also know of a Jewish pilot living in China whose comrades fell in a hail of brine shrimp. Uncle will not stop reminding me how this Chinese Jew even now pursues the Twinkie in her Cessna. There is also a woman in Japan who—"

"So you are saying the God of Potency picks favorites?" Chul asked.

"It would seem so. The Americans, Iranians, Chinese and many other countries have sent out their navies to search for the Twinkie of Destiny. But in each case the sailors have contracted scurvy, consumption, rotgut and anal leakage. It seems only a matter of time before they all return to port. Our own navy has tasted defeat in this way. You must admit, this Potency God does have a sense of humor."

Chul's nostrils flared like a gladiator in combat, like an avenging angel mid-smiting, like a heifer in the heat of bovine love-making. His fist crashed against the *Gunham's* granite counter tops as he dealt a mighty blow against Min-sung's improper thinking.

"I admit no such thing! This situation calls for earnest determination and powerful wills, not the ironic musing of traitors and half-wits."

Chul could almost hear Min-sung's eyes rolling. Finally the boy changed subjects.

"It appears you are one of his chosen," Min-sung said. "I wonder why he picked you from all the millions."

Does the Potency God think me a weakling? Chul thought. *Does my son think me a weakling? None who have underestimated me thus far have escaped sorrow!*

"I cannot tell," Chul said. "I only hope to make him regret this decision."

"So you plan to go along with this—this quest? Father, you are no Joseon warrior. Neither are you a scholar. Come home and thank the Potency God we did not suffer the burden of yet another war."

These words struck our hero in two contradictory ways. On one hand, the younger Choi was right to point out Chul's unlikely road to heroism. On the other hand, why couldn't he achieve this greatness in the name of Korea? The final sentiment he dismissed without thought. *What is life if we have no ideals to perish in the service of?*

"One day you will learn the folly of trading peace for honor. And why should I not use this opportunity to avenge our nation?"

"Look at this issue by means of logic, father," Ming-sung said. "The Potency God, a being of near infinite power, who has seemed cunning, offends billions and then offers his enemies the chance to destroy him? Do you not suspect a trap?"

This sent our hero straight into glorious martyr mode.

"If there is a trap and I reach it first, the world will remember the courage of Korea."

"More likely they will remember the gullibility of Korea," Min-sung said. "Please father, if you must go adventuring thus, remain humble. I do not mean to insult you, but it is not hard to influence the mind of a prideful man."

(For the virtue of making decisions while inflamed with a martyr complex, I bless Chul with divinely protected nipples.)

Seeds of practicality, buried beneath the topsoil of fantastic vegetation and the Mongolian Illuminati, slowly broke into the light this morning. The provision of food, water and fuel concerned CJ and, upon expressing these misgivings to Chul, resulted in further worry over how to operate the Gunham's complex navigation systems. CJ frowned and thought. *We might need another crewmember.* A blindingly obvious question followed on this and spilled from his open mouth.

"Where should we go to find this Twinkie?" he asked.

Chul stood up from the leather couch ringing the Gunham's observation deck and bathed in the blue light cast gently down from the polycarbonate roof panels. The Korean wore the expression of a man at once confused and constipated.

"I do not know but…but I think…" Chul paused, almost as if some quasi-benevolent trickster deity were tugging on his nose hairs. "I feel we should see the navigation equipment ourselves."

CJ followed him down to the lower deck near the prow. There he beheld the green glowing sonar screens, the vast, advanced computers and enough meteorological equipment to incorrectly predict hundreds of storm paths simultaneously. However, none of these man-made marvels drew his attention quite so much as the glistening, resplendent opossum standing perfectly still astride the Gunham's communications array.

Chul approached first and poked the animal's flanks. Nothing. CJ likewise jabbed a single finger onto the marsupial's back, causing it to fall rigid to the side. Where he expected to see dangling udders, CJ instead beheld the simple, blacked out elegance of a Smartphone touch screen. He opened the display and saw a yellow icon labeled "call log" with a flashing "1." He looked to Chul for assurance, nodded and dialed.

Tiptoe Through the Tulips rang out on my Heavenly Phone of Awesome and I wrapped divine fingers round the light blue lobster-skin casing.

"Howdy doody, neighbor?" I asked.

"Who is this?" CJ asked.

I had not programmed my caller ID into the heroes' opossum phone—a sadly outdated and unfashionable model in the heavenly ether, but I do hate to throw out old things especially when I can re-gift—because I wanted to answer precisely that question.

"I am the God of Potency, Heavenly Master of Plant Psychology, Divine Manager of Godly Real Estate Disputes and Master of All I Survey. Quake before my might!"

I could feel the rage pumping through CJ's veins, taste the hurt and shame and feelings of helplessness tied up with Jane's death on 9/11. The potency of these emotions sent tingles up and down my back. What passions lie in the hearts of men!

"I have nothing to say to you," CJ said.

The tingling stopped. I was tempted to take him at his word and abandon these two in favor of the Chinese Jew in her Cessna. And why not? The self-righteousness alone warranted censure, to say nothing of their blindness to irony and inability to grasp the greater purpose of my doings. However, I had to consider the reason I'd chosen our heroes in the first place—if I am to examine your species' strange priorities, my subjects will by necessity embody just those odd values. That said, the stupidity of CJ's lie did compel me to curse him with both the sudden formation of a pea-sized kidney stone and the overpowering urge to pee. I heard the phone bounce off the ground and waited for Chul to replace his fallen comrade.

"You are the Potency God?" the greater of our heroes asked.

"I am the Heavenly Master of Plant Psychology, Divine Manager of…anyway, yes. I am the Potency God. I left you that phone because without my guidance your search will be entirely aimless and because I feel it best to offer you access to my wisdom whenever you should require it."

Chul answered with manly belligerence and courageous bluster.

"Do not think you can fool me so easily. I am strong in my purpose and certain of the rightness of my mind."

I chuckled and acknowledged our hero's observation.

"I would never dream of employing so transparent a gambit against a man such as yourself. Surely you suspect me of a cloying sarcasm, a prancing and thoroughly unaccountable dickishness but, I promise you, the quest I've set you upon is no joke. I shall not lie and say the journey ahead of you will pass without incident. As for your strength of purpose and certain righteousness, I should make it very clear that you hazard your beliefs by pursuing me. I am, before all else, a shaker of man's faith. You *will* choose between your certainty and your desire for the Twinkie of Destiny before this is over."

Chul's reply was slow in coming.

"Do not underestimate the strength of my purpose or the…"

"Yes, yes, whatever you say. The important thing now is to focus on upheaval and rebellion in the Omo Valley of Southern Ethiopia. You'll find the necessary coordinates on the Gunham's navigation computer. Go quickly. The object of your desire is already starting to get squishy."

Chapter Thirty Three

88 Days After

Viewed from afar, the young man's slender contours bent, distorted and shimmering through the heat and dust of that particular bus stop. Called Bume, he was literate and, though disliked by his kinsmen, necessarily a spokesperson for the Kara. It was this position alone that afforded him the ability to leave his cattle behind. These new outsiders flailing about the fringes of Mogadishu and asking for transit to the Omo River Valley—obviously not tourists come to see the cultural game preserve from which his tribesmen hailed—would require more vetting than usual.

But he did not go to see these outsiders in the service of his tribe. He went instead because of his skin. The coal black color was not a problem, per se, for it was not far removed from the mean in these parts. No, the problem that concerned this young man centered on his chest's shameful smoothness—the mark of not only a boy, but a boy too cowardly to avenge his fallen brother. Had he earned his scars, should he run his fingers across his breast and find the divots and welts of courage, then his problems would have simply gone away.

The outsiders, possibly gun runners—not very smart gun runners judging by the rumors of their extravagant boat—might be persuaded to help. And while he was not normally one to heed omens, my appearance the night before might have increased his expectations regarding those "weapons smugglers."

Bume's problems had begun years before when the rival Nyangatom had set an ambush for Bume's older brother and maimed him with their AK47s. He'd struggled and limped a hundred meters before the Nyangatom finished him with their machete blades. For this outrage the Kara had demanded revenge. The duty, by custom, fell to Bume.

His mother had demanded the blood and cattle of a Nyangatom warrior (our young man's own father had died in an earlier vendetta, successfully avenged by the aforementioned older brother) and the marriageable women of the tribe had been unwilling to bear the touch of one so weak.

While Bume felt little personal desire for revenge and could ignore the entreaties of his mother and find female companionship in the villages, he could not so lightly refuse the village elders. Were he to abandon his place in the cycle of retribution, they would expel him from the tribe and thus end his work with the *mingi* children. And that would not do at all.

He crested the last in an endless series of semi-arid hills and came down to the Somalian coastline. A great black boat dwarfed the surrounding fishing vessels and spoke of money the likes of which he'd only seen in Pierce Brosnan movies.

These demands fell heavy against the young man's neck and shoulders and made the sweat drip into his eyes. He thought of Jesus bearing the cross and, perhaps with a touch of grandiosity, empathized with Christ's torment. As he stepped onto the pier, values truly ancient and those merely old, those modern and those emerging anew from the fitful and ever shifting river of human identity, made war within his heart.

He breathed in, stepped to the cabin door and knocked.

The greater of our heroes laughed under his breath as CJ expressed his surprise that here, in Somalia, the people drove such "tiny" cars and rode such "puny" motorcycles, many even resorting to the power of donkeys. "You could run this place with a real man's truck," CJ had said. Chul smiled as he imagined filling the fuel tanks and repairing the chromed 20-inch wheels of said real man's truck on a goat herder's income. *Such naiveté,* he thought.

Since arriving the day before, Chul had received no more communications from yours truly. This left him in a state of doubt and impatience. He had no inkling of who or what to meet with, when this meeting would occur or even where to go—waiting of the most helpless variety. As a consequence, a large percentage of his internal dialog concerned fantastic schemes to exact revenge, vigorous intercourse with my eye socket being perhaps most colorful.

The hollow boom of knuckle on carbon fiber sent CJ up from the table and to the door. He looked to our hero and spoke.

"Do you think that's our guy?"

Chul hoped it was so.

"We should find out, I am tired from all this waiting."

CJ opened the door and blocked the opening. *Perhaps he fears intrusion?* Our hero could see nothing but the visitor's shadows, hear nothing but muted whispering and so moved from his table.

"… are not arms dealers," CJ said. "We aren't going to sell you guns."

The visitor, a young Ethiopian with wide cheeks, a flat face and green soccer shirt, motioned to the splendorous exterior of the Gunham.

"Who else could afford a boat like this?"

CJ raised a hand to his breast and set about delivering his sermon.

"People who do honest business and aren't looking to get an easy buck off respectable folks," he said. "People who know how to respect their traditions without losing the thirst for entrepreneurship—"

Chul interjected before the billowing clouds of CJ's idealism had time to induce vomiting.

"You should come inside. We may have cause to cooperate if only we understand your goals more completely."

CJ glared at Chul but said nothing. Chul ignored his companion and motioned for the guest to sit.

"Why do you wish to purchase guns? You look like a man who studies well. You do not look like the rough gangsters or western cowboys who shoot their enemies and throw knives."

"He looks like the gopher for some terrorist warlord outfit," CJ said.

Chul could clearly see that the young man was not a burrowing rodent and thus dismissed CJ's idiotic speculations. He repeated the question.

"Why do you want weapons?"

"I must kill the Nyangatom because they killed my brother. My tribesmen will not allow me to continue my work if I let this murder pass unavenged. But since I do not wish to die and have sufficient means with which to bargain, I come to you, rich arms dealers. I hope you can help me take this revenge cleanly and anonymously."

Hul, our hero thought. *What sort of man says things like these to strangers? What sorts of people allow revenge to displace justice? I suppose it is Africa…*He continued on slow and cautious as a hidden constrictor, not least because he suspected my divine hand in the matter.

"We are not weapons dealers," he said. "We are instead adventurers seeking unusual happenings. You do not know of any very unusual happenings, do you?"

The Ethiopian's eyes opened wide and he flashed a mouth full of over-white, large teeth. He clapped twice before answering.

"I know what you seek," he said.

CJ spoke.

"What did you find?"

"I know a cave," he said. "A cave which is the work of neither man nor nature."

CJ looked to Chul and nodded. *Surely this is a sign,* Chul thought. *Surely the Potency Bastard has hidden the Twinkie of Destiny in this cave.*

"You must show us this cave," Chul said.

The Ethiopian smiled.

"How badly do you want to see it?" he asked. "Or should I ask how badly do you want to find the Twinkie of Destiny?"

CJ replied as if to intimidate the Ethiopian, as if a man from the murderous tribes, raised in seas of lawless chaos, would flinch when faced with a middle aged plumber from New York.

"Who the hell said we were looking for the Twinkie of Destiny?" CJ asked.

The African laughed.

"If you aren't wanting the Twinkie, then my cave will be of no use to you. No, I know what you need, you know what I need. Help me settle the vendetta and I will show you."

CJ bit his tongue and Chul remained silent and so the Ethiopian continued.

"I see that you will take time to decide. Send for me tomorrow. I am Bume and I stay with the Friends of Omo Children."

Bume laughed again and took his leave.

CJ hated feeling like a mark, hated that sneaking feeling that somebody was fucking with him. The prank calls, admittedly, weren't helping, but this Bume bastard raised every red flag CJ knew. The slimy, grinning "sincerity" and deep smooth voice that said "come gently with me" and then hacked you to bits in an alley. The awful Africa-ness of him. The stench of dysfunction and the hopelessness of anachronism dressed up with one state-run propaganda channel, corrupt Chinese money and a $4 cell phone, caked with malarial mud and hippo fatalities. That little shit even wore the too short shorts and soccer jerseys CJ always saw whenever the news showed some new African mass killing, some dark skinned clusterfuck of dying.

Even if Bume proved sincere, CJ had to grapple with the fact that the Ethiopian represented only one layer of "fucking with him" since I too lorded imperious over his quest. Would it make sense to think I'd wrap a scam inside a deception all in order to make him ridiculous? If you have been paying any attention the preceding pages, the answer should be painfully obvious. Still, he had little choice but to go along with my machinations. With these thoughts running furious circles in his head, CJ sat at the dining table and waited. Chul did not join him for perhaps five minutes even after wandering in from the boiler room.

"Can you believe we are even thinking of helping these backwards fucking tribes kill each other?" CJ asked. "I feel dirty."

Chul shook his head.

"I am indifferent to their sufferings. If they wish to extend warfare endlessly into the future, it is their own fault."

"Everyone deserves freedom," CJ said. "Assholes like Bume are keeping their people locked to the chiefs and warlords. If these people had liberty, everything would fix itself."

Chul's face did not change in the slightest as he spoke.

"I concern myself with Korea's honor. The tribes of Africa do not matter."

CJ disapproved.

"Don't you have any ideals? If anybody should appreciate freedom it is a South Korean. Compare your life with the lives of people who endured communist enslavement in the North."

"It is more important that we remain one people than we are rich," Chul said. "While they failed at many things, the North Koreans have at least maintained our race. These Africans have no effect on my people and in any case, I do not wish to interfere in their business."

It had always bothered him before in a way he couldn't quite put his finger on, a vague sense of otherness in those Asian people. The way you could just see them saying "fuck reason" and, in one giant unthinking blob, rush off to some unholy disaster. Almost like woman logic. He hadn't really nailed the specifics of this behavior down before but, now, with the benefit of this close association with Chul, he had a better idea.

They're goddamned insular. The entire world could go to hell if it meant they didn't have to stop using chopsticks. The only things that matter to those bastards are the things happening right in front of their damned noses. How many world wars and invasions and French occupations is it going to take before they realize the rest of the world (especially America) matters to them, as well?

"You're being awfully damned closed…insular," he said. "Jesus Christ, we're all the way out here in Africa looking for the Twinkie and you still think nothing from the outside world matters to Korea? Look around, man."

Chul looked down at his phone and checked a text message as he answered CJ.

"You sound like a missionary."

The greater of our heroes emerged from the hot, dusty cab and handed the driver a small tip. He'd left CJ behind—someone had to guard the boat while Chul "bought fuel"—partly because he feared another lecture on freedom but mostly because he did not trust any idealist to cope with the hard, opportunistic brutality of Bume's existence. When it came time to trade righteousness for progress, he feared the American would sacrifice the Twinkie quest rather than compromise those evidently sincere ideals.

The entry to *Friends of Omo Children* was mercilessly whitewashed and the plaster crushed into oblivion what must have been a million dirty fingerprints on the door jam. Outside, tiny black children ran after soccer balls and threw sticks into the street, laughing as the passing trucks broke them apart. A chicken crapped indelicately by the sorghum plot and a cow languished beneath the one tree big enough to shade an ungulate. Our hero looked left and right and saw how the natives stole secret glances at him and—shuddering as if filled by a million writhing millipedes—felt like a museum display.

The front door opened out and nearly hit Chul. Bume emerged and, clearly not expecting our hero, stepped quickly back and grabbed at his chest.

"Jesus, man. Why didn't you send for me?"

"It is better we discuss your needs alone," Chul said. "Can I go inside?"

Bume pushed the door farther open and stepped aside so that Chul might enter *Friends of Omo Children* first. Our hero could feel those dozens of native gazes lift. He breathed deep and relaxed his shoulders. *Let me conclude my business and escape.*

He sat upon the chair and looked to Bume's desk. Behind the young Ethiopian hung crayon pictures, hand written notes in the uneven, slanting style of young children. One said "Hapy Birthdey Bume" and another, dominated by a purple and green rainbow and featuring three black stick figures, said "I love Bume." These things nauseated our hero and weakened his stoicism.

"You have not brought the weapons," Bume said, gesturing to an old, wooden chair. "But this is just as well. I have considered our situation and decided that it will be you who takes my enemy's life."

Chul remained quiet but not because Bume's demand had shocked him. Indeed, the dirty, ruthless words sat better with him than seeing those children's' drawings. It was more a sense of suddenly returning sanity—a world as it should be rushing in and preventing him from speaking. Bume continued on to fill the silence.

"You seek a God of Potency. Do not bother lying. I spoke with this god or demon or whatever he is. He suggested that I don't need to dirty my hands when I have you."

Chul said nothing.

"What is your answer?"

"It is easier to find another who knows of this cave," Chul said. "I hope your stupid revenge scheme fails before anyone gets hurt. I must go."

Bume shook his head and opened the door once more for Chul. He spoke with a deep, cheerful voice as Chul went back onto the street.

"I will speak with you again tomorrow."

CJ struggled with his shoes. The cheap, plastic backing had broken and now dug into the skin over his ankles and Achilles' tendon. He wanted nothing more than for Chul to return. That way somebody else could take care of the boat while CJ found whatever passed for footwear in these parts. Sadly, when the Korean finally returned he was both eager for lots of foot-tormenting conversation and loath to let CJ leave.

"We should find someone else who knows this cave," Chul said. "Bume is stupid and dangerous."

"I thought you were getting fuel?" CJ asked.

"I only said that because your idealism makes negotiations difficult," Chul said.

What an apocalyptic asshole, and he doesn't even try to hide it? Is casual betrayal the norm for those Asian people? Think you can fuck me and then count on my cooperation? Not going to happen, buddy boy. CJ's anger again rose within but, in what was becoming an increasingly common twist since the Patty situation, he managed to set it aside before speaking.

"Maybe he will get along better with an 'idealist,'" CJ said. "Maybe he thought you would do something immoral and dishonest and that's why your negotiations didn't work out. I should go check for myself, I think. You can stay here while I take care of business."

A certain drawing back of the lips, a sudden increase in muscle tension around the eyes—*is that fear?* A feeling of glory swept over the American. Oh how wonderful to take hold of the evil doer and see his weakness exposed before the forces of righteousness. How satisfying to watch he who imagined himself powerful reduced to infantile dependency. Pissing on Osama bin Laden's watery grave couldn't have been much better. He wasn't even mad about the shoes any longer.

Chul tried to recover, to regain the power his foolishness and arrogance had just cost him. This delighted CJ further and he smiled.

"It would be very unwise to go," Chul said. "You should leave this to me and I will find a suitable alternative."

CJ had to stop himself from laughing.

"No, I think I'll go by myself."

Chul's fear reemerged. Surely the Korean could feel himself marginalized just as CJ felt the glory of newfound dominance? Chul made another, panicked suggestion for the American's enjoyment.

"Then we should go together, or bring Bume here, where we are safer."

This presented the lesser of our heroes with a dilemma. It would certainly be easy to cut the asshole out at this point, go straight to Bume and take the Twinkie for himself. Except for losing access to the boat, there weren't many practical downsides to this course of action. However, if he allowed Chul to remain, he could do so as the dominant party and *my lord* did that feel good. Sure, Chul might try to claw his way back later, but if CJ could dominate him so easily now, why couldn't he do it again and again? CJ spoke.

"I'll send someone to get Bume. You can support me, I suppose."

Chul breathed out. Such relief. Whether from pride or stupidity—perhaps both—the American had not taken advantage of his mistake. Chul shivered and remembered Min-sung's warning. He would not waste a second opportunity.

Chapter Thirty Four

89 Days After

A stumpy, three-wheeled taxi's antique brakes shrieked outside Bume's office. A man jumped out and came to the door. As the driver did so, Bume felt the familiar sub-nausea, the queasy realization that one could succeed only with difficulty and fail with even the tiniest whoopsy fuck. As he feared, the cabbie entered his office and spoke thus.

"There are two foreigners in a big boat. They say I should get you and come back to them."

"Let us get it over with," Bume said.

A short, bumpy ride followed and the sweat-stained cab seats left Bume's best polo shirt wrinkled, his Levi 501s pulled down enough to expose a bit of plumber's crack and his underwear somehow both too high and too low. It was enough to make the Ethiopian nostalgic for his donkey riding days.

He laughed when he laid eyes on the Gunham. A ten-million dollar boat, docked with the finest rigging to a pier made from driftwood. *This is like marrying a beautiful woman, clothing her in silk and taking her to live in a shanty.* But the time for merriment had passed and, beating the composite door skin with his knuckles, his mind went entirely to the work of convincing foreign strangers to murder some other stranger so that he wouldn't have to. While the strange sight of great wealth rubbing against pre-industrial slums tickled his sense of the absurd, he'd long since become inured to the greater absurdities of his tribal duty.

The brown-faced Korean opened the door and frowned. Bume imagined the sharp edged, over-large bolus of pride Chul must have been swallowing. Chul stepped aside and made way for the red-brown, sunburned American. Where Chul moped, CJ beamed. Bume correctly interpreted this as a crack in their unity and prepared his arsenal of rhetorical wedges.

CJ made a broad sweep of his hand and motioned to the brushed aluminum and cherry wood staircase. A wave of envy, deep and primal, rushed over Bume. *If I had money like this…* Bume stopped a moment. He could feel the jealousy drain away like pustule expertly lanced. *If I had money like this, the mingi children would not run barefoot in a dirt lot.*

CJ waved his finger over a motion sensor. This set the motors of an expertly hidden and beautifully crafted door on the roof to work. Soon the gentle light of midday came over Bume.

"Let's go to the deck," CJ said.

They took seats in a sunken dining area. Chul to the left, CJ directly in front and Bume sitting straight on the beautiful but uncomfortable inset seat. CJ noticed this and offered him a cushion. Bume accepted and CJ began the inevitable difficult business.

"So, I hear my partner couldn't make a deal with you. Now, we could try to find another person who knows this cave but I'd rather just make a reasonable arrangement with you."

"You will not find another person," Bume said. "So please, don't waste my time. I am a busy man and your friend has already insulted me with too many stupid mind games."

CJ smiled and looked to his sullen partner. Bume took this as evidence and determined to drive Chul further to the margins of their deliberations. *Combine the Korean's diminished power with the American's obvious appetite for flattery and I will get what I need.*

"I'm sure we can do better," CJ said. "Tell me what you need."

Bume played up the natural, genuine frustrations of his situation in order to appear needy and, more important, morally just to CJ.

"I need a capable surrogate," Bume said. "If I do not complete the vengeance my tribe demands, they will prevent me taking in the mingi children. If I don't take responsibility for these children, no one will."

CJ nodded twice and leaned forward before answering.

"What does that mean?"

Chul folded his arms and stuck his head out, glaring at CJ.

"It means he wishes to do murder but does not have the courage himself. He thinks we should act as gangsters and kill his rival."

CJ looked at Bume and shrugged as one encouraging a tardy employee to explain himself.

"Your friend does not understand my position," he said. "I am a good man and I do good work. I am no gangster, I want to give my people life, not take it away."

Chul cursed in his native tongue before saying of Bume, "he is a stupid bitch, making a dog's sound."

CJ frowned. He didn't like the way Chul was antagonizing this nice, reasonable man. He suggested Chul cease the insults until Bume had an opportunity to completely explain his predicament. Bume smiled gratefully at this and continued the story.

"In my tribe, we have children who are called mingi. A child is mingi if they have any deformity. They are mingi if their top teeth erupt before their lower teeth or if they are twins. If their parents have not wed or do not first receive the blessing of the elders, that child is mingi. Many children are mingi. You are a good man. Does a good man like you not wish to help the innocent?"

"I understand, and I would like to help your mingi," CJ said. "But I don't know what this has to do with our arrangements."

"I will explain," Bume said. "The mother of a mingi baby leaves her child in the brush to starve or throws them to the river as food for the crocodiles. In the case of an older mingi, our elders push the child from the top of a high cliff. They say these children are cursed. They blame any calamity on these mingi. So I ask you to appreciate the madness and wrongness of their actions—both seem obvious to civilized people."

"They are no worse than you," Chul said.

CJ shushed his companion and made a circular motion with his hand. *Go on*, he seemed to say.

"While I think it obvious they are wrong, I would ask that you not condemn their actions. Our histories predispose us to all manner of horrors. I would also kill the mingi, except for my education. So would you."

I would never condone killing children! CJ's righteous indignation swept aside all doubt, all temperance. It rushed with such fury as to obliterate all memory of letters to the *New York Times* wherein he'd extolled the virtues of carpet bombing. It nearly swept aside his desire for the Twinkie of Destiny before he looked at Chul and bit down. He would not let the Korean witness any of his so-called idealistic weakness.

"I can't see how this has anything to do with buying guns or killing some tribal guy," CJ said. "It sounds to me like you should be asking for donations. There have got to be a lot of churches that would help you stop evil."

"Churches are of no use," Bume said. "I take the mingi before they die. My tribesmen send the cursed child away with me only because I am a Kara. But no one can remain a Kara and ignore his people's vendetta. My father died in a vendetta, my brother died in a vendetta to avenge my father and in doing so they made my education—my work—possible. That is why I come to you. You shoot the Nyangatom and I may carry on, protecting the mingi."

"Don't you have to kill him?" CJ asked.

"Are you going to claim the murder in my place?" Bume asked. "I don't think so."

The turn in conversation made CJ queasy.

"I don't know how to kill people," he said. "Even if I wanted to, there's no way I can help you, Bume."

Chul further expressed his admiration for Bume.

"Do you still think it is stupid to find another guide to our cave? Do you still wish to negotiate with this stone head son of a fuck?"

Bume laughed and set his large, white teeth flashing against the sunlight. He stood and spoke down—literally down—to CJ and Chul.

"You arrogant ignorant fools, coming to the shores of Somalia, endeavoring to travel in the Omo River Valley and questioning my judgment here in a land you do not know, surrounded by people you cannot trust and floating among the pirates in your giant boat-shaped bait for thieves. Do you think yourselves the only ones chosen by the God of Potency? I alone know this cave and I will give you nothing until you do right by the mingi."

The mingi. Why did Bume always have to make this glorified mafia hit about children? This left CJ in a tight spot. To accept Bume's proposal meant, well, murder. To deny Bume would surrender all the soul-feeding dominance he'd earned over his companion—what would stop Chul from searching alone? But murder, murder wasn't something CJ could ever see himself doing. He was a good person with principals and morals inviolable. Perhaps he could reason with Bume. Maybe he could show the Ethiopian the folly of doing a bad thing in the service of a higher ideal. If those children were going to get saved, they would get saved through the path of righteousness. *All you have to do is look at history to see how wrong people like Machiavelli and Kissinger really were.* CJ cupped his chin and held out his left hand.

"Can't you see how killing this tribes-dude will just lead to more revenge?" He asked. "Aren't your people doing something wrong?"

"The cycle of vengeance is wrong," Bume said. "It is useless and dangerous. I wish it would go away, but it will not. My father died at the hands of the Nyangatom. My brother avenged my father and in turn died from the Nyangatom's vengeance. I already mourn the man you will shoot. There are very few things in life I more desire than the end of our vendettas. Sadly, the safety of the mingi is one of them."

"Then stop the vendettas right now," CJ said. "Set a good example for the others and they will follow you. Bring civilization to the darkness. Or just stall, when we have the Twinkie we'll fix it for you."

"How will you do that?" Bume asked. "Are you going to brainwash my people?"

CJ had to stop and think. How would he stop people from fighting without destroying their independence? He, a severely limited being, didn't even consider my godly methods. Instead he retreated into cliché and risked the return of scalp acne.

"I will give them freedom."

Bume sat back down and sighed. He kicked his right leg out and put it on the edge of the table. He shook his head three times before speaking in the manner of an old man, tired and beaten.

"You won't do a damned thing, my friend."

Then something changed. CJ watched as Bume's smile vanished, as his eyes bulged out ever so slightly, as his nostrils flared and his fingers clinched into hard balls of bone and malice. He pulled down his feet and leaned forward.

"I know I am killing not only the Nyangatom but my own people as well," Bume said. "Do you think I take this lightly? You imagine I do not care, ignorant foreign pustule, itch on my bullock, arrogant interloper?"

CJ didn't know how to answer and so said nothing until Bume continued.

"I know what I am doing," he said. "I will sacrifice my brothers for the sake of my nieces and nephews. The mingi do not choose their curse, the rest of us do. If you wish to pursue the God of Potency, you will help me do what is right."

"It doesn't make any sense" CJ asked. "Why do they demand revenge? Why can't they act like real people?"

"Would you let an enemy strike your home and do nothing?" Bume asked. "You would seem weak and cowardly. To use reason rather than passion is to make war with ones nature—good, but unnatural and difficult. You, whose people have so long prosecuted the War on Terror, should know this."

Everyone knew that was different and so CJ ignored Bume's comment.

"The smart thing," CJ said, "is to let your brother's death go. Convince your people that this need to prove bravery does no good."

"Your hypocrisy astounds me," Bume said. "But fine, let's consider the pacifism you suggest. Do your people not make war?"

"Well yes," CJ said. "I suppose we do make war."

Bume turned to Chul and repeated his question. The Korean glared and said "of course."

"Then why, if you are so enlightened, so far superior to my tribesmen, do you not simply convince your countrymen that vengeance will do them no good? It must be a simple matter to show them the folly of violence."

CJ was about to say something soothing and mature when Chul interrupted with his unhelpful lectures.

"Do not compare your petty squabbles with Korea's war against Japan," Chul said. "We are innocent and righteous—standing strong against imperialists and war criminals who would steal away our land. The Kara and Nyangatom are gangs. They are worse than gangs, killing children as you say."

So that's the name of Bume's tribe! CJ didn't particularly care about Japan and Korea, but Chul's stuff seemed to at least slow Bume down. *Why not add the infinitely more persuasive case of 9/11?*

"And the War on Terror is different, too. The terrorists wanted to convert the entire world to their religion of violence. They wanted to control us by killing innocent civilians and spreading fear."

"So Korea and America are sure to win?" Bume asked. "They are certain to end the violence forever? Do you think me a fool? Japan is stronger than Korea and America has given up fighting terrorists. The vengeance of the Kara has laid waste hundreds, but your enlightened wars kill by the thousand for no greater gain."

CJ could not, with any honesty, dispute Bume's account of America tapping out and, judging by Chul's silence, guessed the Ethiopian had similarly diagnosed Korea's problems. Still, it was different. Bume once more filled the silence.

"Then why do you question my people's war? The Nyangatom have taken Kara lands, the Nyangatom have terrorized our people. The only distinction I can draw between myself and you is that I understand the madness of my people's war. You are both too isolated in your gauzy, first world cocoons to recognize the brutality and senselessness of your own conflicts. Who should enlighten whom, fool?"

CJ could not help but laugh at Bume's attempt at moral equivalency. When everybody knows something is right or wrong, when it's obvious you should just accept it, even if you couldn't articulate why. He could just feel it. America was above the sort of thing happening in Ethiopia, it just was. Chul interrupted his thoughts.

"We do not come from primitive, tribal nations," Chul said. "It is different. Even America is more civilized than this."

"Listen, gentlemen," Bume said. "I am tired and I am not going to believe your shit, regardless of how many times you restate it. You can help me and in turn find the Potency God's lair or you can leave. I do not care."

CJ cringed inside. He'd have to find some other way to the Twinkie, he'd have to admit Chul was right and——

"Bume, show me where to go," Chul said. "I will do this evil thing."

CJ was shocked. How rash, how filthy, how...courageous?

Chul went down into the Gunham's guts and flipped open the armory's security panel. He entered the code—which CJ did not know—and stood back as the heavy door slid into the wall. CJ and Bume followed as Chul went past the pistols—useless at long range, almost more dangerous while still mounted in their foam depressions—and came to the rifles. Chul knew the Daewoo K2 rifle from his own military days but decided against it. He would use the XM37 "Evicerator."

"We will not even need to see the enemy with this weapon," Chul said. Then, turning to Bume, he said, "to kill from a place of perfect safety. It seems natural that a coward who must turn to others for murder would use such a weapon."

He saw CJ looking fondly at the pistols and rolled his eyes when CJ slipped a .357 revolver into his pants. *Does he imagine John Wayne will attend?* Bume stayed clear of all the weapons, as if avoiding dog shit.

The Ethiopian's evil and the American's stupidity would not keep Chul from his Twinkie. He felt a determination hard as concrete, cold as the Korean winter night. *Fuck Bume, fuck CJ, I will do what I must to right the Potency God's outrages.* He thought of comfort women raped until death by their Japanese captors. He thought of poets shot, queens murdered and Buddhist temples callously broken by the very people whose fetid insignias now spread across Seoul. *I must, I must, I must.*

Chul turned his attentions to the XM37. It had been more than twenty years since he last shot a gun but, lifting the weapon from its foam divot, the sensations came back. The gentle ribbed texture of a machined trigger, the hard plastic stalk and stupid camo paint—he could imagine the familiar pop and jolt, just like his boot camp training decades before.

The gun itself displeased the greater of our heroes. Where the K2 he knew so intimately was sleek and purposeful, elegant in its minimalism, this XM37 looked like a collection of tumors. Sights and scopes and attachments metastasized from every possible surface. Computers and interfaces budded off the barrel and threatened to crowd out the final remnants of heavily besieged symmetry. The only thing to recommend the hideous gun came in the form of a laser sight and targeting system.

The XM37, as opposed to other rifles, used programmable, explosive ordinance. If a victim hid behind the trees Chul had only to aim to the side, program the bullet to explode behind the cover and then pull the trigger. Hopefully, this feature would leave the Nyangatom, or whatever they were called, without any idea where the fatal shot had come from. After all, enemies do not expect air burst rounds and will be hard-pressed to guess the trajectory of a shell that explodes into a thousand pieces. *If we must kill for these tribal stone heads, if we must forge Bume into a warrior, I should at least contrive to escape censure.*

CJ was looking at yet another handgun, the .84 caliber Glock semi-automatic with a special 48-round clip that extended more than two feet out from the bottom of the grip.

"Put it away," Chul said. "That weapon is useless. Take a rifle."

Chul removed a K2 rifle and handed it to his companion. CJ looked like someone had just offered him a steaming plate of month-old salmon and boiled syphilis.

"You expect me to defend myself with an itty bitty round like that?" CJ asked. "I need a man's gun!"

"Experienced men use rifles or carbines," Chul said. "Victims of penis envy use handguns. Choose what you will."

CJ responded by taking all three guns. Bume took nothing and thus aroused Chul's curiosity.

"Are you afraid?"

"I hate violence."

Chul wanted to rip into Bume's massive, gangrenous hypocrisy but stopped. *Fuck it.* The three men stepped out of the armory and Chul closed the door.

"We will begin preparations in the morning."

Chapter Thirty Five

94 Days After

Chul had considered the nature of their murder, its glaring lack of specificity. Since any Nyanga-tom tribesman would suffice, Chul planned their attack around the most favorable location with the assumption that somebody, somewhere, would stumble into the XM37's range if only they waited long enough. The strategy then, resembled that of a fisherman more than an assassin.

He also had to consider the chances of being recognized and worked to minimize them by hiding himself in Bume's trunk as the cowardly Ethiopian tended to mingi pregnancies, mingi tooth emergence and mingi births in different Kara villages. He crossed the Somalian-Ethiopian border four times. Chul finally settled on a canyon opening to the east, heavily covered by light green trees and low, hard scrub that cut skin and smelled of animal droppings. The rising sun would mask muzzle flash and make it nigh impossible for the victims to see the murderers, hidden to the west, before and after they struck. The canyon would spread and scatter the sound, the disagreeable vegetation would discourage any search party.

Chul, had he thought entirely in terms of success and failure, probably would have undertaken the assassination alone. However, he needed Bume present in order to plausibly "credit" him with the death. His distrust of CJ balanced precariously against his desire for a spotter and was finally overcome by a determination that none would escape their outrageous murder with clean hands. He knew well that one or both would likely fail in their duties and drag behind as uselessly as a goldfish turd.

I like that thought. I will call them The Goldfish Turd Gang.

He smiled for the first time in days and called out to Bume. It was thus on this day that all three men set off into the Omo River Valley.

***

CJ ran out of patience almost before they'd begun. How long could anyone endure bouncing in the trunk of a 30-year-old Mercedes, breathing dust and coughing up muddy mucous, jammed against the wall and pressed against another man? Worse yet, he'd been in no position to protest when Chul said things such as this.

"I am going to use your pant leg as a tissue."

The hours clunking along Somalia's awful dirt roads echoed endless in his ears and ceased only for two gas stops—he could hear the fuel rushing down into the tank and feel the cold gasoline chilling the fuel filler tube running across his face—and the Ethiopian boarder check. CJ could not understand their language but had to imagine Bume soothed away any of the guards' problematic legal impulses with copious bribery. He'd even fallen asleep, the taste of dirty carpet and Chul's shoe leather in his mouth.

The light of the setting sun, blinding after hours of darkness, burned CJ's eyes when Bume opened the trunk.

It was then, as Chul pulled himself from the trunk and grabbed a hold of the weapons, that the full force of what they were doing came to CJ. He felt a sinking feeling in his gut, a desire to vomit and hunch over and escape back to America, back to sanity. Something like the worst stage fright imaginable. It was only when he saw Bume and Chul standing like men that the persistent *why am I doing this?* gave way to a decidedly more primal *stop being a pussy.*

"Has anyone seen us approach?" Chul asked Bume. "We must maintain the myth of your bravery. If anyone sees me or Dirty Harry accompanying you, we will all have descended into savagery for nothing."

CJ could see Bume brushing the insult aside with a small, annoyed shake of the head before answering.

"We are alone. Now, earn your passage to the Potency God's cave."

CJ felt a paranoid sense that the entire world sat watching. He could feel the malevolent, malarial eyes of Africa peering out from behind bushes. He clutched for the pistols in his pants and nearly snagged a trigger with his pinky. The thought of an accidental gun wound to the leg made him shiver and he quickly tossed the .357 into Bume's trunk. He caressed the big .84 caliber Glock twice and no longer took any comfort in its power. CJ looked to Chul, already walking into the brush, and Bume, going after him, and dropped the gun next to the .357. He set off after the others with only the K2 rifle bouncing on his back. Perhaps Chul had been right.

Our three gentlemen took a meandering path through the Ethiopian scrub. Bume, undeterred by the dark and confident in an entire childhood's experience navigating this land, led them away from established trails so that none would see their party. Chul preferred to walk just below the hill peaks—he wished to maintain the highest ground possible without letting any observer below make out their silhouettes against the sky. CJ could contribute little and so maintained silence. Silence against the sharp stickers in his socks, silence against a hundred biting insects, quiet in the face of blistered toes and aching, arthritic knees. Two hours had passed when Chul stopped, sat on a stone and faced his companions.

"We will strike tomorrow in the morning. The rising sun will blind our enemies below and allow us to escape unnoticed. Now we must conceal ourselves."

He motioned to a clump of light green bushes.

"We can use these brushes as concealment and then retreat here," he pointed to the hill top behind them, shrouded by low, unhealthy-looking trees. "We will not have cause to move again until sunrise which is in six hours. If you want to sleep, I will wake you. Only remain quiet."

CJ nodded and dug his feet into the sand. He laid his coat out on the ground to cover the ever-present stickers and sat. He looked left and saw only faint leaves dancing in the light of a quarter moon. He looked right and saw the great spiraling arms of the Milky Way. CJ closed his eyes and vanished into a tumultuous sleep.

(For the virtue of nearly shooting himself in the leg, I bless CJ Smith with an 18% increase in natural estrogen production. For the sin of nearly shooting himself in the leg, I curse CJ Smith with an 18% increase in appreciation for boy bands.)

CJ adjusted the fine, silk collar on his shirt and brushed aside a barely visible spec of fuzz on his slacks. He looked up to see Chul seated, smoking in front of an enormous wooden book case. He was sure they had not met before, but things were going well and so CJ smiled and introduced himself.

"I am likely the most evil man you will ever meet," CJ said. "I don't know if I mean it, but that does little to pollute the flavor as it rolls off my tongue, if I may take liberties with that particular metaphor. I say it often. Usually under my breath, in the shower, sometimes where others can hear me. I have variations as well. Sometimes I say, 'I'm not that good a person. You wouldn't like me if you knew me. I'll corrupt everything.'"

Chul nodded his head—knowing, understanding—but CJ felt the need to explain further, just a little bit more to make sure no ambiguity remained.

"This probably makes me sound like a self-pitying depressive or an old Gothic with delusions of martyrdom. I assure you I am nothing of the sort. It is, in fact, only with a very strange sense of detachment that these echoes reverberate through my life.

"When my internal dialogue turns toward self hatred, as it often does, I imagine myself well dressed and in the company of important people. I think of judges and members of big city planning commissions. My hair is always perfectly coifed and my shoes glimmer a rich brown in the expensive glow of high society. A beautiful waitress in black stalkings serves everyone Grey Goose martinis to go with our figs, prosciutto and salmon mousse. The jurists take these delicacies off silver platters and gather around me to chitchat. I wink and laugh. I hold out my hand and gesture as if to say, 'wait, I've got a good one.'

Then it comes out, full of cheer and casual as an A-lister adjusting his neck tie. 'I am likely the most evil man you will ever meet.' My guests chuckle and thank me for the amusement and I give them a knowing smile."

Chul produced a packet of sweet smelling, loose tobacco and offered CJ a pipe. CJ accepted and Chul spoke.

"As a connoisseur of self-loathing," Chul said. "I would likewise give thanks for those fine words. You offer such a sophisticated take on detesting oneself."

CJ lit the fine tobacco and took a deep breath before continuing his speech.

"Thank you, it's a relief to know I'm not the only one who appreciates the pleasures of exclusive, rarified self-hatred. But I should continue. I've always partaken of self-hatred in this way and, though it is a very carefully crafted thing, I do not know from where this guilty pleasure arose. If this voice were attended by any real anger or resentment or even humiliation then I would try to silence it. But it's not. It's happy and offhand and shines with an easy cosmopolitan sophistication—like reading the New Yorker in the lobby of a Neiman Marcus, waiting for the tailor to finish your latest designer suit.

It's been this way for as long as I can remember. Maybe my parents taught me speech by running a 24-hour loop of H.P. Lovecraft stories. I don't know and I suppose it doesn't really matter. I tell you this because I don't want you to think it came from the God of Potency interfering with my thoughts. I'd love to blame him, but that voice is as native to my mind as these fingers are native to my hands."

CJ raised his hand and wiggled his fingers, as if to prove that fingers and hands do, in fact, go together.

"*I realize, Mr. Choi, that this is probably not what you expected to hear when you asked me to tell you something about myself, and I know such things are not common topics of discussion upon first meetings, but I wanted to inform you of my own volition before the God of Potency rips it from my cache of secrets.*"

Chul smiled and showed his benevolence, his understanding. CJ's confidence swelled to such rarified heights, such pleasant altitudes. Still, CJ would go just a little bit further; he would absolutely ensure Chul's complete understanding.

"*So please,*" *CJ said.* "*If you judge me unstable or weak, if you think I'm likely to endanger your ship or your mission, tell me now and let's skip the pleasant emptiness of gentle rejection. I am, if nothing else, a lover of true things and I would not want you to think you must coddle my psyche.*"

Chul smiled again and answered at length.

"*Do not fear, my friend. What is life if not a struggle to control one's hatreds and hide one's resentments? And we must consider this time as well. We seek to murder a stranger and not in any courageous sense, either. Who could take honor in a random killing, against an enemy who has no means of retaliation and no time for preparation? Certainly not cultured practitioners of self-hatred like ourselves. But this is not all. Even in this inglorious murder, you lack the strength to take life and leave the responsibility to me. Surely, if ever you have earned the right to despise yourself, it is now.*

CJ smiled, Chul laughed and they made merry among the sweet smelling wisps of tobacco smoke, drinking fine whiskey beneath the shelves of leather-bound books.

Chul wiped a hand across his dry eyes and blinked in the gloom. He looked at his watch and saw 5:37 a.m. The sun would come up in 40 minutes and he had to get the Goldfish Turd Gang ready for action. He roused Bume with a kick to the ribs. The satisfying bounce of boot on coward did much to relieve Chul's fatigue. He spoke before Bume could complain.

"It is time," Chul said. "Get ready."

He next pushed against CJ's shoulder and returned him to consciousness. CJ groaned a little and rolled onto his face. Arms then legs folded under his body and the American pushed up off his coat. Chul could not help but notice that neither companion looked very rested. CJ grabbed at his pant waist and crouched next to the greater of our heroes as he coughed. A few minutes passed before CJ's words surprised Chul.

"I really respect the way you're taking responsibility for this."

Chul said "thank you," but only because he could not think of a better reply. He sensed the strange and not entirely welcome grit of empathy working its way into the precision gears of rivalry—an unwanted complexity staining the simple white cloth of his certainty. *Perhaps my gain will not much longer be CJ's loss. I can use an ally, but it is always easier to tell friend from enemy in a zero sum game.* But these matters could wait for another day and Chul returned his focus to the filth at hand.

"I would like a spotter," Chul said to CJ. "As soon as the light appears, use the scope on your rifle to search the valley below. There is little more than one hour in which we can strike unseen and I do not wish to miss any opportunity."

CJ nodded and lay down among the bushes, looking to the valley below. The small sounds of a rifle barrel jostling against dry leaves came over the camp.

"I can see pretty well from here," CJ said.

Bume then sought Chul's guidance.

"Where should I go? Should I hide or do you want me to prepare something else?"

The greater of our heroes thought for a moment before answering. *Is there anything I have not remembered? Maybe Bume will be of some use with the escape?*

"Prepare two canvas bags," Chul said. "In the first, pack everything except the weapons. Leave the second open on the ground. I want to leave within thirty seconds of shooting your victim."

Bume did as Chul commanded and left him with time to ready his shot. While he only had to get the projectile close and let the explosion work, he figured it would not hurt anything to be precise. Chul gazed into the XM37's laser sighted scope and surveyed the killing grounds.

The Omo River gurgled faintly in the distance, 600 meters according to the range-finder. Chul guessed this was where the victim would likely to go, either to wash, gather water for drinking or to rest his cattle. 400 meters away a small path wound along the base of the hills and cleanly divided the brown, grassy valley floor from the green bushes and trees above. Our hero could also attack any victim passing along here, should it prove more convenient. Finally, a salt lick beloved by all manner of grazing animals shone white against the landscape 140 meters beyond the river. Chul did not wish to test the range of his gun so sorely and resolved to use the salt lick only as a last resort.

The sun, like a gentle hand in the cold night, rose over the mountains and laid the first, warm licks of morning against Chul's head. *The time is near.* The greater of our heroes settled against the grains and smells of Omo earth and took in the sounds of three men trying more than anything to remain silent. In, out, thump, thump, in, out. Biorhythm dominated all aspects of his consciousness.

Something flickered in the corner of Chul's scope. He shook a faint gauze of drowsiness from his eyes and moved the XM37's fatal tip toward the movement. Two Ethiopians—*boys? Yes, boys*—drove cattle along the path at the base of the hills. 400 meters would make a relatively easy shot but Chul would have preferred a greater distance to ease escape. *Alas, opportunity is rarely ideal.*

The first boy, somewhere in that 17-19 year-old range where a man's musculature works against a child's overlarge joints and the last great waves of acne wash over firm, youthful cheeks, walked ahead of the cattle. He wore naught but a skirt tied round his waist and an AK47 dangling from his thin shoulders.

The second, probably 12 or 13, stood a solid 15 centimeters shorter than his companion and, combined with a whisp thin body and bulbous head, impressed Chul as having a very distinctly bobble head figure. He too carried an AK and Chul wondered how anybody could even take a bath without fearing gunplay in this place.

"Which one should I shoot?" Chul asked.

Instead of an answer, our hero heard Bume praying. Pleas for forgiveness, good wishes to the soul of him soon to die, an entreaty that this senseless murder might serve a greater good. Chul only contained his disgust with great difficulty and a renewed focus on the dirty business at hand.

He chose the older of the two. *It is better to end the life of one nearly half my age rather than one less than a third my age. Perhaps the younger will escape the poisonous customs of this damned country. The younger and weaker will, even if his future consists of nothing beyond vendettas and a premature death, flee more easily and follow us with greater difficulty, if he follows at all.*

Chul took aim at the older boy's chest took a deep breath and held it. His finger tickled against the faint grooves in the trigger. A digital message flashed inside the XM37's scope. TARGET ACQUISITION FAILED. EXPLOSIVE ORDINANCE NOT PROGRAMMED.

Our hero threw the weapon to his side and told CJ to "give me your rifle." Chul drew the stock to his shoulder, found the boy again and timed his breathing. The sights moved left with each heartbeat. He compensated right, held his breath and painted the earth red.

I began this narrative by observing that greatness begins with small coincidences, that the path to glory runs past beggars, around cute young things who don't know your name and over aborted career paths. A similar principal applies to the great moments in even a mundane human life. An amateur boxer's sweetest memory revolves, to a shocking extent, around the tiny incidental sensations—the clean feeling of sweat falling from a hot eyebrow, the effortless purity of a left hook against the opponent's chin, the sound of his heart pounding through bruised ears. The novice ballerina does not remember the score or the well wishers clasping hands below. She remembers closing her eyes as the cool breeze brushes her cheeks, she cannot forget the tiny flooring imperfection, snagging ever so slightly against her toe, from which she launched her triumphant grand jeté. So it was with CJ in the moments surrounding this first bloodletting.

As the fancy gun bounced in the dirt and CJ followed commands he didn't fully understand, a sense of dissociation came like fog. Something took control of his hands and set them to work. A mysterious CJ that was not entirely CJ looked downhill as Chul's sharp inhalation signaled death. The rifle's crack filled the air with sulphur and phosphorous, the very smells of hell. The boy below jerked rigidly upright as blood and bone and skin and short, curly hair covered the ground. The cows and bulls dropped low onto bent knees and fled for the river with their wild, empty eyes sucking at the morning light. It was from the space between a panicked cow and fleeing calf that CJ got his only glimpse of the other boy.

The younger one had collapsed on his butt with hands splayed out behind to support his shoulders. His AK47 strained against its strap and pointed off at a weird angle, a potent and grotesque addition to the picture of overwhelmed childhood. If he fled or fell beneath the cattle or pursued them into the hills CJ could not tell.

Scarcely a second passed between the shot and CJ jumping from his belly into a crouch, shoving the guns into Bume's sack. No more than a moment between this and turning into the sun, blinded and blinding, as they scrambled over the crest of that hill and towards the safe anonymity of Bume's trunk.

Chapter Thirty Six

96 Days After

Chul had thought a great deal about how he would greet Bume on this day. Certainly he had felt a strong temptation to stand up from his restaurant chair, spit on the dirt floor, shove the murder weapon into the Ethiopian's chest and bask in the satisfying but ultimately meaningless "take that" it entailed. Eschewing that option, our hero instead employed his free time to plan a more sophisticated course of action. He sat back and ordered a beer from the harried staff while deliberating.

He set aside the satisfying righteous fury strategy largely because of a moral quandary he had tried very hard, and failed, to avoid thinking about. The notion of sacrifice, not of the noble sort, bothered our hero. Had Bume's sacrifice really been so different from his own?

Both had shed another's blood in the service of a higher goal, indeed, they'd conspired to murder the exact same boy. The appointed ends to Bume's and Chul's evil means differed, but not critically. The honor of a nation, the lives of cursed children—our hero thought them both worthy of protection. But could a good person look to their actions and find anything to admire?

Chul had sacrificed nothing of himself but innocence, Bume seemingly not even that. Surely it was the work of cowards to let others suffer in the service of their higher ideals. *When I decided to restore my nation's honor, I did not think I would do it through my own dishonor.* And yet he could think of no other way. Martyrdom would serve no purpose for either man. Without Bume, the mingi return to falling from high cliffs and feeding the crocodiles. Without Chul, the Japanese pollution would never go from Seoul.

Bume and I are hardly the first to face this problem, Chul thought. Indeed, the willingness to sacrifice others in the service of one's own goals seemed the very heart of leadership. What good is a general if he will not send others to die in his place? What good is a king or president who, prosecuting a war, sacrifices himself and leaves his nation leaderless?

And yet this realization did not entirely satisfy—satisfy his what? He could not call them moral qualms in any logical sense. More the *feelings* of morality. The mingi children, the great Korean people whose heads bowed with shame, these things seemed so far removed compared to a single teenager whose life was no more. How did this question of proximity come to mean so much? How was it that the lives of people nearby came to count for so much more than the lives of people diminished by virtue of their postal codes alone? How strong was this effect that it moved Chul even in a place as evil and backwards as the Omo River Valley? He took a drink from his beer as Bume opened the door.

"I had not wanted to see you again," Chul said. "But I do not hate you as much now as before. Please sit."

Bume took his seat but maintained rod straight posture, formality not usually seen in a bar.

"I know you cannot see now," Bume said. "But you have done a good thing and I thank you for it."

"You have taught me an important lesson about leadership," Chul said. "I am unhappy with our actions, but I understand your mind. Do not fear my retribution."

"Where is the American?"

"He is coming soon." Chul stopped and emphasized the rest of his reply. "We will wait for him. I do not wish to appear underhanded."

Bume smiled. He suddenly looked more relaxed, happier than when our hero had last seen him. This bothered Chul.

"You look better. How could that be, following on our evil doings?"

Bume closed his eyes and collapsed back into the chair.

"Will you never stop? I am better because I continue my work with the mingi. You don't know how close the elders came to stopping me. There is a vendetta against me, now, so don't think I will not suffer for the sake of my cause, if that is all you care about."

An awkward silence came over the table and lifted only when CJ came through the door.

"Are we ready to find this cave?" CJ asked.

"I doubt it," Chul said. "Nevertheless, let us go."

I descended from the heavenly ether in order to personally improve the furnishings in Bume's cave of wonders. Before I led the Ethiopian to this place, I had allowed *Drosera* to decorate. The super-plant chose an unfortunate pastel and gothic theme. Behind the small, natural cave mouth in the hillside, *Drosera* went with a smattering of soft, pink stone buttresses, dozens of gargoyles with powder blue accents and mother of pearl religious iconography in every corner. Clearly these things were insufficient for heroes of Chul and CJ's stature.

I poured the totality of my monumental intellect into renovating this cave. Out went the iconography and in came white leatherette. In place of flying buttresses, tables and countertops made from the clearest glass held high bounties of soju and tropical themed shot glasses. Where before gargoyles scowled into the darkened corners of *Drosera's* cave, posters of Def Leppard and Poison held court over glimmering boom boxes, stacks of the finest parachute pants ever made and fragrant mounds of Colombia's two most famous exports. Where *Drosera* had left behind musty prayer books and a towering pulpit, I substituted classic episodes of *Miami Vice* and the spiritual works of MC Hammer. I covered the floor with thick, white carpeting and zebra striped rugs which could hardly do less than take our heroes' breath. I stocked the ivory encased refrigerator with delectable treats and installed a karaoke machine complete with a disco ball.

For the *pièce de résistance*, I called into existence a great glass plinth. I shaped each of the four legs like a seductive woman's arm. Each corner I adorned with an overturned starfish, puckering passionately at the ceiling. I covered the translucent top with tasteful pink and blue light strips. On top of it all I set out a prize so valuable as to separate drunkards from their liquor, distract children from their snot-stained computer consoles and inspire awe so deep as to silence the eternal debate as to whether Texas or Alabama has truer barbeque.

The party arrived at the legendary Hill of Fatuous Fraudulence and beheld its majesty. Dark and beautiful, the obsidian strewn HoFF's flanks swept upwards like the swollen haunches of an aging Italian beauty. An even darker depression sank into the south face and beckoned to our travel weary adventurers. Justice against my villainy—so close at hand!

CJ looked up at the mountain and sighed. His knees had not recovered from the, what shall we say, from the *sacrifice*. All his thoughts centered on swelling so strong that a joint looses all form so that it bounces against any bending. He considered the horrid crunching noises only damaged cartilage can make and shuddered. His companions did not seem to suffer in any similar way. so CJ remained silent lest they see his weakness.

Shale, obsidian and slate sloughed out from under his feet with each step as he struggled up the hill—a sort of one step forward half a step back as the ground gave way under his weight. He resorted to grabbing whichever vegetation looked strong enough to pull himself upwards. When CJ looked at his hands he saw long chlorophyll stains smeared with sweat. He wiped them on his pants and pointed at the cave entrance.

"Is this where we're going?"

"Yes," Bume said. "Go in and take your prize. I will stay here and drive you to your boat when you return."

CJ bent down and took a deep breath. Partly because the HoFF had, as your great wordsmiths say, kicked his ass, and partly because he wanted to savor his moment of victory. He looked to the side and saw Chul likewise gathering his strength. *This is where it all ends.*

Heavenly light pulsed in the darkened entranceway and beckoned to the lesser of our heroes. He stepped inside and sent his eyes to probing the darkness. A semi-translucent square glowed in the dark near Chul's shoulder.

"What's that?" CJ asked.

Chul touched it and in doing so set to work all the lighting fixtures of my amazing cave. The kitchen and posters, boom boxes and furniture emerged from the gloom. The many white accoutrements shone so brightly as to momentarily blind CJ. Chul spoke as CJ's eyes adjusted.

"This place reminds me of my army and college years. I do not recognize the musicians, but this singing machine—these carpets and the soju. I took my first sex in a place like this."

CJ had not taken his first sex in a place like this. He'd rid himself of virginity in his parents' bed during the waning hours of a high school party, intoxicated near to the point of vomiting, but it did remind him of those long, boozy nights when plumbing still seemed like an exciting new career, when the intricacies of hair spray and perfectly creased Wrangler jeans occupied him for hours on end.

My blue and pink counter-lit plinth soon pulled CJ from his reminiscing. The thing's majestic size and central location suggested the Twinkie of Destiny could not be far away. He approached with reverent steps and shoulders bowed. Up the stairs he went and, reaching the top, he looked down onto my glorious glass monument. Dead center an elegant plastic box, with a single red button, sat upon a silk handkerchief on which I'd expertly embroidered "push me."

CJ pressed his finger down and heard a click as unseen contacts met deep inside the plastic box. A blinding light shot out from each side and forced CJ to turn away. A sizzling sound emerged from behind, the faint smell of

ground beef cooking in a sea of olive oil and ground pepper, honey and soy.

CJ turned to the kitchen as the light decreased and saw
a rotund man in a red suit with oddly elegant legs. He, or
rather I, was cooking something lovely.

Welcome, gentlemen," I said. "I am so pleased that
you have made it to my little cave of wonders. I
should congratulate you on overcoming so many ob-
stacles, persisting through so many trials. Truly you deserve—"

"The Twinkie of Destiny?" Chul asked.

"No," I said. "Truly you deserve freshly baked pizza,
the finest reasonably priced beers and Gongju-style bibimbap! Please, take a seat. It is not often mere humans
dine courtesy of divine cookery, particularly when those
humans are not particularly bright or exceptional or, indeed, sexy. But we should not dwell on those unpleasant
realities surrounding your silly little lives. Let us instead
eat."

Chul sat cross legged upon my fabulous zebra rug
and CJ bent against his aching joints just far enough to
collapse onto one of my fastidiously white couches. I ignored their accusatory gazes and suspicious glances. For
CJ, I presented Pizza Margherita, crisp and delectable,
dripping with savory sour juices and creamy mozzarella.
For Chul I set forth a hot stone bowl, filled with carefully
cured Korean beef, the finest fish roe, diced carrot and cu-
cumber, fermented fern, savory pepper sauce and white
rice slowly caramelizing against the scalding dishware.
Neither man touched that which I'd specifically designed
to tempt him and, guessing the root of their evidently

considerable angst, I quickly moved to soothe their troubled minds.

"You are struggling with the death of that boy, aren't you?"

CJ answered before Chul had a chance and startled me. I could hardly contain my surprise on finding a multinational enterprise in which the American speaks most!

"You made us kill that kid," he said. "You—goddamnit you put us in an unnatural situation. Decisions are supposed to be clearer than this. How many times, really, do we need to choose between bad and worse without a third option? You made it this way."

I smiled but did not answer. I thus created a conversational void I hoped Chul would fill. He did not disappoint me.

"CJ, he is a torturer. The God of Potency has tortured our nations and is not satisfied. Now he tortures us with unnecessary sacrifices. The sooner we rid the world of him, the greater our happiness."

"Did you expect the honor of your nations to come without a price?" I asked. "Surely you are not so stupid as to assume the honor of *any* nation exists without suppression of outrage, without the glorification of naked power and the uplifting of bloodshed. Surely you are not so naïve as to believe your sacrifice unusual. Surely you are not so ignorant of your own species' history as to suggest good men and women can do great deeds without also doing destruction, without doing injury to at least someone. If you two really are that naïve, ignorant and stupid then I have taught you a valuable lesson, gentlemen. If you are not, then please, put on your big boy pants."

I paused to check Chul's bibimbap and crumble a block of feta cheese over CJ's pizza.

"I have simply shown you a very small example of the sacrifice every polity must make. Furthermore, I do not at all accept your protestations of outrage. I'm sure that what actually bothers you about the boy's demise rests solely with the TV editing, geographic distance and death by proxy you have grown accustomed to—and which I removed. Do not pretend you would have cared about his death had you not been compelled to watch. Your empathy and morals, it seems, have severely limited range. Even more so when there are national allegiances to consider."

CJ took a bite from his pizza. Chul, who had thought something very similar earlier in this chapter, pushed aside his doubts and continued the indictment against me.

"There is no reason we had to kill that boy," he said.

"Sure there is. Bume cannot save many if he does not sacrifice a few. You know this. I merely relieved you of your illusions, removed your obfuscating innocence."

"His country is broken," Chul said. "Why have you chosen to humiliate our countries instead of fixing his?"

"Oh, but I am fixing countries."

Chul's anger grew.

"You fix Korea by memorializing and glorifying an entire race of rapists? You fix Korea by lifting up the most brutal dog-fuckers this world has seen? And you do it in the same country those Japanese nearly destroyed?!"

I laughed.

"You misunderstand me, Mr. Choi. I did not dishonor Seoul to strengthen or glorify the bond Japanese people enjoy with their history. I did it to challenge the connection you feel with Korea. CJ, I would extend the same observation to you. Do you really think I mock the site of your wife's death because I wish to glorify al Qaeda?"

Chul couldn't speak and I continued by addressing both of our heroes and setting an elegant notebook on the plinth.

"You must imagine that the New World Trade Center's lighting arrangement and Seoul's ambience are the stakes in our little game, but it is not so. I have arranged these trifles because I want something much more precious.

"I want your ideals, gentlemen. I want to take away the nebulous, unexamined nonsense you call your humanity. I want to repossess the identities you've stolen from those long dead and, one way or the other, I *will* take my prize."

I patted the notebook.

"But enough of this dreary, serious talk. This cave, I'm afraid, is not the end of your journey. Go next to China. I have included all the necessary information here. In the mean time, eat up."

Belly full and tired from the trip back to the Gunham, CJ turned to Chul and asked a question extremely natural, overwhelmingly obvious.

"Did you understand any of that?"

Chul took a moment before answering.

"I do not know. I believe—I am sure that he intends to break us."

A Search for Human Flesh

It is the desperate moment when we discover that this empire, which had seemed to us the sum of all wonders, is an endless, formless ruin, that corruption's gangrene has spread too far to be healed by our scepter, that the triumph over enemy sovereigns has made us the heirs of their long undoing.

- Italo Calvino

Chapter Thirty Seven

129 Days After

Why the hell did he send us to Harbin?" CJ asked. "I don't see anything special here. Do you?"

Chul said no but, really, this northeastern Chinese city seemed almost like home after so many months floating in the sea, walking the cowboy and urchin filled streets of San Francisco and the blood stained dirt paths of East Africa. That they'd made initial landfall in the North Korean port of Sunbong—thanks to the largess of Mongolian investors, Sunbong boasted an entire paved road!—had certainly added to this feeling. In addition, Chul had only spoken his mother tongue over the phone since *Drosera* made a snack of Hwang Nara. Granted, the Northerners spoke weird Korean, to say nothing of the Sino-Koreans living in northern Manchuria, but it was better than using English all the time. *Damn those illitating riquid consonants.*

"I've never seen so many Asians in one place before," CJ said.

Chul ignored him. The landscape, too, reminded him of home. Blocky, 15-story apartment buildings rising without warning from acres of flat and not terribly pro-

ductive farmland, white and identical, with quaint almost
Victorian style roofs covering their elevator hoists. Re-
freshingly vertical, especially after seeing the way Americans waste all their space on parking lots. The cold that,
thanks to ample humidity, bit far harder than its tempera-
ture would indicate, flat little buildings on the side of the
road where stinky people made stinky things. He, in a
moment of absent mindedness, reached for the keys to
his Ssangyong Chairman luxury sedan back home.

"Everybody looks gay," CJ said.

Chul refused to dignify that with a response and continued in silence. Architecture and climate aside, perhaps the single biggest reason this place felt like home
revolved around a phone call he'd made three weeks before.

M y son, where are you these days?"
    *"I must remain in Kilchu. My unit is to care for
the nuclear facility. I spend so much time translating for
Americans I could die."*

"I only translate for one."

*"You have received many blessings. The Katusas for-
ward every request for information the Americans have.
I get a dictionary-sized stack of inquiries every day. How
many times can they ask about terrorists?"*

"I was a Katusa before you were born."

"I know."

"..."

"Father, why did you call me?"

"I only wished to speak with you."

"I do not believe you."

*" Alright, it is this. I am not so sure as I was before.
But I am old and change does not come easily to me. You*

are younger and might bend with the winds of change. I will break…"

"*It is thus.*"

"*Maybe you did not hear. I am losing my certainty.*"

"*Good.*"

"*What will I have if not certainty?*"

"*Lots of things. Where are you, father?*"

"*The Indian Ocean, near to Sri Lanka. But I will be within convenient distance of you soon. The God of Potency has sent us to Harbin, in Manchuria.*"

"*I have free time in three weeks. Would you like me to come to Harbin? I can bring mother.*"

"*You come, but do not trouble mother.*"

"*Who will babysit your American goldfish turd?*"

"*Hmm. You are wise for one with such poor taste in music. Bring mother and tell her my goldfish turd needs help for his aching body. That should occupy him for as long as we need.*"

"*I will see you in three weeks in Harbin?*"

"*Yes.*"

Click. Beep-beep-beep.

Our heroes, after three weeks, left the boat and as soon as they'd left the dock, Chul motioned towards a squat, smiling woman. He maintained his customary stone-faced stoicism even when CJ turned to him, raised his eyebrows and generally took on the affect of a frightened cat. *What the hell does he have planned for me?* CJ thought.

"I want you to meet my wife," Chul said. "She is very excited to make your acquaintance."

"반갑습니다," Mr. Choi said, bowing very shortly and turning to her family and clapping. "진짜 미국인이다!"

Mrs. Choi blushed and covered her mouth with her hands. CJ had no idea what the hell she'd just said and looked to Chul for translation.

"She says she is very happy to meet you," Chul said. "She has never spoken to a real American before."

CJ attempted to combine the traditional Western greeting, a wave, with the traditional Eastern greeting, a bow. This resulted in his looking very much like a back pain sufferer attempting to heil Hitler. Chul motioned to the young man on his right.

"This is my son, Min-sung."

"My pather talks about you bery much," Min-sung said, his accent rendering "th" as "s," "v" as "b" and "f" as a sort of mangled "p" sound. "It is nice to meet you in person."

CJ bowed unnaturally to them both and said that he, likewise, was happy to make the Choi family's acquaintance. Mrs. Choi spoke very slowly as she continued, evidently hoping the power of enunciation alone could open the mysteries of the Korean language to CJ.

"시재 씨 몸이 많이 아파서 목욕탕과 한의원에 같이 갈께."

At this point Mrs. Choi forgot about the power of enunciation and the words flowed from her mouth like the currents of a flood gorged mountain stream.

"그 다음에 한국식 피자 같이 먹어요. 헐, 콧수염이 엄청 못 생겼어. 미용실에 꼭 가야 되. 여보, 언제까지 계세요? 여덟 씨까지? 그래."

Chul nodded and stifled the tiny hint of what seemed to be a smile creeping over the corner of his mouth. He translated for CJ thusly.

"My wife would like to take you to see some—some of the things in Harbin's Koreatown," Chul said. "She hopes you will enjoy it very much."

Mrs. Choi turned to CJ and, with a great deal of enthusiasm, nodded her agreement. She then used exactly half of her English vocabulary in conjunction with a brushing away sort of gesture.

"Go," she said. "Go."

He obeyed with but one panicky glance back to the greater of our heroes. Chul smiled and offered these words of encouragement.

"My *sarangsurowoon anney* will take care of you. She is very attentive. Go, enjoy your recreation time."

When they had gone out of earshot, Chul switched from English to Korean, turned to Min-sung and offered to buy lunch. Min-sung agreed and the Choi men walked to the nearest stir-fry specialist.

The restaurant was, compared to what Min-sung had grown used to in Kilchu, the height of luxury. Wooden tables with varnish half a centimeter thick, aquariums full of clownfish, puffers, pink and green gobies and even a ringed octopus. The prospect of eating a spicy, fried mix of fresh snow peas, tofu, eggplant and beef made Min-sung's mouth water. *It is not cafeteria food!*

Chul took a seat opposite him and asked what sort of intoxicant the young man would prefer.

"I will take beer."

Soon a great variety of foods, red and chunky and smelling of spice, brown and smooth and drowning in sauce, all savory and delicious, emerged from the kitchen and steamed before them. Min-sung took something that looked like duck and set it upon a bed of rice and went merrily about its destruction. Chul laughed and asked for another bowl so they would have a place to put the bones.

"I see this meal pleases you?" Chul asked. "Do not eat too quickly. It would damage my dignity past the point of repair should I be forced to perform mouth to mouth resuscitation on you."

Min-sung smiled and almost laughed. *He's making a joke?* The younger man shook his head a little bit. If anything, he'd expected Chul's chronic self-righteousness to worsen on a voyage to save Korea's honor. *Who would guess chasing all over the globe mellows my father?* Min-sung slowed down on the delectation and smiled again.

"What have you done since I saw you last?" Chul asked. "Soldiering could not have taken all your time."

"Nothing to of note," Min-sung said. "My life is not interesting."

Chul didn't appear to believe that.

"But you are a young man. Do you not dance in the nightclubs and drink alcohol with your army friends?"

"I do not like nightclubs. We go to the *noraebangs* on base and do playing with the beer-girls, but this is nothing of importance. I do not even go to the *noraebang* often these days."

Chul smiled and answered with a distressingly on-target question.

"So you have a girlfriend?"

Min-sung said nothing.

"You do have a girlfriend! Tell me about her. I must know, does she have double eyelids? Does her nose have a high bridge? Does she have a V-line jaw bone and shapely hips? You are a handsome boy, she must have double eyelids."

If only it were single eyelids and small hips that made me reluctant to discuss her with you, Min-sung thought. He grimaced and salvaged what he could.

"She has a nice V-line and she is very kind."

"Have you done fucking with her?" Chul asked.

Min-sung was used to such forwardness in his father, indeed in older Korean men generally, so while he did not particularly want to answer the question, he was also far from surprised at hearing it.

"No."

"So she is a heavy Christian?"

"No, she is Buddhist," Min-sung said. "Religion has not prevented us from doing fucking. It is because—it is different."

Chul leaned back and smirked.

"Have you grown shy, my flower?"

This stung Min-sung more than it should have, indeed far more than Chul had likely intended. *Heewon is special!* He glared at his father and did not answer.

"I am only joking, Min-sungah. If you do not want to talk about her, I will not force you."

Min-sung skipped a beat as he considered the answer. He picked up a bone and twirled it on greasy finger tips. This vaguely disturbed Min-sung and he dabbed his hands onto the cloth napkins to remove the pollution.

"I liked her before I lusted for her," he said. "That is not the usual way for me."

"I do not see the difficulty," Chul said. "If she meets the standard of lust take her to a motel and enjoy yourself. If she meets both standards, buy her chocolate afterwards."

"That would not feel right."

"It would feel like fucking—is she fat?"

Min-sung said nothing.

"That is okay, if she is fat but you like her, it will be alright. Fat women will often perform acts their skinny sisters will not—"

"Must you make everything a vulgarity?"

"I had a fat woman who would consent to almost anything. One time we—"

"Father, I do not wish to know."

Chul stopped smiling and said that he understood. Min-sung responded with a remark the stupidity of which became clear as soon as it had passed the threshold of his lips.

"It would feel like getting away with a crime if I were to seduce her now. I—I do not wish to cheat Heewon. I cannot believe I said that to you."

Chul sucked his chin back into his neck and raised his eyebrows.

"It is no crime to do fucking with the one you love."

Min-sung, with reluctance and no motive beyond fostering the odd honesty with which he and Chul had conversed recently, shot a poison-tipped question straight into his father's heart.

"How would you know?"

"I," Chul stopped and cringed like one shipwrecked midway between the barren island of shame and the pitiless cliffs of shock. "I would not know."

"I am sorry, that was cruel."

"It was true," Chul said. "I have underestimated your mind, it seems."

"I love you and mother and—"

"But you do not want to live as we do?"

"It is thus," Min-sung said.

"I am proud of you, my son. I admire your finding of a separate path. That takes courage, I think."

Chul paid the bill and led his son away to a terrace where they might drink tea and look over what, six months hence, would rise into a city of ice and light. On this day, however, the summer heat warped the daylight and created little thermals on which to buffer the flying insects.

"The port master tells me they build an entire city from ice here, each winter," Chul said. "Directly in front of us, they make a miniature Great Wall from clear blocks of ice and set green lights aglow within. Beyond the wall and to the left, they erect a blue and green Parthenon and a Space Needle filled with translucent pink and blue, red and yellow. I am sad we did not come in the winter."

"To come in winter would amaze my mind," Min-sung said. "Particularly after my time in the former North Korea. In a place like this, it is obvious people value themselves. In Kilchu I see how disposable life can become. It sickens me."

Chul thought of the skinny boy bleeding into Ethiopia's sucking dust and cringed. The matter of human worth had, understandably, taken a prominent place on his list of interests, neuroses and shames. He urged that his son should continue.

"In what way did you see disposable lives?"

"There are many I—how shall I say?" Min-sung asked. "It is a matter of perspective, I think. In one sense, our countrymen knew the enemy would kill a certain percentage of draftees and they sent us here anyway. One could even say you sent me here to die by your voting. This is a mild example, though. It is right young men should die first."

Chul, before he thought it through, liked his son's con-clusion. *If anyone had to die, that older Ethiopian boy was the natural choice.* However, the pitiless cold with which Min-sung, by implication, labeled himself an acceptable loss disturbed our hero. Chul rubbed his legs and bit his tongue.

"I have come to know a few of those who used to main-tain the Kilchu nuclear facility," Min-sung said. "None of them had proper protection from the radioactivity, not even the colonels. But they were lucky compared to the prisoners. When someone needed to fix a leak or go into a contaminated hole, my predecessors would pluck one of the children from a labor camp. They could always get another. It makes me question, I do not know, it does not seem like the world—once you go beyond the laws and proclamations and religions that are changing all the time anyway—it seems like the universe does not care if we live or die."

Chul nodded and replied to his son.

"I have thought a great deal about sacrifice since I left Ethiopia. I think one cannot lead without destroying oth-ers. Because of this I am afraid."

"Do you think another will sacrifice you, Father?" Min-sung asked. "You are middle aged and prosperous. You are worth more than me; indeed you are worth more than most people and so should not worry."

Chul could hardly bear to look upon his son in such a light. *In what poison soil had Min-sung grown so cynical? How could he so brutally cast aside his own innate worth for the banker's calculation? We are human, we are special, we are worth—we are worth more than a black-skinned teenager.* And yet this was not all that troubled our hero. The source of his fear demanded explanation.

"I am afraid it is I who will sacrifice others," Chul said. "I set out upon this journey willing to suffer. I wanted to sacrifice of myself for the sake of our nation. But I fear I will continue on in comfort and let ones like you suffer in my place. Indeed, I fear my own sacrificing will amount to nothing."

Min-sung cocked his head a few degrees to the left.

"I suspect there is some particular sacrifice that troubles you."

Chul restated for emphasis.

"I wanted to be the one to sacrifice."

"You do not have to tell me," Min-sung said. "I only thought it was something you wished to discuss."

"I have succeeded in tracking the Potency God's thing—I do not want to say its silly name—this far and I have given up almost nothing. Leisure time, some of my comfortable moral assumptions, perhaps, but these are nothing. That boy in Africa, he paid for the blessings I have received. Even the conspiracy theorists—have I earned nothing?"

"What noise is this?" Min-sung asked. "The boy in Africa?"

"The one I shot."

"Fuck me, you shot someone?"

"He could not have been even as old as you are now." Chul tasted defeat with each word. "He died because, because justice had also died."

"Father, please, why did you shoot a *heukin*?"

"I had to. I did not want to, but neither my American nor the Ethiopian had the courage to dirty their hands. Do not blame them, though. I believe my 'courage' has already done far more evil than good."

Min-sung clearly wanted more details and, with cunning beyond his years, used silence as a lever to pry at his father's secrets. Finally our hero could stand no more and spoke thus.

"The God of Potency gave a man called Bume secret knowledge regarding the Twinkie. Bume would not give us this knowledge until we settled his tribe's vendetta."

"So you settled a feud for a tribal enforcer?" Min-sung asked. "And you did not even get what you seek in return?"

"It is not so easy to dismiss Bume for a gangster or evil man. He at least suffers for his evil, far more than I."

"I think you should give up this quest. The Potency God toys with your spirit and corrupts your mind."

Chul found himself in unfamiliar territory. How many times had he, strong and sure, dismissed the complexities of life in favor of clarity? How many times had he cut through the tangles of nuance with the sharp blade of conviction?

"Bume did not wish to continue his tribe's feud," he said. "He did what he thought necessary to protect the greater good. His people lay waste many children. They do so because they believe in magical curses. Bume removes those children before the superstitious elders harm them. The tribesmen would not let him continue unless he killed a rival. I performed the act in his stead."

Min-sung opened his mouth to speak but seemed to think better of it. Chul continued.

"And so you see how I came to lose my certainty."

"I do see. With what have you replaced certainty?"

"Questions," Chul said. "A million questions. This frightens me, I feel like I am once more a child lost and uncomprehending."

"You have made a difficult decision, father. These things are necessary, I think."

"It was senseless, Min-sungah. The tribes kill the children for things the children cannot control, things they were simply born into. Bume partakes in the feuds because that is the tradition of his people, a tradition he was born into. That boy died at my hand because he was born into a rival tribe. All of this death, all of it meaningless, all of it the accident of birth."

Min-sung answered.

"Are you not forgetting your own accidents?"

"I do not follow."

"I have thought about our conversation in Ddang-Ggeut Village," Min-sung said. "You spoke to me of our ancestors toiling against the difficult Korean land. You inspired me with awe at their determination and labors."

"It is true we live as we do because of a hundred Korean generations' exertions, though I do not understand why you have mentioned this now."

"Does fate give us only evil things?" Min-sung asked. "How much luck that we have lived in a time and place where the people can understand writing and take antibiotics?"

"So you think everything is coincidence?"

"No, I do not think so, though, maybe, I do not know. That is not important. I was thinking that your *heukin* earned his death no more than I earned my blood type. These categories, we are born and we get them automatically. I do not like the conclusion to which this brings me."

"What did you conclude?"

"That of everything we will ever become," Min-sung said. "Most is determined at birth."

"This is very depressing."

"It is. Let us talk of something else."

Chul picked up his tea and took a sip. The leaves had brewed for too long and left the drink bitter and unpleasant. He dumped the contents over the terrace railing.

"I thought of something hopeful," Min-sung. "It may not be true, but I think it will help you with the matter of sacrifices."

"I would like to hear it."

"I do not think you will need to settle all your accounts with suffering. I am sure you will need sacrifice so long as you live, but there are other means to success. I am certain you might find them."

"That is comforting. Thank you, son."

Chapter Thirty Eight

130 Days After

Chul woke to the sound of a violently closed refriger-ator door. It could have been Min-sung, wandering the *Gunham* for a late night snack, perhaps Mrs. Choi and CJ returning from their litany of traditional Oriental healing rituals. Our hero turned over and wrapped the blankets tight around his shoulders. He was near to un-consciousness when his wife's small, freshly manicured hand ran up inside his shirt and settled over his scapula. Smoothed fingernails drug lightly over his skin.

"CJ wants to speak with you," Mrs. Choi said.

Chul was going to suggest they do something more than back scratching before Mrs. Choi turned on the TV. Our hero knew his powers of seduction to pale before the mighty allure of "Queen Seon Deok." He rolled out of bed before answering his wife.

"What does he need?"

She did technically turn her head to answer him, but her eyes remained locked on the Queen's resplendent tower of hair.

"How should I know?"

Chul stood up, tucked his chubby under the waistband of his sweat pants and walked into the kitchen. CJ sat next to the table, an unopened beer before him, hugging his elbows and smiling vacantly. A combination of horror and 'what the hell' you'd expect from seeing a giant space flea dance the tango with Serena Williams' severed head or waking up to discover the striking likeness of an elderly Leonard Nimoy branded onto one's breast.

"Did my wife take you to the traditional doctor?"

"Yeah man, she took me to the doctor and I drank this stuff made from deer horns and it was kind of weird but, you know, that's okay but the thing that really—"

"Did she teach you how to burn herbs and spices over the aching joints in your body?"

"That stuff that smells like weed?"

"What is weed?"

"Never mind. She had me light these little sticks on fire and that was fine but—"

"Did you enjoy the traditional chicken and ginseng soup? I see you no longer have that unkempt beard."

"Man, the soup was fine. I don't give a damn about the fucking soup. She took me to this place where they, like, I don't even know what to say, they sort of *rubbed* me."

"Ah, the *mogyoketang*," Chul said. "They removed the layers of dead skin dirtying you."

"Everybody was naked."

"Of course. You are shy?"

"Yeah, I'm a little shy, but that's not why I had a problem. If it was just walking around naked with a bunch of other guys I could handle it but—"

Chul resisted the urge to laugh.

"Please, start from the beginning."

"Okay, so I sat down in this bath and one of the guys working there made this 'follow me' sort of gesture. So I did because I think I'm doing something wrong and because I'm trying not to make a scene, which is kind of stupid since I'm butt ass naked and the only white guy for miles."

"I know this feeling from Africa," Chul said. "It is unnerving when the natives stare. I include myself in suffering from this discomfort."

"Yeah?" CJ asked. "I honestly didn't mind the attention. But damn it Chul, stop interrupting. So I go to this table thing and the guy starts scrubbing my lower legs and that kind of feels good."

Chul nearly interrupted again but stopped when CJ gave him the international sign for "zip it."

"Then he starts scrubbing my knees and getting all that weed stuff off from before and that feels really nice so I kind of relaxed. I, you know, laid my head back and closed my eyes. And so I'm not really paying attention and the guy just grabs my nuts and lifts them up and starts scrubbing."

Chul maintained his silence through the mighty exertion of willpower. The muscles holding his mouth straight and eyes open strained even harder as CJ shuddered once, twice, three times.

"Have you ever been so surprised you can't move? It was like somebody paralyzed me for two minutes solid. And this guy acts like it's the most normal thing in the world. The really crazy thing is I'm sitting there and I just kept thinking to myself, 'that man who scrubs my nuts has got to have the worst job in the history of earth.'"

Chul could not help himself.

"Are you not invigorated?"

"I feel violated."

"Violated, yes, but invigorated as well?"

They stared at each other in silence for a moment and then a moment longer.

"You set this up, didn't you?" CJ said.

Chul smiled and did not answer. Mrs. Choi emerged from the bedroom—it must have been a commercial break—and bowed to CJ. She clapped her hands and smiled, looking from Chul to CJ and back as she spoke.

"정말 재미 있었소," she said. "CJ씨는 즐겨 드셨어요?"

CJ grit his teeth and slunk back into the chair. Chul smiled and translated for his companion.

"My wife wishes to express her admiration for your open mindedness and invite you for further adventures in Harbin's Koreatown. She will be very disappointed if you decline."

"I hate you," CJ said. "I hate you like poison."

Chul took on what the great poets of your generation aptly call the "shit-eating grin" and translated, in a manner, for his wife.

"CJ 가 즐겁게 많이 드셨어. 도와주셔서 고마워, 여보"

"What did you tell her?" CJ asked.

"I said you enjoyed the day a great deal and that you wish to try acupuncture."

"I want to hurt you."

"Think of the good stories this will allow you tell, later in life when you are an old man, surrounded by your grandchildren and in the company of your daughter."

"I'm going to punk you so hard," CJ said. "You dirty, rotten son of a bitch."

"What does 'punk you' mean?"

"Oh, you will know it when you see it."

Mrs. Choi smiled at CJ and returned to the bedroom. Chul laughed and explained his true mind.

"I did not think they would scrub you," he said. "Your experience has been more authentic than I intended. Truly, no more than 30% of mokyoketangs do that these days. And I did not actually tell her you are going to the acupuncturist, only that you enjoyed your day."

"I'm still going to punk you."

CJ skipped several beats.

"By the way, I found this in my wallet after the horror in the spa."

"A floppy disk?" Chul asked.

CJ slapped it against the heel of his palm and sent a thin cloud of dust into the air.

"I know, I haven't used one in years. It was wrapped in this paper with all these numbers. They don't look random, but I have no idea what they're for."

"Does this have significance?" Chul asked. CJ didn't know.

"I suppose we will need to go looking for computer stores tomorrow," Chul said. "In the mean time, I wish you an *invigorating* night's sleep."

(For the virtue of using scrotum treatments as a ritual of male bonding, I bless Choi Chul with an aggressive Internet admirer possessed of a massive Cupie Doll collection, an assortment of rashes and a deep, abiding fondness for nude self-portraiture.)

Chul, Min-sung and CJ set off into Harbin's grimy suburbs—the sort of place where old infrastructure crumbles under the weight of modern commerce—in search of a computer expert who could decipher the mysteries of the floppy disk. The towering Electronics Paradise didn't look promising, filled as it was with counterfeit Apple products and disposable MP3 players. They pressed on and came to a dirt and asphalt alley wherein petrochemicals bubbled up through the mud and slickened the heroic shoes. A dark little computer repair store rose above the pollutants on a foundation of cracked concrete. Chul turned sideways and squeezed through a small pathway left between piles of broken computer waste. He knocked twice before an old Korean man opened the door.

"Yeah? Go in," the store owner said in Korean.

"Thank you, older brother," Chul said. "But we need only to know if you can help us read this floppy disk. We no longer have a computer capable of understanding such things."

"I have one, give it to me."

They followed the man into a yet more crowded room that, it seemed, drew its light from nothing except a single, bare incandescent bulb. Chul lifted his collar over his nose to combat the smells of soldering, electrical grease and a thousand stale cigarettes. The man pressed the floppy into an ancient computer that, now decidedly brown, was once presumably a light grey color. The disk made a solid "plunk" and set to motion some internal drive that was, from the sound, lubricated with grains of sand. Chul looked to CJ and saw him grimace. The old man turned on a newer laptop with a green, tentacled dragon graphic—or was it a plant of some sort?—and connected it with the sand trap.

"It is forty dollars and I will include a thumb drive for free," the old man said.

"That is robbery!" Chul said.

"You have insulted me grievously," the old man said. "May you never find another repairman in possession of a functioning A-drive. I will not submit to your abuse!"

"Fine, I will take my business elsewhere. Give me my floppy disk."

As the old man turned, a sudden sound like blood-thirsty wildebeests stampeding through the Himalayan mountains came from the old floppy. The disk drive burst into flames and bolts of lightning shot like tendrils from the monitor. The laptop with the dragon design writhed and shook. Plastic melted over the motherboards and disc drive and, just when it looked ready to catch fire, the dragon burst free of its moorings and hovered, shimmering with glory as my—I mean "its"—tiny wings beat the air.

"Mortal," it said. "This place is an irredeemable dump. Why have you not used the profits from your obscene markups to at least buy some air fresheners?"

Instead of answering, the old man fled. A rear door, previously unseen in the clutter, flew open and flooded the room with natural light. The dragon turned as if to follow before pausing to address our heroes.

"Search through the ashes of that sacred laptop and, in doing so, make yourselves legendary!"

It flew out the open door. The old man, cursing and yelling, ran somewhere out in the distance. Then silence followed after a single, high scream as our heroes shuddered. CJ grabbed the burnt laptop and made for the front door. Chul followed after but stopped when he saw Min-sung walk to the back. Chul emerged into the field, at his son's side, just as the plant dragon grabbed the old man by his shoulders and flew off into the clouds of coal smoke.

CJ stood on the deck of the Gunham and shook the ruined laptop. Little bits of slag and burnt plastic poured from the wreck and danced in the breeze. He wondered what the hell he was going to do with it. He imagined months repairing broken circuits and listening to mouth breathing geeks obsess over "the condition of the motherboard." Just the thought of all the techno-babble, all that unbelievably tedious computer bullshit he would surely have to learn—

"What have you found?" Chul asked.

"Not much," CJ said. "Everything is pretty well cooked. I think we're going to need someone who can do data recovery. Is Min-sung any good with computers?"

"He is expert in many computer games, but I do not think he will be of use in the case of fire damage. Perhaps we should take it inside and look more closely."

Chul pressed a recessed button to open the cabin door and stepped inside the Gunham's kitchen and dining area. A bright moon shone against the polished granite table tops and cast thin shadows on the walls. Min-sung sat along these tables drinking shots of soju. He looked over from time to time and, eventually, moved to sit beside CJ.

CJ turned on a light and looked over the computer once more. *There must be something I can do.* The plastic shroud that surrounded the keys looked like it might come off with a minimum of risk. He pressed a finger under the melted edge and lifted. Nothing. *I can't get any damned leverage.* CJ produced a small screwdriver from his Swiss Army knife and tried again. He could feel the mechanical strain building up in the shroud, the plastic bending and the retaining clips working slowly free from their holds. *Just a little bit more.* The first retaining clip popped loose, then a second then—

"Shit!"

The mangled cover broke almost exactly down the middle. CJ was about to restart the screwdriver prying when he noticed something strange. Brownish-red and textured like somebody had shaped it with a brush, denser than plastic but not quite as heavy as the metal framework. Min-sung ducked down to look inside.

"What do you think it is?" Min-sung asked.

"Some kind of ceramic, it looks like."

"That is a strange place for ceramics." Chul leaned in as well. "I think it is clay."

CJ blew ash and broken plastic from the computer and reached for a magnifying glass. *That is clay. I'll be damned.* On one of the edges he could just make out letter.

"There's some sort of message on the clay," CJ said. "I'll bet that's where our clue is. Do you want to pull this computer the rest of the way apart?"

All present agreed it best to continue with disassembly and soon four tablets, each adorned with thousands of tiny letters, emerged from the wreckage. Once properly shuffled for the correct sequence, CJ read the contents of these sacred texts aloud to Chul and Min-sung. Mrs. Choi, while within earshot, had once more fallen under Queen Seon Deok's spell and seemed unlikely to join.

B eowulf Two, Beauty Never Rests
    Laura Gillespie Fieldbinder, aka Midnight

Suddenly, Beowulf heard the portal gate suck shut wryly. He cringed cryingly with fear, tears of blood running down his cheeks. Ever since he'd taken a job as a pool boy he was scared horrifically every day. The space wives could be really moody and he cringed with fear because the space wives were fearsome and he thought that was scarily aweful. They sometimes wiped him mercilessly with their horse-wipes so long that it would make his muscled, sexy back bleed bloodily.

A spaceship with very special things on the outside and futuristic stuff inside opened and a stunningly beautiful space beauty got out insalubriously. It was...GRENDEL'S MOTHER!

Beowulf was scared because he thought she would still be all mad about how he killed Grendel back before he stopped violence and materialism and polluting the environment.

She grabbed his golden, long hair and pulled his head back sexily but angrily, too.

"I am all mad about the way that you killed Grendel," she moaned groaningly. "But I know that you stopped violence and materialism and polluting the envinronment," she said non-materialistically with peacefulness and environmental friendliness gushing everywhere. "I'll bet I could forgive you with...THE POWER OF LOVE! And by the way, I changed my name, I'm Melancholy Sirah now because it's all weird to just name yourself as the mother of some guy who is even dead now anyway."

"That's amazing, Melancholy Sirah," Beowulf retorted, amazed. "But how can I get the power of love when I was so bad and violent before?"

Mary Suzanne grabbed his short ginger Mohawk passively and pulled his head up peacefully. She kissed him tongue-ily and there was a lot of swashing noise from where their mouths were sexily exchanging spittle wetly. Her lustful lady lump surged warmly and moistly while his boy's boomerang went powerfully up achingly.

"I will help you forget your sinful past," she forgave forgetfully. "Come to my chic Manhattan penthouse and I will love you a long time, but not in a racist way."

Beowulf threw down his blood-soaked spear angrily and repented to Jesus genuflectively. The light of redemption came down heavily to him like cherry gumdrops dipped in cherry. He could feel the sins of the past lifting professionally off him and the feeling was like feeling a good, clean shower after a long time feeling dirty beause of people who smoke and pollute the environment filthily. His soul cleansed purely and brightly in forgiveness, he stretched strongly his muscled bicepts.

"Melancholy Sirah, you have redeemed me before God. Let's fornicate," he lusted purely. "I will give you another son to replace the first one and you can be happy forever."

Melancholy Sirah—blessed be thy name—grabbed his mid-length black combover and pulled his head back lustily with lots of sexiness added on. She pursed her lips like a cow's nostril and was about to kiss him wetly again when a very evil man with evil in his heart rode his wild stallion haughtily to the front gate of the space mansion. It was...HYGELAC!

"Hygelac!" Beowulf hissed, dragging out each sybillant like a sausage tube that you find on the ground but still think you can use to make more sauzages because it's really not that dirty and you don't want to waste resources wastefully like some fucking prep.

"What are thou doing here?" Hygelac sneered scoffing. "Why art thou scrubbing pools for BITCHES when thou couldst be living the American Dream?"

"I gave up materialism!" Beowulf proclaimed proudly. "I want to live a good life that is good and to be with my goddess, Melancholy Sirah!"

Melancholy Sirah—all glory and power be unto thee—wanted to support Beowulf. To show the support she wanted, she walked behind him and slid her hand sexily down his pants and between his sexy, sweaty pool-boy's ass cheeks.

"But look ye at all these material riches," Hygelac proposed possesively. "They are rich beyond your wildest imagining and they can be yours if only you pollute the environment a little bit."

The riches were monied and rich and Beowulf thought hopefully about all the things he could buy beautifully for Melancholy Sirah—Peace Be Upon Her—to show clearly the true and deep love they had developed deeply in the last ten long minutes. It had to be love! Why else would Beowulf allow her to finger bang him in public? He's not a perve, you sicko, he totally loves her.

"Don't do it," Melancholy Sirah inserted surprisingly. "He is only offering you those riches because he knows that the power of our love will distoy them all, the bad guys."

"It's just one aerosole can," Hygelac sprayed sputteringly. "Point it at the ozone and say 'suck on this, greenhouse gasses!' Do this and then I shall give you all the unimaginable wealth I hath here on my wild stallion and you will be rich beyond your wildest dreams. And I shalt kill Melancholy Sirah!"

A Roman storm trooper rode imperially by on his Harley Fatboy just then and Melancholy Sirah screamed "no!" loudly and Hygelac was watching her lusciously and started masticating vigorously on his horse and Beowulf was so disgusted he pulled her finger out of his love anus lubricatedly and grabbed strongly the Portugeese pirate and tore off his arm brutally and threw it fastly at Hygelac powerfully. The arm hit Hygelac in the head so hard that he died messily. The Burmese Warlord was really mad about losing his arm disgracefully and jumped off bouncily and tried to attack them violently.

Melancholy Sirah used her powers of telekenisis intelligently to read his mind though and so, since she had control of his thoughts totally, made him jump off the ocean cliffs suicidally instead. But! Lots of people came curiuosly and looked angrily and Beowulf was really scared badly again so he and Melancholy Sirah stabbed them all in the face funnily and ran really fast quickly to pick up all the riches efficiently and put them on the motorcycle happily.

Vampires attacked hungrily and Beowulf revved the Harley's engine loudly so that a cloud of smoke made their stupid penta-gram-shaped eyes water bloodily and peeled out all manly and they rode triumphantly all the way to the Parthenon of Rome where lions ate all those Christians back in olden times martyrily. They got off satisfiedly and a lady with Egyptian eyes just like Cleopatra stood powerfully in front of a hotel. It was...CLEO-PATRA!

"Hi," Cleopatra greeted.

"Hello," Beowulf pleasantried.

They went into the hotel directly and got to the presidential suite in the Bellagio sexily. The Cuban themed frontroom had jungle cats and an elephant. The dining room had Theodore Roosevelt riding a pony masculinely. The bedroom had beds with condoms but they didn't need to use those because Melancholy needed to replace Grendel.

"It's time to commence with the lactation of my phallus," Be-owulf was also a scientist and knew how to use scientific words like that scientifically. "Give me head, in layman's terms!" He laid out headily.

Melancholy Sirah dropped harshly to her knees and used her telepathy lustfully to tear off Beowulf's pool boy shorts rippingly. His quivering man-missile stood ready to plunder her mouth like a true Scottsman. She moaned like a thousand moaning walrus bulls and bit down on his throbbing lust snake. Melancholy Sirah chewed it gently like leathery gum as Beowulf reached his climax.

"That was the best ever," he ejaculated satisfactorally. "Let's do some real sex, not just this childish game."

Melancholy Sirah used her levitation to incinerate her black leather bra and lacy panties hotly, revealing a chain-mail g-string and nothing else nudely against her sexy body. Her elegant, floral fun bags bounced like hamsters and her enormous, cavernous va-gina beckoned Beowulf passively like an impact crator back on the moon next to Melancholy Sirah's space mansion back where he'd been working as a pool boy only hours before.

He stuck his car keys into her ignition and started her engine. He swished his candy cane around her Mrs. Claus' workshop like an army of Christmas Elves. The seeds of conception exploded fertily from his man-spoon and sent 43 huge gametes powering slitheringly into her bulberethral tubes, hunting pro-creatively for lady-eggs like old people for the cross word.

They lived happily ever after, then Strider and Gandalf came in and

I am glad it has finished," Chul said. "I cannot decide whether I more want to vomit or laugh. And my IQ, I am sure it is lower now."

"Because my English is weak," Min-sung said. "I am frustrated when I cannot understand all of a person's English speaking. I think I should feel lucky in this case instead."

"Personally," CJ said. "I thought the bit about the thousand bull walruses and moaning lust snakes was kind of erotic."

"This is your true feeling?" Chul asked.

"No. Hell no. My opinion of celibacy has never been higher."

"Then you should not lie," Chul said.

"It's sarcasm," CJ said.

"You should not use sarcasm. It is deceptive."

"Fine, how the hell are we going to use this to find the Twinkie of Destiny?" CJ asked.

Everyone fell silent for a moment until Min-sung came up with an idea.

"Show me the numbers on that paper you received."

CJ fished the crumpled note from his wallet and revealed the following. Min-sung spread it out and adjusted the light so all could see.

121-16, 225-10, 361-11, 625-9, 2500-9, 3721-10, 4225-11, 4624-15, 5476-17, 7744-10, 19881-12, 38809-16, 49284-17, 75625-11, 84681-10, 88804-9, 90000-10, 90000-13, 90000-14, 99225-17, 101761-9, 106276-11, 117649-12, 126736-9, 131044-17, 131044-20, 149769-10, 178929-19, 181476-14, 184900-16, 194481-12, 200704-10, 228484-9, 263169-11, 267289-12, 276676-11, 287296-12, 321489-13, 334084-10, 335241-16, 346921-14, 360000-12, 383161-12, 400689-15, 434281-11, 444889-12, 455625-11, 458329-11, 516961-9, 518400-12, 537289-11, 543169-11, 574564-12, 589824-9, 638401-9, 640000-9, 657721-11, 659344-14, 725904-11, 734449-13, 763876-12, 793881-12, 795664-10, 797449-14, 1036324-19, 1216609-9, 1364224-16, 2005056-11

The younger man scratched his head and sucked his teeth.

"It could be a book code," he said. "Let me take this story and I will try to understand the meaning. We can speak later when I have solved this riddle."

Chapter Thirty Nine

138 Days After

In works of horror, there exists a common plot device I shall call death by common sense. Writers, directors and artists use this device because, in the large majority of horror productions, the slutty teenage girlfriends and stoned, cynical boyfriends could seemingly escape their grisly fates by just leaving the idiocy alone for a short while. Such aggressive stupidity tends to result in unsympathetic victims, who in turn tend to populate films, books or comics remembered more for their unintentional comedy than their scariness. To avert this problem, the creators often insert a character whose job it is to make an intelligent suggestion and then die immediately as a result thereof.

We can invent an example and call him Max. Max will notice that the psycho killer is out to murder them all. He who, alone among his companions has not been smoking marijuana or having sex with a detestable skank fond of crushing kittens and opposing cancer research in her spare time, suggests that, instead of screaming, splitting into small groups and abandoning the easily defended homestead in favor of the dark woods, the group should instead stay together and use the phones to call for help.

Max thus presents the horror maker with the solution to their unlikeable victim quandary. Remember, the artist producing said work of horror needs dumb characters in order to provide a steady stream of victims for his villain's over elaborate and always gruesome death traps. However, if the victims are too stupid, his audience will want them to die and thus, instead of cringing and screaming when one of the cynical boyfriends gets run over by a demonically possessed lawn mower, they point and laugh instead. The artist solves this problem with Max's demise. If the phones carry a curse that summons the eat-your-face monster and Max, as a result of his sensible plan to call for help, loses his face, it proves to the audience that dip-shittery is the only option from that point forward.

I mention this as an explanation of sorts for the code I've inserted above. Book codes don't really need to be very complicated. As long as the person you are communicating with is the only one who knows which book you are using, you can simply number the page, the word and the letter, or any combination of the three. However, I decided to make the task much more complicated because Min-sung was entering dangerously Maxian territory with regard to my quest.

You see, Min-sung has continuously approached my problems and dilemmas with far too much intelligence and as such threatens to derail my entire glorious adventure. I sent this code to him for the express purpose of making him count pen strokes, define letter orders both from front to back and back to front, calculate the square roots of 69 numbers, apply all these processes to both the multiples and divisors of each of said 69 numbers, abandon that enterprise, try shuffling the order of the tablets, and decide that they actually do go front to back. I made him speculate on the statistical probability of all those nice, rounded numbers appearing at such high values and use this suspicion to divine the mathematical treatments I had applied. I caused him to spend hours wondering why the second number set was never lower than 9 and why the first seemed to follow an exponential curve while the second did not. If all this math wanking were not enough to drive him to despair, my task also forced young Min-sung to learn "Beowulf 2" more intimately than pretty much any other thing in the world. As methods of disposing of intelligent characters go, this is kinder than letting loose the eat-your-face monster, but not by much.

Min-sung's head hung down under the weight of enormous fatigue. His eyes were red and itching, his mind numb from exertion and boredom. He wanted soju but could not summon the will to leave his desk.

"You must be finished," Chul said. "It was not such a difficult matter after all!"

"It is all finished. Look on the paper and go. I must sleep."

"It is not so bad, come with us to—" Chul stopped to look at the decoded message. "This presumably Chinese man's place of business."

"I miss reading the affidavits in Kilchu," Min-sung said. "I think those will be better. I will return to duty early, I think. And mother, who will watch Queen Seon Deok with her if I go? I need to stay."

"When you feel stronger we can continue this adventure together."

Min-sung did not answer, preferring instead to bury his face in the pit of his elbow.

The business establishment in question was located outside Harbin's Korea Town and thus put our heroes in something of a linguistic bind. CJ called attention to this as they approached the business.

"I don't know a word of Chinese," he said. "How are we going to talk to this guy?"

"You are an American and thus we assume you do not know foreign languages," Chul said. "Do not worry, however. My studying is good not only in English but Chinese and Japanese too."

"Okay, alright, I guess I'll let you do the talking."

The business establishment overlooked a small garden. Floor to roof windows stretched along three sides of the interior—indeed the building seemed to have only one wall in the traditional sense. Bottles of wine protruded from holes built into the only normal wall and reflected light from a fashionably stainless kitchen wherein chefs unrolled balls of peppered beef. A bank of brand-new, expensive and professional looking computers served the silent, heavily be-sloganed customers and formed the far boundary of the business. Polished steel chairs and tan colored wooden tables dotted the floor space. Chul wandered off to find the owner and CJ took his place at one of the tables.

"I'll wait for you," he said.

CJ looked around and smiled. *Who would imagine anything in a communist country to rise this far above the level of frump?* A waiter came with the menu and CJ pointed at the picture of an ambiguous but sumptuous looking meat dish. He was more than a little excited as he considered the odds of his meal containing grilled cat or boiled musk rat.

Chul returned at this moment with a Chinese man following close behind. The owner wore a causal suit coat and brown slacks with a red beret. CJ didn't know how to say hello and so contented himself with a bow. Chul pulled out a seat and the Chinese owner sat between our heroes.

"迎到的小隔, 花男孩" Chul said. "意外被放演的 的候，我用我的橘色尿液射向."

"你说什么?" the Chinese man asked.

"你会说英文吗?" the business owner asked.

"的噪音在里?" Chul asked.

"Do you speak English?" The business owner asked in English.

"Yes," Chul said.

"Please, let us speak in English. Your Chinese is hurting my head."

Chul seemed to go out of his way to avoid looking at CJ before coughing, pounding his chest and answering in the table's one shared language.

"Certainly," Chul said. "It is better we speak so that my friend can understand in any case."

CJ picked up the fallen reigns of conversation.

"You are Wang Zeng, am I right?"

"Yes," he said. "Please tell me how I might help you. I would ask, however, that you not involve me with your companion's urine streams, regardless of their color."

"It is a poetic expression," Chul said.

Wang Zeng nodded and gestured that CJ should continue.

"I'm sure you know about the God of Potency and the Twinkie of Destiny?" CJ asked.

"The Potency *thing* has indeed made itself known to the Chinese," he said. "May he receive the just rewards of his labors."

"This sounds kind of passive aggressive," CJ said. "I don't understand why you guys are angry at the Potency God. He didn't actually do anything to you, did he?"

"Your knowledge of world affairs staggers me," Wang Zeng said. "To behold such genius—"

"Man, don't be shitty, I'm trying to understand."

"You are trying to understand? Can an American son of imperialists understand our traitors without cheering them on? Can you hide away that laugh and smile when the Potency *thing* breaks apart China in just the same manner as your grandfathers before you? I don't think it likely."

Wang Zeng stood up.

"Gentlemen, enjoy your dinners. If you will be so kind as to allow it, I should take my leave before this discussion becomes unpleasant."

"We seek the Twinkie of Destiny," Chul said. "We could use it to help you."

Wang stopped and bent at the waist. He turned slowly and forced a thin smile.

"Far be it for me to doubt your sincerity, but in any event I am sorry to say I have no particular knowledge of the Twinkie. Enjoy your food, valued customers."

Chul took his time leaving the restaurant. This was partly an act of aggression, a stinky bag of "fuck you, trying to intimidate us" for Wang Zeng's enjoyment, but it was even more from the sneaking suspicion that there had to be something in this café, something about the owner or the staff or even the building itself to provide direction. He particularly wanted to watch those people using the public computers. Something just didn't seem kosher with the way none of the customers—overwhelmingly young, male and upper middle class—could be seen browsing sports, entertainment, fashion or even email accounts. And those were awfully nice machines for the general public to use. Chul had stopped to look more carefully when he heard someone call out "older brother, come speak with me" in Korean.

A fat man of perhaps forty beckoned over his plate of mixed shellfish. A spent mussel rang out against his bowl of discarded mollusk and caused some small alarm in his companion, a similarly portly woman of similarly early middle age. The accent seemed Sino-Korean to our hero's ears.

"Please, sit and share my wine," the man said. "I cannot speak your friend's language, so say that he also would do well to share drinks with us. It seems you are lost and I would like to familiarize you with Harbin's attractions, particularly its digital attractions."

The woman stood up, smiled, and offered CJ a chair from a neighboring table which he, apparently confused, accepted without a word. Chul frowned, straightened his jacket and took the other empty seat. No one ever did get round to translating for CJ.

"A gregarious gentleman like you must make friends wherever he goes," the man said. "I am not mistaken?"

The woman had seemingly checked out of the conversation already, focusing on how to get CJ's napkins properly arranged. Chul saw this and narrowed the scope of his conversational observations, focused on but one source of threats.

"You could say such a thing. You are very generous to invite my friend and I to your table. At least let me buy wine for your enjoyment."

"Very kind of you," the man said. "But I fear, following your linguistic tour de force, it is best we not arouse the envy of those who—filled with petty ambition—wish to make you uncomfortable. In any case, it is better to discuss our business somewhere with more sunshine."

This quasi-euphemistic way of speaking, to our hero, signified several things at once. First, the fat man surely meant to imply a level of danger within the café—perhaps from Wang Zeng or, more intriguing, from the customers. Second, there would be no need to disguise his meanings if at least some of those nearby could not, in addition to Chinese and English, also understand their Korean. Last and most obvious, it strongly implied they had found whatever line of evidence I'd buried in Beowulf 2.

"I could take joy in more sunshine," Chul said. "But I would not dream of separating you from your clams."

"That we can share," he said and, raising his glass to toast. "To gregariousness!"

The couple lived in an apartment near downtown Harbin. It overlooked a hospital emergency room, three separate and very small parks and a grocery store. While comfortably middle class, these people clearly spent their money outside the home. The woman, called Ji-hye, and the man, called Jung-su, offered Chul and CJ their sofa. The two sat as Ji-hye, speaking Korean, went straight to business.

"You were clearly searching for something in the course of irritating Mr. Wang," she said. "It would be better if you ask us and leave the Chinese alone—I do not think he likes you."

"Does anybody speak English?" CJ asked.

"No, they do not. Be still and I will translate for you later," Chul said in English. He turned to his hosts and continued in Korean. "We had reason to believe objects or information of importance would be waiting for us in his café. However, we had no idea what, specifically, we should find."

"Is this some sort of espionage?" Jung-su asked.

"No, it is worse. We search for the Twinkie of Destiny."

Ji-hye pressed her husband's leg and presented an expression that very clearly meant "we should help." Jung-su nodded and addressed Chul.

"Well, I do not know what sort of things help you find the Twinkie, but I can explain the happenings in Wang Zeng's café if you wish."

"Doing so would please me very much."

CJ fiddled with an ornamental shrimp made from jade and abalone shell while Ji-hye continued her husband's line of conversation.

"Wang Zeng is, if you think of it a certain way, an advocate for justice. We do not have legitimate courts in China. We cannot go to the newspapers. If we wish to hold a villain accountable for his evil doings, we must make it thus by our own exertions."

"I do not follow your meaning," Chul said. "Perhaps if you explain in more detail."

Ji-hye and Jung-su both answered at once and, for the length of one or two syllables, their voices ran one over the other's to such an extent that our hero could understand nothing. Ji-hye apologized and smiled while Jung-su began anew.

"My wife is worried you will get the wrong opinion of Wang Zeng," he said. "She is wise to take this into consideration, given your citizenship. The Chinese's work is imperfect and, while it would not be necessary in Korea or America, the Chinese have no alternative. Please keep this in mind and do not judge him with too much harshness."

"My curiosity has grown ravenous," Chul said. "You must tell me now."

"The Chinese offers his powerful computers and stores of digital resources, free of charge, to those conducting human flesh searches," Jung-su said. "You saw just such a search while leaving his café."

"Do you speak of cannibalism?"

Ji-hye waved her hands and pursed her lips. She shot a quick look in Jung-su's direction before answering the greater of our heroes.

"My husband is over-fond of literal translations," she said. "A human flesh search is merely an attempt by Internet citizens to find and expose the personal information of an individual. Last year, Wang Zeng's netizens brought ruin to a corrupt official in Beijing. This man was fired and imprisoned for taking bribes. Wang Zeng found a drunken son of the police commissioner whose reckless driving killed a bicyclist, an adulterer who drove his wife to suicide, an idiot who made web videos complaining that earthquake coverage interfered with her favorite soap operas. All have received punishment for the crimes they otherwise would have gotten away with."

"So Wang Zeng is a vigilante?" Chul asked.

"It is thus," Jung-su said. "Though, as I said before, we do not enjoy recourse to legitimate authority in the manner of Koreans or Americans. Do not think we always approve of his human flesh searches, but they are not the product of an evil mind. They most often do good."

"For which human's flesh does he now search?" Chul asked.

Jung-su shook his head and sighed.

"This is one of those searches we do not like," he said. "They are searching for a girl. She might not even be a woman, but they think she is female. Her Internet name is 'Hairpiece.'"

Ji-hye continued.

"Hairpiece wrote a blog post saying that the separation of Tibet, Taiwan and that place with the Muslims—Jung-su, my beloved, what is that place with the Muslims who are always unhappy?"

"The Uyghur territories, sweetheart," Jung-su said.

"Ah yes, the Uyghurs. Anyway, this Hairpiece person said that losing all of these territories represented something of a blessing in disguise. If I remember correctly, she said the Chinese had, in trapping these dissatisfied minorities under state control, been begging for revolt and, at the very least, continuing the oppression of people whom the Han Chinese majority has systematically victimized. She said China would be better broken into 100 slivers and at peace than whole and fighting continuously with these minority peoples."

"This sounds reasonable," Chul said. "A mild provocation, perhaps, but surely nothing deserving of punishment."

"We would agree with you," Jung-su said. "But the Chinese are touchy about this. They feel great shame about their past, weak and carved up by the Japanese and Westerners. The Chinese believe China should never be divided, regardless of the reason. They tie it all up with the millions of people the Japanese killed during their occupation, with British opium and the Boxers, I think. No, this is not true, they mostly do not even think to question why. The government, of course, stirs up their patriotism to make things worse. This is not like Dokdo, it is not something vital. These outlying territories, they are specs of dust, but do not try saying so to a Chinese. It is utterly impossible to reason with them in such matters. It is like the Americans and their terrorists—your friend cannot understand us, right?"

Chul laughed and assured his hosts.

"My friend speaks only the tongue of his birth. Do not worry."

"I am glad to hear it," Ji-hye said. "You cannot speak reasonably to a foreigner about his own country. All their patriotism shades their perception and blinds them to the truth."

"Your words are well chosen and agreeable," Chul said. "Please do not think it rude if I change our topic of discussion. I think that if my previous dealings with the God of Potency can serve as a guide to his future actions, we should find this Hairpiece before Wang Zeng and his friends do."

"How will you do that?" Jung-su asked.

"I do not know," Chul said. "What does Wang Zeng know about this woman now?"

"He protects the details," Ji-hye said. "I am not sure how close he is to finding Hairpiece. It sometimes takes months, sometimes only a few days."

"Do you know where he keeps the detailed information?"

"We do not."

Chul clenched his jaw and nodded. *This is annoying unto death!* he thought.

"Thank you for helping. If we come across more information on Hairpiece, will you translate it for us?"

Jung-su and Ji-hye would. They sent our heroes away with a bottle of rice wine and a box of dried ginseng. When Chul took to his bed that night he was frustrated, but he had no idea the upwelling of anxiety he was going to get.

H ello Chul,
   It starts like a creeping realization that you are not alone. That's what you want, is it not? Togetherness. And now that you have it…

There's an almost touch in the night from he whom you have not invited to share your bed. It is wet and soggy and rotting and smelling like dead mice down where you are. The bricks are slippery and covered in moss—moss that has died from lack of light and become food for the slime molds. You look up and watch them pass by the opening of his hole. Who are they? What do they want? It is no more possible for you to know their motives than to see their blurry, washed out faces, but this is because you are not thinking so straight these days. They had once been your friends. Are they still friends? Some of them, more maybe. Stop being paranoid, Chul. There must be one, mustn't there?

The enemies or friends, if there are any friends (there aren't any friends, Chul, not anymore because they hate you, hate you like poison, hate you like death), pass over the hole you cannot escape. They spit near you and smile and say, "go over there (far from me, you fucking creep) and see how you like it." They say, "you should try this new way (that will at least lessen your fetid inadequacies) and see if it works for you." They pitied you, did they pity you? "I know you are having a hard time. I know these days are not easy for someone (a weak and ambitious parasite, a tapeworm of greed) like you, you, YOU!" How you hate the pity, if it even is pity. If only you could read their intentions, if only you could discern their motives. If only your eyes had not failed you.

Now you can only hear and you hear your son. Does he hate you so much he'd choose a radioactive hole over your company? Your wife, do you hear her silence, do you hear the void of her concern, the silent confirmation of "I never cared when you went missing?" What else can you hear, Chul? Whose voices whisper down your well?

It is dry and hot and bright now, in this place I have taken you. The sun blasts straight into your eyes and obscures my face. For this you are glad, for I am a man with a voice hot and violent as the earth's molten core, shoulders broad and irregular as a crow's outstretched wings, hands hard with sweat and sebaceous oils. We sit at an aluminum table roasting in the UV, burning the undersides of your forearms. You want to move them somewhere cooler but you cannot. You cannot because I own you, Chul. I own your arms and you will leave them on the aluminum, you will burn for my pleasure, because I enjoy that dull look of pain on your face, because I am kind and did not think to burn you elsewhere.

"These people," I say. "They are like books for you, are they not? They are like the instruction manuals that come with each new television. They are like the business textbooks you read in high school. But you must read them, you must understand the words. Because these people, they are so dangerous, most of them, all of them. If you do not understand, they will crush your bones until you are chalk *and blow your burnt memory over the ocean to be sub-sumed like stillborn plankton, like the ashes of the quickly forgotten grandfather."*

I stop and wait for your slow, slow mind to comprehend. Your lips become hungry leaches and bite one into the oth-er. I look on as the upper locks onto the lower with killing teeth. I watch as the bottom clung to the top with fingers like surgical hooks. You do not scream because you cannot. It is better this way.

"You are illiterate now," I say. "I've changed your books to Sanskrit. I've written your people in Chaldean. And so what can you possibly say? I take your mouth full of igno-rance and close it. You who know nothing, you who learn nothing, you who are nothing."

The people with no faces come from behind you. There is laughter and anger and contempt and affection and ha-tred so sharp it makes the air bleed. I see the whites of your eyes as you struggle. I look on as they pat you on the back (I want your money, Chul, I'm gonna take it all) and tell you to back off (you fucking disease) and ask if you need a receipt (you cocksucking tightwad).

"You are lost and alone," I say. "They are everywhere; the people you love (do you?) and hate (do they?) and work with (we call you the load when you aren't around) and it doesn't matter, Choi Chul. It doesn't matter because you are so lost nothing can ever get you back. There is only me, now."

Chul awoke and coughed hard. He coughed like he had pneumonia. His wife's arm stretched over his chest and her fingers dangled in the sheets. He quivered and withdrew from her touch and went to the kitchen where he could get something for his dry mouth. Oh god, his mouth, he felt for his lips and found nothing out of the ordinary. Chul took a glass of water and spilled most of it because of the shaking.

CJ finished listening to Chul's translation—edited to exclude anything patriotically inconvenient to an American, naturally—of the previous day's meeting. The twists and intrigues gave the lesser of our heroes an idea. *Wang Zeng must be a technophile, or he probably is, right?*

"Did they tell you where the Chinese guy lives?" CJ asked. "I'll bet we could figure out what he knows about this Hairpiece girl if we go to his house."

Chul seemed a beat slow in answering. Something ever so slightly off in his posture, something askew in his expression.

"I do not know where he is, but I can ask when I return to Ji-hye and Jung-su's home this afternoon, if you think I should. Do you think I should? I think you should say what you think I should do, it will be better that way."

CJ bunched his eyebrows, tilted his head and said "uh-huh" before continuing.

"If I were Wang Zeng, I would hide my important information on a computer in my house. It only makes sense."

"Why would he not use an online storage system?" Chul asked. "Not that I am expert in computers, I know little, but do not think me an ignoramus. I do know some and I can learn quickly enough."

Okay, right, moving on.

"I guess he could use an online service. Well, wait, no, think about it. He has those hacker wannabes in his café all day long. Would you rather hide stuff from them on the Internet or in your sock drawer behind three or four real life locks?"

Ben Garrido

"I see your point. Of course I see your point. What do you suggest?"

"We break in and rob his house."

Chul drew himself up as if preparing for an Everest excursion and not a thirty minute walk into a nice part of a nice town. CJ finally asked the question that, over the last five minutes, had become increasingly necessary.

"You okay?"

The Korean turned and walked towards his bedroom.

"I will get my coat so we can leave," Chul said.

They set off, a few hours earlier than planned, for the house of Jung-su and Ji-hye. Chul talked and CJ sat on the sofa and, before long, Wang Zeng's address followed them back to the Gunham.

(For the virtue of realizing the limits of his knowledge and embracing the ambiguity of human existence, Chul blesses himself with truly vast wisdom.)

Chapter Forty

Wang Zeng's suspiciously modest apartment building wedged in between a corner convenience store, another drab apartment building and a taxi mechanic. His actual apartment, from the information they'd gathered, seemed to be on the sixth floor. Each floor had three apartments, save the top, which had only one large suite. The first story doors were made from glass and featured electronic locks that shot metal bolts from the top of the door frame into corresponding voids in the door. An electronic keypad embedded in the glass controlled this lock. Three minutes of loitering at the convenience store and looking over shoulders told CJ that the code was 7714#. Entry would pose no problem at all, but the security camera behind it certainly would. CJ pointed at the little glass eye and nudged Chul.

"Can we sabotage the building's power supply?" Chul asked. "You work with your hands. Certainly you can cut the necessary wires."

"I'm not that good with wiring," CJ said. "And regardless, power outages draw attention. We don't need repair crews or residents poking at the fuse box." He shook his head and looked down the street. "Do you see how the buildings are really close together?"

"Yes."

CJ pointed to the apartment building immediately to the east of Wang Zeng's.

"How much taller do think that is? How far from the other wall?"

"Maybe two meters for the drop," Chul said. "The gap between the buildings is, should I guess, about a meter."

CJ cupped his chin in his hand and considered the logistics. *It might be easier to go in through that neighboring apartment, walk up to the roof and then jump down onto Wang Zeng's building. That way, there wouldn't be any record of us coming and the video won't get anything but the backs of our heads when we leave.*

"What do you think of jumping down from the roof of that other building and then going in through the roof access?"

"I suppose we should make a new plan," Chul said. "Or maybe I should ask if you truly want to continue. I am not sure I do."

"I'm not done," CJ said. "I'm nowhere near being done."

He pointed to a corner mini-mart with plastic chairs set around a yellowing plastic table. Chul acknowledged this and followed him across the street. CJ pulled up a chair while his companion remained standing.

"You are acting weird and I don't like it," CJ said. "Maybe you have no reason to stop this Potency fucker, but I do."

"My reasons for vengeance are greater than yours," Chul said. "You seek to avenge a *single* attack on your nation. It was not even a large attack. I have simply been thinking and—"

CJ could feel his inhibitions slipping. He stood up and jammed his index finger into the hard cartilage of Chul's sternum.

"You don't have the foggiest goddamn clue what you're talking about. I hope for your sake you don't understand what an asshole you're being."

Chul looked like he might bite his tongue. This surprised CJ. He expected at least some form of face-saving. He breathed out and lowered his hand right as Chul turned back and spoke.

"You need to get over it."

CJ turned so fast he could feel the centrifugal force pulling on his hair and on the looser part of his cheeks.

"Two thousand and six hundred and five people, you prick," CJ said. "Two thousand and six hundred and five people who were just trying to do their jobs when those fucking camel humpers decided to import a little of the theocratic misery I wish they'd just fucking drown in. Get over it, my ass."

"Two thousand and six hundred," Chul said. The numbers seemed to roll around inside his mouth. "That is about as many as died in the 5-18 Gwangju Massacre. Do not insult me by pretending you have heard of it."

CJ said nothing.

"Your freedom-loving, what do you say?—'men and women in uniform'—even helped our dictator to kill the people of Gwangju," Chul said. He paused for a second before continuing in a voice flat as the Utah salt pans. "9/11 was America. That is the only reason we must pretend to care. Worse things happen every year, many times in most years."

"You don't understand," CJ said. "It's different."

"It is not different," Chul said. "You need to get over it."

"Do you know how my wife died?"

Chul didn't answer and so CJ continued on.

"The terrorists killed her in that itsy bitsy little attack of no great importance that I should 'get over.' Fuck you."

Chul nodded.

"That at least makes more sense—your motives being selfish. But I wonder if you would chase around the world if some random man had killed her instead of the Arab terrorists."

CJ didn't like that "selfish motives" part, or the insinuation about Arabs, or indeed his reasons for doing any of this.

"I would," he said. "I would chase him wherever I had to."

"Really, this is your true heart?"

CJ felt doubt pressing on the edges of his anger and, following that, fear.

"You know what? I'm done with this shit."

CJ walked alone to the Gunham, embracing anonymity with each duck of the head, each lift of his collar. CJ felt like he'd gone to work naked, he'd crapped his pants or walked in on a sibling in delicto flagrante. He remembered my talk about shaking men's faith and despaired.

Chul knocked on the door to CJ's bedroom and waited for some kind of sound. A groan, stocking-clad feet and the clicking of a door lock followed soon after. CJ's eyes were red and droopy and he had dried spittle at the corner of his mouth.

"I was not entirely honest with you regarding the conversation in Jung-su and Ji-hye's house," Chul said. "I want to tell you everything in the hopes it will help you understand my mind."

"Is this an apology?" CJ asked.

"Not in the way you expect," Chul said. "Though I am sorry for the way in which I spoke, I do not believe I regret the content of what I said."

CJ let out a laugh that almost cracked from the dry heat of his cynicism.

"You sure know how to mend fences."

Chul had never repaired fences, or any type of barrier, in his life. Indeed, he could barely use the baby fencing back when Min-sung was a child. Regardless, he ignored the American's odd, incorrect and irrelevant observation in the interest of civility and continued.

"I asked them about the nature of Wang Zeng's anger," Chul said. "I asked them because I could not understand why the Chinese take so much offense at what, to you and I, is almost nothing—to lose Tibet and the other territories, I mean."

CJ yawned before answering.

"You told me about this."

"But what I did not translate are their observations about you. They did not dislike you or even distrust you, but they were worried you might be able to understand our discussion. It is because when Ji-hye tried to explain why the Chinese feel so strongly about Tibet, she compared the un-reason of their feelings to the un-reason of America. She said it is impossible to speak rationally to a Chinese about his own nation in the same way it is impossible to speak calmly to an American about terror. I have reflected on her words. It is obvious to me now that she was right."

CJ shook his head, seemingly too tired for outrage.

"You don't understand how bad 9/11 was for us, Chul. You can't relate to how I feel because you aren't an American."

"You are right," Chul said. "I cannot understand because your reactions do not make sense. I do not think anyone can understand except in the emotional way but, I also think it is impossible to understand in the emotional way without—how should I say?—losing perspective."

No answer.

"This is why I am sorry. I should have known you could not handle a reasoned discussion of your own motives regarding 9/11. That I did not take your blindnesses into account reflects a thoughtlessness and selfishness in myself."

CJ cocked his head for a second and raised one corner of his mouth.

"You guys are worse," he said. "You Koreans and your rocks out in the ocean—it's not like you are capable of reason either."

Chul surprised himself when, insulted thus, he felt only a flitting sense of intellectual curiosity. It was with a calm, quiet voice he answered.

"I suspect you are right. Go to bed. I have decided to help in the robbery after all and do not wish to suffer Chinese prison for want of sleep."

CJ shook Chul's hand, yawned again and closed the door.

Chapter Forty One

152 Days After

Chul had wanted to buy a ski mask and gloves for the break-in, but CJ prevented him by means of the following argument:

"We are going to draw tons of attention like that," he said. "It's bad enough I'm white, we don't need to look like freaks on top of that."

Chul lifted his beer from the sidewalk and swirled it.

"But what of the security cameras?" The Korean asked. "We will win no Twinkie in prison."

CJ anticipated this line of questioning and hesitated only long enough to shift his buttocks against the concrete.

"Don't turn around in the lobby. We can face away from camera the entire time and there won't be any record of us entering. We just need to look innocent."

"What if something goes wrong? They will see our faces if we do not wear a disguise."

"We can just act confused," CJ said. "White guy in a foreign country, remember? It won't be that hard to convince people I'm lost. That won't work if we dress like Batman and Robin."

Chul put on a solemn look before answering.

"I would dress like Batman, of course, and you would wear the red and green tights."

"You wish, homo."

Chul ignored this and continued on as if philosophizing at a dinner party. He went so far as to stroke the stubble on his chin.

"I think you would look very cute in green tights like one of those elves in a Disney movie."

"I'll wear a Robin costume if you wear George Clooney's bat nipples," CJ said.

"What is that?"

"Nothing," CJ said. "Don't worry about it. I don't think we should use disguises. If we're dressed normally we can just be stupid tourists if somebody sees us."

"What if Wang Zeng sees us?"

"Then we're fucked."

CJ fell silent for a moment to consider this problem. They could surveil the house for a while, become more sure of the Chinese's habits, but that would take time and they had no way of knowing how close the searchers were to getting Hairpiece. *There really is no reason we both have to go in.*

"If you stay on the roof you can watch and call me if he comes home," CJ said. "It will be easier for me to play dumb, too. You don't look like a foreigner here. And anyway, I'll bet you don't know how to pick a lock."

Chul cupped his chin once more and said "hmmm."

"We should start in the morning when it is darker."

We in the Pantheon of Deities allowed human guilt to form in a way that, upon first inspection, seems almost counter-evolutionary. Indeed, it serves almost no function for the individual other than to make him miserable, assuming of course that acting guilty doesn't get him caught in the first place.

Imagine a caveman hungering for his neighbor's leg of mastodon. In a morally normal human, the thought of stealing that delightful mastodon chaud froid causes a stress reaction. It casts eyes downward and increases muscle tension. It makes our caveman speak abruptly and generally draws suspicion from all present. In other words, it dramatically increases our caveman's odds of getting a blunt instrument across the bridge of his nose.

If the thief is lucky enough to escape with his prize, guilt strikes again. It sucks the joy from his accomplishment, sours the taste of his dinner and makes him lie to his mother. It causes him to consider returning the stolen goods and voluntarily facing "justice." Again, it makes him much more likely to receive that traumatic rhinoplasty.

Indeed, were he blessed with sociopathy, our thief would find less danger and greater reward whenever his neighbor brought home some tasty grubs *flambé*, moose tongue *ju de viande* or leaf litter *mirepoix*. It is only when considering the social nature of humanity that guilt starts to make sense. It is only when considering the survival of the group in favor of the individual that guilt begins to function in the interests of teamwork, trust and harmony.

It was thus on the eve of his first theft that CJ, believing himself the ultimate pursuer of human harmony and society, went to war with that same pro-social impulse most likely to destroy him.

CJ tapped Chul on the shoulder and motioned to the convenience store opposite Wang Zeng's house. The attendant hadn't seen them and seemed preoccupied with his cell phone. They looked right, looked left and saw no one else. *Game on,* CJ thought.

The neighboring apartment didn't have a lock or security cameras. Just a quick push against the cold glass and an accompanying squeak as the hinges cycled through their rusty tracks. Stones, coming apart at the joints and polished smooth by thousands of feet, formed a single narrow stair case. Chul went first and CJ tried to look inconspicuous. They need not have bothered as none of the residents had yet woken. They reached the top floor in silence so deep that the hum of distant air conditioners seemed omnipresent and the scrape of his own leather soles on the floor deafening. Chul tried to open the roof access door. Someone had locked it.

"I will break it open," Chul said.

The Korean stepped back and started for the door before CJ stopped him.

"Let me try a credit card."

CJ slid his American Express between the latch and door jam. There was not quite enough room to angle the card correctly and CJ had to improvise.

"Do you have a knife?"

Chul did. CJ cut a V-shaped notch in the card near its far edge. This time he was able to catch the angled side of the bolt with his notch. He smiled as the door popped open. Wind broke apart the quietude, whistling in the cracks and moaning against the air-conditioning towers. CJ put his hands against the concrete rail ringing the building's circumference and looked down on his goal. He had to jump out perhaps one meter, which did not seem like a problem. The bigger obstacle was the green algae, slick with the morning mist and covering the roof of

Wang Zeng's apartment in an ooze of varying viscosities and, presumably, multitudinous smells.

"There's a good chance I'm going to fuck my legs up jumping onto that slimy algae shit," CJ said. "You might have to follow me and to hell with the lookout if I get hurt."

Chul nodded and said nothing.

"Remember, text messages only if he comes home, no contact otherwise."

CJ first hiked up one leg, then the other, onto that narrow concrete barrier. He crouched, took a deep breath and shot out over the gap. Weightless for a moment, arms out and knees bent, his heart pounding a one-note song in his ears—then *thwack*.

He felt the impact run up his legs and into his torso where it pushed the air from his lungs. His right leg shot out in front and something popped. His left knee slammed into the concrete and his right hand slapped the algae and concrete hard enough to bruise. An obscenity, some bastard offspring of words united only by filth, slammed hard against his teeth, against the need to remain undetected. Chul spoke quietly in his direction.

"Are you hurt?"

CJ didn't answer because he really didn't know. His hand hurt the worst, but it seemed to be working. He rolled to his stomach and tested his knees—a big bruise and the sudden inability to completely straighten his left knee, but it seemed structurally intact. It was only when he tried to stand that he realized, with a nauseous certainty, exactly how screwed he was.

"I broke my foot," CJ said.

"Can you walk?"

CJ rocked back on his heel and put weight on that damaged left foot. *Damn, damn, damn.* The pain came in big, dull waves—pain he could feel in his teeth and at the base of his dick. *God this hurts!* He hyperventilated as the nerves in his temples and cheeks joined those in his foot. He was feeling light headed when the white noise of agony ceased and, in its place, a solitary emotion. Pride. He was too proud to let this beat him. This pain—just his foot, for chrissake—was no match for his manly resolve. CJ bit down hard and clenched his fists and growled into the wind. He hobbled to the mercifully unlocked roof access door on Wang Zeng's apartment building and leaned against the door jam.

"I'm gonna see this through," CJ said to Chul. "Wait there."

CJ went inside and closed the door behind him. He heard somebody on the stairs, but they sounded like they were going down. The lesser of our heroes wiped the goo and algae from his pants and tried to look as normal as possible—at least as normal as any dirty, ethnically inappropriate man hopping on one foot could be.

He made it down the first flight of stairs but stopped to rest at the first landing, two stories above Wang Zeng's apartment. *Look like you belong, look like you belong.* An apartment door opened and a Chinese woman wearing pajamas stepped out. Seeing CJ, she uttered the following:

"你受伤了吗?"

Damnit, she just saw my face, he thought. *Go away!* CJ turned abruptly and hopped down the stairs like a caveman about to get caught with stolen mastodon meat.

"嘿，你要去哪里?"

CJ ignored her and sped up his hobbling. He heard a cell phone in the background as he reached Wang Zeng's door. The dead bolt looked like trouble and CJ reached for his lock pick. The adrenaline was really flowing and this dulled his pain. He squatted so he could get a better look at the lock. *Five tumblers, brass, not very tight fit for the cylinder——five minutes max.*

The American reached to his back pocket when he noticed something between the look and door jam, or rather, a lack of something. *He didn't lock the deadbolt!*

The lock picks stayed in his pocket and the mutilated credit card came out. A quick, lubricated click of the door handle and the lesser of our heroes had his entry. He closed the door and texted Chul.

"Any news?" he wrote.

The reply came not even 15 seconds later.

"Nothing. Take all hard drives/USBs. Hurry."

CJ pocketed the phone and explored the living room. No drawers, no computers, just the remains of a rotisserie chicken, dozens of cigarette butts and a notebook which CJ stuffed in his backpack. CJ found an older laptop in the bedroom and didn't bother to separate the hard drive. He just dumped the entire thing in his satchel. The kitchen alone remained.

At first, the kitchen seemed to contain little beside empty beer cans, unwashed dishes and suspiciously stained copies of *Maxim*. Just as he turned, a bit of red caught his eye. Under the table, covered by a blanket of dust and partially hidden behind a *Men's Health* magazine, sat a desktop computer.

CJ pulled it into the center of the floor and removed the multi-tool from his belt. He'd almost gotten the cover off when he felt the phone vibrating in his pocket.

New text message: Choi Chul—You must leave. He is coming in the door. He is running.

CJ said "fuck me" under his breath and tore open the casing. He wasn't sure what was what inside and so he ripped out everything that looked even vaguely like a circuit board. He zipped up the bag, turned Wang's radio on to half volume and hobbled into the bathroom, next to the door. Maybe Wang wouldn't see him if he stayed still? Maybe he could slip out of the door unnoticed? CJ looked in the sink cabinet and saw pills, razors, a box of laxatives and spray-on deodorant—he could use that.

He heard footsteps on the landing and braced. The door opened and Wang stepped past CJ into the kitchen. The Chinese was looking at the living room table, muttering what CJ assumed were profanities. Our hero stepped out of the bathroom, tapped Wang on the shoulder and, when the Chinese turned, sprayed the deodorant into his eyes.

Wang called out like a wounded boar and fell to the floor. CJ stood back, turned up the volume on the radio and left the apartment. A wild sort of confidence came over him, a certain jauntiness with each painful one-legged hop. A friendly smile for that woman in the pajamas, a pat on the head for somebody's young son. He passed out of the first floor lobby beneath that security camera and into the street where Chul waited.

"I think we have it made," CJ said. "I really do, I mean, we got this son of a bitch." He paused a second before continuing. "Let's go before I pass out."

Chul knocked on Ji-hye and Jung-su's door and wiped his forehead. CJ needed a hospital but it seemed likely there'd be police waiting for them. Indeed, he could only pray the Chinese-Korean couple would be willing to help.

"Oh my God," Ji-hye said in English as she opened the door. She tried to continue speaking so CJ would understand but gave up after a few mangled words.

"Can you take him to a hospital far from here?" Chul asked in Korean. "Wang Zeng, if not the entire police force, will be looking for an injured white man."

Jung-su looked at his wife and said nothing. Ji-hye pulled up a chair for CJ and said "jus a momentuh" in Konglish before the couple disappeared into the bedroom. Chul looked back to his companion and saw the bloodless cheeks of a cancer patient, the strained expression of a dying dog. He grimaced and walked to the porch so he would not disturb either CJ or his potential accomplices.

They are all suffering, Chul thought. He didn't have time to go anywhere with that thought before Jung-su and Ji-hye returned.

"We can drive your friend to the hospital in Mudanjiang," she said. "But please do not come here again. You may leave the materials you took from Wang Zeng, and we will be happy to send you the translations, but we should not meet in person any more. You will also want to move your boat to another city. You two are very conspicuous."

Chul agreed and asked where the car was.

"It is lucky we have a garage," Jung-su said. "Here, I will help you with your friend."

The stepped back inside and went to the American. CJ made a pained grunt as Chul and Jung-su hauled him first from the couch and later into to the family's Buick sedan. Chul settled into the back seat next to CJ and came to an odd realization. These trials, the crimes and broken bones and the murder in Africa, did they not seem much more real than his life before?

Chapter Forty Two

155 Days After

CJ flicked the cotton fuzz sticking out of his cast and reached for the mystery opiates. The bitter pills stuck in his throat and left a knot behind even when he chased them with a glass of water. Min-sung was gone now and so was Mrs. Choi. Chul was wrapped up in navigating Manchurian rivers. He'd said something about Russia and the open ocean. It was hard to tell through the narcotics. Bored and stoned, CJ flipped open his computer in search of Internet pornography. Only a new folder, arranged dead center in the middle of his desktop and labeled "FOR CJ," stopped him.

The first document explained that Jung-su and Ji-hye had translated all this from Chinese to Korean, and that Chul had, through several hours of hellish and massively selfless labor, translated that into English for CJ's convenience.

You need not give thanks, Chul had written. *Even if the amount of guilt you feel for needing so much help from me becomes overwhelming. Truly, do not worry about it, not even when you imagine the hours I spent ignoring my own wants and needs to provide this, and it must be said, a wide variety of medical services as well. Please do not think you owe me greatly, do not mistakenly believe I will remind you of this favor for as long as you live.*

CJ smiled and moved to the second document where he learned exactly how far Wang Zeng had gotten. The Hairpiece was a student at Eastern Liaoning University where she studyied economics, spent a lot of time using the free Internet at Tesco and had a grandmother named Zhiang who lived in Yanji. There seemed to be a group of people doing a pretty damned good job of protecting her and the searchers were frustrated at how her BBS posts suddenly stopped. It seemed Wang Zeng's human flesh searchers were getting ready to abandon the electronic stuff and make a road trip.

The third document, awkwardly titled "Their Seriousness," interested CJ more. This contained Internet conversations regarding the Hairpiece, mostly referencing a desire to hang her from bridges or strip her naked to be shamed in the town square. The most interesting, though, was a chat transcript including her original offense.

Separatist Trash, May They Rot in Their Own Filth

Patriotic Dragon Wrote:

We are always seeing videos of the separatists wallowing in filth, disrespecting our nation. They are always glorifying their treason and waving their hideous flags. And now those Tibetans and Taiwanese still among us dare to complain of their rough treatment?

The separatists should stay in the collective fields where they belong!

No speakey the fucking Mandarin!? Then go the fuck away!

Sacred Duty Wrote:
With the bird flu scare, I don't think they should even be in the fields. Minorities that distance themselves from the rest of us by REFUSING to learn and speak Mandarin …That is RACISM!!!!

Spirit of Joy Wrote:
It is all the work of America. They brought about this "Potency God" because they feared our restoration to glory.

Shining Light Wrote:
Spirit of Joy is right, the West must be restrained from its constant attacks on China and trying to turn our women into prostitutes and our young men into homosexuals, plus turn everyone into alcoholics and druggies to mention only a few of the degeneracies rampant in the West. The traitors wish to degenerate us.

Hairpiece Wrote:
Some of the separatists broke away because the Han Chinese disrespect their religious practices. Some left because we oppressed them. Some rebelled because we are colonizing them. We see China as inseparable, but there is no reason the minorities should share our view.

Dutiful Mother Wrote:
You are so quick to disparage the right ways of thinking. You must have very low moral character to miss what is so obviously evil. Don't you feel dirty?

For the morally normal people reading this, I have a question. I went to my son's open house at his school last night and found out that his math teacher is a Tibet sympathizer. He has a picture of himself and one of those separatist traitors displayed on his desk. It made my stomach turn. I would like the picture removed. What can I do? My son is in the second grade, by the way.

Shining Light Wrote:
Religious freedom, huh? I have a religious right to stone subversives like you for treason. What do you think of a shallow grave, bitch?

So Cute Wrote:
I'm a new netizen here, and I'll start by saying that I'm staunchly patriotic...I'm a real Chinese, and I believe in China, and I'm pretty sure it is just a matter of time before scum like Hairpiece make it so Chinese patriotism will be outlawed. American consumerism will be the law of the land, most likely with some pockets of Buddhist and Christian extremists hanging on to what they have deluded themselves into thinking is their morality, of course minus any and all familial duty.

Shining Light Wrote:
The secretary of the party is married to a Taiwanese wife. She probably is an agent for the Taiwanese government.

Hairpiece Wrote:
You obviously cannot challenge my facts. It's okay, you're all stupid and you probably can't help that, so I don't blame you.

China will be stronger when it does not have to waste energy oppressing people who do not want to be Chinese. Let them go and focus on improving our economy instead.

Outraged Moralist Wrote:

I love how you twist reality. We have always shown the minorities great kindness. What we are not tolerant of is crime and promiscuity, which in case you need reminding, RUNS RAMPANT in their communities. Minorities are just as likely as Westerners to be infected with AIDS! Isn't that shocking that they are just as immoral as Americans or Japanese?! They contribute nothing positive to China and should have been shipped off to Africa or dumped in the ocean.

Hairpiece Wrote:

My dearest most beloved friend and number one fan, Outraged Moralist,

If they contribute nothing, you should be glad to see them go. Whoops, didn't think that far ahead, did you? If we'd be better off dumping them in the ocean…you know what, the normal type of discourse is too advanced for you. But don't worry, I will condescended so far even as to lend monoliths of inferiority like yourself assistance.

You see, I was thinking about your tragic intellectual situation when I came to a revelation. You, my beloved friend, are a cephalopod. How else could it be? You can obviously type, as evidenced by your large bodies of inane blathering on this very bulletin board service. This almost precludes the possibility of you being a literal imbecile—as in having an IQ between 26 and 50. However, we still must account for the shocking stupidity of everything you write. I confess I was, for a time, at a complete loss.

Then it dawned on me, you are either a squid or an octopus—perhaps a cuttlefish. Your highly defuse nervous system has 8 to 10 nervous ganglion controlling each of your prehensile limbs, granting you the dexterity necessary to splatter idiocy all over the Internet. You then "control" these arm brains with a tiny, donut-shaped head-brain surrounding your esophagus.

How else are we to reconcile your demonstrated physical dexterity with the utter inanity of your writings? The only question remaining is to figure out who brought a computer to your spawning grounds. And how they water-proofed it, I suppose.

Outraged Moralist Wrote:

I don't have time to deal with your traitorous lies. I hope a human flesh search finds you and has you thrown in prison.

Brave Anonymous Warrior Wrote:

The Hairpiece cannot answer because she is prostituting herself to the Dalai Lama. Aint nothing free, especially sex. Women have ruined that too.

Subversive bitches like this are stalkers. They follow you around like a viper spreading their venom. They relish every opportunity to unleash their hatred for both China and proper morality, and the homosexual ones are the worst! I speak from experience!

Hairpiece Wrote:

What is there to answer? You didn't say anything. My God, isn't anyone familiar with the ad hominem FALLACY?

Hand of Virtue Wrote:

You are a plague, and I relish the world changes that are now in effect that will destroy you. Soon. I really have no other reason for you to continue to exist in my peoples' world. I have friends and we are going to find you.

Shining Light Wrote:

Ad hominem? What sort of Western lie is this? Let me make it as simple for you as I can. I hope you die. One day... you will see the fruits of your ideology. When I face you down and crush you. Personally. Because yeah. Sometimes, it does come down to man vs. ... whatever you are. And whatever your self-claimed ideology, you won't have what it takes to survive. I hope you're ready to face the world.

Empty Afterlife Wrote:

Killing Tibetans is foreign aid...throw those logs on the fire.

Particularly Fine Wrote:

Literally, if I were to hear Hairpiece died tomorrow falling into an open manhole cover, I'd celebrate and call it an act of divine justice.

Hairpiece Wrote:

Fuck your ancestors for 18 generations. You can't even write intelligently and you think you'll find me. Ha! Try your best. Scrunch up your stupid faces like rotting cunts and fail.

Free Tibet! HAHA!

CJ wiped his nose and rubbed his chin. This Hairpiece, even if she did have a point, seemed awfully prone to overplaying her hand.

Chul stared out from his captain's chair, over the muddy river banks and through the lung-wrecking coal smog. He flipped open the calendar app on his phone and checked the time. Three hours until his lunch date with Kong Qing, Professor of Song Dynasty Poetry. He did not intend to mention urine streams to the Professor, regardless of how poetic, and thus decided to conduct his interview in English. In addition, CJ figured to be useless for another couple days, until they could arrange to remove the pins from his foot, and so he would have to work alone.

Chul remembered the man from his dream and shivered. *I am not well equipped to deal with solitude.* He shook out his hands and eased the *Gunham* into a flooded, mud-covered dock that was both barely worthy of the name and, at its farthest extent, impassably submerged 30 meters from any dry ground. The boat's huge diesel engines shuddered to a stop and left the lapping of small waves against the hull as the only sound. Chul had to think.

He jumped onto the wood and tied the boat to a concrete abutment. A thick, pungent organic goo smeared up his slacks and besmirched his leather shoes. Our hero said *sheebal,* looked left and made for the stand of trees clumped together in the tidal mud. The goo sucked at his shoes and he had to curl his toes to prevent a barefoot return trip. Still, the trees were not far and seemed to have trapped stronger varieties of soil with their roots. Chul hauled himself onto the lowest of these trees, found a sturdy branch parallel to the ground and removed everything touched by filth—shoes, socks, pants. He lay down on the branch and stretched his arms. Amorous, winged insects chased tail over the water, water birds speared small, silvery fish with their sharp beaks, wind set the leaves into a discordant symphony of cellulose. Chul took a deep breath and closed his eyes.

I wanted this so bad in the beginning. A bit of sunshine shot through the trees and warmed his cheek. *I do not know if I care any longer. It is like I am no longer the same man. The Choi Chul of 6 months ago—he was so lonely, so angry. His priorities were so abstract. Ancestors and blood guilt, Korea's honor. Are these things real?*

Resolving these questions required more energy than Chul wanted to expend and so his mind drifted onto the men and women who'd peopled the previous six months. Bume with the dirty hands and good intentions—perhaps not unlike what he had expected in Africa but, somehow, real. A bad man with good reasons for his sins, with people who loved him and depended on his success. The Hairpiece persona and her enormous ego. So repulsive and yet rooted in a keen respect for logic. Jung-su and Ji-hye and their second language of sideways glances— the subtle rise and fall of eyebrows. Wang Zeng and his witch hunts for justice's sake. Min-sung's quiet rebellion and unexpected maturity. CJ and his bluster, covering up a sad boy's search for approval. Were these things not more important? Chul smiled and, as he drifted to sleep, entertained one more question.

How can I convince Professor Kong I am no human flesh searcher? He smiled again. *I can think of* one *idea.*

Professor Kong sat grading his student's papers. One particular *child* vexed him to the point of anger. *Stupid pup has the gall to question my poem's rhyme scheme?* He wrote in red pen along the bottom of the student's paper.

"Your talk is not pertinent, you dog-like traitor! Shut up or I will see you punished for your insubordinate rebellion."

His important meeting that evening with the foolish but well connected graduate student at the center of all this Internet vigilantism was not for another two hours and so he made himself comfortable. The unimportant meeting—dusting off one of those damned human flesh do-gooders—was scheduled to take place in 3 minutes. Kong released his jutting belly by unbuttoning his slacks. Two knocks on the door and Professor Kong said, "come in."

A short-ish man of middle age, wearing a formal dress shirt and with incongruously weathered skin walked in and stood beside Professor Kong's guest chair. Probably one of those dreary, ignorant farmer peasants in his town-hall best, filled with outrage and determined to defend whatever primitive beliefs he'd gotten from his cave-dwelling kin. Kong stood first, buttoned his fly second, half heartedly offered his hand third.

"So you must be here to find the Hairpiece. I am sorry to waste your time, but I'm not going to help you."

The peasant surprised Kong by answering in English.

"I am a friend," he said. "I came because I want to stop Wang Zeng from exposing your student."

Kong also switched to English.

"I am sorry, who are you?"

"I am Choi Chul. I come from Korea and I believe the Hairpiece can help me. It would be a large understatement to say that I do not sympathize with the human flesh searchers."

Kong laughed. *How delightfully fun—a break from all that dull, strongly held belief bullshit—this looks like subterfuge, with a foreign devil to boot!*

"Wonderful," he said. "Please, explain to me exactly how you plan to use the Hairpiece in your goals."

"I think I, uh, I think—"

"I think Wang Zeng should prepare more before he sends idiots like you to me," Kong said. "Truly, Choi Chul—if that really is your name—do you take me for an idiot?"

Professor Kong rose to show our hero the door but paused when Chul answered with an odd sort of challenge.

"I have risked much more than you to help the Hair Piece," he said.

"Do tell, Mr. Chul," Professor Kong said.

*Y*ou *can convince him,* Chul thought. *Or if you can't, there's always Chinese prison.*

"Check the newspapers in Harbin," Chul said. "There was a break-in at the home of Wang Zeng."

Professor Kong held up his finger and returned to his chair. Chul leaned back and gathered a deep breath. The Professor tapped his IPad twice, typed something and looked up.

"Alright, what is this supposed to mean?"

"Did the article mention the nature of the crime?"

"Only that the thief stole computer parts," Professor Kong said. "That he was injured and a western devil."

"The thief is living on my boat," Chul said. "I can show you pictures if you like. The injury was a broken foot. The thief, alerted by myself looking on from a nearby apartment, disabled Wang Zeng by shooting armpit deodorant into his eyes."

"How am I to verify this?"

"Surely a man powerful enough to protect the Hairpiece has friends in the police force," Chul said. "That is how it works, no?"

Professor Kong said nothing and so Chul continued.

"If my story is true, you will know I am no friend of the human flesh searchers."

"If you are telling the truth, why should I expose this person, assuming I am protecting the Hairpiece in the first place, to you?"

"Because I have come closer to the Twinkie of Destiny than anybody else," Chul said. This could have been true, though he wasn't sure. A small, ironic smile bent his lips as he thought of the Chinese Jew.

"So," he continued. "In short, you might receive patronage in my moment of triumph."

Professor Kong held his chin then spoke.

"Very well. I will check your story and consult with the Hairpiece. Leave your number and, if we decide it prudent, we will call you soon."

Once the foreign devil had left, Professor Kong placed a call to a private phone line on the 6th floor of the main dormitory building. A short while later, a young woman appeared and sat down in front of Professor Kong's desk.

"Ching Shih," Professor Kong said to the one better known as Hairpiece. "Your Internet ravings are a pain in my ass. Even the Koreans are searching for you now."

Ching Shih's thick eye brows fled north and her broad nose south across her moon shaped face. Her lips turned up at the corners and she laughed before answering.

"Is he a former North Korean? This is exciting, I feel like a celebrity."

"A celebrity known for foolishness," Kong said. "Truly, your father's influence only goes so far. Do not provoke the good netizens or their peasant agents any more. These wrong beliefs will do you no good."

"If they are wrong beliefs, you and the nationalists should disprove them in the open, using logic and rhetoric. You cannot, so you do not. This does not make me think myself wrong."

"To answer your foolish points is beneath my dignity," Professor Kong said.

"Bullshit."

"You have an odd way of showing gratitude to your protectors."

Ching Shih said nothing.

"I have called the police chief in Harbin," Professor Kong continued. "It seems the Korean robbed and assaulted your human flesh searchers in his desire to meet you. Will you see him?"

"Is my emergency contingency still ready?" Ching Shih asked.

"The materials your father provided are in my desk."

Professor Kong opened his drawer and produced a plane ticket to Hong Kong, a passport under the name Mu Nianci, 10,000 US dollars, an equivalent sum in Euros and a full assortment of Mu Nianci's credit cards.

"Your privilege astounds me," Professor Kong said. "I wonder if you would be so brave if you had to make your own way in this life."

"I deserve more," Ching Shih said.

She took the contingency plan, tucked the cash and documents into her shoulder bag and rose as if to leave.

"Tell the Korean I will meet him tomorrow in the morning," she said. "I am getting tired of hiding, in any event."

Chapter Forty Three

156 Days After

She looked strange there with her Oakland A's baseball cap, blue button-down shirt and white rimmed glasses. The three bulging duffle bags to her side suggested travel, the scowl impatience. Chul girded his loins and approached.

"You are the Hairpiece?" he asked. "Would you like a fruit salad? I am going to get lunch for myself and would be happy to treat you."

The Hairpiece answered in English.

"My name is Ching Shih. You are Choi Chul?"

"Yes."

She smiled and tilted her head to the side. There was something uncommonly aggressive in her manner.

"No, I don't need you to buy me salad," she said. She paused a beat before continuing. "Do I look impoverished to your eyes?"

Chul didn't know how to answer beyond simply saying "no." *This feels like a grappling match already.* He sat and listened.

"I have in my possession the means to destroy the human flesh search," she said. "I have a plan to shock my soft-headed countrymen and will need to leave China when it is finished. Give me the use of your boat and I will render Wang Zeng incapable of following either of us."

A sort of cruelty came over our hero. A small malevolence borne of injured pride and sustained on a minor urge to *shut that arrogant bitch's mouth.*

"You seem confused," Chul said.

"How?"

He prepared the rhetorical killing blow.

"I am here because I want to use you," our hero said. "I would prefer the human flesh searchers not find you, but I really do not care very much."

She seemed surprised.

"My father didn't send you to protect me?"

"No, he did not."

Chul smiled and continued.

"I want to find the Twinkie of Destiny. I have reason to suspect you can help me. If I am correct, then we can discuss your needs. If I am not, then I will wish you luck and be on my way."

"I don't need you," she said. "I can just fly out of China."

"I am sure you can," Chul said. "But you want to leave on my boat. I wonder why. Could you be worried about enemies waiting at customs? I would worry about customs if I were you. Let us stop this game. You know what I want. I know what you want. We should trade."

She stopped for a beat to consider his words.

"Okay, how do you think I can help you?"

Our hero relaxed, assuming he'd proven himself formidable and thus earned a measure of safety.

"Did you meet with the God of Potency? The last person I dealt with met the little bitch and saw his face. A cave, too. There was a cave."

"I have not seen anything out of the ordinary," she said.

"No strange messages, visitors?"

"Aside from you?"

"No friends or family acting uncharacteristically?"

"My father has been perhaps a little more helpful than usual, but that was my doing. I may just buy a boat of my own."

Chul was coming near to despair and, indeed, used his internal dialogue to describe yours truly with a long and imaginative string of obscenities. When the final imagined insult passed, a thought occurred to him.

"How did you come to possess this weapon against the human flesh searchers?"

Ching Shih rolled her eyes and brushed the hair back from her forehead.

"I found it in the mail," she said. "My daddy had the driver give it to me with the care packages he delivers every week."

Chul stopped to wonder how one so spoiled could live without offending every nose in creation. *It doesn't matter.*

"Did you see your family's driver leave the…whatever it is?"

"Do I look like I have time to deal with trivialities?"

You look like a person who deals with nothing but trivialities, Chul thought.

"Of course you do not," Chul said. "I would like to see the…whatever it is. If you do not mind too much."

Ching Shih sighed and rummaged through her bag and produced a green thumb drive with an unusual, vine-like decoration.

"You can't have this," she said. "I am not going to let a stranger hold it, but if you like I will demonstrate it on your computer."

"Don't use a nice one," she said. "The damage from my little weapon is not reversible."

Chul thought this an excellent idea and bid the young lady adieu that he might find a sacrificial laptop.

"I will see you here tomorrow," Chul said.

CJ lay on his bed, foot propped up on several pillows when he flipped the channel. Some stupid home economics show with Martha Stewart and—*what!?* CJ recognized Stewart's new assistant as the old man from Harbin, the grumpy computer repairman I'd swooped up via dragon. CJ leaned closer to the TV and listened as Stewart jumped right into the meat of her program. She held a brownish, frilly wreath and spoke into the camera.

"Do you have any idea what this is made from? I'm going to make one of these beautiful wreaths for each of my windows and today, I'll show you how to do the same thing for your own home."

The old man set a coffee machine on the counter next to Stewart and offered her a cup.

"My friend Wei Zhang is giving you a clue. Yes! You're absolutely right, nothing but used coffee filters."

Stewart stopped to thank Wei Zhang and take a drink from the coffee.

"That's right, a coffee filter wreath. These are so much fun to make. They come out absolutely gorgeous and if you tie a ribbon around it, you can hang it from the door—"

Stewart froze in a blizzard of electronic interference. CJ scooted toward the TV to check the cables. On the second scoot Wei Zhang's mouth began to move, then his head, then his entire body. The repairman strained against the stillness and, with an abrupt jerk freed himself from the suspended animation gripping Stewart, the wreathes and even the windblown trees visible through stage windows. He made eye contact with the lesser of our heroes and addressed him in perfect, unaccented English.

"You must think this is going to work the same way as the Bume situation, but you are mistaken," he said. "That girl is giving Chul everything you need right now. You can just throw her away, if you wish. No need to compromise, no need to shoot a boy."

Martha Stewart suddenly set down the coffee filter wreath and joined the computer repairman's lecture.

"This is about you two," Stewart said. "You are going to have to decide exactly what you want. Is this still about your injured nations? Is it still about what a man is made from or have you suddenly started caring what man makes of himself? Think about it."

The TV blacked out for an instant before flashing back.

"—and be careful not to tear the filters when you run the needle like this through the—"

CJ turned the TV off and leaned back. He and Chul needed to talk.

Chul returned with the sacrificial laptop, ordered a fruit salad for himself and made a point of not offering Ching Shih any refreshments. He pulled up a hard, plastic chair and produced the bottom of the line, six-year-old HP. As he set it down, he asked a question with no particular relevance to the task at hand.

"Why are you causing all this trouble?"

Ching Shih answered immediately.

"I want trouble. I want to be *alive.* Don't you understand? I want to fight and know the primalness of a real
life."

"You are joking."

"No. I mean it."

Chul rushed to build a dam against the tsunami of his
outrage. The pressure became too great and escaped under his breath.

"Child."

"What?" Ching Shih asked.

"I asked how," Chul said. "How are you going to get
your excitement?"

"I am the daughter of an important official," she said.
"If I out myself as the Hairpiece it will cause a big controversy."

A student carrying a tray of steamed vegetables
bumped Chul's chair and dropped a floret into Chul's
fruit salad. The boy was half-way through a panicky apology Chul couldn't understand when Ching Shih sent him
away. This small kindness made his next statement harder
to get out.

"I am glad you are not my daughter."

"My father will be fine," she said. "He can figure something out. You don't understand, I am—"

Chul cut her off.

"Bored?"

"This world is full of really, really stupid people," she
said. "I mean, the sorts of who, should they have a thought,
would see it die from loneliness. They are like sediments
in a river, these idiots. They fall wherever chance drops
them and cover up whatever they land on—gold, gems,
beautiful shells. If there are not people like me, who come
along and disturb the layers of sediment, the treasures of

life will be lost forever beneath their dull, brown nothingness."

She took a breath.

"My countrymen are not capable of thinking clearly about the opportunities the God of Potency gave us," she said. "They are lazy, emotional and stupid and they cannot see the world with clear eyes. I will present an alternative with my example."

Chul held his chin between finger and thumb. *The Chinese are foolish regarding their territorial disputes. That is obvious. And she makes a valid point about disturbing the complacent. But this child, can she not see how her arrogance, the way she betrays her father and professor, does she not know how easy these evil things will make it to dismiss her ideas?* Chul imagined a crowd of outraged Tibetans pelting Ching Shih with rotten produce and chanting, "stop helping us!" He kept this to himself and changed the subject.

"Did you bring this weapon for use against the human flesh searchers?"

Ching Shih produced a USB drive and slid it across the table. Chul tapped it twice before picking it up and plugging it into his used laptop.

"Is there anything I have to do?"

"Just turn it on."

The startup screen showed nothing out of the ordinary, ditto the Windows desktop.

"Am I missing something obvious?" Chul asked.

"Try to use the computer," Ching Shih said. "It will become obvious what my virus does."

Chul chose a word processor. It opened normally but, when he tried to type, a cascade of text came down from the menu and covered the document with the phrase

The Fluffenflapper's in Hamburg thousands of times. He watched the page counter on the word processor running ever higher—44, 135, 229, 501, 1107, 2486. Finally, with the document at nearly 10,000 pages, the computer crashed.

"This is what happens for any type of input," Ching Shih said. "Internet browsers will open hundreds of empty pages at the address *thefluffenflappersinhamburg.com* until the system crashes. You saw the word processor. Video players do the same thing. The worst is if you run a virus sweep. The damned thing logs onto the Internet, opens your email account and sends everyone in your contact list twelve hours of pterodactyl pornographies. I did not even know pterodactyl pornography existed until my mother called to complain."

Chul nodded and thought. *I am reasonably certain that the child has given me all I need.* He had not finished weighing the implications of this revelation when Ching Shih spoke.

"I can send this virus to the human flesh searchers tonight," she said. "Announce my Internet identity to the foreign news outlets tomorrow morning and sail with you tomorrow evening. All I need is the hard drive you stole so that I can get inside their system. Bring it to me in two hours at my dormitory."

She handed him a map with her dorm labeled in red. Chul nodded and left without saying anything further.

CJ stood with the aid of his crutches upon the Gunham's deck. He looked restless, so Chul suggested they might retire to a more stimulating locale.

"We should go to the dormitory at Eastern Liaoning University," he said.

"Is this going to be another instance where you tell me the entire story?" CJ asked.

"Yes, though I think our discussion will cause you less discomfort than the last. It is, at the least, not about your wife."

"Lead on."

The click-click of aluminum on plastic broke the silence as they walked, or hobbled as the case may be, along the sour-smelling backstreets of Dandong. This empty sonic environment pleased our hero enough to overcome scarcely breathable air and crumbling old houses.

To his right the dormitory glowed a gentle green in the gloom. To his left a small pond, probably polluted judging by the lack of frog calls, lapped against mud shores. Chul turned to CJ and broke the silence.

"To whom are we loyal?"

CJ said nothing.

"The Hairpiece—her real name is Ching Shih—has given us power. It was only through her foolishness and ignorance, but the fact remains that we will decide who suffers and who profits in this place."

"I already know we don't need her," CJ asked. "Should we play along regardless?

Chul sat on the grass and looked over the pond. CJ joined him after a brief struggle. Nearby a single insect rattled the chitinous joints of its exoskeleton and sent small cracking noises over the water—*amore* in arthropod. CJ produced a bottle of Gatorade from his bag and offered a sip to Chul. Our hero declined. CJ took a big drink and spoke.

"We don't need her anymore."

"I think I agree. Her weapon against the human flesh searchers is a virus. That virus is a name and city and nothing more. Well, it is also pterodactyl pornography, but I do not think that important."

CJ seemed confused but Chul paid him no attention.

"We can just leave," Chul said. "But I do not think that ethical."

"Why? What will happen?"

"She wants to show China her views," Chul said. "I do not dislike this. Do we agree that the Chinese are reacting irrationally to their lost territories?"

"I think they're nuttier than squirrel shit."

Chul did not think Chinese people looked or smelled like nuts but ignored CJ's idiotic observation in the interests of the conversation.

"Then we can help her and perhaps introduce some reason into their disputes."

"Sort of a freedom of speech type deal?" CJ asked. "We could help her advance the open society?"

Chul nodded.

"Yes, and this is noble, but I do not think Ching Shih can succeed. She plans to out herself as the daughter of a high government official. This will make a big controversy and force the people to discuss her argument on the merits, she thinks. I think it will ruin her family and make her reasoned opinions sound like the rantings of a traitor."

CJ took another drink from the bottle before answering.

"Her dad's a communist party official?"

"I would assume," Chul said.

"Then fuck him."

"True, he is probably the son of a dog," Chul said. "But there is also the girl's mother and whatever family she has. Professor Kong would likely suffer as well."

"And this is just if we stay out of it?" CJ asked.

"If we stay out or if we help her. It does not matter which."

"I say it's really not our responsibility. We have what we need and we can let these people figure things out for themselves. I don't think we can do much else anyway."

Chul took a deep breath and said something he would never have imagined saying only a few months previous.

"We can defuse this situation," he said. "We *can* stop her. We will probably silence her in the process, but we can stop her."

"Do what you think is best," CJ said. "I trust your judgment. Just tell me the plan and I'll back you up."

Chul imagined betraying his own family and was filled with terror. To destroy a family like Ching Shih sought to do, that kind of person will be alone—that kind of person should be alone. He could live with hurting that kind of person.

"I think I will teach Ching Shih consideration," he said. "Will you accompany me to Professor Kong's office tonight?"

"I'll be there," CJ said.

Chul heard the insect again, creaking in the darkness. Then another, then another and then a frog. Perhaps this place was not so polluted after all.

Professor Kong rolled over in bed and slammed a soft, plump fist into his ringing cell phone. *Who is calling me at this hour?*

"Speak!" he said.

"Professor Kong," his teacher's aide said. "The Korean from before and a *gwai lo*. They want to visit you tonight. They say it is important."

"Is it important enough to call me at two in the damned morning?"

"They say Ching Shih will make much trouble for you."

Professor Kong groaned like a water buffalo in musk. His toes chilled in their brief trip from under the covers to inside the slippers. He let out one more noise best left to the imagination before answering the TA.

"Give them my address."

"I am glad you consent," the TA said. "They will wait outside your door."

Professor Kong hung up and made his way downstairs and opened a bottle of rice wine. He poured himself a glass and rolled its sour biting goodness around his mouth. Then another, then another. *They can fucking wait.*

A pleasant sort of fog rose up from the venerable professor's brain stem and enveloped his entire head. The tension in his back and neck released and, suddenly, the idea of entertaining uninvited foreign devils in the very early morning did not seem quite so repulsive.

He put one heavy hand on the door handle, twisted and stood in the doorway where his guests—then huddling under the date tree in his yard—could see him silhouetted against the warm light inside.

"Professor Kong," the Korean said in his accented English. "We have news of great importance to you."

"Yes, I am sure you do," Kong said. "It is very, very late so come inside. Show me how this *intrusion* is not a colossal waste of my time."

The foreign devils exchanged glances and walked up the steps on his porch, past his outstretched arm and into the drawing room.

"Please sit down," Kong said. "I want you to be comfortable and well rested so that you can leave without any tired muscles to slow you down."

The American *gwai lo* leveled a half-disguised glare at Professor Kong. This filled the educator's spirit with joy as he continued.

"So, what is so important you interrupt my sleep?"

"Ching Shih is going to betray you," the *gwai lo* said. Just like that, all impertinence and smug superiority. *How dare you condescend to me when I'm condescending to you!*

"She is going to out herself as the daughter of an important official and the protégé of a famous scholar," Choi Whatever-his-name-was said. "I assume this will reflect poorly on you."

Professor Kong, through his drunkenness, finally grasped the meaning of the *gwai lo*'s statement and turned his attentions to Ching Shih. *That attention grubbing, entitled little whore!* His anger reached such heights as to defy containment. He wanted to yell, he wanted to scream and he wanted to smash his glass of rice wine. Instead, he laughed.

"And here I believed her when she said she wanted to remain anonymous!" Professor Kong said.

He shook his head and looked to the ground. *I cannot do anything directly unless—yes, I can preempt her.*

"I thank you for coming to me with this news, even if your manners are somewhat lacking. Is there anything you need as payment for this kind deed?"

"You haven't told anyone about our crime-spree in Harbin?" the *gwai lo* asked.

Professor Kong shook his head and said no.

"We're leaving port tonight," the *gwai lo* continued. "I'd ask you keep what you've learned about us quiet. Past that, I don't care what you do."

The professor looked to the Korean and could not repress his curiosity.

"Why did you tell me this?"

"Ching Shih is reckless and shortsighted," Chul said. "I do not want the innocent people of her family or your family to suffer for her naiveté. But more than this, I think, I do not want to see the good words she speaks ruined because they come from such a horrible speaker. It is uncommon to meet the man who, hearing wisdom from the mouth of a fool, does not consider the former polluted by the latter."

Professor Kong laughed again. *Good words! Ha!* The professor briefly toyed with the idea of doing nothing and letting Ching Shih discredit her own cause but stopped. *I will not suffer for the sake of an ungrateful child.*

"I will take your words under consideration," Professor Kong said. "In the mean time, please, take of the hospitality of my home. I have no food ready, but there is an excellent all night pizza establishment not far from here. Remain in my house, enjoy my wine and I will get delivery."

They again exchanged glances before the Korean answered.

"We must go, Professor," he said. "Thank you for your offer and please, be a good steward to the power we've given you."

"Of course," Professor Kong said. "Thank you again and go well."

The foreign devils left our esteemed scholar in peace. That Ching Shih planned to betray her father made matters easier, for sure. Big Ching was not the sort of man poetry professors could challenge but that didn't matter, he would make a natural ally in this situation. Still, he could not harm the girl. Her father would likely want to stuff that spoiled girl away, secluded somewhere, and that could work assuming she never had another computer or phone in her life. *So, in other words, that won't work at all.*

He shifted his girth against the sofa and shook his head. This sort of planning would not help. *I need to think of this in terms of threats. Ching Shih wants to destroy me by outing herself. The human flesh searchers want to destroy Ching Shih by outing her. They are, in a sense, allies. The chat room transcripts were, of course, the explosive charge. Ching Shih's true identity the detonator. I cannot destroy either but, perhaps if I can permanently separate the two…*

Professor Kong looked at his coffee table, at the corrected student essays waiting to be returned. The horrible essay of that one student who, in his hubris and ignorance, criticized Professor Kong's poetic verse, sat atop the stack. He considered this for a second and came to an idea. He called his poor, beleaguered TA once more.

"I want you to check a student's records," Kong said. "I must know if his parents are important."

"Who should I check?" the TA asked.

Professor Kong looked down to the paper once more and rubbed it in an attempt to clear off some of the red ink obscuring the student's name. It took two licks of the thumb and about a minute of scrubbing to render the name legible.

"Professor Kong, have you hung up?"

"No I have not, I am simply busy," he said. Kong squinted and finally made out the name. "He is called Chi Sung. Yes, I'm sure it's Chi Sung."

The TA went quiet, presumably for the purpose of searching Chi Sung's records. He was, in actuality, muting the pterodactyl pornographies playing on his office computer—but I digress.

"Okay," the TA said. "It says that his mother works in an electronics factory and that his father is a clerk. He does have an uncle in Hong Kong who deals in foreign currency swaps."

"Fucking traitor," Kong said. "Is the uncle connected in the mainland?"

"It doesn't seem so."

Kong hung up and smiled. He could work with these circumstances.

Chapter Forty Four

159 Days After

The *Gunham* powered through mild ocean rollers, 300 kilometers east of Ching Shih, Professor Kong and the me-damned Chinese smog. CJ was watching a flock of sea birds from the pilothouse and thus left Chul alone with his kimchi soup, his soju and cell phone below deck. The greater of our heroes was contemplating the mysteries of his liqueur when the cell phone lit up and said "ka-kao" in its annoying little computer voice. The messenger program displayed the following message.

"Hammered Head says 'Choi Chul?'"

Our hero typed his answer on the touch screen. The soju mixed with his sweat and the built up grime on the phone to create a brownish slurry. He thus kept his answer on the short side and cast about for a wet tissue.

"Yes, I am Choi Chul."

He found a moist towelette and was scrubbing the touch screen when the next message appeared.

"You dirty, duplicitous turncoat."

"Ching Shih?" Chul typed.

A long delay followed as our hero pictured Ching Shih, scowling and breathing hard, pounding a long diatribe into her computer.

"Who else do you think it could be? You cowardly, stupid, dull little man. Who do you think you are? I am a mover and shaker, I am this > < close to being a revolutionary figure and you fuck it all up. You told the fat-ass poet? You told my father? Do you realize what this means?"

Chul tapped on the virtual keyboard fast, pressing harder than strictly necessary as if to emphasize the righteousness of his words.

"It means that your family will not suffer for your stupidity. It means that Professor Kong will not lose his job. Most important, it means that your worthy ideas will not have a traitor and spoiled child for their spokesperson. Everything you say will be despoiled because you say it. Everything."

Chul was proud of that last bit and swaggered a little as he made a run to the refrigerator. When he came back this text awaited him.

"You were worried about the spokesman? Hahaha, you have failed at the tasks of life! Did you ever think how Kong would stop me? He can't just arrest me like some fishmonger's daughter—he had to be more creative. And creative he was, he arranged a great spokesman!"

He went public?! Another message popped up on the screen.

"Kong told everybody that some shit farmer's son is the Hairpiece. Now that poor bastard is getting purged and arrested and you can guess how long he took to renounce my brilliant beliefs."

Chul dropped his soju bottle and pounded the counter tops with his fists. *Not again.* The despair fell upon him with a sudden splat, like a soggy blanket dropped from high above. *Oh please, not another one.* A part of him wanted to grab that girl, that child, and squeeze her until she popped.

"Who suffers in your place?" he typed.

The wait while Ching Shih typed was almost too much for Chul. He had tried to be righteous, he had done all he could think to avoid harming the innocent and yet—

"As I said, it is the son of some shit farmer. He pissed off Kong by making fun of his poetry or some stupid thing like that. What does it matter? He's a fucking nobody. What does matter is because this patsy of Kong's doesn't have the courage to sacrifice for the sake of ME. God, I hate dullards like you! And now, because of you, I'm locked up in this stupid country house with no friends, no clubs and no life. Are you happy now, you self-righteous little prick?"

Her words washed over Chul. Washed away his anger and left behind only regret. That was two—he'd sacrificed two now. A tired sort of vengeance came over our hero. Not so much a desire to punish me, but a sort of obstinant pride. *I am not your plaything,* he thought. As such, Chul redoubled his resolve and set himself to finding "the Fluffenflapper in Hamburg."

That Which is Broken

There is nothing more difficult to take in hand, more perilous to conduct, or more uncertain in its success, than to take the lead in the introduction of a new order of things.

-Niccolo Machiavelli

Chapter Forty Five

CJ lay face down on his bed. He had not slept well the previous night, nor the night before. A certain nervousness, a tightness just short of nausea had gripped at him more and more regularly since he'd left China. The phone sat buried halfway into the sheets next to a pillow, under a depressing, Old Testament-inspired novel he'd picked up in Italy. Its screen flashed once, twice, and an electric motor buzzed somewhere inside. CJ closed his eyes, dreamt of sleep and said "shoot me" into the pillow before checking his text messages.

"Hey Dad," Patty had said. "Haven't talked to you in a while. Call me."

CJ considered her words, poured himself a glass of orange juice from the Gunham's kitchen fridge, went to the top deck and looked at the gray-tipped North Sea rollers off Bremerhaven. There was something harsh, stinging about these skies. Like a jellyfish dragging poison tentacles through the sky. CJ picked up the phone, stretched and dialed Patty. It would be good to get out of adventure-mode, even if only for a short while.

"Hey Dad," Patty said. "How are you doing?"

"I'm okay," CJ said. "Well, it's complicated. I might give you a run for the money in the gimpy Olympics next time we meet."

"What happened?"

CJ was pleased with the joke, but didn't want to talk too much about himself, especially considering Patty's much more serious physical problems.

"I broke my foot in China. Speaking of feet, how is your physical therapy coming along?"

Patty paused a beat.

"I can walk again, mostly."

"I'm so sorry," CJ said. "I promise I'm going to punish that Potency fucker for what he did to you."

Patty said nothing.

"I won't let him get away with it."

Silence.

"Patty?"

"I'm here," she said. "I understand, I—thank you, but you don't have to do anything."

"Honey, it's the least I can do."

Patty's voice strained against sadness, against loss, against the scar tissue and sutures and broken youth.

"Daddy, please, if you do get that thing, use it to make something good. Don't waste those fifteen minutes on punishment."

The silence stretched long and hard through time like piano wire, broken only by the soft sounds of exhalation.

"Where have you been?" Patty finally asked. "I've not heard anything since you sent that email about leaving Africa."

"We went to China," CJ said. "I met Chul's family and that was nice. We ended up saving this stupid girl from herself."

"What kind of problem did she have?"

"She pissed off this poetry writer and was set to make a lot of enemies in the Communist Party. It was actually pretty sad. The entire mess ended up getting pinned on some random college student. That poor kid's probably sitting in jail, scared shitless, wondering what happened."

"Wait, a poet did this? Framing people for crimes doesn't sound like something a man of the arts would naturally do."

"Think about that, Patty. When I say poet, what do you think of?"

"Neck beards, God-hating, sodomy—okay, I guess I can see that."

CJ smiled and continued.

"We're in Germany right now, have been for a while. We're supposed to meet this person with a name I can't pronounce. Fluffyflappy or something like that. Anyway, he is on some vacation in Slovakia and we have to wait for him to get back. But I can't complain too much. German beer is the best and I like the North Sea. You'd like it, I think. Speaking of which, are you headed back to work?"

"As soon as I can. Or at least as soon as this contractor I hired to remodel our house is finished. Cranky old bastard doesn't take directions worth a damn. I think he might have been one of the people involved in that General Buildable scandal. I don't really want to leave him alone in my house, if you know what I mean."

"Wow, sounds like an *interesting* guy," CJ said. "I am surprised to hear you want to go back to Pakistan so soon, though."

CJ's internal dialogue continued that sentence. *I'm surprised you still believe in those fucking towelheads after they tried to start World War Three.*

"You're thinking about it the wrong way," Patty said. "This is an exciting time for people like me. I mean, all the turbulence and uncertainty—that stuff the Potency God has disrespected and destroyed—I just feel like there's so much opportunity to make something better."

"That's one way of looking at it, I suppose."

Patty responded to this by waxing philosophic.

"I think we're naturally conservative. I don't mean that like Democrats and Republicans, I mean that in the literal sense. In the sense that we don't want change of any type. This is okay sometimes, but when stupid gets legitimized it tends to stay legitimate. Pakistan was *really* conservative and because of that, they had integrated a lot of stupid. Now they're dealing with a loss of identity, with national humiliation and the destruction of their traditions—that's really the only time people can get rid of the dumb stuff that's built up. It's like when your computer crashes. You lose some good things, but you also have the opportunity to start fresh, without all the viruses and cat videos you didn't want anyway. The Pakistanis can reformat the whole damn country, if they have the courage. They couldn't do that two years ago."

CJ's heart sank a little bit when he thought of her going back. *Why is she putting herself once more in danger for these people? Is it some quixotic desire to reform a region, a religion so naturally deformed? Can't she see they'll always be a mess? Can't she give up?*

"So you think you can help?" he finally asked.

"Probably not very much, but maybe. I don't know, I feel like we're doing the same thing in the State Department."

CJ held his tongue and looked at the ground. That vague sadness rose higher and higher, covering first his mouth and then his nose until he could not resist breathing it into his lungs. Patty's hopefulness seemed disastrous, naïve and beautiful, like a young bride dancing ecstatic in a pit of poison snakes and broken glass. *I can't—I hope she's right.*

(For the virtue of properly appreciating poetry, I bless Patty Smith with a wide selection of the finest in pretentious indie rock albums.)

Chul was shopping for vegetables in a suburban Edeka supermarket when he got the following text message:

"This is Dr. Fluffenflapper. My assistants say you have been waiting to reach me. If you are available, I can meet you at my office in two hours. If you are not available, I'm sure we can arrange another time next week."

When Chul read this he grabbed hold the nearest bag of tomatoes, made his way to the cashier and completed his shopping with the bare minimum of courtesy. If traffic wasn't too bad, a cab ride could get him to Fluffenflapper's offices just in time to change his shirt, use the restroom and get through the receptionists. Unfortunately traffic was too bad and he arrived three minutes late, needing to pee and adorned in coffee-stained, light blue polo shirt.

"Meezter Chuey?" the receptionist asked. "Ze Doctor is vaiting for you in ze office. Please follow me und I vill show you ze vay."

Chul had trouble with the accent and thus depended more than normal on body language. Therefore it was not until the secretary motioned that our startled hero began his walk down the hall.

The receptionist opened a pair of piano black doors and held them for Chul. In front of him, the conference room impressed with its unabashed modernism. Structural elements painted a bright white were the sole decoration to the left—an I-beam here, a large ventilation tube there and pretensioned cables connecting the roof to the structural parts of the walls. In front and to the right it was as if Lord Vader had melted down his wardrobe and sprayed it over the conference table, the walls and stairwell. Computer screens, in a perfectly straight line and perched atop aluminum pedestals, glowered over each chair. Above it all, a floating office with a huge front-facing window did, in Chul's opinion, a fine, cubist impersonation of the all-seeing eye. A large man, framed in blonde teak wood and burnt orange furniture, stood behind that glass.

"Ze doctor vill see you here," the receptionist said. She pointed at the stairs and left.

Chul made a small bow to the man upstairs. The man returned the gesture, took a few steps to the side and held the office door open.

"Please, come and join me in this office," he said. "I am sorry if you had difficulty communicating with Ms. Crankybottom. She assures me that your English is excellent and that any misunderstandings are the result of her second language struggles and not yours."

Chul nodded and thanked the doctor.

"You flatter me," he said. "I have asked to meet you for very complicated reasons. Personal reasons. Therefore, I hope you will—"

Dr. Fluffenflapper interrupted at this point.

"Is it because a particularly nasty yet oddly whimsical computer virus mentioned my name and place of employment?"

"It is."

"I have been expecting you," Fluffenflapper said. "I must emphasize that I had nothing to do with the creation of that virus. You may check with the authorities if you wish."

"I believe you," Chul said. "I do more than believe you, in fact. I know you are telling to truth. Do not make yourself worried in this way."

The doctor leaned back in his chair and smiled. Chul was about to ask why when Fluffenflapper preempted him.

"I presume that you're after the Twinkie of Destiny," he said. "It is a pleasure to finally meet an adventurer of your caliber."

"You are expecting me?"

"The God of Potency has acquainted with the details of your voyage so far and I have been given the opportunity—I would like to stress that I did have a choice—to speak with you. As I said before, I'm very happy to see you. The great deeds you and your friend have done!"

This did little to constrain Chul's suspicion, not to mention remind him painfully of that boy in Ethiopia, the student in China. *Great deeds—what dog's noise is this?* Dr. Fluffenflapper continued.

"Please, call your friend and invite him to share lunch," he said. "There is much I wish to tell you."

That, at least, seemed like an intelligent course of action.

The good doctor's heart fluttered with excitement. He loved the importance, adored the complexity and freshness of the discussion he was about to have. Fluffenflapper called downstairs and had a selection of artisan sandwiches sent up. He provided Chul with unfiltered microbrews and made small talk until, after no more than one hour, the other adventurer came through his doors. Dr. Fluffenflapper stood and greeted CJ.

"Please sit," he said. "I am very eager that I not waste any of your time. Your business must be very important and I will therefore go straight to the matters concerning you."

He paused for effect.

"So, I shall begin by saying that I am 64 years old."

Fluffenflapper stopped to look at his audience. CJ stared uncomprehending and Chul seemed more interested in his sandwich. *To the point! Brevity, brief brevity with no more than the absolute minimum of words. No games, just the straight narcotics (or was that dope?) and unvarnished truth. No need to introduce everything before——*

"Okay?" CJ finally said. "Are you going somewhere with this?"

It's okay, you have practiced this, Dr. Fluffenflapper thought.

"I am 64 years old," he said again. "You must have guessed my approximate age by my appearance and the sound of my voice, but I give you the exact number because it will prove useful in explaining why my country has thus far escaped from the God of Potency's—what should I say?—alterations."

Chul answered, seemingly more from a desire to move the conversation forward than any curiosity.

"Please explain."

"As I'm sure you know, persons of my approximate age, particularly the educated men, wield the greatest power in any industrialized society. It then follows that when you look at Germany and pass judgment on our country, you are really passing judgment on my generation."

CJ tilted his head and held his chin before answering.

"Okay, I guess that kind of makes sense."

"Since you know my age," Fluffenflapper said. "You have no doubt deduced that my infancy passed among the ruins of the Third Reich. I am, in this sense, a child of de-Nazification."

The doctor noticed CJ squirming noticeably while the Korean moved only so much as was necessary to brush a crumb from his pant leg. The Nazis, it seemed, were less a global shame than a uniquely Western embarrassment. He resolved to write a long, philosophizing article on this subject at a later time.

"What this means for you," he said. "Is that the children of my generation grew up intensely ashamed of our parents and grandparents."

"You should have been ashamed," CJ said.

"I disagree, but not for the reason you suspect," Fluffenflapper said. "But I should explain what de-Nazification meant for my people."

From his look, it was obvious CJ had not considered the meaning of de-Nazification before. *Good.* Chul may or may not have cared. *Not good.*

"De-Nazification is the process of systematically destroying somebody's heritage," Fluffenflapper said. "It's taking all the things in their blood, their birthrights, the mystical virtues of their ancestors and lighting them on fire. It is pissing on the ashes. It is mocking a proud culture, turning young men against their families and breeding shame in the hearts of entire generations. De-Nazification is a field trip to the killing fields where your parents and uncles, neighbors and friends, melted gold from the teeth of the innocent. It is a Sunday matinee where the villains—who look and talk just like you—herd starving families into cages that they might inhale poison gasses. It was a long, thorough process of making the terms 'German' and 'evil' synonymous."

"That sounds like a trauma," Chul said.

"For the older generations," Fluffenflapper said. "But while they had the patriotic feeling beaten from them, my generation simply grew up without any. And we prospered."

Dr. Fluffenflapper paused to gauge the adventurers' reactions. Chul finally seemed to be paying attention, at least.

"I have looked into your Korean history and observed the Americans at Stuttgart and a dozen other military bases. I could not help but notice how different it must have been to grow up as a German.

"You Koreans had vengeance and tradition and the desire to show the world you were more than the regional door mat for your more advanced Japanese rivals. And the outrages they committed against your countrymen! I shudder to imagine them. That they have not apologized and admitted their guilt as we did, this is truly unforgivable. I can see how your people have come to embrace such rigidity.

"And the Americans, too. The way empire fell on your ancestors, the way fate time and again defeated your attempts at isolationism, you almost have to embrace it. But we Germans had little but our own reinvention to embrace and, at least partly because of said reinvention, we are now the nearest thing Europe has to a master. This also means, perhaps more to the point regarding your quest, when the time comes for a quasi-malevolent trickster deity to humiliate the nations, he finds little to target in Germany."

"But your history is bad," CJ said. "And your patriotism would be wrong."

Fluffenflapper thought that funny and let loose a high pitched chuckle before continuing.

"All histories are bad, to one extent or another," Dr. Fluffenflapper finally said.

"It is different," Chul said. CJ nodded in support for his companion.

"How is it different?" Fluffenflapper asked.

"Because you have national guilt," CJ said. "You guys did some of the worst things the world has ever seen. You're empty, in this way, but you haven't shown you can handle the responsibility of loving your country."

"*I* have never hurt anyone," Fluffenflapper said. "Of all the torments I face, guilt is certainly not one. I wasn't even an embryo when the SS men threw Hitler's body in a ditch and lit him on fire.

"You know his meaning," Chul said. "You are a part of the history, you have to accept that."

"No, I don't," Fluffenflapper said. "Not unless you intend to dig up some medieval notion of hereditary guilt."

CJ waved his hands and then pointed at Dr. Fluffen-flapper. His face looked steely and determined, like an avenging angel or vindicated martyr.

"I get it you guys have seen the bad side of national-ism," CJ said. "But there's a lot of richness you Germans just don't get to experience. You just don't know. You can't. I kind of feel sorry for you. It's got to be empty living without a love of country."

Dr. Fluffenflapper smiled and answered.

"I am interested to hear, specifically, what you think I lack. However, it is best if I give you time to mull over that question and instead address a more immediate concern."

He sat forward in his chair and pulled the wallet from his pocket. Inside the leather folds Dr. Fluffenflapper found a single, plastic business card with a phone number and the name "Ines Snyder."

"This is for you," he said. "This young lady would like your help. I do not understand how she relates to your adventure, but the God of Potency seemed to think her important."

CJ harrumphed but arose nonetheless to accept the card. Chul addressed his companion thus.

"You should start searching for this woman now. I want to speak with Dr. Fluffenflapper alone."

CJ nodded, pulled a cell phone from his pocket and left the room. Chul turned back to Fluffenflapper and ducked his head down——the gesture equivalent of "just between you and I."

A feeling like heartburn rose in our hero's breast. It was a discomforting little something Min-sung had said long before, over the phone and doctor's discussion had caused it to resurface in the manner of a noxious burp.

"Doctor," Chul said. "Do you think we are all just accidents?"

"No…"

"It is a thing my son said months ago. He thinks traditions—even less than tradition, inertia perhaps—make 95% of our lives even before we are born. What you said, it reminded me of my son's words. I think he is right, and this causes me sadness."

Dr. Fluffenflapper lit a cigarette and opened a small window. He looked to our hero and spoke before taking his first drag.

"It's a disgusting habit," he said. "I hope you can forgive me."

"I am Korean," Chul said. "I am accustomed to smokers."

He sat looking into the overhead lights. A big inhalation brought the tar and nicotine deep into his lungs and thus, when he spoke, wisps of grey smoke accompanied each syllable.

"You must see me as a counterpoint to your son's observation," Dr. Fluffenflapper said. "People like me, at least, have to invent a little bit more than the 5% other people do."

Chul said nothing.

"Honestly Chul, I think of it as an opportunity. We *can,* if we're brave, make ourselves a product of will. Nothing says we have to stay on the path we're born to. There's an awful lot of room in the world for deviation."

Our hero considered these words. He did not like deviation. Something about the implications. The opportunity, the newness—these things appealed to Chul, but the deviation. He frowned but did not wish to insult the doctor.

"That is an encouraging way to think," Chul said.

With that our hero shook Dr. Fluffenflapper's hand and took his leave.

CJ, standing atop the Gunham, adjusted his belt and looked to the pier. Chul, walking slower than normal and looking at his feet, approached.

"Come here," CJ said. "I want to show you something."

"What is the matter?" Chul asked. "Is something wrong because of the Potency God again?"

"No, nothing like that. But we do need to talk before we decide to trust this Dr. Fluffenflapper."

As soon as Chul made it aboard, CJ went inside and roused his laptop computer from sleep mode. A quick click on the web browser brought up the following, helpfully translated from German into English via an online service:

Welcome to pan-Germanic Alliance, a unified front on the Festival's classic collection. My name is Iglooflit Fluffenflapper, doctor of philosophy, Germany is the editor of a quarterly cooking and modern architecture lovers. I edit and I think the best Germanic (and the world) poetry and fiction, and then comment out the collection. All the versions presented here in proper historical context, contemporary criticism and modern interpretation of the notes. Here are all the materials provided free of charge, we only ask for and share it with your friends, and we all left that debt accumulated wisdom of the late geniuses spreads.

"I wonder why the doctor of philosophy," CJ said, "has not deduced how difficult that name makes it to take him seriously."

"Your names all sound the same to me," Chul said. "I am interested in his work though. What is the Pan-Germanic Alliance?"

"A publishing group, technically. They seem to be a nationalist propaganda outfit."

Chul didn't miss a beat in answering.

"That is odd considering what Fluffenflapper said before. I share your suspicions. We should understand his mind before we act on his suggestions, I think."

CJ moved on to the other bit of literature he'd discovered.

"Fluffenflapper also wrote an essay about how some people are like deep sea sponges," he said. "That translation was even less comprehensible than the crap I just showed you, but it didn't look good."

Chul sucked his teeth and looked to CJ.

"I share your suspicions," he said. "Perhaps it is wise for you to investigate Dr. Fluffenflapper's business dealings while I look into Ms. Snyder."

"That's a good idea, but first, beer."

"Of course, beer," Chul said. "And the weekend as well. We should not overextend ourselves by working on the weekends."

With that our two heroes set to the serious business of drinking, eating pizza and watching spoof films.

Chapter Forty Six

215 Days After

It did not take much effort to organize a second meeting with Dr. Fluffenflapper. CJ had only to speak with the secretary, mention his name and choose a time. No questions, no delays, amazingly little in the way of screening. The lesser of our heroes decided on the law library at Hamburg University as the meeting place, 3:30 pm as the appointment time.

Our hero chose this location because the librarians had proven themselves both universally bilingual and unusually patient. And further, what better place can you imagine in which to check Fluffenflapper's story than a research depository?

Rectangular glass windows of irregular size, colored orange, green and blue covered the entire exterior. Carved, regency style wooden bookshelves clashed amusingly with the hyper-modernist architecture. CJ chose an aluminum desk with an integrated electrical outlet for his computer, a light for his papers and a view of the river for his serenity.

CJ saw Dr. Fluffenflapper appear exactly on time at the library help desk. He appeared to be apologizing in that flittering, nervous way that insecure people mistakenly believe makes oneself endearing, modest or in some way less annoying. The librarian pointed at CJ, who then made eye contact with the doctor and the afternoon's discussion began thus.

"Good evening Mr. Smith," Fluffenflapper said. "I hope you have found my information regarding Ms. Snyder helpful."

CJ thought about that for a second and wondered how Chul was doing. *He'll be okay.*

"I don't know yet," CJ said. "I'm honestly more worried about you."

Fluffenflapper said nothing.

"I want you to explain why a guy like you—with all your talk about being a child of de-Nazification and freedom from nationalism—ends up working for the Pan-Germanic Alliance."

Dr. Fluffenflapper grimaced but did not answer and so the lesser of our heroes continued.

"And what is this about saying some people are subhuman, like sponges?"

"This must all look very hypocritical to you—"

"Damn right it looks hypocritical," CJ said. "What the hell kind of scheme are you trying to pull on us? Are you some kind of new-age, different label for the same thing Nazi?"

"I am certainly not a Nazi, I am—"

"Then you'd damn sure better start saying things that make sense," CJ said.

The doctor cringed and retreated, an action that made the lesser of our heroes want to hit him even more. A silence followed as CJ clenched his jaw and Fluffenflapper composed himself.

"My employer is a very wealthy man," Dr. Fluffenflapper said. "He has an interest in cultural preservation that I do not share—"

CJ interrupted him for the third time in four sentences.

"So you're a sellout?"

"Well, yes," Fluffenflapper said. "I will go against some of my preferences in exchange for money. It's hard to find a boss with whom you agree perfectly, isn't it? And I really think you are misunderstanding the nature of my employer. It's really closer to a historical preservation society than a Party for Freedom, PVV-like organization."

"Then explain the subhuman stuff."

This, oddly, improved Fluffenflapper's mood.

"I would love to," he said. "I haven't gotten the chance to discuss that essay in a long time. Where did you find the translation? I didn't think that was ever available in English."

"I, uh, I used an online translation program."

"Ah, so you didn't really have an opportunity to read it?" Fluffenflapper asked. "In that case, and if you have time, I will summarize."

That awkward sensation when a mighty, public rage peters out, dissipating with neither a target nor a reason for being, came over CJ.

"It was a philosophical exercise," Fluffenflapper said. "I wanted to learn the exact meaning of humanity. I decided to pursue this question by way of comparing us, in many ways the most advanced animals, with sponges, the most basal members of the animal kingdom.

"I thought about this at length and took pains to avoid anthropomorphic bias. I considered metabolism and genetics. Although different in a sponge and a human, our metabolic processes do exist on a fairly neat continuum through worms, non-vertebrate chordates, archosaurs, monotremes and finally our immediate ancestors. Indeed, I might be overstating our divergence from sponges. 70% of sponge genes have an analog in humans. In this sense, we are very similar.

"This brought me to the realization that, by raw material, by enzymes and cell structures and DNA strands, all life is merely variations on a theme. You worried that I am a secret Nazi? The genetic differences between German and Jew are so tiny as to be meaningless. There is far more variance within the German population itself than there is between the average German and the average Jew. Nazis, or any group advocating racial hierarchies, simply have no idea what they're talking about with regards to genetics."

Fluffenflapper paused, presumably to make sure CJ was keeping up with his dissertation. CJ nodded that the doctor might continue.

"Shape seemed like a superficial difference. Instinctual behavior also, in evolutionary terms, changes very quickly. It seems, in this way, a form of window dressing. So how then do we characterize the essential differences between ocean creatures easily mistaken for rocks and the mostly similar organisms that built the Great Pyramids?"

CJ shrugged and held up his hands. "I don't know, doctor."

"Agency!"

"Come again?"

"Agency!" Fluffenflapper's hands flapped, as if fluffing a pillow. "We can be more than the product of our circumstances. We are not passive! Think about it."

"You should really explain it a little more," CJ said.

"I will rephrase," Dr. Fluffenflapper said. "If you are a sponge, literally every single thing in your life came to you as the result of chance. Tides, water temperatures, the plankton blooms and marine snow on which you feed—all just coincidence. The sponge is glued to fate every step of its life. But we are different. We can build cities and explore the laws of nature. Where a sponge must depend on the ocean currents, we can make our own. This, Mr. Smith, this is the defining difference between a human being and a sponge!"

CJ saw in this an opportunity to re-take the conversational initiative, to strike at the slick bastard before he could talk his way completely out of trouble.

"If that's all you wrote, what is the subhuman stuff about?"

"It's almost inescapable," Fluffenflapper said. "If you accept my explanation about passivity separating humans from sponges, you must create two Platonic ideals by which to measure humanity. The positive ideal, the consummate human, would then be the least passive possible organism. This human ideal would actively change, choose and believe everything it came across. The sponge ideal, though, would be the least active possible organism."

CJ nodded, unsure where this was going.

"Therefore," Fluffenflapper said. "If you pay any attention at all to the world around you, you will know that many people are much nearer the sponge ideal than the human ideal."

"Germans shouldn't talk about subhumans," CJ said. "People might get the wrong idea."

"Yes," he said. "People who think like sponges could get confused. That, CJ, that is what I'm fighting against. If you assume I'm a sponge, that I'm just a German, that I'm just a man, that I'm just a Protestant, then yes, I should shut up about different levels of humanity. If I'm a real person, if I'm capable of reaching beyond these accidents, then who am I to remain silent?"

"So that's how you tie it into the stuff you said in the office," CJ said. "All your self-determination and no patriotic feelings stuff. I think you're underestimating how much good stuff just comes to people. It's not always bad to be a sponge."

"Who said sponges are bad?"

"Wait, what?"

"Sponges aren't bad," Fluffenflapper said. "They aren't, they're just more forces of nature than real, essential humans. No judgment, we wouldn't exist without the forces of nature."

CJ leaned back and held up his hands.

"We should probably just wipe out the subhumans, right?"

Fluffenflapper didn't like that question. His face puckered like someone had just shoved a handful of powdered aspirin into his mouth.

"That is a stupid suggestion," Fluffenflapper said.

"Really? Do tell me why you're not just another psycho Jerry with eugenics fantasies."

"The sheer number of false assumptions you needed to reach that conclusion, for one," Fluffenflapper said. "Really, I am disappointed."

"Oh, well in that case, fuck you."

Fluffenflapper shook his head like someone had just slapped him across the cheek.

"Have a nice evening, Mr. Smith."

As he rose to leave, CJ sent a single word chasing after him.

"Coward."

Fluffenflapper, for the first time, appeared more angry than timid. Part of CJ relished violence, hungered for conflict—this part was salivating as the doctor sat back down.

"I'm going to improve on your frankly appalling education," Dr. Fluffenflapper said. "We're going to start at the beginning. Do keep up. Culture is a tool for survival. That's all. When it breaks, throw it away."

CJ said nothing.

"Birth is an accident from the individual's point of view," the doctor said. "Am I going too fast for you?"

CJ just looked at him.

"This means the individual is not bound to respect or adopt the culture of his or her birth. So, unless you are going to tell me how you chose to be an American and I chose to be a German, it's time for you to take that 'Germans shouldn't say' stuff and shove it up your cornfed ass."

CJ harrumphed. He wanted to say something cutting and nasty but words failed him.

"Tradition as inertia is a lazy, dangerous way to build one's identity. It's how lower animals and plants function. It is the way not humans behave. A person who takes the culture and norms of their ancestors without question is not unable to make their own way in life; they are too lazy to even comparison shop. It's like being a 50 year-old, underachieving plumber who let's a decade-old tragedy control every aspect of his life."

Fluffenflapper paused to glare at CJ before continuing.

"Someone who comparison shops and picks bits and pieces from other cultures is more active, a bit more human. Someone who is willing to create a new belief or novel moral system is even more active, even more human. Is your empty little head hurting yet?"

CJ didn't respond.

"Humans think and invent. They are active. Sponges are passive, do not think. Sometimes people act like sponges. Sometimes people act human. Everyone does both at least some of the time. So explain to me why a person who has been given the gift of basic literacy would interpret my admonition to be more human, more of the time, as a call for eugenics?"

CJ glowered but said nothing. Fluffenflapper stood up and gathered his bag. "I will not speak with you again, Mr. Smith. Tell Mr. Choi I'm tired of dealing with children."

Chapter Forty Seven

218 Days After

It was raining and sleeting and grey on the sidewalk. Chul did not want to stay outside any longer than necessary, and so half-ran through the streets in search of CJ's favorite McDonald's. One tug of the red and yellow door handles and our hero was out of the downpour. *Roofs are very underrated,* he thought.

He found CJ the back corner with a stack of papers and an old file. CJ made notes on one of the papers and did not notice Chul approaching.

"I finally found her," Chul said. "She's a gardener and office clerk in Urnfield. What are you doing?"

CJ startled and pushed the papers quickly but carefully back into the folder. He turned it over and thus obscured the folder's label.

"Just a project I'm working on," CJ said. "So are we going to Urnfield?"

Chul wondered what kind of project CJ was attending to. *Perhaps Professor Kong has awakened his inner poet.*

"No need," Chul said. "The secretary at Geschenke der Natur Spirituellen Gartenbau's office said Snyder is visiting family in Kiel, near the Danish border."

"They gave you this information?" CJ asked.

"With Snyder's permission," Chul said. "That is why it took so long. I made other preparations as well. If we walk two minutes we can use the car I bought and go directly to her."

"You bought a car?"

"Yes, it is red and has a voluptuous interior," Chul said. "I am thinking of shipping it to Korea and giving it to my son when our travels are over."

The Mercedes Benz looked to date from about 1976. It was indeed red and the interior was indeed voluptuous, especially if quilted leather counts for volup. It also had gold trim in place of the original chrome, lizard skin in place of the original wood pieces and fringed, velvet curtains hanging from the back windows. CJ's initial impulse upon touching the exquisite leather seats was to go immediately to the nearest clinic and get a syphilis screening. That, however, seemed likely to cause the wrong sort of impression with Chul and so he said this instead.

"This car is very…elaborate."

"It would strain your credulity if I told you how cheaply it came into my possession," Chul said.

CJ doubted that very much but played along.

"How much?"

"No more than two thousand Euros! But let us go now. We can discuss my triumph on the way. "

CJ sat in the back and, after a period of revulsion, grew very fond of the velvet curtains. Good taste was not a precondition of concealment.

(For the virtue of adventurous car buying, I bless the entire Choi family with a lifelong subscription to Donk Magazine.)

Ms. Snyder appeared to live on a leftover *Sound of Music* set. The cottage sat atop a snow-dusted, grassy hill overlooking a conifer lined meadow. White lattices overflowed with bougainvillea and honeysuckles. A rounded doorway trimmed in yellow and green peeked out from the vegetation and, along with the two, softly glowing windows, formed the only breaks in the overwhelming floriculture.

Chul parked the car near several large tomato planters and walked to the front door. *I hope Fluffenflapper's information is good,* he thought. Our hero felt the sharp granite chunks grind beneath his feet and poke at the soles of his shoes. With his fine car glimmering in the winter sun and a new sport coat hugging his waist he could not help but feel more refined than usual.

Knock, knock, knock.

The door opened with a wood on wood creaking sound to reveal three women, all of whom appeared to be in their 30s. The nearest, dressed in a flowing sundress, a floppy straw hat and galoshes, smiled and welcomed our heroes in.

"Welcome, welcome!" she said. "Would you like some tea? Perhaps some sandwiches? Marijuana?"

"Tea," CJ said. "If you don't mind."

"Tea for me as well," Chul said.

"Hilda," the first woman said to the second, similarly attired woman nearest the kitchen. "Could you get some tea for our guests?"

Hilda could and disappeared into a back room. The first woman proceeded to introduce herself and the third woman.

"My name is Ines Snyder and this Nadine," she said.

"To what do we owe this visit?" Nadine asked.

"Sie erinnern sich Fluffenflapper?" Ines Snyder asked to Nadine. "Er ist der Mann, der uns all die schönen gesendet Schalotte Glühbirnen im vergangenen Jahr. Sie erinnern, nicht wahr? Du nicht? Du bist so vergesslich Nadine. Ehrlich gesagt, habe ich fast Lust, werfen Sie Ihre heilige Brunst Cups."

Whatever she'd just said, Ines Snyder seemed disappointed in Nadine.

"Sie würden es nicht wagen, Hündin!" Nadine said.

"Ich bin die Hündin?" Ines Snyder asked. "Sie sind derjenige, der nicht einmal lenken den Geist der Mondgöttin, ohne sich selbst in Vaseline eingeseift!"

"Ich bekomme Scheuern und Sie wissen es, Sie schmutzige Schlampe. Und wer bist du denn? Der Gestank des ungewaschenen Arsch Alleingang zerstört unsere Sonnenblumen. Verwelkte ihnen, so dass dein Arsch ein Sukkubus, hinter Sonnenblumen trocken und tot wie ein gepresster Pickel!"

Nadine stood up and stared death at Ines Snyder. Chul searched for escape routes. Nadine broke her tea saucer on the table. "Sie ein zit aufgetacht!" When she closed the door, the entire house shook.

"I'm very sorry about that," Ines Snyder said. "Nadine wouldn't know the glow of arcane energy if it bit her spirit guardian's behind."

"I think we all know someone like that," Chul said.

CJ shot a bewildered look at Chul, adding the following.

"Yeah, don't we all?"

"Well," Ines Snyder said. "I don't really know why you are here. Mr. Fluffenflapper is not someone I know well, and he was vague about your purpose. If you perhaps told me a bit about your desires I might be of more help."

Chul thought it best if these strangers didn't know the exact nature of their visit, but CJ appeared to disagree, answering thus:

"We are after the Twinky of Destiny," he said. "I don't know for sure, but I get the feeling we're really close, too."

Ines turned her head to the side and smiled.

"Oh really?" She asked. "That's fascinating. I think I know why Fluffenflapper sent you, in that case. I'm very sad to say I think it is my ex-inamorato."

"What's an inamorato?" CJ asked.

Ines Snyder flashed a cheerful smile before answering.

"It's a fuck buddy, you silly boy!"

She waited a beat before continuing.

"He was such a sensitive, brooding boy. You know the type—poetic, sad eyes, brilliant but trapped in his own spiritual angst."

Chul was about to say something but Ines Snyder hadn't finished.

"I always felt for him," she said. "The way his subtle, complex mind isolated him from the common people. He was so misunderstood, so tortured by his art. I used to think the torture came from his hand-rolled clove cigarettes, coconut water and vegan food, unwashed hair and overly tight pants but I now see that I was wrong."

"He sounds lovely," CJ said. "If you're into that sort of thing, I guess."

"There was this one time he gave me just such powerful insight," Ines Snyder said. "And it was so beautiful, so inspiring I remember it even now. He was talking about how cruel the world is, how uncaring and calloused. And I asked, 'how do you bear it?' And he said 'nature is my muse.' Then I said 'tell me more' and he looked to the ground and his eyes were so sad. He touched my hand and said—'If you fall in the woods, at least you know the trees won't laugh.'"

Chul failed to grasp the profundity but nodded, smiled and moved on to the part of Ines Snyder's life he actually did care about.

"That is very interesting. So what makes you think this man is important for us?"

"I think his torment has finally gotten too much," Ines Snyder said. "He left me—well, he left a book for me in Munich."

She folded her hands across her lap.

"It is a dark, disturbing work," she said. "Naturally, it is full of genius and yet, and yet I fear it contains an awful secret. If you give me perhaps a week, I can retrieve it for you."

"Ms. Snyder," CJ said. "I don't know if we can do anything with this. I don't speak German and neither does my friend."

"Neither does my love," she said. "He's from Vancouver."

"Oh."

(For the virtue of using toxic fumes, lanced pimples and succubae in the same extended simile, I bless Nadine with the Moon Goddess' everlasting approval.)

Your species has no clue what the word evil means. You wrap it up so completely in your silly, constantly changing little world views and ignore the context, brush aside the conflicting facts. Hitler was "evil" because he killed so many people. Charles Manson is "evil" because of his psychopathy. Kim Jong-il was "evil" because of his cruelty. This is, frankly, so many tons of horseshit.

I say this because the impulse to ignorance is natural to your species and, mixed with the fuzzy nothingness of moral principle, means that you can and do justify pretty much anything. Hitler thought he was serving the greater good and all he had to do to convince himself was to develop a distaste for the "lesser races." He saw himself as a savior, and tens of millions of perfectly normal people across Europe agreed with him. They agreed strongly enough to die in his service. This was no monster, this was a normal man with a moral vision people found exceptionally appealing. Because of this normalcy, because people could relate to him, he was vastly more dangerous than any truly evil person could ever be.

Kim Jong-il was much the same as Hitler. He believed his nation would fall apart without his steadying hand. He hesitated to betray the birthrights of his loyal family. He did what was necessary to protect the former North Korea from its numerous enemies. How else can you explain 20 million people consenting to his leadership for nearly two decades?

Charles Manson is even less evil because, unlike the other two, he is a psychopath. His mental shortcomings make him incapable of empathy, automatically ignorant of the suffering his actions inflicted. If he is a monster, he's an oblivious one.

To be truly evil requires an uncommon ability to rise above this sort of self-deception and inborn blindness. It requires the ability to set aside the pliable justifications of morality. It requires a deep and nuanced understanding of suffering. The truly evil woman cannot lie to herself at all. The evil man must look at the likely consequences of his actions objectively, understand their totality, without retreating into the muck of moral justification, and commit them anyway.

This type of self-directed honesty will necessarily alienate the truly evil person from their moral, self-deluding peers. It will render them unable to relate or attract followers and thus far less dangerous than a normal person. Indeed, there is almost nothing to recommend true evil excepting, perhaps, a certain clarity of vision afforded by their deep personal honesty—a strong point not exclusively or even mostly present in the truly evil.

A person of this type, both aware and malevolent, occurs with only the greatest infrequency. Indeed, if you are searching for an evil person, you will come closer with this story's protagonists. It is thus unfortunate for our heroes that they would not be looking for someone evil. Instead, this adversary came complete with the normal powers of self-deception and an extraordinary desire for life and, thus, posed a much greater threat.

Chapter Forty Eight

235 Days After

CJ called Chul to his desk in the cheap hotel room. CJ pushed a chair out so his friend could more easily access the scattered papers and reference books.

"How can it be so difficult for you, a native speaker of English, to read this book that Ines Snyder gave us?" Chul asked. "It has been several days."

"The obvious answer is that it's damn near a thousand pages long," CJ said. "Beyond that, it's just so fucking pretentious. I mean, I really, really want to punch this guy."

Chul grabbed the book and opened to a page somewhere near the middle.

"It cannot be that bad."

He stared at the page for a solid five minutes. *Oh yes it can be,* CJ thought. The lesser of our heroes took on a bit of a shit-eating grin as he waited.

"This passage is about a washing machine?" Chul asked. "Why does he refer to Walt Whitman, post-modernism and Marx? And why does he not understand those things to which he makes reference?"

CJ ventured a guess.

"Because he's a douchebag?"

"It is impossible a feminine hygiene product could write," Chul said. "In any event, I do not care. You have read this, why does Ines Snyder give it to us?"

CJ smiled again before answering.

"Well, depending on how autobiographical you think this is, the story is either a massively self-absorbed novel or a massively self-absorbed confession of murder."

Chul frowned.

"I do not like to act on such flimsy evidence," he said. "I know the God of Potency is steering the situation for his own, perverted ends, but I do not wish to depend to heavily on assumptions."

"I do have an idea," CJ said. "I was worried that maybe, I should get a second opinion before I draw any conclusions. This shitty book thing is really subjective and I could just be reading too much into it. That's actually one reason I took so long to finish reading it. I wanted to make a shorter version without all of the unnecessary imagery, pointless metaphors and digressions so that you could read it, too. I mean, your English is really good, but I was afraid that if this was almost too big a mess for me, you might not make it through."

Chul nodded and answered.

"You are right," he said. "Do not think you have offended me."

"Okay, so I cut out a *lot* of stuff and here," CJ patted a stack of papers on the desk. "Here are the remnants. Just what I think is important."

Chul seemed surprised and picked the stack up by its edge, peering underneath.

"I thought you said the book was more than a thousand pages long?"

"Get rid of the fluff and it's closer to ten," CJ said.

Chul sucked his teeth and shook his head.

"Are you starting to appreciate how much pain I just endured?" CJ asked. "No more shit about 'why did it take you so long?'"

Instead of answering, Chul patted CJ's hand, took the papers and leaned back in his chair.

CJ had wondered off to get dinner and left our hero to his thoughts. Chul looked to the first page and read the following, complete with CJ's annotations.

Alright, this guy's name is Mannus. He thinks himself some sort of tortured artist type. He certainly tortured me with his art. This is from his time in the Master of Fine Arts Program in Lower Vancouver Community College.

Deserts of Apathy, Oasis of Syllables—
Like gorgons in a pool,
I rage at the closing of the light.
A poet's life,
forever poetic as all hell.
Oppressed, yes oppressed by the 1%.
Stealing my meaning,
Life is shit.
Blinded like a phoenix
Living in Phoenix
Where it's really sunny, usually
I lean back in my leather chair
Turn on the flat screen.
1,000 channels
Naught but sluts and fascists.
Sluts, with their slapping slits slithering.
Make them groan.
Groan like late capitalism

Ben Garrido

Under the jackboot of fascist sluts.
Fascist Nazis say
buy my exploitative company's unjust
products of rampant consumerism and
the sluts will come to you,
for you,
on you,
inside you,
behind you,
above you,
face down in your bathtub."
That last part, perhaps not so bad,
even if they are fascists.

That slut Dr. Grimswald and her "creative writing class" is oppressing me again. But I learned why. She wrote this bourgeoisie, pretentious little "memoir" about being molested as a girl. She's not over it and hates men, hence the B- for my transformative poetry.

A Vision—
I stand before the academy. I grimace under the weight of their misunderstanding, their misaimed adoration for my art. The tentacles of their expectation hammering my consciousness like a train bound for the deepest pits of purgatory. They say, "conform, conform." They approach the threaded nozzle of my expression with the screw-on caps of censorship, seeking to constipate the flow of my shimmering art. And yet they demand more from me. They demand more of the genius they will never understand. I go to the podium and make a point to recognize the real heroes.

"I'd like to recognize all the smart people and minorities here tonight," I say. This crushes the fascists and sluts. "I like

to think my art is the truest kind—that which goes beyond mere meaning to the endless fields of pure expression. Form without function, context without content, masterpieces without meaning—these are what make me such a transformative artist.

"You can try to tie my pureness to all of your silly little interpretations, but it hurts me. Can't you see how much I suffer to bring you my insurmountable mountain of genius? How can you understand so little of that which, from it's very revelation onward, contains nothing to understand?"

I smash the hundreds of awards and trinkets the fascist pigs put before me and flee before the massive and adoring public can torment me further with their oppressive lowness. They are so, so common!

A Study in Courage—

The corporate fat cats oppress us common people with their corruption and greed. Greed! Greed! Is money all that matters to you, soulless automaton of the stock exchange, slave master of the slave market of late capitalism? Shame, shame on you.

I am joining an Occupy Wall Street protest this weekend. Unprepared I have gone not! I had arranged a new set of fatigued clothing so that I will appear more authentic. I have my well loved copies of The Anarchist Quarterly *and pre-mixed Gatorade and vodka. With these all safely packed into the passenger's seat of my BMW, I set off bravely and stoically, ready to endure all manner of insults and oppression for the sake of the poor, the downtrodden, the victims of Wall Street greed. The wooded lanes of my suburb went away behind and gave way to the concrete oppression of downtown Vancouver. Sweaty, disgusting men in unwashed wife-beater tank tops swung hammers against the institutions of finance, selling out their own lowly class for money so that the banksters can remodel their corrupt dens of exploitation, exploiting those same ignorant laborers from within the comfort of their freshly remodeled banks, said remodeling being the work of aforementioned class traitors even now using greasy tools in exchange for their pitiful wages. I shuttered at their lack of vision. But even this horrifying automatonish behavior would not turn me back, accustomed as I am to horrific artistic suffering.*

I flipped open my new iPad and checked my emails in the few blocks before our rally point. A pedestrian yelled at me, but fuck him.

Our roster of brave souls were: Barry Jane, poet, organic quiche farmer; Kelly Brianne, conceptual sculptor and professor of fine art at the Lower Vancouver Community College; Pat Merry, conceptual weaving artist and recent graduate from the Columbia MFA program; Henry Branston, our virtuous minority, drummer and experienced criminal. Our extended group included Elijah Clare, a librarian at the Rockefeller Library for the Fine Arts; Lindsey Cray another conceptual artist and writer at bS^2 Literary Journal.

Before we'd come, we all shared an email about getting arrested. One person couldn't get arrested because they had a lecture the next day on eradication by corrupt politicians of entire populations of the beautiful, natural organism Simulium yahense. *Another, Angus, was scheduled to appear at an interpretive dance festival. I had no such pressing engagements and determined to be the best civil disobediencer possible, though.*

We began the protest with the standard chants. "We are the 99%," I yelled to the banksters. "And so are you," Barry Jane answered to the passersby. The banksters in their slick suits and fancy cars sneered at us and walked into their fortresses of oppression. Nothing can get through to those people. Nothing. Henry the virtuous minority redoubled his drumming and blocked the path of the next bankster. The bankster tried to move around him to the left, but Henry the virtuous minority scooted sideways so he couldn't go past.

"We are the 99%," he yelled and motioned to the rest of us. We joined him and formed an immovable blockade to trap the bankster, who got scared of all our justice and called out to the nearest Gestapo corporate slave policeman.

The Gestapo didn't say anything. They just formed a wall, pushed us out of the street and went back to their previous positions. Henry the virtuous minority retook the street. He sat down in the middle of the road and dared the Gestapo to oppose him. A Gestapo told him to get up, but Henry wouldn't. Then the Gestapo tried to pick him up. Henry the virtuous minority would have nothing of that sort of oppression and intimidation. He pushed the cop back and yelled, "We are the 99%!"

Their oppression was swift and brutal. They tackled him to the ground and tore his shirt. Blood came from his mouth and knees but it didn't look serious. He would be fine and anyways, we were savvy to the Gestapo's evil ploy.

The Gestapo probably thought they could goad us into violence, some crude physical defense of our most vulnerable member and a virtuous minority to boot. But we were a peaceful, vegetarian crowd. We documented the abuse with our iPads and camera phones. Pat Merry started up a new chant of "shame! Shame!" and we all joined in as they hauled Henry the virtuous minority to the prison truck.

As the day progressed, it became clear that the Gestapo, fearful of our iPads and camera phones, would limit their oppression to people standing in the street. I asked Kelly and

Elijah if they wanted to try out getting arrested. They said they did. We stepped into the street, over the outstretched arms of our fellow 99%ers. We sat on the center divider as the crowd, in recognition of our courage, let out a cheer. Even the Gestapo had to admire our civil disobedience. When they arrested us, they maintained perfect manners, sliding on the plastic handcuffs like wedding rings.

In our first prison cell, there were only protestors. We broke into small groups and had extremely deep and meaningful conversations about European history, wars fought by foreigners and the plight of the North American small, post-industrial city.

Non-protestors, mostly recreational drug users and minorities, filtered in and sat down silently. They didn't ask what we were protesting about. Their loss. Finally Kelly could stand no more of these criminals' wandering in the wilderness of ignorance and lectured at length on capitalism and the tyranny of student debt. An anarchist named Larry explained the glory of revolution and overthrowing the entire corrupt, corporate hierarchy. Elijah spoke to the eternal ideals of our inviolable rights and, to top off his moving speech, went to the door and yelled to the guards.

"What's the delay? What's the delay? WHAT'S THE DE-LAY?!"

A minority with consumerist tattoos and big muscles spoke up.

"Hey, I don't care if y'all wanna say your stupid shit in here, but there aint nothing them guards can do except delay your paperwork. And my paperwork. And if I'm still here in the morning then you're gonna have something real to complain about—my foot up your dumb ass."

I had to let that sink in for a second. I was a tourist here, indeed, I'd gotten arrested largely because I wanted to see the stinking underbelly of the corporate state. This minority had probably seen the insides of prisons a dozen times before. He just wanted to get out, not make some larger point about injustice.

This lack of ideals in our lowest classes is, frankly, both a disappointment and a form of suicide. No group of people suffers more from the corporate culture of exploitation than minorities and poor people. And yet who is it too worried about getting home to sacrifice for his ideals? The minority. Who is so quick to sell out their class for a pathetic wage? Those grease-covered laborers selling their souls, remodeling away on the banksters' palaces.

I despaired. Even now, when these laborers and minorities had such a great opportunity to improve their lots, nothing. Even when the transformative artists, anarchist thinkers and drummers of the world came to rescue them, still these lowly people would not embrace our salvation. Regardless, I would struggle on, I would bring rescue to these people whether they wanted it or not.

As if to prove the tattooed minority wrong, a prison guard came at that very moment to release us protestors. Angus, who'd earlier declared himself ineligible for arrest, redeemed himself by greeting us by the jail. He performed a touching interpretive dance rendition of "In the Future There Will Be Robots" for us as we went down the steps to the sidewalk below. We all embraced and then, without much more fanfare, went our separate ways. Some of us went to a rave in Langley, more headed for Washington State in order to participate in another Occupy Wall Street Occupation. I myself went to Whole Foods. The Gestapo, of course, had offered us nothing in the way of organic or vegan selections during our unjust imprisonment. Barbarians.

Chul turned the page and saw CJ's handwritten mast-head "the music phase."

I took a new lover today. I think her name is Esther or Erica or Ines—something like that. She appreciates my art as translated into the musical medium, she serves as a muse for my creativity, she tolerates butt sex and completes me so that I can escape the all-encompassing melancholy and loneliness constantly threatening transformative artists like me. That she performs these functions is all that matters to me. I will suffer any other of her shortcomings for the sake of our love.

My new project is called "In tHe PreSenT TheRe WilL Be RoBotS." I lead this project, of course, and write all the lyrics. Our first song, "Diabolic Curtains, It All Ends," is my translation of "Deserts of Apathy, Oasis of Syllables" into robotic beeping sounds. We performed it last night in front of the Germans. They were shocked into silence, rendered speechless by my genius, laid bare by the power of our art. The bartender was so overcome that he encouraged me to share this art with other bars and pubs, particularly those of his competitors.

Our success is sure to follow, not that the regular people will fathom it.

Ines' friends do not fathom my art. I had just finished the chorus line to our second song, "The Conical Fascist of Steel," when Nadine came to our stage and looked up at me. The looking was really intense and distracted me from my art. I was already mad about this when the song finished. Then the Philistine waved for me to approach, cupped her hand and asked.

"Why do you make robot sounds, like beep-bop, beep-bop, instead of using words?"

Oh how I wanted to grab her cup of wheat grass and pour it over her dreadlocks. How could she miss the symbolism? How was it that my sublime references to post-pre-intramodernist roboticized Hindu thought somehow went unnoticed by this cretin? Ignorance, naked ignorance. Is there no one capable of appreciating my genius?

Nadine's ignorance bothers me so much I've decided to dump Ines. I can't have a lover who is bringing around "friends" who will only interfere with my process—constantly failing to fathom my art. Losing me will be a blow, I'm sure, but Ines will overcome the crippling void of living without me eventually.

Chul put the papers down and shook his head. *How much dog's noise is this?* Chul could feel his brain going numb and decided to take a break. It was not obvious why CJ thought this important and thus our hero decided to wait until he returned.

Chul went to the refrigerator and decided to indulge a little of his own creativity. He toasted some naan, covered it in kimchi, added a slice of cheddar and scrambled eggs to create one of the most international sandwiches ever constructed. *Surprisingly good, actually.*

Our hero had just finished washing his plate and knife when CJ opened the door. The American dropped a shopping bag full of hotdogs, bread and bananas on the *Gunham's* glistening kitchen counters.

"This is all very interesting," Chul said. "If only in the sense of watching a house burn or reviewing earthquake footage. However, I do not understand why you think this son of insanity committed murder."

CJ frowned and cocked his head to the side.

"Really?"

Chul tapped the stack of papers and answered.

"I saw nothing but occupations, poetry, a very brief mention of Ines and a tendency to confuse robot beeping sounds with music."

"You didn't read the part about becoming a homosexual?" CJ asked.

Chul frowned but did not answer.

"That's the most important part," CJ said. "Did I misplace it, I wonder?"

CJ shuffled stacks of paper, checked the pockets of his briefcase, searched his desk. CJ bumped his laptop and in doing so displaced the machine enough to reveal a slim stack of copier paper peeking out to Chul.

"Is that it?" Chul asked.

He lifted the laptop and removed the papers before CJ could respond.

I've decided to be gay. It will be a struggle for me, due mostly to the yuckiness of it all. I mean, gross. That said, if I'm ever going to escape the conformist, exploitative conditions of this modern, consumerist world, I need to do it.

I am the direct descendent of Don Carlo Gesualdo. This would explain my innate genius and musical inventiveness. That man knew true art, and he let nothing get in his way. When the Gestapo tried to restrain his genius he, with the high rank of his birth and genius art, beat them back with his inborn impunity, his natural contempt for the laws and norms of those dreadful, dull masses that could not fath-

om his art. I am the second coming of Gesualdo, no earthly power can judge me, who the hell do they think they are? Nothing will stand in the way of my expression ever again, I swear to it!

I found a gay lover. I chose him because he wears pink silk shirts, frosts the tips of his gelled hair spikes and speaks with a lisp. He's so gay everyone will know I've rebelled, which is the most important thing. The sex wasn't as difficult as I thought. I simply instruct Stuart to speak in a squeaky falsetto, give him a naughty nurse costume and outfit him in a selection of fake breasts and pubic reshaping devices. Once I turn off the lights, the yuckiness becomes almost tolerable. Stuart initially found this demeaning, but he appreciates my need for true expression and no longer questions my demands. The common people of course do not understand us, even the common homosexuals have joined in oppressing me. Fucking faggots.

Stuart is growing distant. He isn't even trying with the falsetto these days.

I know how Gesualdo felt when he discovered his beautiful wife in the arms of another. I know how betrayed he must have been, seeing her flopping around in the heat of passion. I know because Stuart, ungrateful little strumpet, left me for another.

IS THERE NO ONE WHO UNDERSTANDS?

That selfish, awful man. How could he rob me of my muse? How could he deprive me of my rebellion? He will soon learn the consequences of hurting the expression a Gesualdo genius. Tonight, Stuart, you will learn first hand.

The Subtle Blade—A Poem in Verse, Meter and Rhyme
Wherefore did the Rose blossom unfaithful to me?
In the sewers of the gay bar, gay bar, gay bar.
Where did the fascist slut go to deny me my muse?
The gay bar, gay bar, gay bar.
Where did the gay whore go to get a new boyfriend?

He went to the gay bar to hook up with some stupid ran-
dom guy who "doesn't try to make me act like a girl or treat
me like a stage prop."

Wherefore   did   the   selfish   fucking   loser   go?
Into my basement.

Where did the girly man go?

Into a pool of scarlet crimson, wet like water and spilled
on the floor just like in those awful exploitative CSI shows
on TV, exactly like the victim in season 6, episode 8.

Why fore did the unfaithful whore Rose go unto a pool
of CSI blood?

For dumping me, that fucking asshole.

He totally deserved it and I got my revenge.

See about double crossing me, I straight fucked you up,
cut you open and wore your intestines as a motherfucking
necklace.

And the metaphorical Rose I so skillfully mentioned ear-
lier now feeds the literal roses in my neighbor's front yard,
along with that jerk he was screwing.

I have what I was always meant to have, impunity-ee so
sweetiny-ee .

Amen.

While Chul had to admit, that last poem sounded suspicious, he also thought it a flimsy foundation on which to base an amateur homicide investigation. If, on the other hand, if there were more indications that such a murder did actually happen, that might warrant further exertion.

Chul called the local INTERPOL office and asked if there were any disappearances involving homosexuals in the area. Predictably, the officer provided the minimum of legally required assistance.

"Yes, Mr. Choi," the officer said. "Gay people sometimes get murdered, too. I'm sorry I cannot offer you any more help."

"His name was Stuart," Chul said. "Can you search for a missing homosexual called Stuart?"

"No, Mr. Choi, I cannot."

"야, 좆 빨아봐—너 씨발새끼야."

"I'm sorry?" the officer said. "I didn't understand you."

"I mean, thank you for your time."

Chul groaned at the phone before hanging up. An Internet search seemed likely to result in thousands of wild goose chases. Our hero went to CJ and proposed the only solution he could think of.

"I cannot tell if this story reflects truth," he said. "Maybe we should visit to Ines once more."

Chapter Forty Nine

CJ put down the phone and palmed the keys for Chul's ghastly Mercedes. He tossed the keys to Chul and exited through the Gunham's carbon and glass doors. The darkness would make it harder for outsiders to see him inside that rolling brothel and for this he was vaguely thankful.

"Ines said she'll meet us at her studio in the old Snyder Foundry at 10:30," CJ said. "Let's get going."

A cool breeze blew over the river and brought with it smells of pine, wood smoke and baking. CJ smiled and stepped into the car. Chul followed soon after. They set off into the countryside, gliding through the moonless night beneath the bright stars. Cattle and forests eventually gave way to a poorly lit yard within which industrial revolution-era brick buildings stood like coal-stained ghosts of the long dead.

They stopped and opened the Mercedes' gold-trimmed doors. CJ marveled at the silence in this old factory. Utter peace, as if the clattering and smoke-belching of the factory's previous life had permanently sucked all possible bustle from the atmosphere.

"I think that's the one," CJ said. "Over there, next to the smoke stack."

The white-washed door glowed beneath the gentle light of a single bulb and gave way with a small push. Inside the corridor the walls were plastered with posters from a hundred indie rock shows. A guitarist laying prostrate in a field here, a drummer releasing white doves there, roughly nine million *distinct* posters with a floral and tattoo art theme. Had someone combined all the white guy dreadlocks depicted those posters and arranged them together, CJ imagined the resulting book would check in at an Oxford Dictionary length. Poking through holes here and there were ticket stubs for slam poetry, ads for eco-conscious coffee and fair trade quiche. CJ noted a horrifying poster of a bloodied woman holding a mutilated animal by the leg with the slogan "this is the rest of your fur coat" that covered an old metal door off to the side.

"I can see why she and Mannus got along," CJ said. "It's like Ziggy Marley threw up in here."

CJ opened the next door into what he assumed would be the studio proper, took one bewildered step backwards and felt a rifle butt break his nose.

Chul could barely move, the surprise was so great. A few seconds passed as he looked at CJ on the ground then up at Ines holding a huge knife and that other woman—Nadine?—standing behind her and brandishing a bolt action hunting rifle.

They didn't seem to see him at first, being so focused on CJ. Chul took one step back, then two, and then Nadine looked up.

"Fang ihn!" she screamed.

Chul ripped open the old door with the skinned animal poster and stumbled into the darkness. He turned and crashed into some sort of brick structure, perhaps a bellows or chimney. Blood poured from his lip and he pulled his shirt up to avoid leaving a trail. If nothing else, he could get farther from the door before the women came to find him. He finally crawled behind a huge, rusted machine that, presumably, had once been used as a forging die.

As his eyes adjusted to the gloom he heard a peculiar sound. It sounded like dragging a sack of rice across the sidewalk. As he looked towards the door he saw a woman bent over, pulling something behind her. Three concerted pulls later, Chul was able to make out exactly what the woman was dragging.

CJ awoke to a profound sense of pressure in his head. As he lay prostrate on the concrete, CJ wondered if this was what it would feel like to go a year without blowing one's nose. It must have been the pressure that woke him from unconsciousness. He tried to move the muscles in his cheeks to ease the pain. The sounds of pulverized sinus bones grinding together stopped him. Mouth breathing—he let his jaw hang low, loose, like he might let it fall off.

Fingers snaked through his hair, grabbed hard and pulled his head back. Small hands, not particularly strong. A woman yelled into the darkness of the studio.

"Where are you going?" the woman asked. "I hold all the cards, you can't do anything except piss me off."

There was a pause as the woman holding CJ's head whispered to someone else nearby.

"Look in the forge works. I can handle this one."

Chul saw Nadine leave CJ and begin a search of the building. Ines squatted over CJ's back and held up the American's head as she continued her string of threats.

"You don't want his death on your conscience," she yelled. "Just give me the Twinkie and you can both go home."

He felt fear but not as much as you'd expect. This was more confusion than anything else. What did these people want from him? What could he do? Was CJ alright? Another thought hit him so hard it forced the air from his lungs. *Am I abandoning my friend?*

The greater of our heroes reached for his phone and dialed 110, the German emergency services number. To speak might give away his position, so he whispered "help, help" and left it on the ground.

But then what? Chul checked his pockets and found only his keys, his wallet and a wad of ruined receipts. *Shit.* Nadine or whatever her name was appeared in the murk and seemed to be vaguely on his trail. *Shit, shit, shit.*

Chul pulled the keys from his pockets and arranged them in his fist so that the hard, sharp ends poked out between his fingers in a sort of improvised set of knuckle-dusters. If Nadine got close enough, he'd at least have some chance of survival.

CJ spat out enough phlegm to clear his mouth. The elastic blob shimmered next to his cheek as he spoke.

"Hey," he said. "Hey, there's no reason. Just…"

He looked down and speech failed him. The knife against his throat must have been a foot long. The kind you see on nature shows when somebody has to gut a deer. CJ thought of his wife, how she fell. How the heat and smoke had grown too much. Oh, how clean she must have felt when she reached out into the air. How cool.

The woman holding his head yelled something about impunity to a presumably concealed Chul and mentioned that stupid Twinkie. A part of CJ's heart fell. This was beyond fear, this place he had gone. It was sadness like a frozen lake. He could die with honor, but please not now. Not after so much growth. Not before he could say goodbye to Patty. Not before he could purge the hatred and bitterness from before. There was so much more to do.

CJ made a single, strong movement to stand up and he felt the woman sliding off his back. His thoughts turned to escape and then his neck opened and the blood came out into the silence. Fast, strong, like a pitcher turned on its side, like warm shower water spilling down his chest. The pain was not like the mucosal filth in his nose. This was clean. He stretched his hand and touched his eyes. And then he was empty. And then he was gone.

Chul watched as CJ collapsed to his knees and then onto the floor. Our hero's heart dropped and he nearly fell over. Not another one. Not another sacrifice. *Not my friend.*

The sound of Nadine's feet against the concrete brought him back to the present. She still hadn't seen him. He crouched in preparation for—for what? Chul unambiguously hungered to do murder, but he also wanted to help CJ. He saw a sandaled foot from the gap between the ancient forging die and the ground. His body coiled and he cocked his fist back. The barrel of the gun emerged from the darkness and swung in his direction. Chul grabbed the barrel, pulled the woman off balance and threw a punch so hard it broke one of the keys.

Police sirens blared in the background as Chul looked into his friend's lifeless eyes.

Chapter Fifty

427 Days After

It was early September when he knocked on Patty's door. While no less than 14 degrees Celcius, the San Francisco fog gave even this minor chill appreciable teeth. He shivered twice as he waited. A man in a wool sweater, wearing black-rimmed glasses and Birkenstocks opened the door.

"Are you Mr. Choi?" he asked.

Chul nodded.

"I'm John, Patty's husband," he said. "She has wanted to talk to you for a long time. I'm very glad you could come."

John shook Chul's hand. Our hero could not help but notice how small, how soft John's hand felt in his own. *No wonder CJ didn't like him.*

They stepped inside the house and Chul deposited his coat on the tiny, antique rack. Sounds of aluminum clicking against wood came from round the corner. He pulled an envelope containing CJ's final letter to the *New York Times* and held it in his hands. A woman called from the next room.

"Is that him, John?"

"Yeah, Patty," John said. "He made it."

This was a large woman. Not fat, but big. She had the shoulders of one who climbs rocks and the calloused hands of a cyclist. It seemed incongruent that such a woman would need crutches.

"Can we get you some coffee or tea?" she asked.

"Tea, please," Chul said.

John went to the kitchen and left them alone. Chul's throat tightened and he swallowed painfully. The muscles in his chin, those tiny fibers that shake just before a man weeps, began their flutter.

"I have dreaded this moment," he said. "I have injured you grievously and I am sorry. I am so sorry."

Patty didn't say anything and Chul continued.

"I do not know what else I can say."

Patty's small frown and little nod seemed like the prelude to something more. Perhaps a condemnation, perhaps questions, perhaps leaving the room.

"I didn't know how to say this before," Patty said. "But I think I should thank you. I don't know what you and Dad did, I don't know what happened in Germany, but I do know how he changed when he met you."

"Your father was my responsibility," Chul said. "I saw how bad things followed on my actions but I did not stop. Your father was not the first to suffer grievously for my gain, he was the third."

"Did you sell him out?" Patty asked. "That's how you're making it sound."

"I would never!"

"Then how are you responsible? My father was a grown man, he knew."

Chul's shame rose once more.

"I do not mean this to speak ill of CJ," Chul said. "But I made most of the decisions. I led. This alone makes me responsible. We would not have met with those murderesses if I had been able to anticipate their trap."

He stopped to look at Patty. Her dominant reaction seemed to be pity. He accepted the resulting humiliation as just rewards for his failures.

"It is worse than failing," Chul said. "By the time your father died, I *knew* what it meant to lead, and I did it regardless. I *knew* that a leader is one who sacrifices others for the sake of his own goals, and I did it anyway. My leadership had already brought death to a boy and imprisonment to an innocent. I have learned that I am without honor."

John entered the room with two empty mugs and a pot of green tea. Patty used this interlude to take a drink from her cup and change the subject.

"What happened in Germany?"

Chul wanted to say *I failed, I let him die.* He looked to John, took a seat next to Patty, and said this instead.

"You already know of Ines?"

"The woman who killed my Dad," Patty said. "I know who she is, but what happened?"

"Your father was too brave," Chul said. "He had too much courage…We were going into her studio to ask her questions about 'Mannus.' I see now that she deceived us from the start. Whether she is in league with Mannus, or if Mannus even exists, I cannot know. Regardless, she knew we pursued the Twinkie. She thought we had it, or knew its location. The meeting was a trap and our delay investigating the book simply gave her time to prepare.

"When your father went into the studio she hit his face with a gun. I am a coward. Instead of protecting him, I hid behind some machines. I was not able to reason with her, nor did I have time to bargain. I wanted to explain we had no Twinkie. Your father heard her raving and tried to escape on his own.

"He must have thought I needed help. I remember his eyes, when he got up, when she cut his neck. They were clear and calm and blue. There was no struggle. I do not think he suffered long—he just turned off."

Patty nodded while John put a hand over her shoulder. She put her tea cup back on the saucer and surprised Chul with her words.

"I'm sad my father died, but I wanted to say that I'm glad you and he met."

Is she trying to spare my feelings? Chul wondered. *This cannot be true.* Patty continued.

"When Mom died, something broke in my dad. The daddy I knew who did fake ballet to make me laugh and smelled like mint and kissed me every night before bed— it was like he died. And my god did I miss him. I wanted the dad I loved to come back again *so bad.* But he was gone. There was so much bitterness and hatred in him afterwards—he was this monster of revenge. Revenge on me, revenge on friends, revenge on whoever happened to walk by. I basically disowned him. I kicked my own father out of my wedding, that's how bad it was. I thought he was gone forever.

"But then he met you. He changed in that last year. He started to let go of his—I don't even know what. I almost felt like I got my dad back. Whatever you did, however you and he were, thank you."

Chul took hold of the envelope and extended his hand toward Patty.

"I think you should have this," he said. "Your father was working on it when he died."

Patty set the envelope on the table and took another drink from her tea cup.

"By the way," she said. "I think you're right about leadership and sacrifice—that a leader sacrifices others for his own goals. But I don't think it's bad in itself. Just make sure those goals are worth the price."

Chul looked to the ground and held silent. He felt as if he'd just finished a week-long march. His emotions were somehow flat, shapeless. His hands and legs weak, his head heavy. He stood, bowed to his hosts and left the house.

"I have one more thing I must discuss," he said. "Though I am reluctant because it seems trivial."

"I doubt it's trivial," Patty said.

"I found the Twinkie," Chul said. "I had thought it so important in the time before but now I feel nothing but disgust. I am of half a mind to give it to you, half a mind to destroy it."

"Where did you find it?"

"The God of Potency left it on the seat of my car in Germany," he said. "No speech, no note. Only a *yuht-mug-neun* pastry. I suppose he wished to mock me, giving me my prize only after destroying my appetite."

Patty nodded, put her hands to her chin and offered an alternative explanation.

"Perhaps, he felt that you'd earned it."

Chul thought on this, thanked Patty for her time and asked to leave. When he heard the door close behind him, the greater of our heros opened his briefcase. The locks squeaked and hurt his teeth. The soft, interior lining pressed the flesh of his fingers painfully over his nails as he spread the hinges open. The Twinkie of Destiny shimmered a warm gold and our hero held it up against the hazy, grey light for a moment. He thought of restoring Korea's honor and taking vengeance on me—those same things he'd vowed to do not even a year before. No, what had been done could not, should not, be undone.

He thought back to Dr. Fluffenflapper and Min-sung. He considered Bume's dilemma. He did not wish to be a sea sponge. He did not wish to erase the freedom of other minds. How, then, to procede? He considered this and bit into the greatest pastry ever made.

Give me the wisdom to sacrifice well..

Patty opened the envelope and read.
Dear Editor,

This is the eighth time I've written you on the anniversary of 9/11, and this letter marks the official end to my career as an avenger of injustice. I've realized, finally, just how tired it made me. I've wasted so much time hating people. I wanted to see them burn for what they did to my wife. If I'm honest, I wanted to see people who hadn't done anything to my wife burn, too—I thought that would help somehow.

I was so certain last year. I was so sure I could put myself and my country in this unambiguous box of rightness and that the world was filled with lots of other people in the villain box. I've learned that life just doesn't work that way.

I think it's mostly a matter of me learning about myself. There's a darkness inside each of us. It was just a change of scenery away from taking over for me. I take that back. It was already out, I just couldn't recognize it because I was so caught up in my stupid narrative about good and evil. We are all thieves in waiting, cheats and murderers. I've seen it happen too many times over this last 18 months.

Being wrong—and just look at my old letters to your organization to see how wrong I can be—isn't the problem. It's the certainty that makes us into monsters because certainty is denying the most basic truth there is—this is a big, complicated world and we don't know shit. Lie to yourself about that and the rest is easy to lie about as well.

I miss my wife. I miss her everyday and I will continue to miss her until I die, but I'm done with the retributions. To hell with justice. I'm tired of the heroes and villains. My daughter said something to me recently that I think applies here. She said upheaval is the key to renewal. She asked me not to waste my time on punishment and to make something beautiful instead. I thought she was being naïve at first, but she was right. The world isn't fair, it isn't just. I was the one being naïve to believe it should be otherwise. I'm done with the judgments. I'm done with the outrage and the expectations. I just want to make my part of the world a little bit better while I'm around.

The next time you offer your readers some neat little theory to explain everything, I pray you set it aside. There's so much out there to understand, so many things to discover. Do not cover the beauty of existence in some collection of beliefs. Embrace the wonder, embrace the complexity, do this so that in a hundred years our grandkids can be just a little less fucked up.

Sincerely,
CJ Smith

Easter Eggs

An Easter Egg, in video game parlance, is a non-essential but amusing little extra hidden by the developers for the player's benefit. I've borrowed this concept for *The Potency!* The following contents are not necessary to understand the story and, indeed, I would discourage you from reading them until you've finished the main story. However, if you would like to see some interesting bits of research, think over some of the concepts I was playing with while creating the book or just generally find out how this particular sausage was made, the Easter Eggs below should provide at least some amusement.

Chapter 1:
"over a bounty of expensive liquors ..." Kim Jong-il, at the height of his powers, was going through about a million dollars a year in Hennessey Cognac.

Chapter 1:
"While the great leader Kim Il-sung is both dead and the official head of our country ..." The current official ruler of North Korea has been dead for, as I write this, more than 20 years.

Chapter 1:

"… I will modernize our nation and help *Joseongook* …" This is an official name North Korea calls itself. They take the name from the Joseon dynasty, the royal leaders of united Korea from 1392 until the Japanese occupation officially began in 1910.

Part One, section quote:

"I must make a fresh start in life …" This is a quotation from Lu Xun's novella "Diary of a Madman." I chose this quote not only because it fits the thematic tone I'm trying to set for Part One, but also because I want to expose you, my readers, to a few giants of Eastern literature who, despite their immense talents, remain mostly unknown in the West.

Chapter 2:

"… the lush forests and rusty minefields …" A consequence of the long North/South standoff along the DMZ is that the area between the two Koreas has been almost completely undisturbed since 1953. If you can ignore the machine guns, anti-tank mines and certain death for anyone crossing the fences, it's a lovely nature preserve.

Chapter 5:

"The time 400 days from now will come …" I conceived the God of Potency character by imagining what would happen if Oscar Wilde became all powerful.

Chapter 6:

"Dear reader, pardon my intrusion …" What is justice? Why is it so slippery and variable across both time and location?

Chapter 7:

"… the sixth floor of Gwang-woo Byeong University's …" You might find some joy by typing "광우병" (Gwang-woo Byeong in the original Korean) into an online translation program. Suffice it to say, "Gwang-woo Byeong" is a controversy taken very seriously by many Koreans.

Chapter 7:

"Colonel Moon Doong-lee's …" As with the previous example, you might want to look up "문둥이" (Moon Doong-lee) in an online dictionary.

Chapter 7:

"We have made a deal with the Americans …" This deal isn't so different from a supposed agreement between the US, China and South Korea that WikiLeaks spilled in 2010.

Chapter 7:

"The Japanese set about finding …" Kim Jong-il faced a shortage of fluent Japanese speakers and this compromised his ability to spy on his neighbors. The Dear Leader thus did what any responsible ruler would do in his position—send special forces aboard miniature submarines to kidnap random Japanese children for service in his intelligence agency.

Chapter 8:

"… perverse love of artistic portraiture …" Or, as I sometimes refer to it, MFA-syndrome. Am I the only one who finds "literary" novels full of imprecise poetry and navel gazing to be really, really dreary? Please, literati, have something to talk about when you "pen your next tome" and, for the sake of all that's holy, fall out of love with "beautiful sentences" that even you can't understand.

Chapter 8:
"… smear blood on my face and ululate …" I would like to thank the gifted novelist Paul Beatty for this idea—I will never forget Negritude.

Chapter 8:
"We made it with abalone and goat cheese …" Incidentally, this really is a delicious pasta sauce. Seared abalone with pine nuts, olive oil, thyme and crumbled feta cheese over rigatoni is pretty much heaven.

Chapter 9:
"Decorative cabbages …" The people of Korea love to plant purple and white cabbages on the sides of hills, in parks and along highway dividers. I've actually seen political campaign slogans written in cabbage.

Chapter 9:
"For the first time since …" South Korea is shockingly safe by American or British standards and Korean "drug problems" are so minimal as to be barely worthy of the name. East Asia, in general, has very few drugs, excepting alcohol, of course. In the case of Korea and Japan, it's largely because non-alcohol narcotics never got established. In China, it's because Mao executed junkies who didn't reform quickly enough. Whatever the means, you just don't see the addicted underclass so common in the West.

Chapter 9:

"Ya! Son of a fuck, shut your flapping fish lips!" One of the things I did to make the Korean characters sound Korean is to, wherever possible, use direct, literal translations of Korean idioms, profanity and customary ways of speaking. Keep your eyes open and you will see dozens of examples of this throughout the book.

Chapter 9:

"However, she was a vengeful woman and 'forgot' to call the daeri-oonjun men ..." American entrepreneurs, get on the daeri-oonjun thing. The convenience of just calling a man who will drive you and your car home would put traditional cab companies out of business for as long as people enjoy drinking. At the very least, you'll have my business.

Chapter 10:

"He picked up the new edition of "Guns and Ammo" ..." Yes, gun people, I know that the firearm described here would be nearly as dangerous to the person firing as the person being fired at. I also know that you don't actually want a bullet to penetrate seven people. However, in this particular incident, I felt it more desirable to mock the penis compensation segment of the civilian gun market than to deliver a physics-of-ballistics lecture. I beg your forgiveness.

Chapter 10:

"For the sin of using zombies in a narrative ..." If zombies and/or vampires are not remembered as this generation's nauseating cliché of supreme awfulness, I will turn in my writer's license.

Chapter 10:

"… racing cow breeder …" This is a real thing. Some rural Indian communities have competitions in which cows blast through flooded fields with farmers mud surfing in their wake. It's absolutely epic to watch.

Chapter 11:

"The velour curtains are most tasteful …" Man cannot live on kitsch alone, but that doesn't stop some Korean bars from trying. It is a callous hearted person who cannot chuckle upon witnessing the delightful tackiness of third rate Asian "business rooms."

Chapter 12:

"Patty dialed the embassy and smiled as the cuts …" How do you react to an adrenaline trip?

Chapter 12:

"Bleeding edge processors and the latest sensors fed Kareshi's 563 instruments …" I imagine the engineers responsible for Windows XP had a strong presence in the Mohawk Helicopter's design process.

Chapter 12:

"… Victoria's Secret for Pious Muslim Wives …" I wish this was a real thing. Unfortunately, the only actual connection between the lingerie maker and Islam I was able to find concerned a Muslim woman pouring acid over a Victoria's Secret employee.

Chapter 12:

"… third world hellhole's national pride …" You would think that people would only feel patriotic if they belonged to a successful country. You would be wrong. Indeed, the most venomous patriotism in the modern world tends to distribute almost randomly across income levels, stages of human development and international prestige. Since it's clearly not accomplishment, which the individual would be hard pressed to take credit for in any case, why do you think people are proud of countries in general and struggling countries in particular?

Chapter 13:

"… Korea's mighty navy …" Japan actually has a long history of getting curb stomped by the Korean navy. I'd highly recommend readers do a little independent re-search on Admiral Yi Soon-shin. Or they can read chapter 6 of my book "Critical Thinking for Leaders" if they prefer. Admiral Yi is probably the most successful naval commander of all time.

Chapter 13:

"Shik In-jong …" Korea has had a long, impassioned love affair with inspirationally titled bureaucracies. There were Departments of Cooperative Spirit and Royal Envoys for Encouragement since at least 1590. Also, if you plug Shik In-jong (식인종) into a translation program, you'll get either a fun little joke or a deeply symbolic key to true understanding, depending on your mood.

Chapter 13:

"Long experience has shown me no surer way …" This is an idea I got from Machiavelli's Discourses on Livy. I'm a huge Machiavelli fan and I think Livy is pretty easily his finest work.

Chapter 13:

"… Shik first threw a plastic cup at Domestic Minister Lee …" The South Korean parliament is notorious for debates in which verbal pugilism gets a little bit more literal. If you can get past the average Korean's mortification at the mention of these brawls, it's pretty fun to watch rich, conservatively dressed old people trading haymakers on the floor of parliament.

Chapter 14:

"As the sun rose over the Eastern Sea …" Also known as the Sea of Japan. I call it the Eastern Sea here because I'd prefer not to be lynched by my neighbors.

Chapter 15:

"I just received word they launched an invasion of Korea …" The Japanese have invaded Korea twice before. Both times they based their forces in Busan and pushed north toward the real prize, China. The first time, between 1592 and 1598, the heroics of the previously mentioned Admiral Yi Soon-shin led Japan to ultimate ruin and preserved the Joseon Dynasty, which was a mixed blessing at best. The second time, officially from 1910 but actually since 1870s, Imperial Japan did some good things like modernizing the Korean economy, and some truly awful things. They forced hundreds of thousands of Korean men to fight and die in WW2, which is normal and okay, and also pressed thousands of Korean women into sexual slavery, which is abnormal and not okay.

Chapter 16:

"I am a professor of emotion-based psychology." One of my stranger attempts to learn the Korean language involved joining a group of mostly elderly women as they studied emotion-based psychology. The idea was so fun I couldn't keep it out of the book.

Chapter 16:
"Video shot from the deck of the Korean fishing boat "Ddong-jeep" showed …" Ddong-jeep is 똥집 in Korean. You might want to Google it.

Chapter 16:
"Our hero cheered aloud as the Yushin Maru capsized …" The real Yushin Maru starred in a villainous role on Discovery Channel's series "Whale Wars."

Chapter 16:
"The reporter said "I'm sorry, I'm sorry, I'm sorry" and our hero shut off the computer." How can it be normal for Chul to cheer watching young men die on the Yushin Maru but clam up when young men die in Busan? How can it be normal for me to cheer when special forces shoot Osama bin Laden's sons, but fall into silent reverence when a vaguely remembered Marine I met once dies in Kandahar? What is patriotism actually doing to us in these situations?

Chapter 17:
"The cellular phone played two verses …" I've never understood why patriotic Americans play this song during July 4th celebrations. In case you've never listened to the lyrics, it's a song in which British drug addicts reject the corruption of American culture.

Chapter 18:

"… drove him to a Homeplus department store …" Homeplus is a joint venture between Samsung and Tesco. Think a slightly upscale Wal-Mart or Target with more food.

Chapter 18:

"Shit-eating Dokdo…" Hearing a young Korean person talk this way about Dokdo would be freakishly rare, like hearing a young American give a similar speech about why he doesn't give a damn what happens with al Qaeda. Why are these seemingly realistic stances so hard to take? What realistic stances does your patriotism prevent you from taking?

Chapter 19:

"Listen, whatever your name is …" How would you react if someone "crapped all over" your heritage? How would you react if someone crapped all over somebody else's heritage? I'm guessing those are two very different answers. If I'm right, it might be fun to ask yourself why.

Chapter 19:

"Sir Ethelred Leofric Westminsteringham III Esq. PhD …" I really wanted to put some of my useless knowledge into the book here. Did you know that Lady Godiva's real name was Godgifu, her father was Ethelred the Unready, her son was Ralph the Timid and her husband was Leofric? I hereby denounce the lack of awesome Old English names in our corrupted, dreary times.

Chapter 19:

"Royal skirt servants …" The queen has possessed approximately 5,000 of the finest hats in the world. Imagine how much that cost.

Chapter 19:

"Have you prepared a list of these pollutions I might present to the Loi Toubon Commission …" The Loi Toubon Commission is a real thing. Its job is to hunt down and punish loanwords from German, English, Arabic et al. In France, the grammar police have legislative power.

Chapter 19:

"It is true I have risen to the heights of bureaucracy …" It would be so tragic if a man of exactly this description were the current leader of Israel.

Chapter 20:

"Why can't these people just speak English …" While living in South Korea, I once had the misfortune of going on a blind date with an American ex-pat we'll call "Jessica." After ten minutes of excruciating conversation, I asked Jessica what she thought of South Korea. She informed me that "it's really annoying, you know? I come halfway around the world and these people don't even speak English."

Chapter 20:

"I mean goddamn, how much are these people willing to sacrifice for their stupid historical shit …" How much are you willing to sacrifice for the honor of your nation? This question gets a lot more interesting if you actually add up sums. How much tax money goes into your nation's honor? How many people in your family work upholding the national honor? How much time do you spend on your nation's honor?

Chapter 20:

"Contained inside are memorials …" Worshipping at the Yasukuni Shrine is a pastime of many patriotic Japanese and a considerable irritant to almost every other country in Asia. Current Japanese President Abe kicked off his administration with a trip to Yasukuni, keeping the controversy very much alive. The following is a partial list of war criminals honored in the Yasukuni Shrine.

Hideki Tojo—Waging unjust war and permitting inhumane treatment of prisoners. Tojo was at least partially responsible for about 20 million deaths, mostly in China.

Sadao Araki—Waging unjust war, particularly in Manchuria where he created a fake Chinese attack (the Mukden Incident) as pretext for a full Japanese invasion.

Kenji Doihara—Helped design the "three alls" doctrine—kill all, burn all, loot all. Used his position as commander to flood China with opium, fostered terrorism, deliberately promoted and protected corruption in the occupied territories. He also sent secret agents with addictive drugs out to "cure tuberculosis," thus creating thousands of unwitting junkies. He also forced thousands of Russian women into sexual slavery, for the use of Japanese soldiers.

Kingoro Hashimoto—Like Sadao Araki, he helped set up the Mukden Incident. Also a major player in the Rape of Nanking.

Seishiro Itagaki—Another planner of the Mukden Incident, Seishiro Itagaki also arranged for the starvation deaths of thousands of prisoners of war, mostly in Indonesia, and was part of the Korean comfort women program. Korean comfort women were typically raped a dozen or so times a day by patriotic Japanese soldiers and suffered a death rate of around 75%.

Iwane Matsui—Mastermind of the Rape of Nanking, he did nothing while his troops raped, murdered and looted their way through the city for several days.

Akira Muto—Used torture and indiscriminate slaughter to control conquered territories in both China and the Philippines. He was also one of the lower level commanders running the Rape of Nanking.

Shumei Okawa—Often called the Japanese Goebbels. The name fits.

Ishii Shiro—Ishii Shiro ran U731. By this, it is meant that he murdered hundreds of thousands of Chinese and Russians in grisly experiments. Ishii oversaw the release of bubonic plague, smallpox, and botulism on random villages, the destruction of hundreds of "logs" (including infants), many vivisected without anesthetic, limbs frozen and then shattered with hammers, deliberately infecting subjects with gangrene to study the course of the untreated rot, people tied to stakes in concentric rings around bombs to test shrapnel kill radiuses and innumerable miscellaneous delights.

If you wish to honor these brave and patriotic defenders of the Japanese homeland, the Yasukuni Shrine is open every day from 6:00 a.m. to 5:00 p.m., a mere five minute walk from Kudanshita Station in Tokyo.

Chapter 20:

"I interrupted the Dalai Lama …" The Dalai Lama is not the hippy we in the West imagine him to be. He is, or was, really weird about sex. Any form of sexual activity, even between a husband and wife, that does not lead to pro-creation is misconduct. Masturbation is misconduct. So is having reproductive sex during daylight hours.

Chapter 20:
"Expert on authoritarian princesses…" I'm talking about former South Korean President Park Geun-hye. However, I have to change her name because she's a delicate, litigious flower and it never occurred to her that a career in politics might involve criticism.

Chapter 20:
"Our hero could not help but laugh …" It might be fun to compare Chul's reaction to America's purely symbolic misfortune with CJ's reaction to Pakistan/India/Korea/Japan's symbolic misfortunes. Are they both just hypocrites? Do they both, in essence, simply say "patriotism is stupid and infantile in everybody else's countries, but sacred in my country," or is it something deeper?

Chapter 21:
"The samgyupsal began to burn …" One of my favorite things about Korea is that in most meat restaurants, there is a fire pit in the middle of the table. You can't cook food much fresher than that.

Chapter 21:
"May their sordid conspiracy-rubbing …" This is a linguistic joke my native-speaking friends assure me no self-respecting Korean would ever make. That said, I'm not mature enough to stay away. Conspiracy is "eummo" (음모) in Korean. Eummo also means pubic hair.

Chapter 23:

"AA Bob = Affirmative Action ..." Many people have expressed to me their opinion that minorities in positions of power were, until proven otherwise, benefactors of affirmative action. Since these people vote and feel a lot of resentment regarding racially-based affirmative action, I wonder if we aren't going to see the program either killed or replaced with something that removes the race-test in the future.

Chapter 24:

"To prevent this I caused a flood of ..." This 282 word sentence is actually slightly more intelligible than the lecture which inspired it. The women's studies class in question asked me to believe things like "men are taller than women because of discrimination," "your male children totally wouldn't get their asses kicked if you sent them to school in pig tails" and, my favorite, "evolution is no longer valid because we live in modern times." Dear University of Nevada, Reno sociology department, you can do better.

Chapter 24:

"... had I not caused *Drosera* to ..." This is a real plant, though considerably beefed up for God of Potency duty. I needed a predatory plant for the story and thought the venus fly trap too obvious. Real life *Drosera* are widely available at nurseries. They kill flying insects with their prehensile limbs and sticky bubbles of syrup. They also look pretty cool.

Chapter 24:
"Why only last week you, with no obvious signs …"
Bob O. Gateun (바보 같은) is another bilingual pun you
might enjoy.

Chapter 26:
"Our hero stepped over the threshold and saw tables of
knurled wood …" Many of these knurled wood tables in
South Korea, for reasons supposedly tied up with fertility
charms, are carved to resemble penis tips. Sometimes the
dicks become so numerous they spill out into entire gar-
dens of lovingly carved stone and wood phalli.

Chapter 26:
"The woman drew herself up and …" This is not a typical Buddhist ritual, no matter how much I wish it were.

Chapter 26:
"Now, Sahal, let us …" More bilingual jokes! Sahal
(сахал) is a Mongolian word meaning—well, you're just
going to have to find out for yourself.

Chapter 27:
"CJ ignored the policeman's stupid sermon …" You
really should shut up when it comes to dealing with the
police. They are not trying to help you, they are trying to
punish you as much as possible. Blabbing before, during
or after arrest is one of the worst things you can do, regardless of your innocence or guilt.

Chapter 27:
"Remember, I'll taze you …" This all comes from
real life. The law enforcement officers and inmates of

that fine facility actually did the things mentioned in this scene. One of the book prisoners is a composite and I did change the location from Virginia City, Nevada to Dayton, Nevada, but other than that … The lady officer, in particular, was *very* memorable.

Chapter 28:
"Let us take our interpreter above …" One of the first things a visitor to Korea will notice is that Koreans assign special health benefits to any food that's even remotely traditional. The two most common benefits are healthy women's skin and "endurance," by which they mean "a man's ability to delay ejaculation," but in a sweet and innocent way.

Chapter 29:
"Uncertainty, dark and immense …" According to most cognitive psychologists, the contest between belief and fact almost always ends badly for fact. We are belief machines and our brains, unless we are very disciplined, will almost always function far more in the service of those beliefs than in the service of truth. A fun example of this is the aftermath of a failed doomsday prediction. You would assume that members of a doomsday cult, upon living uneventfully through the "day of reckoning," would question their leader. With very few exceptions, an incorrect doomsday prediction will actually strengthen the belief of the community.

Chapter 30::
"My immortal heart leapt with joy. How exciting …" What sort of a role do you think heroes should pursue in real life? Should they pursue greatness at the expense

of purity or should they pursue purity at the expense of greatness? Should they be like Chul and suffer villainous titty twisters?

Chapter 31:

"He had tied the Gunham …" American made, super-market kimchi is an abomination, in case you were wondering. The stuff they make in Korea, or the stuff you can get in your local Korean market, is as far superior to the American crap as a fine truffle is to old mayonnaise.

Chapter 31:

"It was not an impressive place and Chul worried …" Korea has a much more communal culture than the US. There's a much larger tendency to see everyone and everything coming from the Korean race as representing the nation's honor. The Korean mass apology following Cho Seung-hui's Virginia Tech shooting is a good example of this in action. Chul's defense of Korea's culinary honor is something I've watched unfold several times during my time in Korea.

Chapter 31:

"CJ got the very strong sense …" I won't say that sar-casm doesn't exist in Korea, but it is certainly vestigial at best. This makes communication between world-weary, cynical Westerners and Koreans of basically any type hi-larious to watch from a distance.

Chapter 31:

"Chul thought this a ridiculous thing to name a child …" There is no such thing as Libertarianism in Korea. In my Anglo-American culture classes, it's one of the most difficult and alien concepts to explain to Korean students.

Chapter 32:

"The effect is not unlike the hydraulic computers …" There were a number of aborted development paths for computers. There were computers based on looms as early as the 18th century and purely mechanical computers, such as the antikythera, from as early as the third century B.C. Hydraulic computers are, by comparison, relatively modern.

Chapter 32:

"While the causes for Chul's outrage struck CJ as being …" Every single Korean I've shown this work to assured me that the God of Potency's punishment of Korea was *far* worse than any other nation's punishment. Every single American assured me that America's punishment was *far* worse than the others. Why do you think that is?

Chapter 33:

"Chul's nostrils flared like a gladiator …" One reason I had so much fun writing The Potency is that the subject matter gave me an unlimited supply of "straight men." In comedy parlance, a straight man is the person who reacts seriously or normally in comic situations. As an example, Monty Python, with their straight-faced and pseudo-dignified idiot characters, used straight men particularly well. Because the God of Potency is messing with patriotic symbols, and because patriotism and a sense of irony are mutually exclusive, I can have everyone treating absurdities with deathly seriousness at basically all times.

Chapter 33:

"The self-righteousness alone warranted censure ... I intend to make you choose, I'm afraid, between your certainty and your ..." What is the Potency God's greater purpose, in your opinion? What would you rather have, confidence in your beliefs or power?

Chapter 34:

"His mother demanded the blood ..." The Omo River Valley is a real place. The Nyangatom and Kara are real tribes in the area. The "no sex or place in society until you continue the cycle of revenge" things is, sadly, also real for the young men of those tribes. Even worse, I actually toned down the awful things happening to the mingi children. They literally feed infants to crocodiles and shove tweens off of cliffs if they show signs of "being cursed." It kind of irritates me when righteous idealists treat the question of whether foreign powers should or should not respect these cultural practices as either simple or obvious.

Chapter 34:

"You do not look like the rough gangsters or western cowboys ..." Having spoken to hundreds of Koreans, Japanese and Chinese people about tourism, the most common reason I've heard for not vacationing in the US was the second amendment. Gun control has a much better reputation in the East than West.

Chapter 34:

"I am indifferent to their sufferings ..." Both CJ and Chul are pretty seriously flawed characters, but which set of flaws do you prefer, CJ's flighty idealism or Chul's myopic pragmatism?

Chapter 34:
"I only said that because your idealism …" Chul is being a dick here, but not as much as a Westerner would think. In a lot of Confucian traditions, there's a major emphasis on harmony above all else. Chul probably thought he was, to an extent at least, avoiding unnecessary conflict with his little maneuver.

Chapter 35:
"The pale-faced Korean …" I'm deliberately echoing the language native groups used to describe white imperialists. Why do you think that is?

Chapter 35:
"The mother of a mingi baby leaves her child in the brush to starve …" Remember, less developed people are morally superior to modern, degraded man.

Chapter 35:
"Everyone knew that was different …" Remember, rich-nation citizens are more enlightened than primitives.

Chapter 35:
"He thought of comfort women …" The Japanese, between 1910 and 1945, ran institutionalized rape camps for the amusement of the rank and file. A plurality of the victims were Korean women, most of them lured away with the promise of work. Very few survived the dozen or so daily gang rapes needed to fortify Japanese fighting spirit. I also referenced the Japanese murder of poet Yoon

Dong-ju, the ninja-assassination of Queen Myeongseong and the large-scale Japanese practice of literally carrying away buildings they found interesting. There are valid reasons that the Koreans are still mad at Japan.

Chapter 36:

"I am going to use your pant leg …" One of my favorite, subtle methods Koreans use to say 'fuck you' is to politely inform the victim of an unpleasant action said victim has no power to prevent.

Chapter 36:

"What is life if not a struggle to control one's hatreds …" Henry Adams wrote that "politics, as a practice, whatever its professions, has always been the systematic organization of hatreds." Do you think organizing hatreds is limited to politics?

Chapter 37:

"Indeed, the willingness to sacrifice others in the service of one's …" Most modern people are wed to the idea that all lives are equally precious. I very much doubt this and will provide an example to explain why.

We have four people. The first is the leader of a first world country, we'll call him Barry. The second is a blonde, middle class girl from the US, we'll call her Jonbenet. The third is a Hispanic boy also from the US. We'll call him Jose. Last, a 35 year-old farmer from Somalia, whom we'll refer to as Muhammad.

Barry has a cadre of highly trained body guards who protect him 24/7 at great expense. If he dies, multi-billion dollar corporations will scramble to rearrange their business strategies, stock markets will plunge, enemies will seek to exploit military weakness—often going so far as to launch territorial incursions - and the nation will mourn his death on the front page of every newspaper and magazine for at least a week.

Jonbenet has a police station a mile down the road filled with highly motivated professional investigators and officers. If she goes missing, those people will conduct a several-month long manhunt attempting to find her. She will be on a fair number of front pages for a fair length of time regardless of the outcome of her case.

Jose has a police station three or four miles away filled with relatively demotivated professionals who likely see him as a future problem but will attempt to protect him based on a sense of duty. If he dies or goes missing, those demotivated professionals will look for a week or so before giving up. However, since Jose has both black hair and a penis, he is replaceable and not worth monopolizing department resources over. He will probably get a short story on page 4 of the local newspaper when somebody finds his body.

Muhammad has a theoretical police station somewhere filled with people who very well might be carrying out a pogrom against his tribe. If he dies or goes missing, his family will be very sad and take the time to bury him in a shallow, unmarked grave. Outside of his immediate family and neighbors, nobody is likely to notice his demise.

Now for the horrible part, try to rationally justify taking away Barry's "valuable person" treatment and giving it to Jose, or spending Jonbenet resources on Muhammad.

Chapter 37:

"Truly you deserve freshly baked pizza, the finest reasonably priced beers and Gongju-style bibimbap …" Those of you versed in Korean culture will note that Gongju-style bibimbap is not a thing. Indeed, Gongju is perhaps the largest city in Korea that is *not* famous for some type of food or another. I preserved this error as a sort of homage.

You see, in 2013, I arranged a family trip in Korea so that we might experience the finest bibimbap, which is from Jeonju. However, in failing to check, I instead took the entire brood to Gongju where, unable to find bibimbap of any sort, we settled for the Korean equivalent of Pizza Hut.

Chapter 37:

"I have simply shown you a very small example …" The God of Potency is clearly embracing the insensitive dick side of his nature here, but does he have a point? Is murder bad, on the emotional level, only when we have to look at it?

Chapter 38:

"I've never seen so many Asians in one place before …" Talking to other ex-pats living in Korea, one of the most common things they think upon returning to the UK, USA or wherever is "look at all those white people." My Korean ex-girlfriend, upon returning to Korea after a month in Oregon, immediately remarked to me that it was weird seeing so many Asians in Seoul.

Chapter 38:

"She says she is very happy to ..." Chul starts out translating relatively honestly, towards the end of the conversation—not so much.

Chapter 38:

"We go to the noraebangs ..." A beer girl or prostitute, engaged in the company of one's new army friends while visiting a karaoke bar, is a very common means for losing one's virginity in Korea. This sort of thing is, to say the least, not nearly as stigmatized in East Asia as it would be in London.

Chapter 39:

"Our hero knew his powers of seduction to pale ..." Queen Seon Deok is both a real queen of ancient Korea (then called the Shilla Dynasty) and the subject of a wildly popular modern soap opera. So-called *sa-guek,* or historical dramas, are an amusing fixture in the living rooms of pretty much every middle aged Korean woman.

Chapter 39:

"Laura Gillespie Fieldbinder, aka Midnight ..." Fan fiction is a thing wherein people take the characters and settings of established fictional universes and then make their own stories in said frameworks. Due to the obvious copyright issues, fan fictions are rarely published in any way that can result in profit for the author. As such, the authors of fanfictions tend to be horny virgin girls in the 14-16 years-old range. I borrowed from three notorious fan fics and a fake fan fic as inspiration for my own.

Laura is the author of "legolas by laura" wherein Legolas discovers and adopts a baby named Laura. Laura is kidnapped by orcs and taken to "Mondor" but, thankfully, rescued from a "posion" injection by Legolas, who then marries his 10 year old adopted sister. I was inspired by this fic's "enigmatic ending" when writing the ending of Beowulf 2.

Tara Gillespie is the author of "My Immortal," a notorious Harry Potter fan fic. In it, all of the members of Hogwarts align into either "prep" or "goth" factions, Harry turns gay for Draco, Hermione is randomly a suicidal vampire and Gandalf calls everyone "mediocre dunces." This fic's creative spelling, random cameos from completely different story universes and general idiocy permeate Beowulf 2.

Midnight is the genius behind "The Human Centipede, Love at First Bite." Midnight writes some of the most disgusting, anatomically impossible and unintentionally hilarious sex scenes I've ever been exposed to. If you think Beowulf's love for Melancholy Sirah gets graphic, believe me when I say I've significantly toned down Midnight's original. My debt to her is profound.

Finally, I wanted to pay tribute to David Foster Wallace's fake fan fic detective "Monroe Fieldbinder." Unlike the other three, I would actually recommend you read "The Broom of the System."

Chapter 39:
"121-16, 225-10 …" This is a functional book code. Everything you need is contained in this set of numbers and the text of Beowulf 2. If you, my groovy audience, are half as nerdy as I think, you will need no further assistance in finding the secret message.

Chapter 40:

"迎到的小隔, 花男孩" Chul said. "意外被放演的候用我的橘色尿液射向 ...'" This is every bit as linguistically innovative as you'd suspect, but it's at least professionally idiotic. Thanks to Dan-ryeon for translating my nonsense into Mandarin.

Chapter 40:

"My husband is over-fond of ..." Human flesh searches are real, and all the examples in this paragraph are taken, unmolested, from actual online vigilante activities in China. As you would expect with regular folks forced into the realm of amateur justice, the results are very hit and miss.

Chapter 41:

"It is not different," Chul said. "You need to get over it ..." Is Chul just being insensitive or does he have a point?

Chapter 41:

"She said it is impossible to speak rationally to a Chinese about ..." Can you talk to another about their country rationally or does patriotism make that impossible?

Chapter 42:

"I broke my foot ..." I actually broke my foot in real life shortly *after* writing this section. I can tell you that the real thing, at least as I experienced, was not quite as bad as what I describe here. The pain was long lasting and annoying, but not that intense.

Chapter 43:

"Separatist Trash, May They Rot ..." I got most of the following polemics from an online forum called perspectives.com. Seeing that most of the perspectives.com members are Westerners, I had to change the names of the various trash, scum and traitors, but the rest I left alone. Most of the rest I got from the few Chinese BBS transcripts I could find in English. I'll bet you can't tell Western nationalistic outrage (with the names changed) from Chinese nationalistic outrage, translated into English.

Chapter 43:

"Three hours until his lunch date with Kong Qing, Professor of Song Dynasty Poetry ..." This character is based on a real person. Search for Kong Qingdong if you're interested. The traitorous dog thing comes directly from the good professor.

Chapter 43:

"'Ching Shih,' Professor Kong said ..." The real Ching Shih was probably the most successful pirate in world history. At the heights of her powers, this former prostitute commanded a fleet of pirate ships so powerful it crushed the Chinese Navy. It's a nice story of girl power, so long as you don't mind putting girl power and literally eating the hearts of your slain enemies into the same narrative.

Chapter 44:

"Well, it is also a pterodactyl pornography ..." I would love to tell you that we, as a species, are above making erotic movies about extinct archosaurs and have not, in reality, created such a horrifying thing as pterodactyl porn. We aren't and we have. Consider yourself warned.

Chapter 44:

"He is called Chi Sung ..." The real Chi Sung was better known by his Christian name, Metrophanes. He was the first Orthodox Priest martyred during the Boxer Rebellions. Like the Chi Sung in my book, he got caught between those looking to open China and those looking to preserve it from foreign contamination.

Chapter 46:

"Neck beards, God-hating, sodomy ..." I studied briefly with some aspiring poets in college. They were easy to make fun of.

Chapter 46:

"I am, in this sense, a child of de-Nazification ..." The process of destroying patriotic feeling in post war Germany is much less discussed than I think it should be. Germans learned that they were heirs to a shameful tradition, that their ancestors had been monsters and the troops they had supported were worse than common thugs. What, I wonder, were the effects? On a practical level, the destruction of heritage coincides with the very prosperous and responsible Germany we see today, but were there spiritual costs? What was the cost to systematically annihilating a peoples' heritage? Wouldn't it be fascinating if the answer is 'not much?'

Chapter 46:

"We *can*, if we're brave, make ourselves a product of will ..." What sorts of people do you think are most the products of will? What sorts are least the products of will?

Chapter 48:

"She's a gardener and office clerk in Urnfield ..." The Urnfield culture was one of the oldest settled groups in Europe. As far as I know, there isn't actually a city thus named.

Chapter 48:

"'If you fall in the woods ...'" My goal in writing the Mannus chapters was to mock the institutions of higher education, hopefully to straddle the line between laughing and cringing. What follows in the Mannus stories are mostly real anecdotes shared with me by friends and family. The trees won't laugh story came from one of my sister's professors who discussed this concept, in all seriousness, for several minutes during one of her philosophy classes.

Chapter 49:

"Desert of Apathy, Oasis of Syllables ..." A special thank-you to fellow writer Anne Merritt for providing me with the inspiration for Mannus' poetry. There was a young man in her creative writing courses who found inspiration in his twin muses, sluts and fascists. He couldn't understand his low scores and thus decided himself a victim of blind misandry and a cabal of evil molestation survivors.

468 Ben Garrido

Chapter 49:

"A Study in Courage—" I went searching for the most patronizing, clueless white-curtain asshole on earth and found Keith Gessen, editor of n+1 magazine. The infuriating condescension and self-righteousness following in this section mostly come from Mr. Gessen's "jail tourism" article "Central Booking."

Chapter 49:

"I took a new lover …" This (mostly) true story also comes courtesy of Anne Merritt. The spurned lady in Ms. Merritt's story, I think, did not lose much in the long term.

Chapter 49:

"However, I do not understand why you think this son of insanity …" I love to literally translate cursing. "Son of insanity" sounds pretty goofy in English, but it's like saying cockcuntfuck in Korean.

Chapter 51:

"By the time your father died …" If Chul is right that leadership is the art of sacrificing others for your own gain, do you think it is possible to be both good and a leader?

Thank you for reading and I hope you enjoyed *The Potency*!